BAMBOO ISLAND

THE PLANTER'S WIFE

ANN BENNETT

Third Edition 2023

Cover design: Coverkitchen

All Enquiries to: andamanpress@gmail.com

❀ Created with Vellum

In memory of my mother, Jean Bennett

PROLOGUE

Ceylon 1938

'Shall we go ashore, Juliet?'

Rose and I were leaning over the rail of the liner, staring open-mouthed at the scene on the dock below us. The ship had put in at Colombo to take on cargo and fuel before sailing on to Penang, and it was our first encounter with the East. The teeming sights and sounds and sheer colourful confusion of the place was overwhelming. Porters ran to and fro with baggage balanced on their heads, hawkers cried out on the quayside, all manner of people pressed forward selling their wares, carrying goods or begging for money.

'I'm not sure.' We only had a couple of hours, but Rose was insistent, pouting a little as she always did if she didn't get what she wanted.

So we made our way down the gang-plank onto the dockside and were immediately surrounded by rickshaw-wallahs clamouring for our trade. After much gesticulating and haggling, we managed to single one out, and for ten rupees he agreed to give us a whistle-stop tour of the neighbouring streets. It felt unnatural sitting on board a little cart pulled by a human being who was dressed only in a loincloth and running barefoot between the two shafts like a beast of burden. But the other Europeans around us, lazing back on the seats in their spotless white clothes and solar topees, made it seem like a perfectly normal way to be conveyed about town.

He took us down a narrow alley opening off the dockside. It was lined with shops with open fronts that sold every type of produce there was, from fresh fruit to jewellery, from colourful silks to live fish. People were squatting on the pavement, frying delicious-smelling meals in woks over open fires. The sights and sounds were astonishing, but it was the smell that I really took in: a mixture of exotic spices, wood-smoke and open drains. It was the smell of the East, one which I would quickly grow to recognise and to appreciate.

Between two of the shops was the covered entrance to a temple. Rose leaned forward and asked the rickshaw-wallah to stop. 'Come on, let's have a look,' she said, jumping down and smiling at me, beckoning me on. I followed reluctantly as she rushed towards the temple pavilion between long rows of stalls selling flowers and cheap trinkets.

Halfway along the alley, we saw an old woman sitting in front of a little tent, her face withered and wrinkled. 'Fortunes told for five rupees,' proclaimed a notice beside her. Rose turned to me smiling. 'Let's go in, Jules, I'd love to have my fortune told,' she said.

I hesitated, but Rose persisted and was the first to go inside the tent with the old woman. I waited outside in the steamy heat, breathing in the incense that wafted down from the temple, listening to the low chanting of monks inside.

When Rose came out she looked visibly shaken. The colour had drained from her face.

'What's the matter?' I asked, worried.

'It's nothing. You go on in.'

Feeling apprehensive, I entered the dark little tent, with its oppressive heat and heady smell of smoke and candle wax. I sat down on a rickety chair opposite the old woman, who took my palm in her leathery fingers. She studied it with bloodshot eyes.

'You'll have a long life, my dear,' she croaked finally. 'Long and healthy ...'

Then she paused, and gripped my hand, 'But wait ... There is something else here too,' she studied my palm intently. 'Pain. I see pain here. There will be many painful moments for you. And loss too ... Much loss and sadness.' Her tone was so dramatic that my instinct was to laugh, but as she looked into my eyes, a sudden chill went through me, even there in that stuffy tent.

'My father died a few months ago,' I said. 'Perhaps, that's it?'

'I see that. I see that, my dear. He was a good man, wasn't he? I see that. No ... It is not your father. I see other men in your life. One you love deeply.'

'Really?' I felt a little reassured. There was no-one; she must be making all this up. Again she gripped my hand with her bony fingers.

'I also see a woman. I cannot see her face but she is very brave, full of love and kindness.'

Now I smiled and relaxed a little. She must be talking about Rose.

The old woman let go of my hand and sat back. 'You must not worry about what I have told you, my dear,' she said. 'There *will* be pain and loss and suffering. But you need to be patient and wait for a long time. I cannot see what they are, but there will be rewards too. Wonderful rewards if you wait.'

I stared at her. With life as it was now, embarking on a trip to experience the exotic East, I could hardly begin to imagine a life of pain and heartache. But I thanked the old woman, put some coins on her table and emerged into the alley. Rose was waiting outside, still looking pale.

'Shall we go on into the temple?' I asked.

'I'd rather not, Jules. Let's head back to the ship.'

As we made our way back to the rickshaw, we passed a stall selling trinkets: key rings, model lions, tiny ebony elephants, cheap jewellery.

'Look, Rose,' I stopped to pick up a silver charm delicately engraved with a tiny Buddha. I held it up to have a closer look, then showed it to her. 'Would you like one of these as a memento?'

The stallholder smiled at me. 'They are amulets. Good luck charms, madam. Will keep all evil spirits away. Very, very cheap.'

'I'll take two.'

Rose was already sitting in the rickshaw, her face pulled into a frown. I put my arm around her shoulders and gave her a squeeze. We emerged from the narrow alley onto a wider road with broad pavements lined with neat trees and grand white colonial buildings. Bullocks plodded along, hauling huge loads on covered wagons, jostling for space with pony carts, rickshaws and the odd open-topped motor car. I looked at Rose. She looked a little better now and was staring at her surroundings in wide-eyed wonder.

'It's fantastic, Jules, isn't it?' she said, warmth finally returning to her cheeks.

I nodded. 'I think we're going to enjoy the East.'

Later, in our cabin, as the ship cast off from the docks, we got ready for dinner.

'What was all that with the fortune teller, Rose darling?' I asked tentatively.

'Oh, nothing really,' Rose said. 'She couldn't find the time-line on my palm that's all. It was ... It was severed apparently, so she couldn't tell me about the future beyond a few years. It must be because I injured my hand when I fell out of that oak tree when I was a little girl. Do you remember that?'

'Of course. Oh, how you screamed! Father had to rush you to the doctor for stitches. That must be it. That fortune telling is all nonsense anyway. It was only meant to be a bit of fun. Those amulets we picked up are gorgeous though, aren't they?'

'Yes, beautiful. I've got mine on now,' said Rose, fingering the charm at her throat. 'After that experience I need all the luck I can get!' she said with a shudder. 'I'm never going to take this off now, Jules, not until the day I die.'

1

Windy Ridge Estate, Malaya, 1962

The big white house dominated the crest of the hill and looked out over the lines of rubber trees to the jungle beyond. It was quite alone, miles from any neighbours, and hardly any traffic ever ventured along the rutted dirt road that ran the five miles between the estate and the nearest settlement, Kuala Lipis. It had been a proud, grand building in the years before the war, its paintwork startling white against the blue of the tropical sky, but now the walls were scabbed and peeling and there were a few gaping holes in the roof where the tiles had blown off during the high monsoon winds.

The deep veranda running the length of the ground floor was shaded with bamboo chicks, which were rolled up near the front door so that Juliet Crosby, relaxing in her deep rattan chair, had a view of the faint breeze playing in the rubber trees. She watched it ruffling the leaves, turning them from green to grey and back again.

She always sat here at this time of day, before the sun had begun its descent behind the jungle-covered horizon, and the cicadas were still chattering in the casuarina trees in the garden. This was the best hour of her unwavering routine. She liked to sit with her afternoon tea tray on the little cane table, her two Dalmatians lazing on the boards of the veranda beside her, and take deep breaths to empty her mind of everything but the mundane business of running the estate, banishing any other thoughts that might trouble her. She loved the sharp light of the early evening. It was as if the sun was burning with renewed intensity before it dipped away.

Today was a day like any other. It had begun before dawn for Juliet, with her routine tour of the estate. As usual she had walked through the trees at first light, the dogs at her heels, to the tappers lines. She knew all the workers on the estate and chatted to them in fluent Malay as she took the roll call, made sure that all was running smoothly and that everyone knew their tasks for the day. She then checked on the workers in the production sheds, assessing the stocks of latex, making sure the machines and presses were running properly. As usual she'd walked out through the lines of trees to check that the maintenance gangs were at work, weeding between the trees, digging ditches for drainage. And like any other working day it had ended like this.

She had grown to enjoy the comfortable rhythm to her life, this pleasing, safe routine that she had been following for twenty-odd years. She rarely saw anyone other than the rubber workers. There was no need. Very occasionally she would take the old Morris from the stable behind the house and drive the bumpy road into Kuala Lipis to visit the few friends who had outlived the war and the Malayan Emergency. They would play a rubber of bridge or two in the decaying building that housed the club, or go for a drink at the bar in the Government Guest House. There were still a couple of survivors from the old days living in Kuala Lumpur, too, and once or twice a year she would take the train down for a short visit. Juliet was always glad to get back to the estate, though, and the comfort of her quiet, reclusive routine.

The old house was rather shabby now it was true, but business was not what it had been, and the estate only just made enough to pay the workers and turn in a tiny profit. There was no money to pay for repairs, but after all what did it matter? It was only her living here now. And after she was gone there would be no-one. It was not like the war years when rubber had been booming and money had rolled in effortlessly. Of course Juliet hadn't been managing the estate then. She had had nothing to do with it. No, it had been down to her husband to run things then. She felt her fingers tightening around the arms of the chair, nails digging into the wood, and her breath quickening at the mere thought of him. Uninvited, an image of him swam into her mind: an image of her first encounter with him that very first evening at the Penang Club. How he had leaned casually at the bar, toying with his glass, watching her, and when he had crossed the room to ask her to dance, her cheeks had burned with anxiety and pleasure. Juliet stopped and checked herself. Sweat was standing in little beads on her brow.

The dogs sensed something before she did. One moment they were lounging on the floor, the next sitting bolt upright, ears pricked, poised for attack.

'What's the matter? Caesar? Cleo?' Juliet sat forward in her chair. She had a dread of unexpected callers. She peered towards the gate beyond the expanse of lawn, just where the garden ended and the rubber trees began. There was nothing there, but both her dogs were on their feet now, whining, wagging their tails.

'Sit down!' she commanded and they obeyed instantly.

Juliet quickly went inside and fetched her leather binoculars from the hall stand. She leaned over the rail and trained them on the drive. She could see nothing. Just the palms waving in the breeze, and the heat haze hovering above the empty drive. She

sighed and was about to put them away when there was a movement, and through the glasses she caught sight of a figure moving
at the limits of her vision. She peered more closely. A lone figure
was moving towards the house, short and slight and carrying a
heavy load.

Who the hell could that be? She put down the binoculars,
afraid of getting caught snooping, and clung to the railings,
confused. Then, beginning to panic, she went inside and closed
the front door. She stood behind it, her fists clenching and
unclenching, her eyes closed, breathing heavily, wondering what
to do. She never had visitors. Who could it be?

She went to the window and peered out, careful to keep
hidden behind the curtain. Whoever it was, was drawing closer
now. There was something in the way the intruder moved, that
way of striding that stirred something deep inside Juliet, something buried beneath the dry layers of long forgotten memories.
As the figure moved closer, she saw that it was a young woman,
with a mop of short dark hair and dressed simply in blue pedal-
pushers, flat shoes and a white shirt. The girl was carrying a rucksack. It was a bloody backpacker! There were too many of them
now, lazing on the beaches of Penang, staying in squalid hostels
in the seedy parts of KL, doing the Southeast-Asia trail. But she'd
never seen one anywhere near the estate before.

Her mouth went dry and she began to panic again. What on
earth would she say to the stranger? The girl was crossing the
semi-circle of gravel in front of the house now. Juliet stepped well
away from the window. She could hear the footsteps on the front
steps, crossing the veranda, stopping at the front door. And then
came the firm knock.

Juliet froze, her back pressed against the wall, and held her
breath. If she waited long enough surely the girl would go away?
She must have come to the wrong place, or was looking for a free
bed for the night. It would be far easier to let her think there was
no-one at home than have to actually turn her away. Juliet waited

and counted the seconds. She had reached forty when there was another knock, even firmer this time. Juliet passed her hand through her hair, agitated. Why didn't the girl just leave? She was still in a state of panic when her elderly houseboy appeared from the direction of the kitchen, making for the front door. She held up her hand.

'It's alright, Abdul. I will answer it.' He shrugged and shuffled away.

She took a deep breath, smoothed her crumpled skirt and opened the door a fraction. The dogs burst through the open door, wagging their tails in excitement. The girl looked into her eyes and smiled. Her face was tanned, and she had eager blue eyes, a freckled nose and white, white teeth.

'Are you Mrs. Juliet Crosby?' Although the girl looked European, she had a strong accent, as if English wasn't her first language.

Juliet nodded. Words just wouldn't come to her. Her throat felt paralysed.

'I realise this will probably come as a shock to you,' said the girl, 'but I think you and I might be related.'

Juliet stared at the girl. She was struggling to grasp the meaning of the words. 'I beg your pardon?' was all she could find to say.

'I think we might be relatives. I know that might be a bit of a surprise, but I can explain.'

'I have no relations,' she said stiffly, her voice cracked and strained. She hardly ever spoke English now and the words felt odd in her mouth.

The girl remained standing there. 'I can explain,' she said again.

'You'd better come in then,' muttered Juliet, drawing back the door.

The girl came inside, eased the backpack off her shoulders and put it on the floor. 'I hope you don't mind,' she said, still smiling. 'It's very heavy. I've carried it all the way from Kuala Lipis.'

'Goodness me. You walked all that way? In this heat?'

'Yes, I came from the station in the town. The place was very quiet. There didn't seem to be any taxis around.'

'Did you come on the train? Where from?'

'From Singapore. I came on the night train. It's taken me nearly two days.'

Juliet had no idea what to say or do. Nothing had prepared her for this. Despite that, she knew she couldn't stand there gawping. Her ingrained good manners took over. 'You must be thirsty. Would you like some water, or some tea perhaps?'

'Oh yes, tea please. If it's no trouble,' the girl smiled gratefully.

Glad to finally find something to do, Juliet rang the little bell by the door, and Abdul shuffled back into the room.

'Could you get this young lady some tea please, Abdul?' The old man shot a curious look at the newcomer before nodding and ambling back into the kitchen.

Juliet turned back to the visitor. 'I'm sure there must have been some mistake. I don't know where you got your information from, but I'm afraid every one of my relatives is dead.'

The girl hesitated, then fixed Juliet with her blue eyes. 'Does this mean anything to you?' she asked then put her hand to her throat and pulled out a silver chain from inside her blouse. Dangling from it was a square silver amulet engraved with a figurine of Buddha.

Juliet's hand flew to her mouth and her knees suddenly felt weak, as if all the blood had drained from her. She sat down heavily in the chair behind her.

'You recognise it, don't you?' said the girl, her eyes still fixed on Juliet's face. Slowly, Juliet nodded.

2

London, 1938

We came out to Malaya for a holiday, Rose and I, and we never went back. We left a few months after Father died. For years we had thought things would never change for us: two young women, living at home in a comfortable semi in the North London suburbs, travelling daily on the Metropolitan line into Central London to work at soul-sapping administrative jobs, returning home to cook supper for Father. Occasionally the routine was punctuated by a trip out to the Regal Cinema on Harrow High Street or an evening spent dancing at the Majestic Ballroom.

I thought life would go on like that forever, at least for myself, and that I would grow to be an old maid under Father's roof. Poor old Father. He loathed his job as much as we loathed ours, but he had been subjected to the daily grind for a lifetime. He worked in middle-management in a giant insurance firm in the City. Every day he would set off for the tube station, briefcase and umbrella in hand, his shoulders drooping in dismay. He was an outdoor man at heart, never happier than on his council allotment, or striding across the mountains of Snowdonia on his yearly walking holiday. But fate had decreed that he would spend his days pen-pushing in a dreary office, worrying about deadlines and office politics, climbing the greasy pole. And fate decreed, too, that the stress of this life would lead him to an early grave. He had been at his desk in the office when it happened. His secretary had come in with his coffee one morning and there he was, slumped over his papers.

After the funeral, Auntie Maude wrote to Rose and me from Penang, asking us to come out on an extended stay. We only had the vaguest of memories of her: an exuberant but negligent carer who had lived with us in the weeks after Mother had died from tuberculosis, before Father had time to fix up a proper nanny. She would allow us to romp around the house in dressing-up clothes and Wellington boots, eat jelly for breakfast, stay up very late in the evenings. Looking back I realise it was because she hardly had been grown up then herself and had no idea how to look after two young children. She disappeared from our lives when she married Uncle Arthur after a whirlwind romance and had set off for Malaya, where he worked as a broker for a trading company.

'I can't promise you much excitement here,' she wrote in her flamboyant, flowing hand. 'Life can be a little dull at times, I'm afraid. It revolves around the club. The ex-pat community is very small and friendly, though. Life here is extremely comfortable, the company pleasant and the scenery beautiful. You should find it a relaxing change from London.'

'Can't we go, Jules? Please?' Rose asked as soon as she had put down the letter. 'Auntie Maude's right. It would be a wonderful change from London. I don't know how much longer I can bear to go on working in that ghastly typing pool.'

I knew she expected me to object, to put up all sorts of reasons why it would be impossible to abandon everything we knew and embark on a journey half way across the world. I was always the practical one, the boring one who curbed her natural excesses. However, I simply smiled back into her pleading eyes and said, 'Of course we can go. What's there to stop us?' I needed a break from our monotony, too. Besides London would only continue to remind us of Father.

Over the next few months we worked hard at emptying the house of our personal belongings. Some things went to jumble sales, some into storage. We rented it out to a respectable school-teacher and his wife, worked out our notice at work, and with some of our inheritance money booked our passage to Penang on P&O Tourist Class.

On the morning of our departure, a taxi arrived to take us to Waterloo Station to catch the boat train to Southampton. As we set off down the road, I turned round and stared through the back window at the house where I had grown up, lost Mother and Father, spent my life so far. It looked just like every non-descript semi-detached house in North London, with its neat little front garden and carefully clipped privet hedge, but its walls harboured all my memories, bore the imprints of the loving years our family had spent there.

The journey on board the SS Cathay to Georgetown, Penang, took several weeks. The first few days crossing the Bay of Biscay proved to be a dreadful ordeal. The weather was stormy, and Rose and I were both seasick. We lay groaning in our tiny cabin, wishing we had taken the train to Marseilles to join the boat there instead of subjecting ourselves to this torment. But as soon as we had passed the Rock of Gibraltar and entered the calm waters of the Mediterranean, the weather improved, and we began to enjoy the journey.

Soon, life on board took on an existence all of its own, as if we were living with our fellow passengers in a little bubble that would never burst. We got to know some of our ship-mates very well in those few weeks: there were several genteel middle-aged couples travelling back from home-leave to manage tin mines,

run factories or return to jobs in the Malay civil service. There
was a dour missionary and his wife, bound for a remote part of
Borneo, who dressed in black even in the sunniest of weather and
kept to themselves.

There was also a group of young men, setting out to take up
jobs running rubber plantations or mining operations, embarking, just as we were, on their first foray to the Far East. They spent
their days lazing in the sun in deck chairs and their nights
drinking and playing snooker in the smoking room. Their ebul-
lient sense of adventure affected the whole company, and as the
weather grew warmer, the delicious anticipation of arriving at an
exotic land increased.

A couple of these young men took a shine to Rose, vying for
her attention at the bar in the evenings and monopolising her at
the occasional dances held in the ship's ballroom. She seemed
happy to return their attention, but there was one man in particular, Robert Thompson, an officer in the RAF, dashing and charming, with whom she seemed particularly keen on dancing. It was
the story of my life, and reminded me sharply of all the Saturday
evenings at the Majestic in Harrow when Rose had been
surrounded by admirers, overwhelmed with requests for dances.
I would stand on the side-lines looking on, drink in hand, trying
not to show that I felt humiliated by the situation, when all the
time I was shrivelling inside with hurt and self-loathing.

But then why wouldn't they pursue her? She had the sort of
looks that made people turn and stare. Her skin was translucent
and her features perfect, full red lips, constantly smiling, and
starry blue eyes with impossibly long lashes. Her lithe, graceful
figure always looked good no matter what she wore, and her
blonde wavy hair framed her face and tumbled around her
shoulders. Our looks were similar, but fractionally different in
every way. While her features were perfectly formed, my face was
a little too long, my cheekbones a little too high to be considered
beautiful, my hair just the wrong side of blonde, sometimes

described by unkind observers as mousy. I was a little too tall and a little too thin, and my dresses tended to sag on my shoulders, whilst Rose's clung perfectly to her shapely body.

But it was as much a question of personality that drew people to her effortlessly. She had a certain magnetism, a lively manner, full of generosity and humour. I didn't have that natural way with people. I was awkward, shy and difficult. People were put off by my lack of confidence.

I tried not to let my jealousy show, so I stood by while Freddy Clarke and Robert Thompson fought it out quite amicably for Rose. In the end they came to an agreement over taking it in turns to dance with her or walk her round the deck in the moonlight. The one who wasn't occupied with Rose grudgingly danced or walked with me while awaiting his turn with my sister. Robert was returning to his airbase in Singapore from a trip to England. He had missed the troopship he should have been on, he explained, having succumbed to a bout of flu. His manner with me was always formal and a little strained. I wondered if he felt out of place amongst all these civilians. But I observed that when he danced with Rose he grew instantly relaxed, and they would spin around the dance floor laughing and chatting like old friends. I struck up a good rapport with Freddy Clarke, a fresh-faced young man from the Midlands, full of optimism about the job he was going to and what the future held for him. But I had the feeling that he was just killing time when he was talking to me.

Father would have understood how I felt. I remembered being a gawky sixteen-year-old sitting next to Father in the school hall watching from the back row as Rose took the audience by storm as Eliza Doolittle in Pygmalion. She was perfect for the part, pretty and vulnerable, witty and charming in equal measure. The wild applause at the end was clearly meant for her; the other members of the cast stood back as she took three curtain calls.

Father clapped and cheered like everyone else, and so did I. Afterwards we went back-stage to find Rose. She was surrounded by a crowd of people congratulating her; teachers, parents and fellow pupils. We waited in the corner of the dressing room for ten minutes until they had all melted away. When Rose finally noticed us standing there, she came forth to greet us. As she flung her arms around my neck and kissed me I felt the heat of her cheeks and the heady beating of her heart.

'Shall we go and celebrate, Father?' she asked as she hugged and kissed him too. 'Will you take us down to Lyons for tea and cake if it's still open?'

'That depends, Rose darling,' he said. 'I know Juliet has school work to do. She's been worried sick about her exams next week. Have you got enough time to pop down to Lyons quickly, Juliet?' He turned to me and gave me one of his warmest smiles. My eyes filled with tears at his display of love and understanding for me. When I nodded my consent I couldn't speak for the lump in my throat.

Later, at home, after our outing, when Rose had collapsed, exhausted in bed, Father came to sit beside me in the living room where I was finishing my history essay.

'Are you alright, Jules?' He put his arm around me. 'I know that sometimes you feel a little bit swamped by Rose,' he said gently. 'That's only natural. She's so ... She's such a big personality, isn't she? But you shouldn't feel like that. You are just as important, you know. You are every bit as lovely as her. You're a wonderful daughter. Kind and considerate. Clever and beautiful.'

'Father, there's no need ...' I began, embarrassed.

'Of course there is. I saw how you were feeling at the play and while we were waiting in the dressing room. You hide your feelings, I know you do, but they're there all the same.'

I had to look away to hide my emotion.

'I just wanted to let you know that I understand and that

you're loved and appreciated, that's all,' he said. 'Don't ever forget it.'

THE HEAT WAS NOW intense and oppressive, and people became even more languid. Drab, grey London was just a distant memory. Our days were filled with sunshine, the relentless blue of the sky and the shimmering, endless sea. It was a delicious sort of limbo. There was very little to do but read books, walk the decks, chat amiably to fellow passengers and eat the regular meals in the dining room. We finally got the chance to reflect properly on Father's death.

In the few weeks after his passing away it had been difficult for either of us to talk about him, but the journey, in both distance and time, was gradually liberating us from our pain. Although we could not recover completely from it just yet, we were learning to accept that it had happened, to be grateful for his life. We were beginning to remember him with love and affection rather than with the intense pain of recent grief. Sitting in our deckchairs under the clear blue sky, with the chug-chug of the ship's engines as background, we spent hours discussing our memories of Father, sometimes squabbling over little details.

'Do you remember that time Father took us to Brighton on the train, Jules?' said Rose. 'I think I was about five. You must have been seven or something. It was really sunny, and we went on the pier. There was a Punch-and-Judy show going on and a whole crowd of people watching. You were terrified of Punch and screamed blue murder. Everyone in the crowd turned round to stare at you, thinking what a dreadful child you were, feeling sorry for poor old Father. But he just ignored all their looks, lifted you up, popped you on his shoulders and pretended to be a horse, and galloped off down the pier leaving them all staring.'

I laughed. 'Yes, I do remember that day, Rose, but it wasn't me

who created such a fuss about Punch and Judy ... It was you! I
was the one left standing at the back of the crowd with everyone
staring, waiting for you both to come back.'

'Surely not!'

'And I remember that when you did come back, Father had
bought us all enormous ice creams with flakes.'

'He was so generous, wasn't he?' said Rose, her eyes shining,
'It must have been so hard for him, especially when we were
small ... Two little girls to bring up, having to entertain us when
he came home from work. He probably just wanted to get down
to his garden shed, listen to his wireless and do his woodwork in
peace.'

'And we always insisted on going to his shed with him to
help,' I said, smirking.

'Do you remember when he was making that doll-house for
us, and he let us help him paint it? He gave us strict instructions
that the walls were to be yellow and the roof red. We'd just got
started when Mrs. Hutchins next door called over the fence to
talk to him about something. They were chatting for ages, and
you and I thought it would be wonderful to paint the walls of his
shed yellow for a surprise.'

'I remember his face when he saw what we'd done! It looked
such a dreadful mess, didn't it? He went bright red for a few
minutes. I thought he might shout at us. But he couldn't be angry
for long, could he? When he saw our faces, he couldn't stop
laughing.'

'And do you remember his bedtime stories? He didn't need a
book. He knew them all by heart. All the fairy tales. And he had
stories of his own too. Stories none of the children at school
knew, about giants and witches and magical kingdoms.'

'And we wouldn't let him go downstairs. We would make him
stand at the bedroom door telling us story after story until we
couldn't keep our eyes open any longer.'

We were leaning over the ship's rail when we first saw the

island of Penang. Rising from the sea, the hills were at first a blue smudge on the horizon shrouded in tropical mists, like one of Father's mystical kingdoms, but as we drew closer we could see that they were covered in deep jungle. The ship steamed through the straits between Penang and mainland Malaya, and as we got closer to the dock we could make out the elegant white buildings of Georgetown lining the sea front. Fleets of small boats filled the busy harbour, and swarmed around our ship, some with sails, some being rowed, some punted like gondolas. And once again, that unmistakable tropical smell floated on the air.

It was with a pang of regret that we realised our wonderful lazy days on the ship had come to an end. Rose said tearful good-byes to Freddy and Robert, and exchanged addresses, promising to write. As the ship docked we could already see that Auntie Maude was there to greet us, standing beside an enormous black limousine with an Indian servant in tow.

'My darlings, how you've grown! What a pair of beauties!' She caught sight of us as we came down the gang-plank, flung her arms around us and hugged us to her ample bosom. She had grown stout over the years with good living, but her eyes were the same, still sparkling with mischief and humour.

'Well, it would be odd if we'd stayed the size we were when you left England!' said Rose, and Aunt Maude burst out laughing.

'Come on, let's get you up to the house. I've got the car here. The syce will take your trunks.'

We stared out of the open windows as the car made its way through the crowded streets lined with brightly painted Chinese shop-houses. It made slow progress, held up at every turn by rick-shaws, carts and bicycles.

Auntie Maude and Uncle Arthur lived on the outskirts of town, in a beautiful white stucco house surrounded by luxu-riant tropical gardens. When the car drew up on the gravel drive in front of the steps I knew I was going to adore staying here. We each had a vast room at the front of the house, over-

looking the gardens, with shutters and mosquito nets at the
windows. Every room had its own enormous bathroom
complete with a vast cast-iron Victorian bath and ancient lavatory that clanked and gurgled with age whenever it was
flushed.

For the first day or two we relaxed at the house, sitting in the
garden or reading in our rooms. Auntie Maude insisted that we
rest properly after our journey. However on the third day, when
we were in danger of growing bored, she told us to dress up. She
was taking us to the club.

It was one of the grand white buildings on the waterfront,
approached by a sweeping drive. Turbaned doormen bowed as
we went in through the imposing entrance.

'Come on, we'll go up to the bar. See who's around,' said
Auntie Maude, beckoning us forward. We settled at a table in the
corner of the bar, which was housed in a cavernous room with
floor-to-ceiling windows overlooking the harbour. Auntie was
looking round, as alert as a little bird, her beady eyes taking in
every detail, and commenting on the people at the other tables.
She seemed to know everyone.

'That's Martha and Joe Robinson,' she gestured to a stylish
young couple as they entered the room and were shown to a table
on the other side. 'He's a big noise in Firestone Rubber. Rumour
had it that they had some marriage problems last year. I think he
was playing away, as they say. But they seem to be over them now.
She's expecting in October ... Oh look, that's Sir James and Lady
Millicent Atherton,' she nodded towards a stout grey-haired man
and his much younger dark-haired wife. 'He runs the court
service. Another pair with marriage problems. It's her this time ...
Oh, and there's Jeremy Brown. He works for Sir James. Terribly
talented lawyer, apparently. No lady love on the horizon.' With
that remark she looked meaningfully at Rose. I looked away,
pretending not to notice. As every club member came and went
she gave them a little wave of her fan, had a private comment for

us and often a little potted history to go with it. She missed nobody.

The evening wore on, and Uncle Arthur joined us. He was a lot older than Auntie Maude, with grey whiskers and was running to fat. He was a mild-mannered benevolent man and smiled at his wife's tittle-tattle indulgently.

A couple of young men entered. One was unremarkable, with brown hair, of medium height and with neat, fresh looks. The other was something else. Tall, blond, tanned and well built. The company seemed to take in a collective breath and fall silent as the two men crossed to the bar and ordered drinks.

'Well, I'll be blowed,' said Auntie Maude, leaning in toward us and whispering conspiratorially. 'If it isn't Gavin Crosby.'

'Oh, that young scoundrel,' said Uncle Arthur with distaste. 'Thought he wasn't welcome around here.'

Auntie Maude gave him a pointed look. 'Yes, he's very unpopular now, since that dreadful business on the estate. Simply no one invites him anywhere these days. And I'm not surprised either,' she said, shaking her head and pursing her lips.

Rose and I looked at each other and shrugged, wondering what they meant. It didn't seem appropriate to ask. I couldn't stop looking at the newcomer, though. I had never seen anyone with quite such perfect looks before. I felt quite safe stealing the odd glance at him. No-one ever looked at me after all, and Rose was on the other side of the table. But the third time I looked, I realised that he was looking straight at me. I felt the colour rising in my cheeks and glanced down at the table quickly, praying that he would look away, but when I looked up he was still watching me, handling his drink absentmindedly and leaning backwards against the bar, appearing to be quite at home.

'Who is he?' asked Rose. I looked at her, wondering how she would react to someone looking my way instead of hers for once. If she felt piqued, she wasn't letting it show.

'Oh, he owns a rubber plantation up-country. Inherited it

from his parents, who both died of malaria within a few months of each other a couple of years back. Doing very well he is, too, by all accounts. That's his cousin, Johnny. He lives here in Penang. In some sort of import-export business. Gavin comes down to stay with him from time to time.'

'And what's the unfortunate matter you were talking about?'

'Hush, my dear,' Auntie Maude whispered, rolling her eyes. 'I can't talk about that now. Far too scandalous. I'll tell you all about it at home.'

Later, a small jazz band struck up on a little raised stage at the end of the bar. They were playing 'Night and Day'. I suddenly felt an unexpected tug of nostalgia for the old days at the Majestic ballroom, even though those evenings had often been tinged with unhappiness. I watched wistfully as a few couples got up and moved around the floor to the music. I glanced across the room and to my astonishment the handsome one was approaching our table. Rose was looking up expectantly. But he came around to my side.

'Would you like to dance?' I couldn't believe he was addressing me. I knew I was blushing furiously. Across the table, Auntie Maude's jaw dropped with surprise.

'What, me?' I asked stupidly.

He laughed. 'Yes, of course. You,' and he held out his hand. I got up awkwardly and let him lead me to the dance floor. I could feel Rose's astonished stare on us as Gavin took me in his arms.

3

J uliet sat there for a long time staring at the silver amulet. The little silver Buddha felt cold in the palm of her hand. The girl was watching her, quietly, waiting for her to speak. Just looking at it transported her back to that noisy backstreet in Colombo, filled with the cries of street sellers and the low chanting from the temple. She could almost smell the incense on the air. She remembered the fortune teller's face, the feel of those leathery fingers on her palm, and Rose's white face as she waited in the rickshaw.

Juliet realised that Abdul was hovering near them with the tray. 'Put it on the coffee table please, Abdul,' she said.

When he had gone she handed the amulet back to the girl. 'It certainly looks as though you've looked after it well,' she said crisply.

'Yes. I take care of it properly. I often clean it. It's my only link, you see. To my family.'

Juliet stared at the girl's face with its frank, open expression. How could she know that Rose's amulet connected them? The girl might have just come by it anyhow. She might even have stolen it. There were five-hundred acres of rubber trees out there that belonged to Juliet. She had a big house. To a penniless back-packer that must look like a fortune. This girl could simply be an imposter, coming here to string her along in the hope of some future inheritance. Perhaps she was even part of some wider criminal network, preying on lonely people to defraud them out of their fortunes. And yet, and yet ...

No, she mustn't let the girl know she was suspicious. She didn't want to get into any unpleasantness. 'Why don't you sit down?' said Juliet, smiling. 'You haven't even told me your name.'

'It's Mary,' said the girl, sitting down in one of the stiff-backed armchairs. 'Mary Batari. That's the name they gave me in the orphanage.'

'Orphanage?' Juliet asked, surprised. 'Where was that?'

'In Palembang, Indonesia. It was run by nuns. It was a very religious place to grow up. It was quite strict really, although everyone there was very kind.' The girl's face took on a serious look. The big-toothed smile gone.

'And where did you get the silver charm from?'

'Well, I'm not quite sure, but I've always had it with me. It was with me in the orphanage. I can't remember anyone ever giving it to me, though. It has been mine for as long as I can remember.'

'And when did you leave the orphanage?'

'About two years ago. I went to Singapore to train as a nurse at the General Hospital there. When I left the orphanage they gave me my papers and got me a passport. That's when I started searching for my real family. It's taken me all this time to track you down.'

'Look, I really don't know how I can have anything to do with someone from an orphanage in Palembang. You'll have to explain why you think we might be connected.'

The girl, still serious, looked down at her lap and hesitated. 'I'm not sure. Not absolutely. I'm taking a chance here. But you are my last hope.'

Juliet seized the moment. 'So, there's room for doubt then.

You might be wrong about the connection. You've been to see other people?'

'Yes. All I have to go on is this charm, and ...'

'And?'

'And nothing. Except for this bit of paper and hours and hours of digging.' She rummaged in the front pocket of her rucksack and produced a large cream envelope. From it she drew out a sheet of paper. She handed it to Juliet.

Juliet felt in her pocket for her reading glasses and peered through them at the typed document: 'September 1942. Baby girl admitted, approximately ten months old. Brought in by missionary from Bamboo Island. Possible survivor of the sinking of the *Rajah of Sarawak*.' Shock went through Juliet like a bolt of lightning. The hairs on the back of her neck stood on end. She stared at the paper until the writing blurred on the page, the words dancing in a black mist before her eyes.

'Are you alright?'

Juliet nodded and swallowed. For a moment she could not speak.

'It was your sister, wasn't it? On board that ship?'

She turned to the girl, suddenly resentful. Why was she doing this? What possible good could come from bringing back the pain of a past that had been buried for years?

'Do you know what happened to them?' Juliet said in a low voice, tight-lipped with suppressed anger and grief.

The girl began gently, 'Well, I've read as much as I can find out about it ...'

'But you haven't lived with it like I have, have you?' Juliet snapped. 'I've lived with it for nearly twenty years. Every day, the horror of it haunts me. The thought of what she went through. What those savages did to her. Her and ... and that beautiful baby girl.'

Juliet's throat constricted in pain and the tears began to flow, tears that had been held back for half a lifetime. And now that she had started, she couldn't stop. She knew what a sight she must look to this strange girl, losing control like that, her face blotched and red, eyes bloodshot and swollen. But she was past caring about that, she could not hold back.

'Why have you come here?' She sobbed bitterly. 'Why have you come to dig up the past? An hour ago, before you walked down that drive, I was happy. At least as happy as I could ever be. And now you've destroyed all that. How do you know who you are anyway? You could have been anyone's baby. Look at the words on here,' she said, waving the paper at the girl. '"Possible survivor". That's all. If they really thought it was true, why didn't they try to find your relatives?'

The girl looked flustered at this outburst. A flush crept up her neck and into her cheeks. 'I really don't know,' she stuttered. 'Obviously Sumatra was occupied by the Japanese for the rest of the war. And after that, who knows? There were new staff coming to work at the orphanage all the time. Maybe nobody ever looked at my papers until I came to leave.'

'So how did you find me?'

'When I was in Singapore I went to the public records office. It was the first thing I did when I had a day off work. I spent all my free time on the search. Eventually I found the records of the passengers on that ship. I started contacting the relatives of all of them. At first it was a bit random, I was getting nowhere. Then I began to approach people who were listed as having babies or children who had died. There were about ten of them. None of them knew anything about this charm and most of the children were older. You're the last. And you did recognise it, didn't you?'

'But that doesn't prove anything. Who knows how you got that amulet?'

The girl looked down, her face crestfallen. For a moment Juliet thought she was going to start crying too.

'I don't know,' she said simply, shaking her head. 'There's no-one who can tell me. There's no-one at the orphanage any more who was working there when I was brought in. I was just hoping …' she trailed off and took a sip of tea.

Abdul came into the room and began to move about, tidying and switching on the lamps as he always did at this time of day. 'How many for dinner, madam?' he asked.

Juliet glanced outside. The tropical night was falling rapidly. Outside, the sky was smoky blue, punctuated with sparkling stars. 'You'd better stay for supper,' she said to the girl. 'Abdul won't mind running you into Kuala Lipis later, will you, Abdul? There are plenty of guesthouses. He can make sure you find somewhere to stay.'

The girl smiled at her. 'Thank you. That's very kind.'

Later, as they sat at the polished table in the forlorn dining room, tucking into one of Abdul's rather hot Malay chicken curries, Juliet asked, 'So, tell me. How did you actually track me down to this place?'

'Oh, a lot of detective work. As I mentioned, there was a list of people who died when the ship went down, together with their next of kin. I worked through those whose babies were listed as having died, and your sister was on that list.'

'What did it say? I've never seen it.'

'It said "Mrs. Rose Thompson and baby Claire". There were two addresses written there. One was Tengah Air Base, Singapore. That was crossed out, and this address was listed beside it. Windy Ridge Estate, Kuala Lipis.'

'That would have been right … When Rose boarded the *Rajah of Sarawak* her house in Singapore had already been bombed. She would probably have given this as her only address.'

'What about her husband? Why wasn't he listed beside her name? He must be my father. I'm that baby. I'm Claire, aren't I?'

'Look, aren't you jumping to conclusions here? There must have been so much confusion on that ship! Not everyone would have been listed as being on board. It was one of the last ships to leave before Singapore fell. People were crowding on board without papers. Perhaps there were some babies that just didn't get on that list? You might belong to one of the unmarried women who didn't want to list a baby for obvious reasons. I think you're really getting ahead of yourself.'

Juliet just couldn't believe that this breathing, living girl was the lost baby. How could it possibly be her? Rising from the dead after all these years? It must be some elaborate scam. Suddenly she felt weary. She had had enough.

'Look, I know this can't be easy for you,' said Mary. 'It isn't easy for me either, believe me. It was incredibly hard to track down those families. Names had changed, people had moved on. Now I've finally found what I think is a link, but you just don't want to give this a chance.'

'I just need some proof that's all,' said Juliet, setting down her fork. 'Something more than just a bit of paper and an old neck-lace. The paper could be a forgery for all I know and—' She stopped suddenly, remembering that she hadn't intended to let it slip that she suspected the girl's motives.

Mary's expression hardened. She pursed her lips and pushed her plate away, dabbed her mouth on a napkin. 'Forgery?' she asked. 'You think I'm some kind of fraudster, trying to take you for a ride?' She pushed her chair back and stood up, lifting her chin defiantly. 'If you don't mind, perhaps I could have that lift into town now? I've lost my appetite. I won't bother you again. I'm sorry to have upset you.'

Juliet stood at the front window and watched the tail lights of the old Morris disappear down the drive. Then, she went to the roll-top desk in the corner of her living room and pulled out an old leather-bound photo album. She had not opened it for years. Looking at it caused so much pain. But now she opened the first page and there they were, the two of them, her and Rose, on their very first week in Penang. They were sitting on deck chairs on the terrace at Auntie Maude's, holding up glasses in a toast to their new life on the island. She sighed and snapped the book shut.

Turning back into the room, something on the coffee table flashed in the light. It was the amulet. The girl must have left it behind in her haste to leave. Juliet picked it up and held it to the lamp. Even more than the pictures, it brought the memories flooding back, as bright and clear as if everything had happened only yesterday, and once again she was reminded of what she had lost. She began to cry, great heaving sobs of loneliness and regret that she could not hold back.

4

Juliet pushed back the sheets, parted the mosquito net and heaved herself out of bed. She crossed the bare boards of her room and drew back the curtains. It was still dark outside, but she could tell from the halo of pale light on the eastern horizon that dawn would soon be breaking. She had barely slept. The past had haunted her all night. The recurring image of Rose's tear-stained face as they had said goodbye in Singapore for the last time had troubled her most of all.

She could hear Abdul moving about in the kitchen preparing her breakfast. She was normally up at six, eating porridge before heading down to the estate. But this morning was different. She had other plans for the day. Jalak, the Malaysian overseer, could manage without her for a few hours.

She went through to the bathroom and washed quickly and efficiently in cold water from the gurgling tap. That was no hardship. The room was hot and steamy. Although there was a ceiling fan above her bed, which whirred and clanked through the night to create a feeble breeze, there was no such concession to the stifling heat in the bathroom. Juliet pulled on some loose linen trousers and a short-sleeved blouse. She glanced at her reflection in the mirror on the dresser. There were streaks of grey in her mousy brown hair now. She brushed it quickly and carelessly and tied it into a pony tail. She could hear Rose's voice in her head: 'You'll get split ends if you use an elastic band.' Juliet smiled. 'I don't care,' she said aloud, slapping some cold cream onto her face. This was the usual extent of her beauty regime, but this morning, peering at her face more closely, she wondered if she should use some powder and lipstick.

'God, girl. You do look a sight,' she said to her reflection, pulling a face. There were bruised smudges under her eyes from lack of sleep, and the lines on her cheeks were deeply ingrained from lying face-down on the hard cotton of her pillow.

As she came downstairs, Abdul looked up in surprise. He was setting the table for breakfast. 'Good morning, madam. Up very early this morning,' he said.

'Yes, good morning, Abdul. Do you know what time the first train to Singapore leaves from Kuala Lipis today?'

'Normally seven o'clock, I think. You go to Singapore, madam?'

'No, Abdul. But I need to see the young lady who was here yesterday. She's going to Singapore by train and she left something behind.'

'You want me to take it to the guesthouse, madam? Save you trouble?'

'No, thank you. I need to pop into town myself anyway,' she said, trying to sound casual. 'You can tell Jalak that I'll be along later.'

He gave her a searching look, and she looked away quickly. He knew her too well. He had come to the house when he was young, as a new assistant houseboy before the war and had been here ever since. He knew everything about her. He knew her moods almost better than she knew them herself. He knew every expression on her face, every passing whim she might entertain.

She wondered how much of the conversation he had overheard the evening before.

'That will be all. Thank you, Abdul,' she said curtly. 'You can bring my breakfast now, please. Then perhaps you could get the car out of the garage? I'd better be getting along soon.'

'As you say, madam,' he said with a slight bow, moving slowly towards the kitchen.

It felt liberating to leave the estate behind and head down the rutted road between the regimented lines of rubber trees. Soon the trees ended, and thick jungle crowded the road on either side; in some places luxuriant bushes grew overhead and met in the middle, enclosing the road in a tunnel filled with green light. It didn't trouble Juliet, being alone in the jungle like this. It was her home and it felt natural to be here. It was almost six-thirty when she arrived in the outskirts of the town. She headed straight for the railway station. The girl might already be there, waiting for the train. She parked in the yard and hurried onto the platform. There were a couple of young men sitting on a bench with backpacks beside them, sipping through straws from fresh coconuts, and a couple of families of locals weighed down with boxes and bundles as they waited for the train. There was no sign of Mary.

Sighing, Juliet returned to the car and set off through the backstreets to where Abdul had dropped Mary off the previous evening. She was not quite sure of the way and took several wrong turns. She began to panic, sweating uncomfortably, her blouse sticking to her skin. Eventually she drew up in front of the Star Guesthouse. It was very run-down, with peeling paint and dirty windows, and Juliet felt a pang of guilt for consigning the girl to this unwelcoming place.

The receptionist was barely awake and yawned that there was indeed a young woman called Mary Batari staying in Room 10. Yes, she was still here and no, she had not yet come down for breakfast.

'Could I possibly have a coffee then? I'll wait for her.'

Juliet sat at a flimsy plastic table in a sparse dining room cooled by noisy fans. A weary looking waiter brought her a fresh coffee, and it tasted surprisingly good. As she waited she assessed the guests at the other tables: three or four Malaysian men, probably down-at-heel commercial travellers, and a western couple dressed only in shorts and vests, gobbling a full fry up as if they hadn't eaten for days.

After a few minutes she saw Mary coming down the stairs and stood up to greet her. The girl looked different today. Her thick dark hair had been backcombed in the style of the moment, and she had made up her eyes with black eyeliner. Despite that she looked younger, more fresh-faced and vulnerable. She wore a short cotton dress and flip-flops. Mary stopped and hesitated as she caught sight of Juliet then began to walk towards her slowly.

'Why have you come?' Mary asked, reaching the table.

'Can't you guess? You left the amulet behind.'

'I know. But I realised that it belonged to you more than it belonged to me, so I wasn't planning to come back and get it.'

'Look, why don't you sit down? We can talk about it.'

Looking troubled and reluctant, Mary sat opposite her at the table. The waiter brought her the menu and hovered over her until she had ordered.

'So?' she asked Juliet when he had gone. 'Why *did* you come?' Juliet noticed that the skin under Mary's eyes was puffy beneath the foundation, and guessed that the girl had probably spent a restless night as well.

'I told you. To bring this.' She held the amulet out and Mary took it, fastened it around her neck and tucked the charm into the front of her dress.

'If you thought I had no connection to you, you would have just kept it.'

'Well, I wouldn't go that far. But yes, perhaps I was a bit hasty last night. I've hardly slept, Mary. I was thinking about Rose and the war all night. I was in shock, you see, when you turned up out of the blue. I just simply wasn't ready.'

'And what about now?'

'I just think we should give it a bit more time. Would you like to come back to the estate with me? We could have lunch and a chat.'

'I'm not sure. Is there any point? You obviously thought I was some sort of con-artist yesterday. What's changed your mind?'

'I've had a bit of time to think, that's all.'

The waiter came with more coffee and a plate of fried eggs on toast. Juliet watched Mary as she began to eat. She tucked in as if she hadn't eaten for a month. Juliet's stomach already felt weak from lack of sleep, and the sight of the runny yokes and their greasy smell made her suddenly nauseous.

'Are you alright?' Mary was watching her.

'Yes. Just a bit tired, that's all.'

'You could always go and rest in my room.'

'That's very kind of you, but I'll be fine. What about it then? Would you like to come back with me?'

Mary shrugged. 'I suppose it can't do any harm, but I'll have to leave here first thing tomorrow. I'm due back at the hospital on Monday.'

'Abdul or I can drop you back here this evening so you can get the early train in the morning.'

'Alright, I suppose I might as well. There isn't very much to do around here.'

On the way back to the estate Mary sat on the front passenger seat, staring out of the window, clutching her knees. She hardly spoke. Juliet began to feel uncomfortable. Had she done the right thing asking the girl back? She was so unused to company, especially young people. How would she entertain this girl for the rest of the day?

'You don't have many visitors here, do you?' Mary remarked as they entered the house.

Juliet bristled. 'I've got lots of friends,' she said defensively. 'But I tend to visit them, rather than have them come here, it's true. There's not much to do here for guests. I'm normally out working on the estate.'

'Would you be working today if I wasn't here?'

'Of course. I work every day except for Sundays. And even sometimes then, if it's busy.'

'Well don't let me stop you. I could come with you.' Mary was looking at her, smiling that wide toothy smile for the first time that day.

Juliet stared at her. Why would a young girl be interested in seeing a rubber estate? Was she just looking for an easy inheritance? 'No, it's quite alright,' she answered stiffly. 'They can manage perfectly well without me. I deserve a day off now and again. Look, let's go and sit down on the veranda. Would you like a coffee or something?'

Abdul brought them a pot of freshly brewed coffee and they sat in the rattan chairs under the fans. 'Did you say you were a nurse?' asked Juliet.

Mary's face lit up in a wide smile again. 'Training to be one, yes. I've got another year to go. It's wonderful. It's what I've always wanted to do.'

'And do you live in the hospital?'

Mary nodded. 'Yes, in a nurses' hostel. Full of other girls of my age. We have so much fun together! We sometimes go to the cinema, or out dancing.'

Juliet smiled, remembering her trips to the cinema with Rose.

Mary broke the silence: 'What happened to your husband?'

Juliet flushed and she put down the coffee cup, her hands beginning to shake. 'He died in the war.'

'Was he a soldier?'

'God, no! He stayed here managing the plantation.'

'And?' Mary asked gently.

'Look, it's difficult for me to talk about the past. Can't you see that?'

'I'm sorry. I'm just curious ... I was going to ask you, and you'll probably say no, but I was wondering if you have any pictures of her?'

'Of whom?'

'Of Rose, of course. Of my mother.'

Juliet had anticipated this. She wasn't going to get the album. That would be too much. She went to the bureau in the living room and fetched a small framed picture of Rose and herself sitting on the veranda here together. She handed it to Mary.

Mary stared at it for a long time. When she looked up tears were brimming in her eyes. 'She was very beautiful,' she said.

Juliet nodded and said, 'Too beautiful to be my sister.'

The girl stiffened. 'I didn't say that.'

'Look, shall we go for a walk?' Juliet suddenly didn't want to sit there anymore. She felt the need to be on the move. 'I suppose I *could* look in on the estate offices and let them know I won't be down at all today, and I'll show you around.'

Mary nodded, brightening immediately. 'That would be super. I'd love that.'

They set off down the drive, through the front gates and turned onto the estate road, which wound through the trees. The offices were a quarter of a mile or so away at the bottom of the gently sloping hill. As they walked, Mary looked around her, shading her eyes, admiring the scenery.

'I don't think I've ever been on a rubber estate before,' she said.

'There's not much to see really. Row upon row of trees just like this, stretching as far as the horizon. I'll show you some tappers lines later, where we extract the latex. That's the interesting bit.'

'What's that building down there?' the girl asked, pointing through the trees.

Juliet followed Mary's gaze, then looked away quickly. Dear God, she shouldn't have brought the girl this way. 'That's just an old derelict bungalow,' she mumbled, trying to sound disinterested.

'Does anyone live there? Can we go and take a look? I just love old buildings!'

'It's not very nice. No-one's been there for years. Mary—' But the girl had already started to stride down the little overgrown path that led to the bungalow in the hollow. Juliet hurried after her. 'I'd rather you didn't go down there,' she said, raising her voice.

'I just want to see. Promise I won't touch anything,' Mary called back over her shoulder.

Juliet ran behind her, but Mary was rushing ahead in her excitement. She was already inside the overgrown front garden, skipping up the decaying front steps, rattling the front door handle.

'I don't have the key. You won't be able to get in,' Juliet protested.

'But the door's not locked.' Mary was already turning the handle and pushing the warped front door open with her knee.

Juliet walked up the wooden steps and stood on the porch clinging to the bannisters. Dreadful images overwhelmed her, of him lying on the boards, blood oozing from a gunshot wound in his stomach. She could hear his yells of pain again, his animal howls. And she had just watched him, covering her ears to blot out the sounds. She looked inside for a moment, and there were the dark stains on the boards where he had bled to death. As she stared at them, they seemed to her as livid red and fresh as that fateful day. And again she heard his yells and moans as he clutched his stomach. Nausea overwhelmed her. She sank to her knees, retching air.

'Are you alright? Mrs. Crosby,' Mary was looking at her with anxiety. 'Are you OK?'

'Not really, my dear. I think I'm going to be sick.'

GEORGETOWN, Penang 1938

Life in Penang settled down into a very agreeable routine. Rose and I would sleep fairly late in the mornings, until we were woken up by Auntie Maude's ayah with a cup of tea. We would then bathe in the palatial bathrooms and proceed downstairs to a buffet breakfast laid out in the dining room: scrambled eggs, kippers, porridge, fresh fruit and whatever else took our fancy. We would then head out to town in Auntie Maude's great black Daimler, to see the sights, wander around the street markets, or just sit on a bench beside the harbour watching the great ships pass through the straits and the flotilla of tiny boats that constantly plied to and fro in the port.

We would make our way back to White Gables, as the house was called, for afternoon tea, a rest in the garden followed by leisurely evenings almost invariably spent at the club.

This routine was interspersed for me by delicious interludes with Gavin Crosby. The day after our first dance at the club, a short, polite note arrived at the house by messenger: 'Dear Miss Edwards, it would give me great pleasure if you would accompany me to dinner at the Eastern and Oriental Hotel this evening. Please let my manservant know your response. If you are able to come, I will pick you up at seven o'clock.'

'How very quaint!' exclaimed Rose when she read the note.

'Perhaps that's just how they do things round here,' I said defensively.

I was desperate to accept the invitation, but found myself remembering the displeasure on Uncle's usually mild-mannered face at the sight of Gavin when he appeared in the club, and Auntie Maude's ominous words about 'that dreadful business'. They had not explained things when we got home from the club that first evening, perhaps because they had realised that I had taken a fancy to Gavin and had wanted to spare my feelings. Now it played on my mind. What dreadful thing could they have been referring to? Perhaps some business matter connected with the rubber estate? It didn't sound like that though.

'You *are* going to go, aren't you?' asked Rose.

'I'd like to, but ...'

'You're thinking about Auntie and Uncle, aren't you? Don't worry about them. I'll keep them occupied.'

'No, it's just ... you know. That thing they mentioned at the club. About the dreadful business.'

'Oh that. It's bound to be nothing. You know what an old gossip Auntie is. There's obviously not much going on around here, and the most trivial thing probably gets blown up into a major scandal. Why don't you ask him about it?'

'Ask Gavin? Don't be silly, Rose. I don't want to get off on the wrong foot.'

Well, *I'd* ask him if I were you.'

'Yes, I can just imagine that. You probably would. But I can't.'

The dining room at the Eastern and Oriental hotel was everything I'd imagined a restaurant in a grand old imperial hotel would be, with its pillars, marble floors, huge potted palms and fans whirring in the high ceiling. It was the epitome of colonial elegance. Taking my seat at the table opposite Gavin, I was very nervous and couldn't stop my hands from trembling as I held the cocktail menu, trying to decide what to order from the multitude of complicated recipes. He leaned over and whisked it away from me.

'Have a Singapore Sling. They're not as good here as in Raffles but it's still the best cocktail you'll find in the East.'

'That sounds lovely,' I said smiling. I was happy to have the decision taken for me.

I noticed that Gavin was watching me closely, contemplating my face, leaning back in his chair and putting the tips of his fingers together. I couldn't help but admire him. He really was blessed with good looks. A well-made face, with perfect features, suntanned skin and serious blue eyes.

'You're not used to getting attention from men, are you?' he asked suddenly, and I felt the colour rush to my cheeks. I looked down at the tablecloth, not knowing what to say.

'I bet your sister steals all the limelight, doesn't she?'

I shrugged and tried to smile. 'She *is* very attractive. It's hardly surprising.'

'But I chose you,' he stated simply. 'You looked more interesting. You've got beautiful bone structure, you know, lovely eyes and you're tall and graceful. Your sister's looks are ... How do I put this without sounding unkind? Rather obvious, I think.'

'It isn't a competition,' I said, feeling uncomfortable discussing Rose like this. He laughed.

'Of course not. And I admire your loyalty. It's just my round-about way of telling you that I find you very beautiful, intriguing even.'

After that, and having downed a couple of gin slings rather quickly, I began to relax and the conversation began to flow more easily. We discovered that we had much in common. We were both the older of two children, and had both been recently bereaved. He spoke of the death of his parents with emotion. At one point I thought I saw tears in his eyes.

'It was only last year. They had both been on a trip up-country into the jungle. Father was looking for land to buy. He was interested in setting up another estate, with rubber booming as it is. We can't meet the demand with what we produce. They were away for a few weeks camping in the hills and they both contracted malaria. When they came back they both went down with the fever at the same time. There was nothing the doctors could do for either of them. It was a virulent strain.'

'It must have been dreadful for you.' He nodded. 'But it must be comforting to have your brother around,' I said, but then saw a shadow of something new cross his face. Was it anger, irritation? He quickly recovered his composure.

'I'd hardly say that. Scott and I don't get on that well, as a matter of fact. He's not there very much anyway. He's in the army now. Only comes back on leave now and again.'

Realising it was difficult for him to speak about it, I didn't ask about his brother again.

When he drove me home, he stopped the car outside the gates of the house and leaned over to kiss me. It was delicious being kissed by those perfect lips and feeling his strong arms around me. I was ready to fend off any further advances but was surprised when he stopped with that rather restrained, respectful kiss.

After that I was lost to him. I had no more qualms about whatever scandal might taint his family name. I put that to the back of my mind.

We saw each other almost every day for the next fortnight. He would collect me in his car in the mornings and we would drive around the island, to the beautiful deserted beaches in the north, or over the hills to marvel at the views of the shimmering ocean stretching into eternity. I had never been happier. I was enchanted by my tropical surroundings and by Gavin. He was right: I had not had much male attention before, and it didn't take much for me to be completely addicted to his company. As we strolled together arm in arm on the beach or on jungle trails in the hills, we talked about our families and friends, about books we had read and films we had both seen, about politics and the worrying situation building up in Europe. There was never any difficulty between us or awkward moments, and when it came to saying goodbye, he would put his arms round me and kiss me on my cheek, just like the first time. He never once tried to go further, rather to my disappointment.

Auntie Maude tried to warn me off a couple of times.

'You know, you shouldn't get too close to Gavin Crosby,' she said, coming into my room as I prepared to go out with him one morning. I was sitting at the dressing table, putting on my make-up.

'Why ever not, Auntie?'

'Because he lives a long way away and he won't be in Georgetown for long.' I knew that couldn't possibly be the reason.

'Plenty of people have long-distance relationships,' I said simply. 'Look at all the girls in love with soldiers. They must be away nearly all the time.'

'Well it's not just that,' she mumbled, sounding uncomfortable. She crossed the room and sat down heavily on the bed. 'That family's not well-liked amongst the ex-pat community in Malaya, you know. There's bad blood there.'

'Bad blood? Whatever does that mean?' I said, trying to make light of it, but I was beginning to get annoyed.

'His father was an absolute tyrant. He was a very bad employer, treated the workers on the estate like slaves. He was a hard drinker too, and a womaniser.'

'But that's not Gavin,' I protested. 'Whatever his father was like, he's different.'

'The seed doesn't fall far from the tree,' Auntie said, pursing her lips.

'What was that business you were going to tell us about?' asked Rose from the doorway. She'd obviously been listening in on the conversation.

'What's it to you?' I spun round to face her, angry now. Wasn't Rose supposed to be on my side? And why were they so against Gavin anyway, when all he'd been to me was perfectly charming and considerate?

'I wasn't going to tell you, as you were so determined to be friends with him,' said Auntie Maude, drawing herself up, 'but I think things are getting serious now. Perhaps now is the time to bring it out in the open. I really don't think you should get any closer to him, Juliet. And when he goes back to Kuala Lipis I think you should forget all about him.'

'Well go on, tell me then. What is he supposed to have done that's so dreadful?'

'I said his father was a womaniser. And so are the sons. The father was always carrying on with one or other of the native female workers, and the sons too by all accounts.' I watched her face as she spoke. She looked deeply embarrassed, not meeting my eyes. She spoke breathlessly, as if she wanted to get the story over and done with as quickly as possible. I felt weak with shock. I put the hairbrush down on the dressing table so they wouldn't see my hands shaking. It couldn't be true. Gavin was such a gentleman.

'The younger brother, Scott, got a daughter of one of the workers ... Well, you know, in the family way. She was very young. Only a teenager, apparently. Rumour has it that he paid for her to ... Well, get rid of the baby, but it all went wrong and she was very ill. Nearly died. The father went up to the house to ask for compensation for her medical bills and there was a huge row. It ended up in Gavin expelling the family from the estate. They lost everything. Livelihood, home, friends. They had to move right away from the area. There was a strike on the estate after that and it went on for weeks. Things only got back to normal a couple of months ago.'

'But that wasn't Gavin's fault, was it?' I said, slightly relieved. 'It was his brother.'

'No, but it might just as well have been, from all accounts. We've heard such rumours about Gavin, too. Besides, he handled the whole thing very badly. He's made himself a lot of enemies, both amongst the natives and the Europeans.'

I was silent, digesting the information. This must be why Gavin was so reluctant to talk about his brother. But I quickly exonerated him in my mind: it wasn't his fault, it was his brother's. If he had handled the workers badly that was because he was young and inexperienced and still reeling from the loss of his parents.

'It doesn't make any difference to me,' I said defiantly. 'It doesn't sound as though Gavin was to blame. And I don't believe what you're saying about him being a womaniser as well. He just isn't like that. I know him.'

Auntie Maude got up from the bed. 'Well, I've told you now. You can't say I haven't warned you. You're old enough to make your own decisions, Juliet,' she said frostily as she walked across the room.

'Don't be like that, Auntie. I'm sorry you feel that way, but I think you should give him a chance. He's really not like you say. Not at all.'

'You know why he's picked you, don't you?' She stopped midway and turned, and I saw a glint of something new in her eye. For the first time I had a glimpse of a different side of Auntie Maude, a vindictive side that must have been borne of all the years of living in this closed community with nothing to do but spread malicious gossip.

'What on earth do you mean?'

Her puffy face was an unhealthy red now.

'He's picked you only because you're new here and you don't know what the Crosbys are like. He wouldn't have a chance with any of the other European girls who've lived here all their lives. And one day he'll need someone to look after him and run that great house for him.'

'How can you say that? That's a beastly thing to say, Auntie.' I burst into tears.

'Because it's true, my girl. You mark my words,' and she walked huffily from the room.

Rose rushed over and put her arms around me, and I sobbed into her shoulder, smarting at the cruelty of my aunt's words yet wondering if there was any truth in them.

5

A week or so after my argument with Auntie Maude, Gavin told me that he would soon have to leave Georgetown. We were sipping coffee in a Chinese café in a shop-house near the harbour.

'They need me at the estate, I'm afraid. I only came down to stay with Johnny to buy some spare parts for our equipment and arrange for them to be transported up to the estate by train. I've been prolonging my visit because of you, but I must get back. We had a bit of trouble a few months ago at the estate. I can't be away for too long.'

'Trouble?'

'Yes. There was a strike. It all got rather unpleasant. It was all over a ridiculous argument I had with one of the tappers. He'd been taking time off without permission but was still demanding his wages. He was one of those militant types. It blew up out of all proportion I'm afraid.'

'Really?'

'Yes, really. Why? Have you heard anything about it?'

'No,' I said, trying to keep my voice level, but I was a hopeless liar and couldn't meet his eye.

'There have been all sorts of wild rumours circulating about me. I know that much. People have been snubbing me in the club ever since I got here,' he was looking earnestly into my eyes as he spoke. 'I'm afraid my father was not well-liked around these parts. The simple fact is he was successful. Too successful. People didn't like that. It isn't quite British. They'll take every opportunity they can to spread evil rumours about my family.' His jaw set bitterly for a few seconds, and I saw a vein pulsing in his neck. But he then took a deep breath and smiled at me. 'You do understand that, don't you? Lots of people here have nothing better to do than to gossip. Some of it is quite harmful stuff.'

'Of course.' Was he telling the truth? I had no way of knowing. He certainly sounded plausible, and I was glad that he had brought up the matter at last. It had cleared the air and I didn't have to worry about the shadow of the secret hanging over us anymore.

'Would you like to come up and stay with me on the estate for a few days next month?' he asked suddenly.

'I'd love to,' I said straight away. But then my spirits sank as I remembered that Auntie Maude was bound to disapprove. 'The only thing is, I'm not sure my aunt would be very happy about it,' I said. 'She seems to think she should behave as if she were my mother.'

'Perhaps I could come and speak to her? Reassure her that you'll be perfectly safe.'

'No,' I said quickly, 'I don't think that's a very good idea.'

'I just can't think of any other way of seeing you. I really need to get back to the estate. I'm going to miss you so much, Juliet,' he said, taking my hand on the table.

'I'll miss you too,' I said, squeezing his hand and gazing into his eyes. 'I'll try to think of a way of talking her round.'

Auntie Maude had been frosty towards me for a couple of days after our argument, but her natural good nature had eventually prevailed and it was soon forgotten. Besides, she had another interest to occupy her by then.

We had been invited to a dinner party at High Tops, the home of Sir James and Lady Millicent Atherton. Being shunned by most of the community, Gavin had not been asked along. I had sat with Auntie Maude at the end of the ballroom, watching other couples as they spun round the floor. We noticed that Lady Millicent spent most of the evening in the company of a tall young man with dark hair

'He's new here,' said Auntie Maude dismissively. 'She'll make mincemeat of him, just like the others.'

Of course all the young men there had flocked to dance with Rose. Although she had her pick of eligible army officers and young businessmen, she seemed to be enjoying the company of one dancing partner more than the others. As the waltz brought them spinning towards where we were sitting, I realised who it was. He looked even more dashing tonight in his dark uniform, sporting the RAF wings on his epaulets.

'That's Robert Thompson,' Auntie Maude noted approvingly. 'He grew up here. Went away to school and to Oxford I believe. I think he's now stationed at Tengah Air Base in Singapore, but his parents live here in Penang. He must be home on leave.'

'I know him, Auntie,' I said, and I couldn't help feeling a little triumphant at her look of disgruntled surprise. 'Quite well, in fact. We met him on the ship over here. He and Rose took quite a shine to each other on the voyage. It's so lovely for her that he's here. They seemed to get on so well.'

It was soon clear that Robert Thompson was completely besotted with Rose and that she was very taken with him, too. They began to spend a lot of time together and of course Auntie Maude was delighted: Robert had a promising career in the RAF and although he had not mentioned anything about it on the voyage, it emerged that his family was very well off; his father owned several tin mines up country. Auntie Maude threw herself into ensuring the success of the relationship. She fawned over Robert whenever he came to the house, visited his mother for afternoon tea, and invited him and his parents over for dinner as often as she could.

When I told her that Gavin had asked me to stay with him, she was in her study sorting through recipes for another dinner party she was throwing for Robert and his family. She looked up from her desk and stared at me vacantly. It was almost as if she had forgotten who Gavin was, as if all the fuss over the scandal about him had vanished from her mind.

'If you must go, you must, Juliet dear. I'm not your mother, and I'm not here to preach. All I can say is be very careful. You don't want to get caught out, if you catch my meaning?'

I blushed to the roots of my hair. 'You needn't worry about that,' I said. 'Gavin's a perfect gentleman.'

She raised her eyebrows and stared at me sceptically for a few seconds before returning with a preoccupied frown to the important business of the menus.

Rose was preoccupied herself, floating about the house with a blissful smile on her lips. When I told her I was going to stay with Gavin, she threw her arms around me saying, 'I'm so happy for you, Jules darling. Isn't it wonderful? Everything's turning out so well here for us. I'm just dreading waking up one day and finding out it was just a dream.'

I was nervous about the journey ahead of me. I had never travelled alone in a foreign country before, and as I stepped onto the passenger ferry at Georgetown with my small suitcase and waved goodbye to Rose from the deck, I felt a certain amount of trepidation. But I need not have worried. The ferry only took about half an hour to cross the straits to Butterworth and it was a short rickshaw ride from the docks to the train station. The train south to Kuala Lumpur was far more civilised than travelling at home. There was a porter in attendance in every carriage, whose job was to bring drinks and refreshments from the restaurant car.

I sat back in the comfortable seat and relaxed. As I watched the countryside of oil palm and rubber plantations unfold, against a backdrop of distant hills, and interspersed with stretches of untamed jungle, it suddenly struck me how far I had come in less than a year, how my life had changed completely. I felt very different now from the shy, buttoned up girl who had led that dreary existence in London.

I changed trains in Kuala Lumpur, not daring to go out of the cavernous station in case I missed the connection on to Gemas. At the little town of Gemas I had to stay the night in a hotel. Uncle Arthur had wired an advance booking for me from his office. The hotel was next to the station. It was sparse but clean and I ate my meal in the almost empty dining room, waited on by uniformed staff who jumped to attend my every need.

The nine-hour-long journey from Gemas up to Kuala Lipis was truly breath-taking. The little steam train climbed steadily through mile upon mile of hills covered in dense jungle, passing the occasional tiny settlement built of bamboo and palm leaves where semi-naked villagers stopped to stare at us as we passed. It then rattled on through steep-sided mountains, with plunging valleys and rocky outcrops, where there were spectacular views of towering peaks and thundering waterfalls.

Gavin was standing on the platform to meet me at the small station at Kuala Lipis. I had not seen him for three weeks. He took me in his arms and held me for a long time. Everything around us seemed to fade away. All that mattered was his touch and the feel of his lips on my face.

'I've missed you,' I whispered in his ear.

'I've missed you too, Juliet,' he said.

When I saw Windy Ridge for the first time it took my breath away. We approached from the jungle road, and drove through regimented lines of rubber trees, bathed in their grey-green light. As we emerged into sunlight, the house was ahead on the crest of the hill, looking majestic but somehow welcoming too.

Gavin looked sideways at me and seemed secretly gratified at my reaction. 'Like the house?' he asked, as if trying to sound casual.

I nodded. 'It's beautiful. I'd no idea it would be so grand.'

'It's not bad, is it? Father built it about fifteen years ago when he started making money from the estate. Before that we lived in a little wooden bungalow down the hill. Do you know, when father first came here he lived in a tent while they cleared the jungle and planted the rubber trees?'

'That must have been tough.'

'He was a tough customer. He was a hard old Scotsman, a pioneer, you know. They were selling land cheap to people who'd served in the Great War and he'd been a fusilier, so he qualified. This was the first rubber estate around these parts.'

By this time we had reached the front steps, and he pulled the car up, leapt out and got my suitcase from the boot. 'Allow me to show you inside,' he said proudly, taking my arm and leading me up the front steps.

The rooms were painted in pale colours, chintzy curtains hung at the windows. It was furnished with low tables and expensive looking furniture. As he showed me round I just kept murmuring 'It's beautiful, Gavin. You're so lucky to live here'.

'Ma designed all this. She spent years planning and decorating the rooms. Everything was brought up by train from Singapore. She only wanted the best for her house.'

I stayed with him for four days and in that time Gavin never put a foot wrong. I slept in his mother's room on the first floor at the front of the house, overlooking the lawns and the jungle beyond. It was a beautiful room with a four-poster bed draped in white mosquito netting, and a carved oak dressing table in front of the window. It felt strange occupying the room of a recently dead woman. I could not help wondering if she had suffered and died here in the bed, and at night I would have disturbing dreams and wake bathed in sweat, imagining that I too had succumbed to a virulent strain of malaria.

By day Gavin took me out riding on the estate. Being raised in London I had never been on a horse before, only donkeys on day trips to Brighton and camels at London zoo, but I found it surprisingly easy, and after a few short lessons Gavin proclaimed me to be a natural.

When he showed me around the plantation headquarters and the factory sheds, I couldn't help noticing that when he entered, a hush fell over the workers, and whenever he went to speak to one of them at work on the presses in the factory, or to one of the tappers at the trees, they would answer him reluctantly in sullen terms, refusing to look him in the eye. But I chose to ignore this, putting it to the back of my mind. I didn't want to think about the scandal or question whether he had told me the truth or not. I didn't want to let anything spoil our time together.

On my last day at Windy Ridge, when we returned to the house for tea, we had to step over a pair of leather boots casually flung aside in the doorway. At the sight of them the colour drained from Gavin's face.

'So, Gavin, old boy, you've finally found a woman who's prepared to put up with you, have you? Hmm, not a bad catch, I must say.' The voice came from the chair in the corner of the room, where a young man was lounging, his shirt unbuttoned and feet propped up on the coffee table. I guessed it was Gavin's brother. He looked like Gavin, but was stockier and shorter and had not been blessed with his good looks. When he smiled, his teeth were a little too large, and his eyes were slightly too close together to be anything approaching handsome. His thatch of hair was darker than Gavin's too.

'What the hell are you doing here, Scott?'

'Regiment's being transferred down to Singapore on Friday, so they've let us have a few days leave. Sorry, if I'd known you had company ...' He took a swig from a whisky bottle and gave me a wide smile. I smiled back at him feebly, feeling uncomfortable.

'Watch it, Scott. It's a bit early to be hitting the bottle,' said Gavin.

'I can do what I damned well like. It's my home as much as yours. Let's take a look at the little lady then,' Scott said standing up and walking unsteadily across the room towards us, still grinning at me.

'Go to hell. Leave her alone.'

I had never seen Gavin angry before, or even heard him raise his voice, but now all that pent up tension I had often sensed simmering there bubbled up to the surface. I saw the muscles in his arms flex under his shirt, and an angry red flush begin to creep up his neck. As Scott carried on swaying towards us, whisky bottle in hand, Gavin took a step towards him and shoved him away.

'Don't you dare come near her,' he said between clenched teeth.

'You don't want her to see you lose your temper now do you, Gavin? That *would* look ugly, wouldn't it?'

Gavin turned to me. 'Go upstairs,' he said, his voice strained with anger. 'I'll come up in a minute.'

I rushed upstairs, a sick feeling in the pit of my stomach. I had never witnessed such an unpleasant scene within a family before. I found it difficult to comprehend. I went quickly up to the bedroom, locked the door and threw myself on the bed. I realised I was shaking all over.

After about half an hour the shouting stopped. I heard the front door slam and unsteady footsteps on the drive. A few minutes later, Gavin walked into the room. He sat on the bed, his head in his hands. He was sweating heavily and his face was flushed.

'I'm so sorry you had to witness that,' he said. 'Scott is always difficult when he's been drinking. And that's all too often nowadays.'

'Why is he like that?'

'He's always been a bit wild. Father tried to beat it out of him. He beat us both, but Scott had it worse than me. Once or twice he got locked in the stables when he'd done something to annoy Father.'

I stared at him. 'But that's dreadful, Gavin. What did your mother do?'

He shrugged. 'What could she do? She was afraid of Father just like we were. She always kept her distance.'

I couldn't understand any of it. Coming from a family where all I had known was love and warmth it was hard to imagine.

'And now Scott's fiercely jealous of me,' Gavin went on. 'Father left the estate to me and only a small sum of money and the bungalow in the grounds to Scott. He can't get over it, but Father had a thing about me being his first-born. He was very traditional. I asked Scott to stay on, said he'd always have a home here and a job on the estate, but he wouldn't have it. Went off and joined the army a few months after Ma and Pa died. It's not been good for him. It's encouraged his wild ways and his heavy drinking.'

I put my arm round his shoulders and stroked his hair. 'What's he doing now?'

'He's taken himself off to the bungalow where he'll probably drink himself into oblivion. At least he's out of our hair now.'

I kissed Gavin on the lips instinctively, and he returned it for a moment but then pulled away from me. He stood up. 'I just need to check something down in the sheds,' he said, crossing the room and leaving. Disappointment and shame flooded through me. What had I done? Was it wrong of me to have shown my love for him at that moment, when he was still angry with his brother? I wondered why he was so restrained with me, why he held himself back. Was it just that he was playing the gentleman, not wanting to take advantage of me?

We didn't see Scott again that night, and the next day I had to leave. His appearance and the angry argument had left a stain on the last few hours of my visit. I wondered why their father had been so unfair to Scott in his will, and why there was such bad blood between the brothers. I couldn't get out of my mind the suppressed violence contained in the exchange between the two of them. All the way home on the train I stared out of the window at the beautiful scenery, and I kept remembering how angry Gavin had become, and wondered for the first time whether I knew him at all.

6

———

Penang, 1939

W hen I got back from Kuala Lipis I must have appeared subdued, because Rose kept pestering me for details about my stay on the Crosby estate. I was non-committal. I didn't want to tell anyone about the confrontation between Gavin and Scott because it might prove that I had been wrong about Gavin all along and that there was some truth in the rumours about the family. I didn't want to admit that, even to myself, so I put on a brave face and pretended to my sister that everything had been wonderful.

I told her about how grand and stylish the house was, about how I had learned to ride, how Gavin had shown me the estate on horseback and taken me through the jungle on tracks only he knew, about how he had lent me a thoroughbred named 'Whisky' to ride around the estate. I told her how he had been considerate and loving, and how he had never tried to do anything more than kiss me, even though we had been quite alone in the house apart from the servants. I admitted to her how I was more in love with him now than ever before.

But she was not fooled. 'There's something you're not telling me, Jules. I know you. What is it? Something happened, didn't it?' Her sharp blue eyes were watching me closely. I avoided them.

'No, nothing Rose. I'd tell you. You know that, we don't have secrets.'

She stared at me for a minute, looking doubtful, but she didn't press me too hard. She had other things on her mind. Robert was due to return to his airbase in Singapore in a few days' time, and she was anxious to spend as much time with him as she could.

'You know what, Jules, I really think he's going to ask me to marry him. Maybe tonight even. He's asked me for a meal at the E&O.'

'And if he does, will you say yes?'

She looked at me with shining eyes and clasped her hands together dramatically. 'Yes, Jules, I think I will. I really think he's the one.'

Rose was right. Robert did propose to her that evening. I stayed awake, reading, waiting for her to come home, and when she tiptoed into my room after midnight I could tell what she was going to say as soon as I saw her face. Her cheeks were glowing and her eyes shining. She ran over to the bed, hugged me and said, 'I was right, Juliet. He did propose.' She showed me the huge diamond ring he had given her.

'It's beautiful, Rose. I'm so happy for you.'

'It was very romantic, Jules.'

'Tell me all about it.' I could tell she was bursting to.

'Well, the meal was wonderful. Rob bought champagne. I can hardly remember what I ate! We were so engrossed in conversation. He didn't ask me during the meal, though, and I was beginning to think I had misread the signs. But when the meal was over, he asked if I'd like to take a walk along the Esplanade. It was beautiful, Juliet, the stars twinkling on the water, the lights from the boats in the harbour. We'd been walking a little way when we came to a bench. He asked me to sit down, and then he actually knelt down there on the pavement and said, really formally, looking into my eyes, 'Rose, I love you, and I'd like to marry you if you'll have me.' And he produced this wonderful ring from his pocket. He said he bought it in Singapore last week.'

'What did you say?'

'I said yes, of course! I said yes straightaway, without any hesitation at all. Then we kissed and wandered along the esplanade for miles, arm in arm, talking about our future.'

Rob's proposal sent Auntie Maude into paroxysms of delight. She immediately embarked upon anxious preparations for the most elaborate celebrations she could persuade the long-suffering Uncle Arthur to pay for.

A week or two later a letter arrived from Kuala Lipis. I recognised Gavin's writing on the envelope and tore it open eagerly:

'My Dearest Juliet,' he began, *'I was so sad to say good bye to you the other day, and I have been missing your company since then. I'm so sorry you had to witness Scott's boorish behaviour. I hope it hasn't changed the way you feel about me. He has re-joined his regiment in Singapore now, and he won't return for some time.*

While you were staying I was trying to pluck up the courage to ask you a question. The appearance of my brother ruined our final evening together and I lost my chance to ask you. So I've decided to do so in this letter. I would like to marry you, Juliet, if you will have me. This might come as a shock to you as I'm not good at expressing my feelings, but it meant so much to me to have you here at Windy Ridge.

I understand that you might need some time to consider this offer, but I truly hope that you will accept it. Please send your response to me by telegram as soon as you have made up your mind.

Your ever loving, Gavin.'

. . .

'WHAT'S THE MATTER, dear? You look as though you've seen a ghost,' Auntie Maude asked, coming into the room.

'Gavin has asked me to marry him.'

'Good God!' She sat down heavily on the nearest chair and began fanning her face rapidly with a magazine.

'But what about Rose's wedding?' she asked petulantly after a moment. 'That's in six weeks' time. I'm not sure I can be expected to run to another spread shortly afterwards.'

'Nobody would expect you to, Auntie,' I said, 'but surely it's not the size of the reception that really matters anyway.'

'No, of course not. I must say I'm surprised, though. I would have thought he would go for someone more ... Well, never mind. He's rich, Juliet, and you've got to know him over these past few weeks. Perhaps we all misjudged him.'

I read the letter again, and felt uneasy. There was something missing from it. And from all the encounters I had ever had with Gavin. There was a restraint there that was disturbing, the feeling that he was holding something back. The only time that I had seen him completely drop his guard was during the argument with Scott before he insisted I should go upstairs. In those few seconds it was as if I had seen him unmasked, exposing his true self, not hiding it beneath some sort of self-imposed control.

And something else troubled me. I scanned the letter again. There was surely something odd about asking someone to marry you when you had never even told them that you love them. The words 'Your ever loving Gavin' neatly side-stepped the issue.

But I didn't allow myself to dwell on these thoughts for long. I forced myself to put them aside and focus instead on the companionship of our rides through the jungle, our candlelit dinners in the big house, the light in his blue eyes as he talked to me about his plans for the estate, and the way a little dimple appeared in his cheek when he laughed. I knew that whatever my misgivings, I was in love with him and I was going to accept his offer.

I ran outside and asked the syce to take me to the main post office on Downing Street near the harbour. Before we had driven a hundred yards from the house I realised that I had not spoken to Rose about Gavin's offer, or my decision to accept it. I was surprised at myself. I usually talked to her about everything. I was tempted to tell the driver to turn back, but reasoned that I had made up my mind and there was nothing Rose could say to change that.

At the post office I sent a simple telegram: 'The answer is yes stop love Juliet stop.'

If Rose had doubts about Gavin or his proposal she didn't say anything to me. She just hugged me in her usual effusive, generous way and said, laughing, 'I'm delighted for you, my darling Jules! Who'd have thought when we set off from home that we'd both be engaged to be married within the space of a few months?'

Rose and Robert were married the following month with as much pomp and circumstance as Uncle Arthur's budget would allow. Rose's dress was pure ivory silk from Siam with a long train. The ceremony took place in St. George's church to a packed congregation. Robert's entire RAF squadron had been invited. The reception was held at White Gables. The house was decked out in flowers and fairy lights, and a jazz band played on the terrace all afternoon and into the evening. Champagne flowed and was served by uniformed bearers who moved skilfully through the guests balancing silver trays full of glasses above their heads. Auntie Maude flapped around making sure that people had enough to eat from the elaborate buffet. The cake was a highly decorated multi-tiered affair shipped in especially from Singapore.

When Gavin and I married a month or so later it was a much more muted occasion. I didn't want any fuss, and I certainly didn't want to try to upstage Rose. Only the front few pews of the church were occupied. Gavin's cousin Johnny and a few scattered acquaintances of his from around the colony came. There were some friends of Auntie Maude and Uncle Arthur's too, and of course Rose and Robert who made the trip from their new married quarters in Singapore. To my relief Scott was unable to get leave from his regiment.

My wedding dress was a simple white gown run up by one of the Indian tailors in town. I wore lotus blossom in my hair and carried a small spray of purple orchids. The reception was a quiet drink at the club. I felt this was a fitting place to celebrate as it was where Gavin and I had first met.

We honeymooned in the Cameron Highlands, in the newly opened Smokehouse Hotel in Tanah Rata. It had been built to emulate an English country pub, and even the gardens were laid out and planted exactly like a country garden in England.

I was very nervous when we arrived at the hotel. Our room was on the first floor with a view across the cottage gardens to the mountain beyond. The bearers brought our bags upstairs. They were tipped and then left, and Gavin and I were alone in the room. It was what I wanted, what I had dreamed of for all the months I had known him, but my heart still fluttered and my body shook with nerves as he took my hand and pulled me towards him on the bed. He was gentle with me as he unbuttoned my dress and kissed me as I lay down on the bed. He was gentle and skilful in a way that only a man with experience could be, but even in all those moments of extreme intimacy, I still sensed a reserve, a sense of him holding something back.

We spent four days in Tanah Rata, strolling along the hillside trails with a guide and admiring the beauty of the mountain scenery. We would come back to the hotel for afternoon tea of scones and cream and tea in china cups, before retiring to our room to make love. Early in the evening we would come down to the dining room lit by flickering candles and warmed by a log fire roaring in the grate. Dinner was usually something English, like a roast or a steak and kidney pie. The hotel was reminiscent of a quaint old pub in the heart of the shires, with walls of white plaster, mock Tudor beams and horse-brasses around the stone fireplace. Strangely enough it didn't make me homesick for England. Instead I found it rather quaint and amusing.

Although he tried to hide it, I noticed that Gavin was becoming increasingly restless as the days passed. On the fifth morning, while we were eating breakfast, he said, 'I really need to get down to Kuala Lumpur as soon as possible. You don't mind, do you? We've done most things there are to do here, haven't we?'

'Why? I thought we were staying for a whole week.'

'Of course it would be lovely, darling, but there are a few things I need to sort out with the lawyers regarding the estate. You could come down with me and we'll find a hotel. When I'm not in meetings we could do some sight-seeing. How about that?'

I shrugged. 'If you like, I suppose.' I agreed because I had no choice, but I was puzzled by this change of attitude and was secretly hurt that he had cut our honeymoon short.

The next day we took a taxi down to the nearest station at Tapah Road and caught the train to Kuala Lumpur. I had never been to a great Asian city before, apart from my fleeting visit to Colombo, and as soon as we were out of the station I could sense the teeming bustle of the place.

We arrived after dark on the first night and checked in to the Majestic Hotel, a grand white building on Victory Avenue just opposite the central railway station. On the first morning, Gavin left straight after breakfast for a meeting with his lawyers. Left to my own devices I wandered down to the reception area. I was going to ask for a map of the city so that I could explore, but the place was filled with a crowd of British officers in uniform. One of them was complaining in a loud, imperious voice to the uniformed bearer on reception about inadequate plumbing in his bathroom, while the poor man was bowing repeatedly in apologetic despair.

I noticed that one of the officers had detached himself from the group and was standing beside the window. He was tall and tanned with close-cropped dark hair, and from his body language I could see that he was trying to distance himself from what was happening. As I hovered on the bottom step he looked across and caught my eye. I could see from his expression that he was deeply embarrassed by the behaviour of his fellow officer. I held his gaze for a moment, but at the same time I caught sight of a box of maps on the concierge's desk beside the front door. I hurried across the reception area, selected a map quickly and left the building.

There was a line of rickshaw-wallahs waiting patiently on the hotel forecourt so I asked the one at the head of the queue to take me to the Padang, which I could see from the map was where all the grand colonial buildings were. He dropped me in front of the Selangor Club, with its mock Tudor façade looking out of place amongst the palm trees. I strolled across the wide green admiring the enormous government building spread out beside the river on the opposite side of the Padang. It looked like something out of a fairy tale, with its Mughal domes, elaborate cupolas and colonnades, not at all like the seat of an imperial European power. But the white men in linen suits and solar topees coming and going from the front entrance were a reminder of its true purpose. I wandered through a gap between the great buildings towards Klang River and began to stroll along the bank. I was surprised at the graceful beauty of the place, and regretted that I had no-one with me to share my first impressions with.

That thought gave me a strange feeling. For the first time in years I felt a pang of loneliness. And the more I thought about it the worse it got. Soon, overwhelmed by the feeling I sat down right there on a bench under a tree. I'd only walked a few hundred yards, but I was already sweating profusely and my clothes were sticking to my skin. Sadness and disappointment engulfed me as it suddenly struck me that I had not only given up my home and everyone I knew back in England, as well as the security and comfort of Auntie Maude's luxurious home and circle of friends, but no longer had Rose by my side.

I realised that I really missed my sister and that this was virtually the first time I had been sight-seeing without her. I remembered the enthusiasm with which she had embraced Georgetown and the whole island of Penang when we first arrived, persuading Uncle Arthur to take us to every temple, church and mosque, every far flung beach and landmark. She seemed to have boundless energy despite the sapping heat, encouraging me to accompany her on the funicular railway to the top of Penang Hill to sample the cool air and experience the spectacular views over the shimmering sea to the mainland. We walked arm in arm through narrow alleys and streets in the Indian and Chinese quarters, crept barefoot into prayer halls, even into one where bright green vipers drowsy from the smell of incense curled around beams and ornaments. Her voice was in my head now: 'Come on, Jules, come and look, you mustn't miss this ...'

Feeling wretched, I got up, wandered aimlessly along the river and crossed a small footbridge. Over the water I found myself in a maze of narrow passages, teeming with people. Stalls groaning with goods of all descriptions lined the pavements, people pushed barrows to and fro and the smell of frying food and exotic spices filled the air. The noise and clatter of people and commerce was deafening. I had wandered into Chinatown. For a while I was distracted by this extraordinary attack on my senses, overwhelmed by the sheer pulsating energy of these narrow streets. I walked on without any regard to where I was going, mesmerised by the surroundings.

I soon realised that I was lost, but looking around there was nobody I could ask to help me. I walked blindly for half an hour or so, taking false turns, trying to find my way back to the Padang. As I turned a sharp corner, I almost bumped into a white man coming the other way. I looked up and recognised the officer from the hotel. The one who had caught my eye earlier.

'Excuse me,' I said, moving aside.

'Are you all right?' he asked, stopping and peering at my face with curiosity.

'Yes. It's just that I've lost my way.' I touched my face, wondering why he was looking at me so oddly, and it was then that I realised I had been crying. I rushed to wipe off my tears.

'Would you like me to show you the way back to the Padang? You can get a taxi there. You are staying at the Majestic, aren't you?'

'Yes.'

'I say, you look dreadfully hot. Would you like to step into this café for a cold drink?'

I felt a bit awkward, but readily accepted as the intense heat of the alleys had made me very thirsty. We sat down in a tiny café across the street, where a few Chinese coolies sat eating with chopsticks. They looked at us with open curiosity as we entered. My companion ordered me a lime juice, and I drank it gratefully.

'What are you doing here all alone?' he asked. He had soft brown eyes, and a serious, intelligent air. I got the impression that he was genuinely interested in my answer, that he was not just being polite.

'I'm not alone really. My husband is with me. He's at a meeting this morning and I thought I'd explore the city. Perhaps I shouldn't have.'

'Are you new to Kuala Lumpur?'

I nodded. 'What about you? Why are you staying at the hotel?'

'Oh, it's only temporary. We arrived from India a week or so ago, to find that our barracks are being refurbished. We officers are being put up in the hotel at the army's expense. I can't say I mind, but some of the chaps aren't too happy with their accommodation.'

'Did you say you came from India?'

'Yes. We're Indian Army, to be precise. A sort of advance party.

We've been sent here because everyone's worried about the Japs invading. There are plans for troops to be drafted in to Malaya and Singapore at the moment. You might have read about it in the papers?'

I thought about this for a moment. I did remember some half-hearted discussion about it at the club in Penang a few weeks before.

'I'm on honeymoon, I haven't been taking much notice of the news,' I said. He raised his eyebrows, and I suddenly felt the need to justify myself, to defend Gavin.

'Of course, I know it looks strange that I'm wandering about here alone. My husband wouldn't normally go off to a meeting. It was something really urgent,' I said, feeling my cheeks growing hot. His eyes were on my face still. Why didn't he look away? His look of sympathy was infuriating. I didn't need that.

'There's no need to feel sorry for me,' I blurted out, the tears threatening again.

'Of course not. I understand,' he said, looking down at the table. 'I apologise if I embarrassed you. You just looked a little lost when we bumped into each other a few moments ago.'

'Well I *was* feeling a bit lost to tell you the truth. You see, I haven't been in Malaya for very long and I was feeling slightly lonely.'

'I'm sorry to hear that,' he said gently. 'The East can be very daunting if you're not used to it.'

'No, it's not that. I love it here. It's ...' I stopped myself. What was I doing? This man was a complete stranger.

'Go on?'

'No ... no. It's nothing. Please, I'm feeling fine now.'

There was an awkward pause between us, filled only by the clamour from the alley and the conversation of the coolies at the next table.

'Do you think it will happen?' I asked at last. 'Do you think there will be an invasion?'

'Lots of people think the Japs aren't capable of it. I'm not so sure.'

When we had finished he walked me back to the Padang and hailed a taxi. As I got in, he shook my hand. 'Thank you so much for helping me,' I said.

'It's been a pleasure,' he said, smiling. 'Tell your new husband to take better care of you in future. I certainly wouldn't let my lovely new wife out alone to get lost in Chinatown.'

As the taxi drew away I looked back and saw him standing on the pavement, his dark eyes watching me. I raised my hand and gave him a tentative wave.

7

J uliet opened her eyes and the world swam back into focus. She found herself lying on the chaise longue in her living room. The blinds of the window were pulled down and someone had put a shawl over her. The fan rotated overhead wafting cool air onto her face.

'Here, drink this water.' Mary was kneeling beside the couch, holding out a glass. She was peering anxiously at Juliet's face.

'How did I get here?' Juliet asked, taking the glass and gulping down some water.

'I ran up to the house for Abdul, and we both helped you back. We virtually carried you. You were completely unconscious for a time.'

'I'm so sorry. That's very unlike me.'

'Please don't apologise. It was all *my* fault! I'm sorry I made you go down to that derelict bungalow. I can be a bit impulsive at times. A bit of a bull in a china shop when I get enthusiastic about something. I really wasn't thinking. It must have really tired you out being out in the heat of the day, especially after your early start.'

'No, it wasn't that. It was ...'

'Please, no need to explain.' Mary took Juliet's hand in hers and patted it. 'Just relax now.'

It felt strange to be cared for like this. Juliet took another sip of water and lay back again, letting her limbs grow heavy. For most of her life it was she who had looked after others; she'd been the one who'd cared for Rose when they were children, for her father, for Gavin. She remembered being looked after like this when she was lying sick with fever in the hospital in Singapore. The ill-fated Alexandra hospital. No, she mustn't think about that now, or she'd begin to feel faint again. She closed her eyes. Images came to her of Japanese soldiers storming through the corridors of the hospital, wave upon wave of them yelling and shouting crazily, weapons drawn, the blood-curdling screams of patients being bayoneted as they lay there helpless in their beds. She screwed up her eyes and took deep breaths, trying to banish those memories.

'Please, try to relax,' Mary said again. Juliet closed her eyes and felt the girl's hand gently stroking her head. 'You have really beautiful hair you know. You should style it so it would frame your face better, bring out your cheekbones.'

'Whatever for?' asked Juliet, irritated. 'I hardly ever go out, and when I do it's just with the old wrinklies in town. We've all known each other for more than twenty- years now. They'd think I'd gone ga-ga if I suddenly started worrying about my looks.'

Mary laughed. 'You should come down to Singapore sometime. Have a change of scene, see the town. Perhaps you could come and stay with me? We're allowed to have visitors. There's even a little guest room in the nurses' hostel. How about that?'

She looked away. Wasn't the girl running ahead of herself? Juliet needed some actual proof of their connection first. That typed bit of paper and the silver amulet just weren't enough to convince her. 'I'm not sure.'

'You should think about it. I'd be able to tell everyone that you're my auntie. I'd be so proud!'

Juliet sat forward. 'But you don't know that yourself, do you? You're really clutching at straws here, Mary.'

'You've seen the evidence. How else could I have come by it?'

Juliet fell silent. How on earth could this situation be resolved? She thought for a long time and at last, propping herself up on her elbow, she said, 'Look, what about this for a suggestion? When you next have some leave, why don't I come down and meet you? We could catch a ferry to Sumatra and go to the orphanage in Palembang together. We could see if anyone knows anything, if there are any more records available. There might be something there other than that certificate you've got.'

Mary shook her head. 'I tried to ask them before I left. No-one knows anything. I told you, the staff change all the time.'

'Perhaps we could even go to Bamboo Island, where the ship went down? We could see if there's anyone there who can remember the day it all happened. It was only twenty years ago after all. There might still be someone left.'

Mary nodded slowly. 'Maybe ... But suppose we don't find anything? What then?'

'If we don't find anything, you must promise me you'll drop the matter. Forget about trying to prove there might be some sort of connection between us. You must go back to the ship's passenger records and carry on searching through them. It might be that you were not even listed as a passenger and that you belong to another family completely. You could start working your way through the other families on the list, start trying to contact them.'

Mary's smile vanished. She fell silent and was clearly turning this possibility over in her mind. After a while, she looked up and said, 'I suppose I could ask for a bit more time off when I get back. I think I'm probably still due a couple of weeks. I could let you know when it will be. Do you have a telephone?'

'Not in the house, no, but we do have one in the estate office. I'll give you the number. You can call there and leave a message

saying when your days off are, and I'll come down on the train to
meet you. How about that?'

Mary smiled again. 'That would be cool. But would you
promise me something? Would you promise me that when you
come, you'll tell me all about how you and my mother came to
Malaya, and about what happened to you during the war?'

'Oh, I'm not sure you'd want to hear about that,' Juliet said
quickly looking away. 'It's a rather long and boring story.'

What she didn't say was that she wasn't sure that she wanted
to share her story with anyone. She had never spoken about the
dreadful things she had witnessed and experienced back then,
and she certainly wasn't going to tell the girl about her journal,
where she had written it all down after the war in an attempt to
purge herself of the memories.

That was why she lived all alone, apart from the servants and
the workers who had no interest in her past anyway. And why the
only Europeans she bothered to keep in touch with were the ones
who knew her story so well that there was no need to ever
mention it. When they met they followed a well-worn routine of
platitudes and bridge, getting mildly drunk and reminiscing only
about the safe subjects.

'Why on earth would it be boring? I'd like to know, really,'
said Mary, watching her eagerly, waiting for an answer.

'You wouldn't want to hear it, Mary. I'm quite sure of that,'
Juliet said firmly.

Later in the afternoon, Juliet felt well enough to stroll
around the gardens. She showed Mary the old stable block. 'We
used to have four or five horses here before the war. I loved to
ride then.'

'Not anymore?'

'The horses all died during the Japanese Occupation, starved
or left to perish of disease. The Japs commandeered this house,
you know. Used it as their local headquarters during the invasion
and the Occupation. They mistreated the horses dreadfully.

When I came back the horses were all gone. I hadn't the heart to buy any more.'

'Were you not here during the war then?'

Juliet shook her head. 'No. I'd gone to stay in Singapore,' she said simply. They strolled out of the yard and across the long sweep of grass behind the house.

'What's over in those trees?' Mary pointed to the little spinney of *angsana* trees in the far corner of the plot.

'That's where my husband is buried. Him and his brother,' said Juliet. Her heart began to beat more quickly. She didn't want to have to speak too much about Gavin or Scott. Not today.

'Can we go over there?' Mary asked. 'Would it upset you?'

'No, of course not,' Juliet said quickly. 'Gavin's been dead for twenty years. Scott for well over ten. I've had plenty of time to get used to the idea.'

Under the great *angsanas* the graves of the two brothers rested side by side. They were together in death even though the two men could not stand the sight of each other in life. It had been her sense of bitter irony that had led her to have Scott buried here and not up in the churchyard in Kuala Lipis alongside their parents' graves.

'Did you say your husband died in the war?' asked Mary. Juliet nodded.

'But he wasn't a soldier, right?'

'No ... No, he refused to volunteer, even though a lot of young men around here were joining up with the Volunteers. He said the estate needed him. That if he left it would go to rack and ruin. He was very stubborn about it.'

'So, why did he die? He can't have been more than ...' She read the engraved headstone and calculated his age under her breath, 'thirty four?'

'I'd really prefer not to talk about it, Mary, if you don't mind. Perhaps one day ...'

'I'm so sorry,' said Mary, turning to Juliet, touching her arm, her face full of concern. 'I'm being clumsy again, aren't I? I don't want to tire you again. Shall we go inside now?'

Later, after a few hours spent chatting comfortably on the veranda and an early supper of *nasi goreng*, Abdul took Mary back to town in the car. Again Juliet watched from the window as the rear lights of the old Morris disappeared through the gates and turned onto the jungle road. She stood staring into the darkness long after it had gone.

This time she had mixed feelings. Contrary to her expectations the girl had turned out to be a thoughtful and intelligent companion. It had been surprisingly pleasant and relaxing to have some female company. She had not realised how much this was missing from her life, and she found herself thinking of Rose. How she ached to have her sitting here beside her, sharing a pot of tea, chatting aimlessly. Perhaps there was something in Mary's wide smile, in her impulsive manner and in the way she seemed to have a natural empathy with people that was reminiscent of Rose? She shook her head and banished the thought from her mind. She was imagining it, letting her mind run away with itself. The girl could be making it all up, taking Juliet for a ride. She began to regret having suggested the trip to Indonesia. Why had she allowed herself to be drawn into that? It could only lead to unhappiness and disappointment.

8

O ver the next few days, in spite of her initial misgivings, Juliet found herself waiting for Mary's call. When she was out inspecting the tappers or checking the workers on the latex presses in the sheds, she kept inventing reasons to drop into the estate office on some pretext or other to check whether Mary had left a message. Finally, on Friday, six days after the girl had visited the estate, the call came. Mary had left word with Jalak, the manager, that she was allowed a week's leave of absence from her work on the ward beginning on the following Monday.

Juliet went into overdrive, preparing for her trip. She packed a small suitcase with sensible clothes which seemed suitable for the journey to Singapore and then on to Sumatra, then realising that a suitcase would probably be cumbersome, she repacked her belongings into a soft hold-all. She didn't possess a backpack.

'That will have to do,' she said to herself, feeling her nerves tingling with a mixture of anticipation and trepidation.

She found Jalak down on the tappers lines and briefed him on what needed to be done on the estate for the next few days. It was a quiet time; they weren't due to send a consignment of latex down to Kuala Lumpur until the following month.

She spoke to Abdul about looking after the house.

'You will be away for long, madam?' he asked, raising his eyebrows in curiosity.

'Not long, Abdul. Probably around a week.'

'That *is* a long time,' he said. 'Madam is usually away for only two or three days' maximum.'

'Well, I'm sure you'll manage just fine without me, Abdul.'

Abdul had the car waiting on the front drive for her before daybreak the next morning. Her hold-all was already on the back seat. As she came out of the house, she remembered something. 'I won't be a minute,' she said, rushing back up to her bedroom and opening the bureau. There it was, under a pile of papers at the bottom of a drawer. She pulled out a blue hardback notebook and flicked through the pages filled with her flowing handwriting. That was it. She needn't give it to the girl, but she would take it with her, just in case she changed her mind.

Abdul drove her to Kuala Lipis station. She boarded the early train and waved goodbye to him. He looked a rather forlorn figure standing there on the platform in his spotless white tunic, waving to her.

She felt a similar thrill of anticipation to the day she had set out from Penang to see Gavin for the very first time. How much time had passed since then, and how much had happened. She felt a completely different person now from that naïve young woman who was travelling alone in Malaya for the very first time. As the train drew out of the station and began to rattle through the outskirts of the small town, she finally faced the fact that she was going back to Singapore for the very first time since she had returned to the Crosby estate after the war. She knew that she had avoided the city for a reason. The place held so many memories for her, memories she had been supressing for years now, memories of the worst of times that she had banished to the darkest recesses of her mind. But buried alongside those disturbing images were bittersweet memories too. She was unable to face them either. Letting them surface would remind her of everything she had lost.

She looked out of the window and as the train plunged south through the jungle, she realised that there was no going back now. She knew though that if she wanted to find the truth about Mary, she would have to face Singapore and along with it her past.

Then, for the first time in years she allowed the image of his face to surface in her mind, and her lips silently formed his name: 'Adam.' He'd promised to come back for her. And then he'd been gone. He had meant what he said, she was sure of it. But as the years passed without any sign from him, not even a letter, she'd finally been forced to admit to herself that it could only mean one thing, that he must be dead.

The day that Juliet decided he would never come back was the day that she'd banished all thoughts of him and of the war from her mind. Since then she'd refused to let them enter her head. But despite that, there was part of her that still watched and waited for him. Each evening, as she sat on the veranda sipping her tea, watching the sun go down, she was unconsciously tuned into every sound on the road, every movement in the trees, hoping to catch the first glimpse of him as he made his way towards her.

～

Singapore 1942

It was early February when I was admitted to the Alexandra hospital. The wards were full and they put me in a tiny side-ward that was hardly more than a cupboard. It was a military hospital, but when I had developed septicaemia and lapsed into a fever, Robert had taken me there from the bungalow on the airbase. Robert had driven crazily through the bombed out streets of the besieged city, and when we had arrived he had used his rank to insist that they take me in. Throughout my stay nurses rushed in and out around me, fetching bedding for the influx of new patients, soldiers wounded in the battle that raged on the edge of the city.

From my bed I could hear the rumble and rattle of guns on the front line, and over the following days, as I gradually recovered from my illness it began to terrify me that the noise of the fighting was getting closer by the hour. I was also aware that the hospital was in chaos. I heard the clamour and panic in the corridors as wounded men were brought in, screaming in pain. Nurses in blood-stained uniforms were running out to collect clean linen, their faces pale and strained. After a time, though, the linen ran out and I was left alone. From my bed I could hear the moans of injured men lying on stretchers out on the corridor and on nearby wards.

Bombing raids were frequent, and the building would tremble and the glass vibrate in the windows as Japanese planes flew low over the city, seeking out targets. Many times I heard the crash of explosions as bombs fell on surrounding buildings, but the hospital itself was spared. A worse fate was in store for it, although no-one knew it then.

On that last dreadful day, the fighting had come very close. I heard the rattle of machine guns below the windows, and from the shouts and screams of the soldiers, it sounded as though the battle was raging in the hospital grounds. For hours on end I lay in bed, sweating and trembling with fear as I listened to gunfire, and several times the sound of shells exploding shook the glass in the windows.

One of the nurses a young Malay woman called Nazira Syed,

had come into the room to check on me. She was just preparing to take my temperature when we heard something that sent chills of terror through us. Nazira dropped the thermometer on the floor and it smashed into slivers of glass, tiny beads of mercury rolling out and spreading round the room. It was the unmistakable sound of soldiers storming along the corridors of the hospital itself. They were shouting and yelling in Japanese. Then came more chilling sounds: a volley of gunshots, followed by the blood-curdling yells and screams of patients. Nazira looked at me with wide, terrified eyes.

'Quick! In here,' she whispered, her voice shaking, her face white. She beckoned me to one of the large wall cupboards where bedding had been stored. We both climbed inside and crawled to the back of the dark cupboard, hid ourselves under the rolled-up bedsheets. Nazira pulled the door closed from the inside. I remember crouching there with her, our breath coming in shallow pants, our bodies shaking all over. There was no air and we thought we were going to pass out. We were too terrified to speak. We squatted there in silence, squeezed together, our bodies moulded to each other.

As we crouched there, trembling, listening to the gunshots and screams, we heard heavy footsteps inside the room and men shouting in Japanese. There was some banging and clattering as a table was knocked over and medical equipment thrown on the floor. I was frozen in terror. Nazira was holding her breath. Her eyes were fixed on the cupboard door. We were expecting that at any moment it would be flung open and a Japanese face full of hatred and murder would fill the opening. But the footsteps eventually went away, and the cupboard door remained closed. The two of us stayed there for what seemed like hours, squatting together, not moving, breathing each other's breath, sour with fear.

When all the shouting and screaming had been over for a

long time, Nazira tentatively eased the cupboard doors open. The room was still and quiet. Slowly and painfully I followed Nazira and clambered out of the cupboard, unfolding my stiff and aching limbs and stretching as I stood up. My legs felt as though they were about to give way. I swooned, and the room went black for a moment.

I watched Nazira tiptoeing to the door and beckoning me forward. I had not walked anywhere for days, so Nazira came over to take my hand and guide me out of the room and along the corridor, stepping over the piles of soiled bed linen and dressings that had built up during the siege when there was not enough water to wash them. There was an unnatural stillness and silence here in the passage.

Then we saw them. Slumped against a wall in pools of blood were the bodies of patients and staff, shot or bayoneted to death by the marauding soldiers, their stomachs messes of entrails spilling out onto the floor. Vomit rose to my throat and I retched as we passed the first one.

'Don't look,' said Nazira and took me firmly by the hand.

We passed the door to a ward and stared inside. Everyone in the ward had been butchered, bodies were lying across the beds or prostrate on the floor in pools of blood. We stopped and stared, aghast.

'I'm sorry but I need to go in there and see if anyone is alive,' said Nazira, her voice shaking. 'Can you sit out here on the bench for a few minutes? I can't just leave them.'

I nodded mutely. My knees were already weak with fear and I sunk down on the bench outside the ward. I watched through the doorway as Nazira picked her way through the debris on the floor to the first body. She listened for a heartbeat, felt for a pulse, then shaking her head moved on to the next one. She went from body to body doing the same thing. My mind was racing. What if the soldiers came back? Surely they would just kill us on the spot as they had all these other poor people. My ears were straining for voices or footsteps, and I jumped at every tiny sound. There was an eerie stillness throughout the hospital though, as if the place was suspended from reality, in a unique bubble in time and space all of its own, the horror of what had just happened separating it from the real world.

At last Nazira came back, her face grey.

'They are all dead,' she said, shaking her head, her voice breaking. 'Every single one of them. I can't believe it.' She sat down for a few seconds beside me on the bench, her face in her hands, taking deep breaths. But quickly she recovered herself and straightened up. 'Come, Mrs. Crosby. We must get out of here. Those murderers might come back.'

We found a fire escape at the end of the corridor and pushed open the door. Cautiously we made our way down it onto a gravel path, terrified that there might still be Japanese soldiers amongst the trees in the hospital grounds. We walked slowly through the hospital gardens and out onto Alexandra Road.

It was late afternoon by now, and the sun was beginning to go down. The air was filled with smoke from the air raids and as we walked we saw that buildings on either side of the road were devastated from the bombings. Some had collapsed onto the street and others were on fire. We made our way past a fire crew trying to douse the flames that leapt high into the sky from a go-down. The men were working with an antiquated pump and the trickle of water from the hoses seemed inadequate for the task. Smoke billowed from the building, making us cough and our eyes smart. People were stumbling about looking dazed and disorientated, most of them covered in black soot from the smoke, some injured from the blasts.

I could still hear the thunder of guns from the front line, and the buzz of engines as Japanese planes circled around, sometimes swooping down low over the streets, opening fire on whoever happened to be there. It took us over three hours to walk to Nazira's home in Kampong Glam. On our way we had to step over

bodies buzzing with flies, clamber over rubble from the devastated buildings, skirt around great craters in the roads. We
walked in fear, terrified in case Japanese soldiers should come
round the next corner. We tried to walk as close to the buildings
as we could so that there was just a chance that we could take
shelter.

'Thank God Rose managed to get away with the baby,' I kept
breathing to myself, to help keep me strong, relieved that they
were out of this hell-hole and on their way to safety in Australia.

I remembered our tearful goodbye at the hospital, when I had
been so delirious with fever that I had barely known what was
happening. I should have been on that ship with them, but I was
too sick to travel. I remembered the last glimpse of my sister as
she lingered at the door of the side-ward with tears in her eyes.
Rose was wearing a bright blue cotton dress. I remembered too
the sight of the baby's tiny head protruding from the blanket, and
wondering when I would ever see them again.

Every so often on that interminable walk, I found that I
simply could not go on. My limbs felt inadequate, my head so
heavy with nausea that I thought I would faint. I had to sit down
on a wall, or on a pile of rubble and take deep breaths, waiting
until I felt able to walk on.

Nazira's street in the Malay district was narrow and lined with
shop-houses, the ground floors of which were open to the street
with wares stacked on the pavement. All manner of goods were
on sale: fruit and vegetables, clothes, bric-a-brac, groceries. It was
thronging with people when we arrived. It felt as if life was
carrying on as before here, and this little enclave was a pocket of
normality, unconnected to the rest of this war torn city. We made
our way down the street between the busy stalls and when we
came to a shop selling metal pots and pans, Nazira stopped and
beckoned me forward between the stalls. She pointed to a narrow
set of stone steps. I put my foot on the first step and stopped. I
simply did not have the strength or the energy to get up the stairs.

Nazira put her hands under my armpits and virtually lifted me up each step until we had reached the first floor. Still panting with the effort, I looked around Nazira's home, its two small rooms and little kitchenette. Louvered doors opened onto a narrow balcony that overlooked the street.

'Do you live here alone?' I asked. Nazira nodded.

'Since a month ago. It was our family home, but both my parents were killed in an air-raid.'

I put my hand on Nazira's arm. 'I'm so sorry,' I said. 'How dreadful.'

Nazira looked down and took a deep breath to steady her voice. 'They'd gone over to Chinatown to buy supplies for the shop. They used to go once a month. When they were in the warehouse collecting the stock, there was a raid and the street was razed to the ground. Their bodies haven't even been found yet.'

'I'm so sorry,' I repeated, taking her hand. Nazira wiped a tear away.

'Thank you. It's been really tough,' she replied. Then she drew herself up and looked at me. 'But please, why don't you lie down? You look very tired. I'll get you something to eat.' She gestured towards a narrow bed under the open window.

I went over and lay down on it and closed my eyes. I felt a sheet being tucked around me, but was already losing consciousness. For a while I was dimly aware of Nazira moving quietly around in the little kitchen, but soon sleep overcame me.

When I awoke, it was morning, and the flat was deserted. Through the open window floated the sound of a melodious voice, calling, almost wailing. At first I thought I was still dreaming, then I realised where I was, and that I was hearing the call to prayer from a nearby mosque. When it finally stopped, I could hear the sounds of the street below. Feeling stiff and heavy with sleep, I managed to sit up and get out of bed.

There was a stone sink with a tap in the kitchenette, but when

I turned on the tap there was no running water. There was a bowl of cold water beside the sink though. Gratefully, I splashed my face. Nazira had left me some bread and fruit on the side in the kitchen with a scribbled note: 'I have gone to fetch food. I won't be long.'

I peeled a banana and took a bite, but my stomach was so taut with hunger that I found myself running back to the sink, retching. When I had recovered, I went to the balcony and looked out. The street was just as it had been the day before when we had arrived from the hospital, filled with shoppers moving between the stalls. I could hear the cries of the vendors and the shouted conversations in Malay and Chinese of the shoppers and stall-holders. I was grateful for the air of normality. I looked around the flat to see if there was a bathroom, but found none. Instead, I discovered a door that opened onto a narrow rear staircase. I groped my way down the stone steps and found that it led to a cluttered back yard with an outdoor privy in a hut in the corner.

Nazira soon returned with some more fruit and some bread and cheese. Her face was full of fear. 'People are saying that the British have surrendered and that all British and European civilians have to go to the Padang to assemble. I saw some of the British soldiers being rounded up by the Japanese and marched away. If they resisted the Japanese would thump them with their fists or hit them with rifles and bayonets. Apparently they are making them march to Changi.'

I felt the blood drain from my face. 'I'll have to go to the Padang too,' I said immediately and began to stand up.

'No, no. You can't go. You must stay here. People say that they are marching everyone to prison camps including women and children. You are still weak. I need to look after you.'

'But won't the Japanese check the houses?'

'I don't know. But if they do, you'll have to hide. You need rest, Mrs. Crosby. You can't possibly go. If you go it will make you very ill. You might even die.'

I stared at her, overwhelmed by what she had told me and by her generosity and kindness. 'I can't ask you to take that risk for me. What would happen to you if they found me? And who knows how long this might last. I can't hide forever.'

'Let's take one day at a time shall we? When you get better we can think again.'

'But why would you do that for me? You could be safe on your own here. The Japs don't have anything against the Malayan people.'

Nazira shrugged. 'I don't have anything left to lose. My parents have gone. They were killed by the Japanese. My job is to care for people. I was caring for you when they came, and I would like to take care of you until you are better.'

Shivers of fear ran through my body. I realised that either way I was in danger. If I went down to the Padang now and joined the rest of the Europeans, I would probably become even sicker on the march to the prison camp. But if I stayed here, the Japs would probably find me sooner or later and then they would kill both of us.

'I can't do this to you. You are good and kind and brave, but what you are suggesting is too much to ask of any human being.' I stood up. 'Look, I'll go now. I'll make my way down to the Padang and take my chances. Thank you for everything you've done for me. You saved my life yesterday.'

'Let me give you some clothes to wear at least. You cannot go in your nightie, Mrs. Crosby.'

Nazira rifled in a wardrobe and brought out a traditional silk blouse and long black sarong. I slipped into the blouse and let Nazira tie the sarong around my waist. She gave me a pair of cheap raffia sandals.

There were tears in Nazira's eyes as we said goodbye and I walked unsteadily down the narrow steps. I began to walk along the pavement between the cluttered stalls, feeling the full fury of the noonday sun on my face, but as soon as I had started walking, my legs felt weak and unsteady and my head light. I tried to ignore it and carried on but after a few more steps black dots appeared in front of my eyes and I began to swoon. Then the black dots were getting bigger. They soon filled my vision, and I felt myself falling forwards, and the road coming up to meet me.

9

——————

When I came to I was back in the narrow bed in Nazira's flat. She was sitting beside me on a stool holding a cup of water and with an anxious look on her face.

'You see, Mrs. Crosby,' she said, 'you aren't strong enough to move yet. You must stay with me and get better.'

I had no real choice then. I had to stay.

Over the next few weeks I remained in Nazira's flat being nursed back to health. I would time and time again remember the nightmare of the hospital, or have a feverish dream about the bloody bodies collapsed on the floor, and would cry out in distress. Nazira would dab my forehead with a damp cloth and open the windows wide to try to ensure some breeze reached me.

She made me rest in bed and waited on me, brought me food and water, made me nourishing vegetable soups and hot tea. She worked tirelessly, but whatever she was doing, five times a day she would excuse herself and go to a private corner of the flat to perform her prayers.

Sometimes she would leave for a few hours and go down to the quay in search of seafood. I would lie there alone, slipping in and out of sleep, the hours punctuated by the sounds from the street outside, the call the prayer from the mosque. Under the Japanese Occupation, food was dwindling fast. I realised that Nazira was having to pay more and bargain harder each time she went out, and felt guilty that I was being supported by this young woman who was already living in poverty.

'I will pay you back, Nazira. When I can go home, I'll send you some money I promise.' But Nazira just smiled and patted my hand.

'It is nothing. I am glad to have someone to care for. Think nothing of it and I would be insulted if you paid me.'

Nazira had to fetch water from a standpipe in the street and there was no electricity any more. The bombing raids had destroyed all the cables, and with the chaos that reigned in the city, there was no prospect of it being restored for the time being. In the evenings we had to light candles in order to see what we were eating. We cooked over a small paraffin stove in the corner of the kitchenette.

Nazira had not dared to go back to the hospital. We realised it would be in Japanese hands by now anyway. She had a trickle of income from the shop downstairs, where a young Chinese boy was still employed each day to sell the dwindling stocks of kitchenware.

We lived in constant terror of a raid on the street, and rumours began to filter through about Japanese atrocities. The newspapers told us nothing. The *Straits Times* had been taken over by the occupiers and renamed the *Shonan Times*. Nazira brought a copy home once and I saw that it was full of Japanese propaganda: how many evil enemy warships the noble Japanese Navy had sunk, how Malaya and Singapore, now re-named 'Syonon', were prospering under the benevolent rule of the Japanese, how the Japanese had released the oppressed population from the rule of the evil British.

Each day, when Nazira returned from her shopping trips, she

would bring back any news she had heard on the streets. She had seen that the Japanese were bringing work parties of British soldiers into the city and forcing them to clear the rubble from the bombed-out buildings and bury the victims of the bombing raids.

'Those poor prisoners. They don't look well-fed,' she said, a worried look in her eyes. 'Some of them are still wounded from the fighting or suffering from illness. They are still being forced to work though. I saw a Japanese soldier thrashing a man who'd fallen down on the ground through exhaustion. It was terrible!'

As I gradually recovered from my illness and regained strength, I prepared myself to leave. Nazira had already done enough for me, put herself in more danger than she had to, and I wanted to spare her the burden of caring for me. However, when she realised what I was planning, Nazira insisted that I must stay.

'If you left now, we would be in trouble anyway. They would ask about why you didn't go with the other Europeans when you had to. They might punish you for disobeying them,' Nazira said, 'and me for protecting you.'

As the days wore on, I began to feel restless being confined in the tiny flat, unable to go out. When I went onto the balcony, Nazira insisted I must wear a headscarf so that I would blend in and people would think I was just another Malay woman. From the balcony I observed that the street below still appeared to be little changed by the Occupation. Although there was less and less produce on the stalls as the days wore on, every day the stall-holders would still set up shop and the customers carried on coming. The street looked so little changed by the Occupation that I often wondered whether it might be safe for me to venture outside. Perhaps my new friend was being a little over-cautious and protective? I longed to be able to stretch my legs, to feel the breeze in my hair.

But I was shocked when Nazira returned one day with a livid

bruise on the side of one cheek. 'What's happened,' I asked, alarmed. 'Who did this to you?'

Nazira sunk down in chair and burst into tears. 'It was a Japanese solider. I had forgotten that every time you pass them you have to bow. I always do it at the checkpoints. Everyone has to. But this soldier was just walking along the road. He was alone. I forgot to bow to him and he turned round as I passed and hit me with his rifle butt. I fell to the ground and he grabbed my basket of food and ran off. I'm afraid we'll just have to finish up the sweet potatoes from yesterday.'

Food was becoming scarce now, and it was rumoured that the Japanese were planning to issue ration cards for rice and other essentials. But the lack of food and basic supplies seemed insignificant in comparison to the stories Nazira brought home daily about how the occupiers were treating their new subjects. Each day those stories got steadily more shocking. One day she came home more ashen-faced than usual.

'All Chinese people have been ordered to report to reception centres,' she said, sitting down.

'Reception centres? What are they for?'

'They are going to interview them all to check for anti-Japanese activists. If people don't go to the centres, they are rounded up and taken away. At the centres everyone is questioned about their past. If they get through they are given a piece of paper saying "examined". If they haven't got one they will be taken away. If they are shown to be anti-Japanese when they are interviewed they are taken away too. The Japanese are calling it *Sook Ching*. It means "purification by elimination".'

'Taken away? What does that mean?' The hair stood up on the back of my neck.

'No-one knows where they go to. They're loaded onto lorries and driven out of the city. Some people say that groups of them have been marched into the sea and shot by firing squad. Whatever happens to them they never come back.'

My mouth went dry and my stomach tightened with shock. This is what would happen to me and to Nazira if I were discovered here. The street seemed friendly enough, and no-one had remarked upon my occasional presence in a headscarf on the balcony, but Nazira had said there were rumours that there were informers amongst the people. There could even be some here on this seemingly friendly street. I decided then that I would not go out on the balcony again.

A few days later, there was a commotion on the street. People were shouting and screaming and a great clattering and banging came from the buildings opposite as if something was being demolished. Nazira and I ran to the window, and I took care to stand concealed behind the curtain. What we saw outside shocked us to the core: Japanese soldiers had filled the street. An army truck was parked at one end. Several soldiers were ransacking a shop-house opposite. We recognised it as belonging to one of the Chinese families who lived in the quarter. The soldiers were kicking over the stalls in front of the house, smashing the windows and throwing the stocks of vegetables out into the road. Then a group of them disappeared into the house. A timid little crowd of onlookers had now gathered at a safe distance, watching in silent horror. Screams and shouts could be heard from inside the shop-house. After a few minutes the solders came out again dragging the occupants out one by one. The grandmother was dragged out by her long grey hair, kicking and screaming, then came the mother, father and three teenage children, all screaming and struggling, their faces bloody and their clothes torn.

Nazira's face was drained of colour. 'That family said they weren't going to report to the reception centre,' she said. 'They were afraid. The father was a Volunteer for the British Army.'

I stared mutely, appalled at what I was witnessing and more petrified than ever for our safety. Would the soldiers search the whole street now? We had agreed that if that should happen, I would hide up in the loft space above the flat. It was quite roomy up there and there was even a little window, but we both knew that it wouldn't fool the Japanese if they were serious about searching the place.

We watched helplessly as the Chinese family was bundled into the lorry and driven off. The rest of the soldiers soon disappeared, and people slowly returned to their shops and houses. But the incident had stunned and sickened everyone on the street. It had wrought a permanent change in the atmosphere. From that day onwards the place lost its vibrancy. People hurried about their business looking cowed and furtive, afraid to speak or to linger.

Soon ration cards were issued, and Nazira was out for long hours queuing for meagre supplies of rice and other staples. We supplemented these with vegetables and sweet potatoes that Nazira bought on the black market with the tiny profits from the shop. The days were long, hot and gruelling. I had little to do but sit alone in the flat, fretting about Rose and the baby, worrying about how Robert might be faring in Changi, if he had survived the final battle.

Sometimes I thought about Windy Ridge and Gavin, and wondered if he had been captured too and was imprisoned somewhere on mainland Malaya. But I could not think about him without having the images of those last few dreadful days on the plantation flash into my mind. Just the thought of that time was enough to make my stomach clench with anger and disgust. Since I had fled to Singapore, I had tried hard not to think about those events, but now that I was alone for long periods it was difficult to banish those disturbing thoughts from my mind.

The endless days of self-imposed captivity wore on, and I teetered between boredom and fear that the Japanese could burst into the flat at any moment and drag me away, just as they had dragged away that poor Chinese family across the street. I would spend restless nights on the narrow bed, sweating and worrying, listening to the crickets in the bushes in the backyard and Nazira's gentle breathing from the other side of the room.

We grew thinner by the day. The clothes that Nazira had lent me had already been loose, but they now hung off me in folds. My arms were stick-like and buttocks so thin that it was painful to sit down on a hard chair. Nazira had been stout when she had looked after me in those first days at the hospital. Now she was gaunt and pale, with a hollow-eyed haunted look and dark shadows under her eyes.

One day, though, she came home looking less beaten than usual. There was even a glint of excitement in her eyes. 'I've found some people who have started up a canteen for prisoners and people who lost their homes in the bombings. They belong to a sort of underground movement. They are sending food and medicines into Changi,' she said in a low voice. 'They've asked me to help them. They want me to take some food parcels and hide them near to where a work party of prisoners is due to be working. That's all I need to do. When the prisoners arrive, someone will come and take the parcels. It's all been pre-arranged through previous deliveries.'

'Isn't that very dangerous?' I was full of admiration for my friend but terrified that she would be risking her life.

Nazira shrugged. 'What have I got to lose? Those men need help. You should see them. They look like skeletons, their clothes are shabby and torn. Some of them are sick. I hardly have to do anything really, just take the food on a little cart to the place and leave it under some bushes.'

The next day before Nazira left, I put my arms around her and gave her a quick hug. Nazira drew back. 'I just want to say good luck,' I said, looking into her eyes, concerned now that I had embarrassed her.

'Thank you, Mrs. Crosby,' she said shyly.

'Please, do call me Juliet,' I said, laughing, giving her another hug.

Nazira nodded and smiled, and returned my hug this time. After she had left I was even more racked with worry than before, and counted the minutes and hours until I heard Nazira's feet on the steps.

It was the same every day from then on. To pass the time and to distract myself, I took down the only book in the place from the dusty shelf, an old but well-thumbed copy of the Koran written in Malay. I found a pencil and paper and began to translate it into English. It took every ounce of concentration and effort as my Malay was still not fluent, but I found that it helped me pass the hours. It also helped me understand the deep faith that motivated the kindness and selflessness of my friend.

Nazira now returned home with a new sense of purpose, with stories of how she had taken food to this place or another. Sometimes she hid and watched for the prisoners to come and take it away. 'It feels good to be doing something for those poor men at last,' she said.

One day she came home unusually agitated, and I noticed she had high spots of colour on her cheeks.

'The people at the canteen have asked me if I will shelter three men. Three escaped prisoners.' My mouth fell open in shock.

'They escaped from a work party on Changi Beach, and they need a place to stay until someone can help them leave the island.'

'Who are they?'

'They are not ordinary soldiers. That's all I know. They are part of some special unit. Some sort of special resistance force. I'm not quite sure what, all I know is they're going to be taken to the mainland to work against the Japanese Occupation.'

'You didn't agree did you?' I asked, feeling my mouth go dry.

'Of course. Of course, I agreed. We must all do what we can to help.'

I was silent and looked away. How could I ask Nazira not to do this, even though I knew this would increase the risk of discovery even more, when she was already risking her life daily to feed and shelter me?

'When are they coming?'

'Today, after dark. One of them was injured when they were escaping, so he might have to stay a bit longer. The others are only going to be here a couple of nights. Please don't look so worried, Juliet. God will take care of us.'

For the next few hours Nazira busied herself preparing for the new arrivals, dragging extra bedding from the cupboards, struggling up the ladder to the roof-space to clear it out and put out matting for the men to sleep on, sweeping the floor, fetching water.

'Can't I do anything?' I asked, feeling helpless.

But the reply was always, 'You must rest.'

'Why don't I just prepare some vegetables? They might like some soup.' So, glad of the distraction, I peeled potatoes and onions while Nazira carried on with her preparations.

At around ten o'clock we heard soft footsteps on the stairs and a discreet knock on the door. Nazira flew to open it, and three very thin men shuffled into the flat. Two of them carried small backpacks, and one of them walked with a severe limp, dragging his left leg. I was surprised to see that they were disguised as Tamil workers, wearing sarongs and cheap sandals. They came in quietly and sat down gratefully on the chairs that Nazira had set out. Under the shoe-polish they'd used as part of their disguise, they faces looked thin and drained.

They introduced themselves as Patrick Murphy, Richard Jones and Adam Foster. At the sound of the last man's voice I felt a wave of recognition. I peered at him closely and then remembered. Even in the gloom I recognised those strong dark eyes. My heart missed a beat.

I stood up and shook the men's hands. 'I'm Juliet Crosby.' To Adam I added, 'I think we've met before. Kuala Lumpur, 1939? I was lost in Chinatown. You bought me a drink and helped me to find my way.'

He rested his eyes on my face and smiled. 'Of course. I remember you very well. You were the lady all alone on your honeymoon, weren't you?'

'Yes,' I said, nervous now, not able to meet his eye. 'It feels a lifetime ago.'

10

The train to Singapore had now entered the final stages of its journey, rattling across Johor Causeway and powering through the outskirts of the modern city. Juliet felt a fresh nervousness about being here again, and wondered why she had made the decision to come. She realised that she had been clenching her fists; there were little grooves in the palms of her hands where her fingernails had been digging into the skin.

The train was slowing down now and soon it was pulling into Keppel Road Station. There was no going back now. As it jerked and squeaked to a halt she got up and reached for her hold-all.

Mary met Juliet on the platform. She was wearing a short cotton flower-print dress and sandals. She wore lots of mascara and pale pink lipstick. Juliet immediately felt scruffy and under-dressed in her creased trousers and old sandals, but Mary put her arms around her and kissed her on both cheeks as if they were old friends. Juliet could not stop herself from going rigid and drawing back. She was not used to such intimacy with anyone these days.

'I'm so happy you've come!' said Mary, smiling her usual wide smile.

They took a taxi to the nurse's hostel on Outram Road where Mary had a small room. Juliet stared out of the window as the car crawled through the traffic. She was stunned at how the city had changed since the war. New buildings had sprung up everywhere, estates of houses, forests of office blocks, and the streets were choked with motor vehicles now. But at least there were still some signs of the old Singapore she had known before the Occupation. Street stalls selling food still lined the roads, rickshaws wove between the cars in the traffic jams, Chinese coolies jogged along the pavements, some with poles on their shoulders and baskets of goods swinging from either side, while others carried the loads on their heads. They passed a row of shabby Chinese shop-houses, bringing the memories of the old days sharply to mind. Most of the bombed-out buildings of the war years beside Outram Park had been replaced by smart new office blocks, several storeys high.

The nurses' hostel was on the grassy campus of the General Hospital. Uniformed nurses bustled about the corridors, chatting in little groups. Juliet shuddered as the smell of disinfectant caught the back of her throat, and she tried to supress disturbing memories. Mary took her up to her own room.

'I'll make you a cup of tea,' she said, kicking off her sandals and busying herself with an electric kettle in the corner of the room.

Juliet looked around her. The room was neat and homely. The bed was covered with a bright pink bedspread patterned with tiny mirrors and fringed with long tassels. The walls were covered in posters. Some looked modern and arty – there was a loud painting of a psychedelic sunset in purples and pinks, and several of overgrown flowers – others were of Western pop stars. Juliet didn't know most of their names or faces, but she did recognise Elvis Presley and Neil Sedaka amongst them. A rail of colourful clothes stood in one corner, mostly very short, very bright dresses, and underneath that a neat row of shoes and a pair of white leather boots. Mary saw Juliet's eyes lingering on them.

'You wear *them* here? In this heat?' asked Juliet.

Mary laughed. 'I love dressing up. It's a weakness of mine, I'm afraid. I spend most of my wages on clothes. It *is* a bit hot for the boots, I know, but they're so beautiful I just couldn't resist them.' She handed Juliet a cup of tea in an orange mug and Juliet took a sip gratefully.

Later, Mary showed her to a small bare guest room at the end of the corridor. They left Juliet's bags there, and after she had showered and changed, they went straight out to eat.

'Let's go down to Boat Quay. There are a few food-stalls next to the river down there. We can sit outside and have a cheap meal.'

They hailed another taxi out on the road and headed towards Chinatown. This was familiar territory to Juliet. Nothing much seemed to have changed over the past twenty odd years. Crumbling two storey shop-houses with washing from Chinese laundries hung out on poles across the streets. Even though darkness had now fallen, noisy markets filled many of the roads, makeshift stalls set up on boxes under umbrellas or awnings, lit by gas lamps and the occasional street light. People thronged the roads, and bicycles and rickshaws pushed their way through the crowds. The cries of hawkers and the smell of spices filled the air.

Being here suddenly brought it all back vividly. She was transported again to that fateful, sweltering day, stumbling weakly through the streets with Nazira, while Japanese planes swooped overhead, dropping bombs on the buildings, gunning down people they saw on the streets.

'Juliet, are you alright?' Mary's voice came from a long way away. The girl was squeezing her hand and staring at her, frowning. 'You've gone completely white. Are you feeling ill?'

'I was just thinking back ...' Juliet said breathlessly. 'Being here reminded me of the war. I haven't been back since then, you see.'

'I'm sorry. I didn't mean to upset you. It must have been dreadful.'

'Yes, but it's all a long time ago now. I expected it to have changed, but Chinatown looks just the same. It took me by surprise, that's all.'

The Singapore River was little changed either. Down on Boat Quay crowds of *twakows* or bumboats were moored up for the night, and the narrow quayside between the go-downs and the river was alive with food-stalls selling seafood. Energetic stall-holders shook woks over naked flames. Again the delicious aromas of spicy cooking mingled with the pungent smell of drains from the river. But at the far end of the quay was an unfamiliar sight; the floodlit banks and financial houses of the new business district loomed over the river.

Mary and Juliet settled themselves on stools in front of a wooden table and ordered plates of *char kway teow*. As they waited for the food to come, three young Chinese men strolled past the table. They walked with a swagger and were dressed in leather jackets and drainpipe trousers. One of them stopped beside the table.

'Hey, Mary!' he said, tossing his head back and pushing his fringe out of his eyes. He flashed her a smile. 'How are you doing? Didn't see you at the Golden Venus last time I was there.'

Juliet noticed that Mary's cheeks were colouring. 'Oh, hello, Li,' she said, lowering her eyes. 'I had to go up to Kuala Lipis, to see my ... to see someone. This is my ... my friend, Juliet Crosby.'

The boy held out his hand and shook Juliet's. 'Pleased to meet you, Mrs. C,' he said, appraising her briefly with his dark eyes, but he quickly turned his attention back to Mary. 'Will you be there next week?'

'Maybe. Yes, probably.'

'Cool. Make sure you are,' said the boy. 'I missed you last time.

See you there then. I've got to run now.' With that he squeezed Mary's arm and hurried off to join his mates who were already some way off down the quay. Mary stared after him.

'Who was that?' asked Juliet after a pause.

'Just some guy I met at a dance a few weeks ago. There's a night club on Orchard Road. I sometimes go on Saturdays with a few of the other nurses.'

'He's rather good looking, isn't he?'

'Yes. He is rather, but he knows it too. He thinks he's God's gift to womankind,' sighed Mary, staring after him with dreamy eyes.

'He seems to like you, Mary.'

Mary looked at her. 'Do you think so?'

'Well, it looked like it to me. Are you not keen?'

'I don't know,' said Mary, sighing heavily. 'There's someone in Palembang, too, a boy called Zaq. We go back a long way. We were at the orphanage together. I know he likes me. I wouldn't want to hurt him.'

'And how do you feel about Zaq?'

'Zaq's great, a really nice boy. I like him a lot. I know he really cares about me, but I'm not sure I want to settle down now.'

'Is that what he wants?'

'He hasn't said so, but you know how you get that feeling? Li's not like that at all. He's so fun. He's like no-one I've ever met before. That's exciting. I know he wants to go out with me, but I just can't make up my mind.'

'Perhaps you can think about it while we are on this trip. You mustn't make hasty decisions. You must give it time, you know.'

A few minutes later the food was brought to the table. Mary turned to her, chopsticks in hand. 'Have you changed your mind about telling me your story? You know, I asked you when I came to your house. You weren't keen then, but I wondered if you'd thought about it. I'd love to hear about how you and Rose came to Malaysia.'

Juliet toyed with her noodles. 'I have thought about it, but I'm sorry, Mary. I find it so difficult to talk about the past. I'd prefer not to if you don't mind.'

Mary's face fell. 'Couldn't you just try? Make a start? See how it goes?'

'It's painful for me, Mary. I'm sorry. Why don't you tell me about your work? I'd like to hear about that. It must be very rewarding.'

Mary brightened a little. She started to talk about the hospital, about the patients she cared for, about their little foibles and needs, and about the other nurses. As she talked she seemed to forget her disappointment, and she smiled as she spoke about the sense of satisfaction she felt when she helped people, when she saw their health improving day by day under her care.

Soon, the crowds had thinned out, and the stallholder was hovering near the table, wanting to clear away. 'Let's go now, Mary. It's getting late. We've got a long journey ahead of us tomorrow.'

Back at the hostel, Mary said goodnight outside the guestroom.

'If you need anything, you know where I am.'

'I doubt I will. I'm completely exhausted. I didn't sleep much on the train journey.'

Juliet undressed quickly, fell into the narrow bed, expecting to fall asleep straight away. But sleep wouldn't come. Perhaps she had been unfair on the girl. Perhaps she should have told her something about Rose and about what happened to them during the war.

After a while she switched on the light and fetched her journal from her bag. She pulled a blouse over her nightdress and went barefoot along the corridor. She listened at Mary's door and could hear the sound of pop music from the record player. She knocked, and Mary opened the door in her pyjamas.

'I'm sorry to disturb you,' she said. 'I thought you might like this.'

Juliet handed the journal to the girl. 'It's all in here,' she explained. Mary took it, looking puzzled. 'It's my journal. I wrote it all down after the war. Everything that happened to me from the time I left London. I find it hard to talk about it. I never have, really. Not to anyone. If you read this, you'll find out why.'

'Thank you,' said Mary, smiling. 'Thank you so much. I feel ... I can't tell you how much this means to me.'

'Well, goodnight then,' said Juliet, feeling awkward. She turned and walked quickly back to her room.

Four o'clock. Moonlight flooded in through the thin curtains and Juliet got up, pulled them back and leaned out of the open window. The night was hot and steamy but the sky was clear and studded with stars. The moon lit up the lawn in front of the hostel, coconut palms casting long spiky shadows on the pale grass. It reminded her of another moonlit night in Singapore, when she had been staying in Rose and Robert's bungalow on Tengah Air Base. She had been awoken by a loud rumbling, like thunder, and got up to look out of the window then too. She loved to watch tropical storms and to throw open the windows and feel the fresh cool air the sudden rain always brought with it. But that night there had been no rain. The boom and rumble had continued, and the sky above the city was lit up in a smoky orange glow and dotted with tiny planes. As she watched, too stunned to move, the planes turned and began to move in the direction of the airbase. The bedroom door was suddenly flung open, and Robert stood there, white-faced, in his pyjamas.

'We're being bombed, come and get under the table.'

She and Rose had huddled on the dining room floorboards while Japanese planes screamed overhead. Everything in the house had vibrated to their echo, and outside they heard the crash and boom of the explosions as the bombs ripped into the airfield. Robert had left the bungalow to run to headquarters. The bombing went on for hours. At day-break they looked out of the window at the craters that scarred the runway and at the groups of servicemen already at work with spades and shovels repairing them hurriedly.

The paper-boy had been very late that day, but then he finally came pedalling on his bicycle, dodging craters in the road. The shocking headline on the *Malayan Tribune* was 'War comes to Malaya, Japanese troops land at Kota Bharu'. Juliet and Rose had stared at each other in mute horror. They knew that their lives would never be the same again.

11

Kuala Lipis, 1939

I didn't see the need to mention to Gavin about getting lost in Kuala Lumpur or about being rescued by the British officer. My husband spent the following morning at the bank and when he returned to the hotel he was in high spirits. He took me in his arms and kissed me, saying, 'I'm so sorry I've neglected you, Mrs. Crosby, but it's all sorted out now. Let's go out and see the sights.'

He ordered a hotel limousine to ferry us in style around the great buildings of the city, and gave me a potted history of each one as we drove. The feelings of loneliness and despair that had engulfed me the day before dissipated, and I caught Gavin's enthusiasm for the capital as he chatted away, pointing out landmarks with one hand and holding my hand with the other. Perhaps things were going to be alright after all.

The next day we took the train back to Kuala Lipis and the old bearer, Mohammed, was waiting with the car at the station to meet us. It was a strange feeling being driven through those gates and seeing the great house again on the hill, realising that it was now my home. There were two new servants: Abdul, the new houseboy, who was gradually going to take over from Mohammed, and Surya, an ayah.

'I don't need a maid,' I protested to Gavin when we were alone. 'I've never needed one before, so I don't know why I should now.'

'Of course you do, my dear. All English women need an ayah out here. It's what's done. If you didn't have one, there would be complaints that we were depriving someone of employment.'

The maid was cheerful enough, and her gentle gossip about the workers on the estate or about what was going on in Kuala Lipis entertained me in a way. But I was wary of her. Occasionally I caught her looking at me with a critical look in her eye, and sometimes, in the months that followed, I had a strange creeping feeling that she was watching me.

The day after our return Gavin rose early, before dawn, and went out onto the estate. He came back for lunch and a siesta in the afternoon, but then went out again and didn't return until after dark. The next day was the same and the one after that. I was at a loss as to how to spend my time in the house. There were no household chores for me to do, and unlike in Penang there was nowhere for me to go. I wandered around the beautiful rooms, touching the elegant furniture, admiring the paintings, trying to get used to the strange feeling that all this was mine now. In the end I found a set of leather-bound Dickens novels in the living room bookcase and settled on the veranda to read Oliver Twist.

'Are you alright?' Gavin asked me when he came home one day. 'You look a bit pale.'

'I'm fine. I didn't get much fresh air today, that's all.'

'Why don't you take one of the horses and go for a ride tomorrow?'

'Couldn't I come with you on your rounds?'

'No, I'm afraid not,' he said curtly, but then his voice softened. 'It wouldn't be practical, Juliet. I'm really busy at the moment. I need to get the re-planting underway as soon as I can. That's what my meetings in Kuala Lumpur were all about. I had to get the bank to release the funds for it. Rubber trees don't last forever, and if I don't do it soon, production will start to decline.'

'Did you need to take out a loan for it?' I asked, alarmed. Everyone had told me he was rich. I hadn't realised he needed to run up debts.

'No, no. I am using the money father had deposited in a trust fund. There were certain things that had to be sorted out before I had access to it that's all. Look, you don't want to bother your head about all that. That's for me to worry about. If you're bored, why don't we go into Kuala Lipis to the club? That will be something for you to look forward to.'

I took Whisky from the stables the next day and rode around the perimeter of the estate. The track separated the rubber plantation from the jungle, and the buzzing of insects and the call of wild creatures from within the dense green depths was deafening. The horse was jittery. He reared when a king cobra suddenly emerged from the undergrowth and slithered across the path in front of us in a great looping motion. I managed to stay in my seat, but unnerved I took the next track that turned away from the jungle and from then on stayed on the inner paths within the plantation.

At the weekend, Gavin, true to his word, drove me along the jungle road and into the little town. The Pahang Club was a small black-and-white wooden building on the top of a hill. It looked a bit like a down-at-heel village hall, very different to the palatial surroundings of the Penang Club in Georgetown. When we entered the crowded bar there was a low murmur, and the place fell silent for a few seconds. People turned to stare. It reminded me of the first time I had seen Gavin, when the eyes of the assembled company in the club had turned to watch him cross the room.

'Good evening, Mr. Crosby, sir,' the Indian barman bowed politely. 'Very nice to see you again, sir,' but others at the bar moved discreetly away from where we stood.

We sat at a table in the corner and after a while a middle-aged couple came up to us. 'Evening, Crosby. It's a long time since we saw you here,' said the man. He was wiry and tanned with receding grey hair and a toothbrush moustache. Ex-military, I guessed.

'Evening, Hatton. Allow me to present my wife, Juliet.'

The man shook my hand and introduced his wife, Beatrice. 'We heard you'd got married Crosby. Many congratulations.'

Beatrice was stout and what I might have described as horsy. She looked as though she didn't give a damn about what she wore. Her grey hair was untidy and her skirt and blouse creased. But she had a kindly face and a warm manner, and I instantly liked her.

'How wonderful, to have a new girl to add to our company at the club! We're rather short of ladies here,' she said brightly. 'Now why don't you two chaps go and have a round of billiards, and I can have a chat to Juliet here.'

So we sat in the corner and sipped our *stengahs* while Beatrice asked me endless questions about my family, my life in England, how I had come to meet Gavin, what I thought about life on the plantation. 'You might find it a bit dull at first, my dear, but you'll soon get to know people on all the estates and mines for miles around, and there's always the club. There's a tennis court outside, you know.'

I looked around me. 'I couldn't help noticing, that people don't seem very friendly here,' I said in a low voice.

She patted my hand. 'You're not to worry. People were a bit cross with Gavin recently because there was a strike on his estate that spread through the region, and some people ended up losing quite a bit of money through it. He made himself rather unpopular for a while. But that was several months ago now, my dear, and people out here have short memories. I think you'll find that now Gavin's got a new wife, people might start to forgive and forget.'

As we left at the end of the evening, Beatrice made me promise to come and visit her at her home on the other side of the town. Her husband managed a tin mine. She told me that she had two horses and she would show me the local forests if I enjoyed riding.

'Thank you,' I said. 'I'd like that very much.'

As we finally left she took both my hands in hers and drew me aside. I felt an address card being pressed into my palm. 'If you ever need anything, my dear, anything at all, or just want to talk, here's where to find me,' she said, with a meaningful look. I realised that what I saw in her eyes was a mixture of pity and concern for me. I felt confused and slightly affronted.

As we walked towards the car, Gavin put his arm around my shoulders and said, 'Don't take any notice of Bee Hatton. She can be a bit of a busybody, but she's a good sort really.'

The days turned into weeks and then into months. Our days were shaped by Gavin's self-imposed routine of work on the estate. I spent my days riding, reading Dickens on the veranda and strolling in the grounds. I even started taking an interest in the food that the servants prepared in the kitchen, learning all about Malay food and cooking techniques. Each morning I went into the kitchen after breakfast and discussed menus with the cook. He taught me how to slow-cook beef in coconut milk, galangal and herbs to make a succulent *rendang*, how to achieve the right balance of fragrant spices and chillies to make a tasty *nasi goreng*, and the right way to marinade and barbecue chicken pieces for perfect *satays*.

Once a week, Abdul would drive me into Kuala Lipis to the Tuesday bazaar, to buy fresh produce. It became the highlight of my week. I loved the atmosphere there, the exotic sights and smells, the cries of the vendors, losing myself in the anonymous crowd, the crush of people at the stalls that overflowed with fresh exotic fruit and vegetables. I enjoyed selecting the best pieces I could find and bargaining with the stallholders. I even made an effort to learn my first stumbling words of Malay to help me get better bargains from the stallholders.

One day, during those first few months, a visitor arrived unannounced at the house. Gavin was out on the estate, and I went into the drawing room half way through the morning to see Scott walking in through the front door. He kicked his boots off and threw his hold-all aside.

'Mohammed,' he bellowed. Then he saw me standing there and smiled.

'Oh, it's my new sister-in-law. How charming to meet you properly at last.'

He walked towards me and before I had time to think had taken my hand and raised it to his lips. He looked into my eyes and said, 'Delighted to make your acquaintance, Mrs. Crosby.' I couldn't tell if he was mocking me, and I felt the heat of confusion in my cheeks. I looked away. He let my hand drop. 'Where the hell is that boy? Mohammed! I'm gasping for a drink.'

'I'll get you something,' I said quickly. 'What would you like? Tea? Lemon juice?'

He laughed loudly, 'Oh, my dear Juliet. I see I'm going to have to educate you in my ways. I meant a proper drink. Whisky, if you have any.'

'The decanter's over there on the sideboard,' I said, not moving.

'Don't give me that look, please. You look like my commanding officer. Now why don't you sit down and join me?'

I hesitated. I had no wish to join him and prolong the discomfort I felt in his presence. I was also fearful of what Gavin would say if he came home and saw me drinking with his brother in the middle of the day. I searched my mind for an excuse.

'No, thank you,' I said. 'I was just about to go out riding.'

He laughed again. 'In that pretty dress?'

'Of course not. I was just on my way upstairs to get changed.'

He eyed me sceptically, went over to the sideboard and poured himself a large shot of whisky.

'Well, have it your own way,' he said, tipping his head back as he drained his glass. 'Now why don't you pop up and change, and I'll come out riding with you when you're ready.'

I felt trapped. As I changed into my riding clothes in the bedroom I found myself dreading the next couple of hours.

The syce saddled Whisky and another horse for Scott, and we set off down the drive. Like his brother, Scott rode well, with ease and confidence. Once through the gates, we turned onto the plantation and rode for a while along the familiar tracks in silence. We neared a crossroads where the route to the tappers village branched off. 'Let's go down there,' said Scott suddenly, pulling his horse to a stop.

'No, I don't think so. I never normally ride through the village,' I said.

'Why ever not?' he asked, and I felt his eyes on my face, watching for my reaction.

'I don't know. I don't like to disturb them,' I said, not wanting to admit the truth. Going through the village made me feel guilty, it brought home to me how poorly paid the workers were, the conditions in which they lived. It reminded me that my very existence depended upon their poverty.

'Nonsense. They don't mind. There's a wonderful stretch of open track on the other side where we can gallop. Come on.'

He kicked his horse on and trotted off down the track towards the village. I followed reluctantly. We rode in silence between the stilted wooden huts, where chickens pecked around in the bare earth and children played under the houses. There were no men about. A few women were preparing food on their porches, or sweeping between the houses. As we passed, they stopped to stare at us. No-one smiled or waved. They just stood and watched as we passed, their faces expressionless, inscrutable. I sensed that Scott was watching me, too, assessing my reaction, waiting for me to say something.

When we had cleared the village and rode out on the other side, the track widened where the rubber trees had been felled for replanting.

'You're tougher than I thought you were,' said Scott. 'Come on. We can gallop here.'

He urged his horse on, whipping its haunches, kicking it hard, and the horse leapt forward into a gallop. My horse followed, jittery and excited. We were soon galloping full tilt, side by side, foam flying from the horses' mouths, flecks of sweat on their flanks. It was exhilarating to feel the breeze in my hair, the energy of the horse beneath me, the reckless motion of the gallop. I glanced at Scott and observed that he was caught up in the moment, too, his eyes focused on the track ahead. We galloped until the horses began to tire and pulled up where the track ended in a clearing. We dismounted and let the horses rest and drink from a stream that ran through the clearing.

I was breathing hard, my heart beating fast. 'You're quite a girl, Juliet,' said Scott. He came closer, and I caught the smell of whisky on his breath. I felt awkward again.

'I think we'd better go back,' I said.

'Nonsense. We've only just started.'

'I need to speak to the cook about dinner,' I said. It was a feeble excuse I knew. He ignored me and stepped closer.

'Gavin doesn't deserve you, you know.' He was right in front of me now, within touching distance. I refused to look up at his face. Instead I turned around and busied myself with the saddle, tightening the girth. To my relief he stepped away and I heard the saddle creak as he mounted his horse.

'Come on then,' he said, resignation in his voice. 'I'll show you how to get back to the house from here. I know all the secret paths on the estate.'

That evening at dinner there was a palpable atmosphere between the brothers. Gavin had not been surprised to see Scott there, drinking whisky in the drawing room when he came in from work. He had just stood over him, his arms folded, and said, 'How long are you staying this time?'

'Only a couple of days. Keep your hair on, old chap. I'll be good, I promise.'

We ate our food in uncomfortable silence, until Scott said half way through the first course, 'She's quite an accomplished rider, your little wife, Gavin.'

There was a pause. I watched Gavin's face. He frowned and put down his fork. 'You went riding together?' he was staring at me.

I opened my mouth to answer when Scott broke in, 'No harm done, old man. We only had a quick turn around the plantation together. She rides very well.'

I saw the vein pulsing in Gavin's throat, but he said nothing more about it. Conversation was stilted and half-hearted during the meal, and before he had finished his desert, Gavin got up from the table and said, 'I'd appreciate it if you'd stay down in the bungalow while you're here, Scott. I've got some work to finish off in the sheds now, and when I get back I expect you to be gone.'

I could barely look at Scott when Gavin had left. I felt so confused and ashamed. He got up angrily from the table, pushing the chair over. 'Damn him!' he said, slamming his fists on the table.

Mohammed appeared in the doorway. 'Everything alright, sir?'

'Yes, thank you, Mohammed,' snapped Scott. 'Everything is just fine. Just fine and dandy.' He walked unsteadily towards Mohammed, who stepped aside. 'You needn't worry. I'm about to obey your precious master and go down to my squalid little quarters. I won't be bothering you again.'

He wound his way between the chairs in the drawing room towards the sideboard and seized the decanter.

'You don't mind if I take the rest of this whisky, do you?' he said, tucking it under one arm and collecting his hold-all with the other. I jumped when the front door slammed behind him, and glanced at Mohammed. He was looking at me steadily, impassively. I looked back down at the tablecloth. What did he know that I didn't? But I knew the answer to that question. He must know everything about this family and their strange warped relationships. More than I ever would.

ONE DAY A NOTE from Beatrice Hatton came through the post asking me over the following week.

'You're not going to go, are you?' asked Gavin when I mentioned it at supper time. 'You'll find it terribly dull. The house is a dreadful mess you know, full of dogs and straw and tack for the horses.'

'I thought I might. It can get rather dull here on my own all day.' I was just stating a fact, and hadn't meant to upset him, but his expression changed. Anger flashed across his face.

'Well, you chose the life, didn't you?' he snapped, raising his voice. 'You knew damn well what it involved. You knew that I had to work on the estate and that you'd be here alone. Why don't you pack your bags and run straight back to your auntie in Penang if you don't like it?'

Stunned by this outburst I went and put my arms around him. 'I'm sorry,' I said, tears pricking my eyes, but he stood up, shook my hands off him and left the room without another word. He went off on his horse into the darkness and was away until after I had gone to bed. When he did come home and slid into bed beside me, I put my arms around him again, but he simply turned over and after a few minutes I could tell by his breathing that he had gone to sleep.

I did go to Beatrice's house the following week. I felt I needed to make a stand. Abdul drove me the twenty or so miles over the rough mountain roads to the tin mine headquarters where the Hatton house stood on the edge of the jungle. Gavin was right: the house was untidy and smelled of dogs, of whom there were about four. But Beatrice was warm and welcoming. We had a light lunch on her terrace overlooking the forest and after that we went to her stables behind the house, mounted the two horses and rode off into the jungle.

'I often go out in the afternoons,' she said. 'Charlie sometimes doesn't get back until after dark, so it's a long time to be on your own with not much to do. I find a ride breaks up the time.'

'Yes,' I said. 'Gavin is out for long hours too. In fact he often goes out in the evenings too.'

At this, she gave me a sharp look, but didn't say anything. Later, on the journey home, thinking back over the day, I began to wonder why she had reacted like that. This thought began to corrode my peace of mind like a cancer. Once I had started I couldn't stop my wild imaginings about why Gavin was out late and what he might be doing. It had never occurred to me before, because I knew very little about the running of the estate, but the more I thought about it, the more I felt sure that all the workers would go home at sundown and the sheds would be closed for the night. Should I ask him about it? Perhaps not; it might make him angry, and I did not want to risk that.

I decided to follow him the next evening. I knew he generally walked towards the factory sheds with a flashlight so I could hide in one of the outhouses and see where he went. He was unlikely to go very fast in the dark, so I should be able to keep up. The difficulty would be slipping out before he left the house.

The next evening, at supper I could hardly eat. My stomach

churned with nerves. I toyed with my rice and Gavin looked at me frowning.

'Are you alright? You've hardly eaten a thing.'

'Actually I'm not feeling at all well. My stomach feels very odd. I think I'll go upstairs and lie down if you don't mind.'

'Of course not. You don't mind if I trot off in a moment, do you? There are some issues with the accounts.'

'No, don't worry. I'll probably just go to sleep.'

I went out of the dining room but instead of going upstairs, went to the back door near the kitchen, opened it carefully and left the house. I crept across the lawn to the edge of the garden, walked quickly through the gates and took the track that forked off towards the factory sheds. I had hidden a small torch in my pocket, but was wary of using it in case it could be seen from the house. Near the sheds was an outhouse where spare parts for the latex presses were stored. I stood against the wall of the building and waited. The sound of night creatures filled the air, and I was worried in case a snake had concealed itself in the shed. My legs were quaking with fear and my heart was pounding. Soon I heard footsteps on the track, and from the footfall I knew it was him. I pressed myself against the side of the shed. I felt as though my heart was beating so hard and my breathing was so heavy that he was bound to notice me. But he was whistling 'Begin the Beguine' loudly as he made his way down the path. Whistling was something he hardly ever did at home.

When I was sure he was far enough ahead I crept after him. I could see the beam from his flashlight bouncing along ahead, lighting up the lines of grey rubber trees in an eerie arc. It was not difficult to follow him at a safe distance. Instead of turning off the track towards the sheds and estate office, he carried on down the hill towards the little settlement where the estate workers lived. I hadn't been there since Scott and I had ridden through, not wanting to repeat the discomfort I'd felt then as every pair of eyes had turned to stare at me. But now in the darkness, it was quiet, except for the few people cooking over fires outside their huts or relaxing on their verandas under hurricane lamps, smoking cheroots.

I realised that it would be impossible to follow him along the track between the huts because I would be seen, so I stopped at the edge of the hamlet. I shaded my eyes, trying to make out where the flashlight was going. Half way down the track I saw it stop and make a turn towards one of the huts. I strained my eyes to see what he was doing. Like all the others the hut was built on stilts. He was going up the wooden steps. As he got to the top step, a figure emerged from the hut onto the platform in front of it. It was a woman, I was sure of that. I could not see what she looked like, but I could make out that she had long dark hair. To my astonishment Gavin put his arms around her and kissed her. Shock hit me like a physical blow, and I stood there at the edge of the clearing reeling, as if I had been slapped. I put my hand to my mouth to stifle my cries and turned back the way I had come, tears streaming down my face.

12

I suppose some women would have stormed across to the hut, marched up the steps, interrupted the embrace and demanded to know what was going on. But I was too much of a coward for that. Instead, I turned and ran blindly all the way back up to the house, my breath coming in heaving gulps, tears streaming down my cheeks, stumbling off the road in the dark and snagging my legs on branches and thorns. As soon as I got inside the house I rushed up the stairs and threw myself down on the bed, sobbing.

The image of Gavin taking that woman into his arms and kissing her kept playing over and over in my mind like a bad movie. My thoughts returned to the events again and again, searching for some innocent explanation for what I had seen. But try as I might, I couldn't think of any reason, apart from the obvious one, why he would take the woman in his arms and kiss her as he had done. There was no escaping it; what I had witnessed was an unmistakably sexual embrace.

I wondered how long he would be out of the house this time. He usually returned around the time I went to bed. I didn't want him to find me crying. I forced myself to get up and go into the bathroom and splash my face with cold water. Peering in the mirror, I saw that my face was horribly puffy, my eyes bloodshot. I couldn't let him see me like that. My pride wouldn't allow it.

I quickly changed into my night-dress and was already in bed when I heard the front door slam and his footfall on the stairs. I lay stock still on the far side of the bed as he came into the room. I realised I was shaking and I felt sick to the core at the thought of him touching me after what I had seen, but I need not have worried – he got into bed and immediately turned over the other way. Within minutes he was asleep, breathing heavily and evenly, but I lay awake staring into space until the first rays of light began to spill from the edge of the curtains.

When I heard him get up, soon after dawn, I pretended to be asleep. He didn't try to wake me. I heard him go downstairs and the chink of cutlery on china, and the murmured conversation between him and Mohammed as he ate his breakfast. After the front door had slammed and I heard him walk around the house to the stables, I finally went to sleep. A little later Surya came in with a cup of tea. She shook me gently, but I turned away. She put the tea down beside the bed and left the room. I went back to sleep. When I awoke again the tea was stone cold. I looked at my watch and realised it was noon and that Gavin would soon be back for lunch. I dragged myself out of bed, washed and dressed quickly and was already sitting at the table when Gavin came through the door after his morning's work.

He looked at me with curiosity. 'Are you feeling any better, Juliet? You look dreadful.'

I shook my head. I couldn't meet his eyes.

'Perhaps we should get the doctor to have a look at you,' he said, sitting down at the table. He didn't sound very concerned, rather I detected a note of annoyance in his voice that I might cause him the trouble and expense of calling the doctor.

'I'll be fine,' I said. 'I've had a bit of an upset stomach, that's all. I just need some rest.' My voice shook when I spoke to him and I still could not look at him. I felt his eyes linger on me suspiciously.

We passed the meal in virtual silence. I couldn't think of anything to say to him.

After lunch I went back to bed and lay down. I felt exhausted, devoid of energy. I did not even have the will to read a book. All I felt was a dreadful sapping hurt, like a physical pain draining my strength and gripping my chest and throat.

Surya came in and looked at me. 'I have herbal remedy for you, madam,' she said, setting a glass down on the bedside table. 'Master say you unwell.'

'I'm just tired,' I said, turning away from the foul-smelling brown drink which was full of herb leaves. The bitter smell caught the back of my throat and made my stomach turn.

'You have bad fever, madam, but you not ill,' said Surya, standing over me, her hands on her hips.

'What on earth do you mean?' I asked, sitting up and staring at her. But she looked away, and I noticed her smiling quietly to herself. What did she know? Did she know about the woman Gavin kept in that hut in the village? She probably did. After all, he didn't seem to care who did know, judging by the brazen way he'd behaved the night before. They probably all knew, all the estate-workers, the house servants. They must all be gossiping and laughing at me behind my back, calling me a fool.

And they would be right. I was a fool. I had thought I knew best, that all the warnings from those close to me and the rumours circulating in the colony amounted to nothing. My head was so turned by the flattery, by the sheer amazement that someone as handsome and eligible as Gavin could possibly want to marry me, that I had deliberately put all those warnings to the back of my mind and rushed headlong into the trap he had set.

What had prompted him to set that trap for me? Why had he married me? If he had a lover already and a house full of servants, surely he had no need of a wife. There was nothing for me to do here. Auntie Maude was quite wrong in thinking that he needed someone to run the place. The house ran smoothly already. Mohammed was the perfect housekeeper and was training Abdul up in his ways. It couldn't be that Gavin was lonely. He was out on the estate all day and spent his evenings in the village with that woman. I thought long and hard but I simply could not think of an answer to that question. He must have had a reason, I concluded, and whatever reason it was, marrying me had been an act of pure cruelty. I had lived a full and free life before, with family and friends and happiness. Here I was like a caged animal. Useless and redundant, without work or pleasure or company. I lay down again, face down on the pillow, sobs of self-pity racking my body.

At some point during that long afternoon I hauled myself out of bed and went to sit at the writing desk in the corner of the bedroom. I had decided to write to Rose. I had the vague thought that if I put the events down on paper it might lessen the pain. Rose and I had written to each other about once a week since we had both left Penang. I cast my eye over Rose's latest letter:

'Isn't it dreadful that Britain is at war with Germany? Just think, Juliet, of how frightful things must be for everyone at home. I can't believe there might be a war here, too,' she had written. 'Rob thinks it might be all a false alarm, but we often hear people discussing it in the clubs and shops, and some people are really convinced it will happen. But with all these troops pouring into Malaya and Singapore, we surely must be safe, don't you think? And there is a fantastic new naval base at Sembawang on the east side of the island. That can't be all for nothing.

But day-to-day life goes on much as before, despite this distraction. We dress up and go down to the officers' mess on the base most evenings and have a drink and play bridge, or Rob plays poker or billiards and I chat with the other wives. It's very sociable, you know, Juliet. I've made dozens of lovely friends and we often go down into the city shopping on Orchard Road, or to the swimming club on the seafront together. Sometimes we go down to Raffles to the ballroom there to dance. It is truly magnificent, you know. Great chandeliers and a big band, and the dance floor is so smooth, you just feel yourself floating on air. I sometimes think back to the shabby old Majestic in Harrow. Do you remember, Jules, what fun it was there? All those gauche young men trying to dance with us? Well this is a different matter altogether. Much more grand and sophisticated and grown-up.'

Her letters always me left me feeling inadequate and with a tingle of the old jealousy. I could just picture her, the darling of the officers' wives, with 'dozens of friends'. I was sure it was no exaggeration. I was sure she was happy, with constant company and entertainment.

I remembered how she had been always surrounded by a swarm of admiring girls at school. They would follow her between lessons and at break times, copy her hairstyle, the way she walked and talked, the ways she wore her uniform. Some would even bring her little gifts in the hope of being admitted into her inner circle. Rose accepted all this attention with genuine gratitude. She could not abide being alone or bored for long.

One summer Father had taken us along on his annual walking holiday in Snowdonia. He had been going there alone for a few days every year since mother died, leaving us in the care of our nanny. It was his one indulgence in life and his greatest pleasure. But that year, he had invited us to join him. We stayed in an ancient granite farmhouse high in the hills, where the farmers' wife took in walkers for bed and board. On the first day we climbed miles through forests and heather into the hills, finally reaching a still clear lake surrounded by towering peaks. We sat beside the clear water and ate our sandwiches. Father took a great gulp of the delicious cool air and remarked, 'Isn't this just wonderful? It's so quiet here.'

'Hmmm, it's lovely, Father,' I said, lying back on the cool grass and looking up at the scudding clouds. The only sounds were the distant bleating of the sheep and the cawing of birds circling high above us.

'Well, I think it's beastly,' said Rose. She was sitting on a rock a few paces away, huddled into her coat, her shoulders hunched.

'Whatever do you mean, Rose darling?'

'There's no-one about,' she said with a shudder.

'But that's the point, Rose. To get away from it all. Have some peace and quiet.'

'Well it gives me the creeps.'

Father's face fell and he finished his sandwich in silence. 'Can we go back to the house now?' Rose asked, bringing our outing to an early end. 'I'm freezing to death.'

Back at the farmhouse, after a huge supper of stew and mashed potatoes, Rose and I went up to our bedroom while Father sat and drank a beer downstairs in the kitchen with the farmer.

Rose threw herself on her bed and stared at the ceiling. 'What are we going to do now, Jules?' she demanded. 'There's hours before bedtime still.'

'Well, I'm going to read a book.'

'I forgot to bring one,' she said, turning over restlessly.

I tried to read a page or two, but couldn't ignore Rose sighing and fidgeting beside me. After a while I gave up and put down the book. 'What's the matter?'

'I don't like it here, Jules. There's nobody to talk to. No-one for miles around. No street lights. Nothing to do.'

'But that's why we're here, Rose darling. Like Father said. To relax and to get away from London for a while.'

She was silent for a few moments, then said, 'But why would we want to do that? I love London. Do you know, Jules? I don't really understand the countryside at all.'

I could not help thinking now as I stared at her letter from Singapore how she would have hated to live my life, here on this remote estate in the middle of the jungle, with no friends to talk to and very little to do. Even though I did not need company like Rose, the solitary existence had daunted me a little at first, too. But I had thought it would all be worth it, that loving Gavin and having him love me back would make up for everything, that our love would render our world complete and my solitary life worthwhile. How cruelly I had been deceived, had deceived myself.

I picked up my pen to write to her, to pour out my grief and frustration.

'My dearest Rose,' I began, 'I'm afraid I have to tell you some bad news. Something absolutely devastating has happened to me. I'm tearing myself apart with it. It is so bad that I can barely begin to write it down.' I stopped writing. How could I begin to describe it? How could I put down the words 'I think Gavin has a mistress' in black and white? How could I tell my sister that my husband was being unfaithful to me with a woman in the workers' village on the estate and that it wasn't just a suspicion, that I had seen the evidence with my very own eyes? How could I tell her that I was desperately unhappy and lonely here and that my marriage had been the biggest mistake I had made in my life?

In truth when it came down to it I did not want to see it written down. I didn't want to admit to Rose what I could barely admit to myself. She would be desperately sorry for me of course, but I didn't want her pity, and I didn't want to impinge on her own happiness either. I stared at the page through gathering tears and with a violent gesture I ripped the page out of the pad and tore it up into tiny pieces so that no-one could ever read what was written on it. I threw it into the bin, took a fresh sheet and began again.

'My Dearest Rose,' I wrote, 'How lovely to get your letter. You sound as though you are having a wonderful time on the airbase. It must be nice to have so many friends and to be able to go dancing as often as you do. Of course I remember the Majestic.

But of course you are being kind, and it was you that the young men wanted to dance with, never me at all ...'

I continued in that vein and after a couple of pages I had almost convinced myself that things here were quite normal. I told her of my occasional trips to see Beatrice and to the club in town. I told her about how I was learning about the local cuisine and the language, and how I usually spent my days riding on the estate. I tried to describe the landscape and the savage beauty of the jungle. When I had finished, my eyes were dry and I was feeling a little better. By the time I slid the letter into an envelope and sealed it, I had decided that this was by far the best way to cope. It was best to ignore the unhappiness that was gnawing at my heart. I would simply carry on as if nothing had happened. There was nothing to be gained by confronting Gavin. I did not want to trigger his anger and have to face the fall-out of such a discussion. No, I would simply pretend that nothing had changed between us and that I had no suspicion of his deception.

13

The battered old ferry was now chugging nearer to the Island of Batam, and Juliet could just make out a smudge of land on the horizon.

'We're nearly there, Mary. We'd better get ready to get off.'

Juliet saw that Mary was staring at the sky with a faraway look in her eyes. 'Are you alright, Mary? You're not feeling queasy are you?'

'No, no. I'm fine. I was just thinking about you and your life,' she said, then turned to Juliet. 'I read your journal last night. Some of it, at least. You know, when I first came to your house a few weeks ago, I would never have guessed in a million years that you'd lived such a miserable life there.'

'Really? I didn't know that I made such a good job of hiding things.'

'For a little while, you did, yes. But it's more about how I see things, myself. When I saw that fantastic house, even though it's a bit shabby and old-fashioned now, I thought whoever lives there really has got to have a wonderful life for herself.'

'Why?'

'Because I've never lived anywhere like that. You know, I've never actually lived in a proper house at all.'

Juliet remembered the crowded refectory of the hostel where she and Mary had their breakfast that morning, sitting at a cheap formica table. Juliet had watched Mary as the girl stood in the queue, waiting for their food and chatting to the other nurses, looking so relaxed, seeming so happy and comfortable. It suddenly struck her that to Mary, living in an anonymous institution like a hostel must feel quite normal. The girl had spent her life in such places. Communal dining and shared facilities were all she had ever known.

'It's crazy, I know, but I used to think that if people live in a lovely place and seem to be well off, they must be happy. It's because of how I was brought up, I suppose.'

Juliet was lost for words. She slid her hand on top of Mary's. Her heart turned over with sympathy for the girl, as she thought about everything that Mary had been deprived of, if indeed she was the baby who had set off in Rose's arms on that ill-fated journey on the *Rajah of Sarawak*.

'I'm so sorry, Mary. Was it a very unhappy place to grow up, the orphanage?'

Mary wrinkled up her nose as she considered the question. 'Not unhappy exactly. At the time, you don't know anything different. But looking back, I suppose it was a bit cold and impersonal. Especially for little ones. All our physical needs were catered for. We weren't ever hungry, we had clothes, and there were plenty of other kids around to play with, but do you know, nobody ever once gave me a hug, or kissed me goodnight. It was only when I left and began to mix with other girls who came from normal families that I began to realise what I'd missed out on.'

'Why don't you tell me about it?'

Mary sighed. 'Oh there's not much to tell really. Every day was exactly the same. We'd be up at six in the morning for prayers. Then we'd have breakfast, then we'd go to the nursery when we were tiny or to lessons in the schoolroom when we were older. During school holidays we'd play in the yard. We'd eat lunch in the refectory. Then back to class until it was time for tea, and then play-time and more prayers before bed. We did this day after day, year after year. Sometimes at weekends or during the holidays we were taken on trips to the market. Once or twice on very special occasions we had a day-trip to the country or the seaside. That was all.'

'You must have had friends?'

'Of course. Fantastic friends. Girls I'll stay in touch with for ever. And there was Zaq, of course. They all made it just about bearable. Because of them I managed not to be crushed by the monotony of the routine or the starkness of the surroundings. You'll see what it's like when we get there, but just visiting the place won't give you a proper idea of just what it was like to be brought up there.'

'I'm so sorry, Mary. What can I say?'

'Nothing. There's nothing you can say. But maybe you could try to understand why it's so important for me to trace my family. I just want to belong to someone. To live a normal life, I suppose. That's why I want to find out all about what happened to you and your sister. I really want to know about your lives. It's because I haven't really had a normal one of my own.'

Juliet watched Mary's face as she spoke. Her expression was frank and serious. She spoke with honesty and passion.

'Of course, Mary,' she said, 'I do understand. But it isn't easy for me, though. I haven't thought about those times for years. In fact it is so painful for me to think about them that up until now I had made a conscious effort to forget. I'm doing all this for you, Mary.'

'I do appreciate it,' Mary said and gave her a hug. Juliet didn't resist.

The ferry drew into the dockside, which was bustling and

crowded. There was much excitement and shouting as ropes were thrown from the boat onto the quayside. Locals rushed forward to help moor the boat and greet family members who disembarked noisily carrying packages and luggage. Juliet and Mary were the last to scramble up onto the quay. Their bags were thrown up to them by the crew. A crowd of touts and rickshaw men surrounded them, badgering them for their trade. Mary immediately took charge and began bargaining with one of them in fluent Indonesian. She quickly secured a ride to the other port from which they planned to catch the boat to Palembang. They climbed on board and were soon making their way out of the busy terminal and down a road lined with dilapidated wooden buildings towards the other port.

'I'm glad you know where you're going, Mary,' said Juliet, clutching her hold-all as they bounced along the rutted road.

'I've done it before. I had to go to Singapore for my interview at the hospital, and when I left there for good, I came this way.'

There was another passenger ferry waiting at the other docks and as soon as they arrived on board and stowed their bags, Mary slipped off to visit a line of food stalls she had spotted on the dockside and returned with two meals of rice wrapped in banana leaves and two bottles of water.

'Packed lunch,' she said, holding them up, smiling.

The ferry rapidly filled up with locals and their luggage and soon set off southwards, down the coast of Sumatra towards the mouth of Musri River. They ate their lunch as the ferry chugged south, hugging the misty slab of land to the portside.

'I've been thinking about Zaq and Li,' said Mary. 'I suppose Li is superficially attractive to me, but he could be bad news. It's a bit like you and Gavin.'

Juliet shuddered. 'I don't suppose Li is anything like Gavin, Mary.'

'No. That's not what I meant. I meant maybe I'm attracted to him for all the wrong reasons. He's good looking, popular. But apart from that, I don't know much about him at all. Whereas with Zaq, I know him so well. He is kind and loving. He cares about me.'

'When did you last see him?'

'Oh, months ago. He came over to Singapore for a few days. He's studying in Palembang now. He doesn't get much time off. I might try and see him while we're there. If you don't mind?'

'Of course, not. Why should I? It might help you make up your mind about him.'

'I'll do that then,' said Mary, smiling her toothy smile.

KUALA LIPIS, 1940

Over the following months my life established itself into a regular pattern of self-deception. I avoided the truth and avoided confrontations with Gavin. I did my best to ignore his comings and goings and tried my best not to anger him in any way. I began to exist like a shadow, fitting in passively with his routines, bending myself to his will, making myself undemanding and accepting.

My only real solace at that time were my visits to Beatrice. I began to see her more often and she occasionally came to the estate to visit me. On one of those visits she said, 'Why don't you pop down to the club one of these evenings?'

'Gavin tends to be busy in the evenings. It's usually really late by the time he comes in.'

Once again she shot me that look, the one that had raised my suspicions in the first place. It was a look which combined pity with disbelief.

'I meant *you*, Juliet dear. You could come along on your own. You could get one of your boys to drive you, or you could even drive yourself. You can drive, can't you?'

I nodded. 'Of course. But I'm not sure.' I felt shaky inside and my pulse was beginning to race at the thought of what Gavin would say when I told him.

Beatrice leaned forward and took my hand. 'You need to get out sometimes, Juliet,' she said gently. 'It's not healthy alone here in the house all the time. You don't look at all well.'

It was true. I had lost weight and my clothes hung even more loosely on my frame than before. I had no appetite and had stopped eating properly. Under the suntan I had built up from riding out on the estate, my skin was sallow and unhealthy. I hesitated. 'I'm not sure. Gavin might not like it.'

It was the first time I had openly expressed any hint of the fact that Gavin was controlling and possessive. Beatrice drew herself up.

'Well, if he doesn't like it, he should jolly well take better care of you himself. He should take you out sometimes instead of abandoning you here all alone. It isn't fair on you. A young wife needs to be entertained. Especially living all the way out here like you do.'

'I'm sure you're right, but ...'

'You're scared of him, aren't you?' Her shrewd eyes were assessing me.

'Of course not, Beatrice.' I tried to look horrified by the suggestion.

'So why not come along? Look, Charlie and I are going down to the club on Wednesday evening. You should join us for a drink and a rubber of bridge. If Gavin can come all well and good, if not, we can rustle up another partner for you I'm sure. You can play bridge can't you?'

I nodded. 'Rose and I used to play with Father and his friends sometimes, but I'm a bit rusty I'm afraid.'

'Don't worry about that. It's just for fun. Well, that's settled then. I won't take no for an answer.'

When Wednesday came, I intended to say something to Gavin at breakfast time, but I was just plucking up the nerve to do so when he got up, dabbed his mouth on a napkin and said, 'Must go now. We're really busy today. There's truck-load of latex bales to get ready to ship down to Kuala Lumpur. There'll be the paperwork to deal with afterwards. I might not be back for lunch, I'm afraid.'

With that he dashed off, leaving me opening and closing my mouth in surprise.

I lunched alone, and when supper time came, I sat down alone again to eat coronation chicken and cold potatoes. One of the estate workers came to the door and told Mohammed that Gavin had been delayed in the office and not to wait for him. I felt so apprehensive about the evening that I could hardly eat. Afterwards I went upstairs and put on a flower-print dress I had brought from London. I made up my face in the bedroom mirror, something I hadn't done properly for weeks. As I came downstairs I asked Mohammed to fetch the car.

'I'm going to the club. I was hoping you could drive me there,' I said. He stared at me for a few seconds.

'Master not go?' he asked impassively.

'No,' I said, returning his gaze. 'I'm going alone.'

I scribbled a note to Gavin. 'Beatrice has asked me to go to the club with her. I meant to tell you at supper but you didn't come back. I won't be late, Juliet.'

All the way there on the dark jungle road I stared out at the wild undergrowth, lit by the headlights, biting my nails, worrying about my decision. I was on the point of asking Mohammed to turn back on several occasions. Already I was dreading the conversation with Gavin on my return. The thought of it made my heart pound and sweat stand out on my brow.

At the club, Beatrice greeted me warmly and ordered me a *stengah* from the bar. Then she introduced me to Major Benson, a tall elderly man with sandy whiskers dressed in a safari suit. He was to be my partner at bridge. We played a couple of rubbers. Beatrice and Charlie played together instinctively. They seemed to know what cards the other one had automatically. I envied them their quiet contentment. The Major was an affable and genial partner. He played gallantly, but he and I lost every game. It was all good natured though and after a few rounds I found myself relaxing and even beginning to enjoy myself. But all the time in the back of my mind niggled the thought of the impending confrontation with Gavin.

All the way back in the car I could think of nothing else. And as Mohammed drove the car up the front drive I saw that the lights were on in the hall. My heart sank. It must mean that Gavin was still downstairs. I went quietly through the front door and slipped off my shoes. I started creeping towards the stairs. Perhaps Abdul had left the lights on for me and Gavin wasn't there after all.

But as I put my foot on the first step I heard his voice: 'So, the wanderer finally returns.' It was slurred with drink.

I stopped and looked across the room. He was sitting in an armchair in the corner. It was the same armchair that Scott had been sitting in the first time I had met him, and it shocked me how much Gavin reminded me of his brother at that moment. His face was red, and his eyes were blurred with drink. He stood up unsteadily.

'Where the hell do you think you've been?' He lurched towards me.

'I've been to the club,' I said, forcing myself to lift my chin and look at him. 'Didn't you see my note?'

'Yes, I saw it. But why didn't you tell me beforehand? It was all very secretive slipping away like that.'

'I meant to tell you at supper, but you didn't come back. Beatrice asked me last week if I would go this evening.'

'Well if you've known since last week, why the hell didn't you tell me?'

'I ... I don't know.' I looked down and realised I was shaking. I was about to confront him about the woman in the village. It was on my lips, but as I opened my mouth to do so, the words just wouldn't come. I couldn't face what he might say or do if I said them to him.

'So you were hiding it from me?'

'It's not as if you tell me where you go off every night,' I muttered.

He came closer to me, and I could smell whisky on his breath and the sweat of the working day on his body. 'What did you say?' he demanded.

He loomed over me. 'Nothing,' I said. I wanted to move away, but was afraid of inflaming his temper further.

'You shouldn't have gone to the club on your own. It's not right for a wife to go out without her husband. People will talk. And besides what did you think I was going to do alone here all evening?'

This was too much. 'What about me?' I retorted. 'You leave me alone night after night without company while you—'

He struck me hard across the face with the back of his hand. His signet ring caught my cheekbone. I cried out in pain, but I stood there staring at him for a few seconds, appalled. Then I fled upstairs. He didn't follow me. Panting and gulping back tears of shock and anger, I ran into the bedroom and slammed the door. I locked it behind me.

I collapsed to my knees, sobbing. When the tears eventually subsided, I got to my feet unsteadily. I crossed the room and looked in the dressing table mirror. My eyes were red and swollen and already a purple bruise was forming on my cheek beneath an ugly red gash.

14

Gavin did not come to bed that night. I heard the stairs creak as he came up well after midnight but he must have slept in the guestroom.

In the morning I got dressed and went down to breakfast as normal. I concealed the cut and bruise on my cheek as best I could with foundation, and brushed my hair forward so the servants would not see the mark. I had even managed to hide it from Surya. When she had come into the room to bring my morning tea, I made sure I was in the bathroom and stayed there until she had gone.

Gavin looked up from his bacon and eggs in surprise as I came downstairs that morning. I took my seat at the table and looked him in the eye. I wasn't going to let him know that inside I felt wrung out and beaten.

Abdul brought me my porridge, and even though I did not feel like it, I forced myself to eat. I knew it would do me good to have something solid in my stomach. 'I think I'll go down to Singapore to see Rose next week,' I said as casually as I could.

Gavin put down his fork and stared at me. 'What the devil for?' he said.

I stared at him, frowning. 'Surely that's obvious. I need to get away. It would do both of us good. Can't you see that? And besides, Rose is my sister. I haven't seen her for months.'

He began eating again. 'What rubbish you talk. All I can see is that you can't wait to get out of here at every opportunity. To the club, to Singapore. Anywhere but here, where you belong.'

'Are you surprised I want to go away? After what happened yesterday?'

I saw anger in his eyes again. He looked around to check that the servants weren't within earshot. 'You're not going, Juliet. Your place is here on the estate. With me.'

'You can't forbid me to go,' I said, raising my voice.

'Shut up, you little fool. The houseboys will hear.'

'Let them. I don't care.'

'Damn you,' he said, and slammed his knife down on his plate, cracking it in two. I jumped at the sound and stared at the plate. 'Stop it, won't you?' he said, menace in his voice.

I turned my face to him in defiance. I wasn't going to let him see that his violence frightened me.

'You don't own me, Gavin.'

'Oh, don't I? I am your husband and you'd do well to remember that.'

'I can't think why you should care where I go or what I do anyway,' I said.

'Because you're my wife, Juliet. Your place is here, as I said.'

I was feeling too low and defeated to fight him then. I said nothing.

Life resumed its normal routine after that with Gavin out for long hours and me lonely and bored at home. I felt like a prisoner on the estate. My only solace were the rides on the plantation and my weekly outings to town with Abdul. I tried not to think about my unhappiness, burying it in a deep dark place inside. After all, hadn't I buried the knowledge that Gavin had a mistress? I could bury the fact that he had hit me too.

A few weeks after the time I went to the club with Beatrice, Scott came back to the estate again for a few days. He didn't come up to the house, but I thought I saw lights from the bungalow through the trees one evening, and the next morning Surya told me that Scott was staying in the bungalow.

I was upstairs getting ready to go into town to the bazaar when I glanced through the window and saw him striding up the drive towards the house. I felt panic rise inside me and wondered what to do. I contemplated shutting myself in the bedroom, pretending I wasn't there. The front door slammed shut and I heard his steps cross the drawing room.

'Juliet?' I heard him shout. Reluctantly I left my bedroom and went downstairs. I didn't want him coming up to look for me.

'Ah, there you are,' he said as he saw me on the stairs, resting his eyes on me, appraising me. 'Looking as lovely as ever.'

I hesitated. He had a couple of bottles of spirits tucked under his arm.

'You don't need to worry,' he said, 'I'm staying down at the bungalow. I know when I'm not welcome. I just came up to the house to get some supplies, that's all.'

'Oh.' I didn't know what to say to him. I just stood there, twisting my hands, feeling foolish.

'Since I'm here, why don't we go for a ride together again? I could do with some fresh air. So could you by the looks of you. You look pale.'

'I don't think so, Scott. I'm just about to go into town to the bazaar. Abdul is just getting the car out.'

'Where's Gavin? Isn't he coming back for lunch?'

'He'll probably eat something down at the office,' I said, shamefaced. I didn't want to admit to Scott that Gavin was rarely back for either lunch or dinner nowadays. He usually came in late, ate something quickly in the kitchen then went out again until after midnight.

'Do you mind if I come along with you into town? I could do

with a trip to the tailors as a matter of fact. I need to order some new shirts.'

'I don't think that would be a good idea ...' I said, remembering how Gavin had behaved when Scott had insisted on accompanying me riding.

'Nonsense. Gavin won't find out anyway,' he said as if reading my thoughts. There was the sound of the engine on the drive, the tyres on the gravel. 'Come on,' said Scott decisively, putting the bottles down and making for the front door. 'Here's the car now.'

Scott sat in the front seat, chatting away to Abdul, regaling him with stories of his regiment, their recent exercises in jungle warfare, their training for a Japanese invasion. I listened in silence. Abdul kept glancing sideways at Scott and nodding politely at his stories of derring-do. They were clearly exaggerated accounts, emphasising Scott's own bravery, and I wondered what Abdul made of it all. Was he secretly as embarrassed as I was at this obvious make-believe?

When Abdul dropped him at the tailor's shop, Scott turned to me and said, 'I'll pop along to the bazaar and find you later. I'll only be a few minutes.'

My heart sank. I had wanted to be alone, wandering through the stalls as I usually did, practising my Malay, bargaining and chatting with the stallholders, who knew me now and greeted me like a friend.

I was buying spices when Scott tapped me on the shoulder. 'Quite the little linguist, aren't you? I heard you speaking the language like a native.'

'Oh, I don't know about that ...'

'Well, I do. You shouldn't be modest. Now what do you say about a quick drink in the club bar before we head back to the estate?'

'No, I don't think so. I need to get back,' I said, not meeting his gaze.

'Whatever for? You said yourself that Gavin won't be back 'til later. What are you afraid of? One drink won't do any harm.'

'What about Abdul? He's waiting with the car.'

'They're used to waiting. He won't mind. I'll bet you he's drinking tea somewhere or playing cards with his mates. You need to get used to being the boss, Juliet.'

'Alright then, one quick drink,' I said reluctantly, following him as he shouldered his way back through the packed market and out onto the road. He waved down a passing rickshaw and held his hand out for me to get in. As we rode through the streets and across the railway line towards the club, he said, 'I meant to ask you earlier, but Abdul was there ... Whatever happened to your face?' He pointed to where Gavin had struck me. Before I left the house, I had applied foundation to hide the old bruise, which had not yet quite faded, but you could still see it if you looked closely.

'Oh, nothing, that's nothing,' I stuttered, trying to hide my nervousness and humiliation, to think of an excuse to give Scott. My fingers rushed to touch the bruised skin. 'I fell over a couple of weeks ago and hurt myself.'

Scott smiled mockingly at me. He knew. 'I worry about you, Juliet. Just be careful,' he said simply, and looked away.

It was quiet in the bar. A couple of old gentlemen were playing billiards in a cloud of pipe smoke, but apart from that the place was deserted. I could tell from the barman's reluctant smile that he was less than delighted to be serving Scott, but he said nothing as he poured two whiskies.

'That's better,' said Scott as he drained his glass in one gulp. 'Another one please, Hari,' he shouted.

I sipped mine slowly. Scott drained his second glass and turned to me, his face flushed and eyes glazed, 'You know when I said that Gavin doesn't deserve you, I meant what I said.'

I smiled awkwardly, trying to think of how to respond,

wishing the time would pass quickly and we could go back to the car. 'There are things you don't know about him, about our family,' he went on leaning towards me and lighting a cigarette.

'Perhaps I already know.' I said, that creeping feeling of discomfort stealing over me again. I didn't want him to talk about what had happened between him and the Malay girl, about the scandal he had caused. I knew all about that already, and I didn't want to hear him make excuses for himself and his family. I didn't want him to tell me what I knew already about Gavin's lover either.

'Perhaps you don't, though. And perhaps you'd prefer to hide from the truth.'

I looked at him, wondering fleetingly if I was wrong and there was something else he had to tell me about. Something other than the scandal or Gavin's mistress. I only had to say the word and I knew he would tell me. I hesitated for a moment, but I was a coward. He was right in a way. Perhaps I didn't want to know.

'Look, Scott,' I began. 'I agreed to come for a quick drink with you. I'd prefer it if we didn't go over all that now.'

He laughed and drew on his cigarette. 'Whatever you like Mrs. Crosby. But whenever you're ready to hear, I'm happy to talk.'

After a third drink he stubbed out his cigarette and said, 'Finish up. You are very slow, you know. Let's get back.'

I finished my whisky, feeling surprised. I had thought he might want to stay there all day.

It was late afternoon and the light was fading as we arrived back at the estate. Scott jumped out of the car at the end of the drive. 'Goodbye, Juliet,' he said, leaning in through the window. 'I meant what I said, you know.' Then he was off, striding down the path towards the bungalow.

I saw that Gavin was already home, drinking tea on the veranda when I got out of the car. I went up the steps slowly. 'Where the devil have you been?'

'Just into town, to the bazaar to get food. I always go on Tuesdays.'

'You were a long time. Did you go alone?'

I stopped on the step. 'Of course,' I muttered not looking at him. He thumped on the table making me jump.

'That's a damned lie.' He pushed back the chair and came towards me. 'Do you think I'm blind? I saw him get out of the car. You went into town with Scott, didn't you?'

He grabbed my blouse and pulled me close. I refused to look at him.

'You've been drinking too. I can smell it. You're no more than a slut.' He gripped my arm and twisted it as far back as he could. Pain seared through me and I screamed. He shoved me backwards against the wall. Then he punched my stomach hard with his fist.

'Leave me alone,' I cried, doubling over and sinking down to my knees.

'I've told you about this before and you took no notice.' He kicked me in the hips with his hard leather shoes. 'Perhaps you'll learn your lesson now.' Then he swiped me across the face again, where he had hit me before. The pain shot through my cheekbone, and I cried out. I heard him walk into the house and slam the door shut.

I crept up to the bedroom, undressed and washed myself in cold water. Then I slid into bed and closed my eyes, trying not to think about what had happened. Trying to ignore the pain still coursing through my body, and to blot the whole day from my mind. Eventually sleep came.

I rose early the next morning, dabbed makeup on the bruise on my face, and went down to breakfast once again as if nothing had happened. Gavin was at the table, reading the *Straits Times*. He barely looked up as I entered the room. Abdul brought me my porridge and I tried to eat. But saliva rushed into my mouth each time I took a taste and I couldn't swallow.

'Gavin, I'd like to go and stay with Rose as soon as possible.' I said at last.

He sighed and looked up from his paper. 'This again? I've told you. You're place is here with me.'

'I don't understand,' I began. I wanted to ask him why he was doing this to me. Why he wanted to keep me here against my will when he had no love or respect for me. He had already looked back at the newspaper. 'Well, if you don't want me to go to Singapore, I'll ask Rose to come here,' I said.

He rolled his eyes impatiently and stood up, pushing his chair back. 'If you must, you must. But make sure it's a short stay,' he said, getting up from the table. 'I've got to go down to the office now.'

I wrote to Rose that very day inviting her over for a stay. Her response came back before the end of the week:

'Rob was a bit worried about me coming away, because everyone here is talking of little else but a Japanese invasion. He's anxious that it might happen when I'm away. But I managed to talk him round in the end. I've already bought my train ticket and will be with you in about a week's time, on Monday on the evening train. I sense from your letter that all is not well with you, Juliet. I hope that isn't right and that I'm reading too much into your tone. I'm so looking forward to being with you and to catching up on all your news. It's been far too long.'

I could not wait for the days to pass and for Rose to arrive. I threw myself into preparations, buying extra food from the bazaar, sitting down with our cook to plan meals. I wanted to show my sister that I had made a success of something at least, even if it was only my knowledge of Malay food. I kept myself busy so I did not have time to think. I kept out of Gavin's way during those few days and he seemed to be doing the same. We only met occasionally at mealtimes and barely spoke then. At night he would come home late as usual; I would hear his footsteps on the stairs and him passing the door to go to one of the other bedrooms. I was relieved that he did not want to speak to me or to sleep in the same room.

Surya and I prepared one of the guestrooms for Rose. It was the room I had stayed in on my first visit, the room that had once belonged to Gavin's mother. We spring cleaned it, polished the floorboards and beat the rugs. Surya put fresh linen on the bed and flowers on the dressing table. I was delighted with the result. I wanted Rose to appreciate the beauty of this place, to be enchanted by the surroundings. In the back of my mind I must have been hoping that it might somehow distract her from noticing reality, the emptiness and unhappiness of my life here.

Mohammed drove me to meet Rose from the evening train on the Monday. I dressed carefully in a cotton print dress and white cardigan, twisting my hair up into a French pleat and making my face up carefully. The swelling on my face had receded a little by that time, and again I covered it with foundation and rouge to be sure it would not show. My nerves tingled with excitement as I waited on Kuala Lipis Station for her train to arrive. The train puffed into the station twenty minutes behind schedule. Rose got off the first class carriage, looking fresh and well-groomed as if she had just stepped out of a beauty parlour, not spent a gruelling fifteen hours on a hot train. We hugged on the platform while Mohammed organised the porters to carry her bags. Then she held me at arms' length and said, 'My goodness, Juliet, you do look glamorous! I didn't realise people were so sophisticated out here in the jungle.' But then she frowned and looked at me more closely, concern creeping into her blue eyes. I quickly turned and tucked my arm into hers, ushered her towards the car.

On the journey back to Windy Ridge, I watched her face as she looked out wide-eyed at the rampant jungle that lined the road on either side.

'You really are in the back of beyond out here, aren't you?' she murmured, and I sensed a shiver go through her. I squeezed her hand.

'Don't worry. You soon get used to it, and the house is beautiful. You'll see.'

'But what about you, Juliet? You don't look at all well.'

'Nonsense. You said yourself I looked glamorous.'

'Yes, but you look thin too. And something isn't right. I can tell.'

'Don't be silly. You just haven't seen me for a long time. You must have forgotten quite how thin I normally am.'

She gave me her sceptical look, but I wasn't ready to confide in her yet. I wasn't sure at that moment if I ever would be. I had wanted to be with her, I had hoped that her vivacious company would distract me and take my mind off my situation, but I hadn't decided yet whether I was going to tell her everything. And besides, here in the car certainly wasn't the right place. Mohammed, despite his amiable and bumbling ways, had a pair of sharp ears, and I knew was fiercely loyal to Gavin.

Rose was of course entranced by the house. She gasped as we drew in through the gates and she caught sight of it dominating the hill in front of us. Once inside I proudly showed her around the rooms and she followed me, her eyes wide with wonder.

'It's beautiful, Juliet,' she kept murmuring. 'You're so lucky.'

Gavin joined us for supper and appeared charming and gallant. He chatted away to Rose, asking her about Singapore, about Rob, about life on the airbase, smiling and laughing at the amusing anecdotes she told about the other ex-pats there. He was playing the part of perfect host. I watched him quietly, wondering at how one man could have so many different guises. It was incredible that this charismatic, handsome host was the same controlling, adulterous monster who kept me a prisoner here and had reduced me to the frightened wreck I had become.

I also wondered why Gavin had chosen me that first time he had seen us at the Penang Club. What had led him, in those crucial few moments as he had stood toying with his glass at the bar, watching our table, to approach us and ask *me* to dance. Not Rose, with all her beauty and charm, and not any other woman there, although he could have had anyone he wanted. It had been inexplicable to me at the time and was even more so, since I had learnt the secrets behind his good looks and superficial charm, the night-time trysts with his Malay lover and his carefully hidden violent temper.

On the first day at the estate, Rose and I took a gentle stroll around the garden. Our gardeners were busy at work, trimming the lawn with scythes, pruning the bougainvillea that tumbled over the veranda, watering and tending the exotic shrubs in the borders.

'It's so beautiful,' said Rose, looking around, her eyes shining. 'Do you know, it's made me think of Mother? She would absolutely love it here, Juliet. Do you remember how she used to love the garden at home?'

'Of course,' I said. 'With Father it was always his allotment, but the garden was her pride and joy.'

'Especially her beloved roses.'

I smiled. 'It's why she gave you your name.'

We walked around the borders arm in arm, in silence. I pictured Mother in her little suburban garden, looking graceful in an old jacket and baggy trousers under Wellington boots, her blonde hair tucked neatly into a headscarf. She would work away for hours, pruning her beds of beautiful roses, weeding around them. She had a tiny greenhouse next to Father's shed in the corner, where she cultivated seedlings. In the springtime she would plant them out and fill the garden with colour and delicious scents: marigolds, sweet peas, pansies and lobelia. She had a real talent for it; whatever she planted seemed to grow in abundance.

She bought Rose and me tiny garden tools and taught us how to plant and water the seedlings. We would potter around after her, trying to copy what she did. She persuaded Father to buy a table and chairs for the garden, and on summer evenings when he came home from the office, she would set the patio table and bring the supper outside. In my memory those evenings were perfectly preserved: after we'd eaten at the table, Mother and Father would relax in those chairs, smoking cigarettes, sipping fruit punch and chatting for hours. Rose and I would play together on the lawn as the light gradually faded and until it finally got so chilly that Mother would get up, rubbing her arms, saying briskly, 'It's time for bed now, girls. Run upstairs and get ready, and I'll come and read you a story.'

After she died nobody used the garden furniture. It sat out there on the patio for years, decaying and mildewed. Weeds gradually choked the borders, the roses grew rampant, the lawn untamed and full of dandelions.

When Rose and I returned to the house we sat on the veranda, and I fetched my photograph album. I turned to my favourite photograph of Mother. It was taken on the patio by Father shortly after we had taken delivery of the garden furniture. She was sitting in one of the wooden chairs with Rose on her lap and me standing beside her. All three of us were smiling broadly for the camera.

'Things would have been so different if she hadn't died,' said Rose, pensive suddenly.

I took her hand. 'We mustn't think like that, Rose darling. We always had each other. And Father. And she gave us more love in those few short years than some mothers give in a lifetime.'

ON THE SECOND DAY, I lent Rose a pair of jodhpurs and some riding boots and took her down to the stables. I had asked Abdul to saddle my usual mount Whisky, as well as Brandy, an old horse who had belonged to Gavin's mother and was by far the quietest and safest animal in the stables. We took the horses out into the yard, and I tried to teach Rose how to mount.

'Look, you put your left foot in the stirrup like this, hold onto the saddle, and hoist yourself up.' But try as she might, she could not heave herself up into the saddle. After several failed attempts she collapsed in giggles, saying it was impossible. We had to lead the old horse to stand next to a wall so that she could step on easily from there.

We then set off. I rode in front and guided her horse with a leading rein.

I could not help smiling. Rose's teeth were clenched and she looked truly terrified. Her whole body was stiff, but even so she could not sit up straight in the saddle and could not move with the rhythm of the horse as it walked. Every time the horse lifted its head or stumbled even slightly, she let out a shriek, which spooked both the horses and then terrified her even more. We had only ridden for half a mile or so before she called out in a thin voice, 'Juliet, do you mind very much if we turn back now? I'm never going to get the hang of this. I'm a city girl, you know. I can't think how you ever mastered it yourself.'

I smiled quietly, but I did not tell her that I hadn't needed to master it. As soon I had got into the saddle the very first time, it had come as naturally to me as breathing the air. I didn't need anyone to explain how to sit, or how to get the horse to walk on; I had an instinctive feel for it from the first.

As we turned and went back to the stables, it occurred to me that this was probably the first time in my life that I had shone at something where Rose had not. It was a surprising feeling. Here was something that I could do better than my sister.

Back on the veranda, after a hot bath and change of clothes, Rose stretched back in one of the cane chairs.

'It must be very lonely here with Gavin out all the time,' she began. I could sense what was coming. Whenever she had tried to ask me so far if there was something wrong, I had immediately clammed up and assured her in a smooth voice, without looking her in the eye, that everything was fine. But now I was tired of lying, of maintaining the pretence. Hadn't I wanted her to come here partly so that I could tell her of my troubles?

She was due to leave the next day, and I couldn't put it off any longer. I turned to her and began, 'Well actually, Rose, there is something—' I was cut short when Abdul suddenly appeared on the veranda carrying Rose's camera carefully, as if it were a delicate piece of cut glass.

'Madam, you want photograph? I take for you?'

'Yes, please,' said Rose. 'You don't mind, Juliet, do you? I asked Abdul to come out and take our photo. Let me just explain what to do.' She showed him how to point the lens and focus it. Then the two of us sat close together and smiled as he pointed and clicked the camera.

'Thank you, Abdul,' said Rose. 'I'll take it back to Singapore and get it developed. Then I'll send you a copy, Juliet.'

When Abdul had gone I thought the moment had passed, that Rose would leave the next day and I would not have told her the truth about my life here, but she turned to me and said, 'You were about to say?'

I hesitated then took a deep breath. 'Things haven't been going well for me here, Rose. I've been trying to act as though everything is alright, but the truth is I really think I made a dreadful mistake.' The tears threatened to come then, but I swallowed hard and battled on through them. I told her about how Gavin was out late every evening and how I had finally become suspicious and followed him one evening. How I had seen him in the arms of a Malay woman in the workers' village. I told her about how controlling he was, how he didn't like me to have friends or to go anywhere alone. How he had even stopped me from going to Singapore to see her. And then, with stumbling words, I told her about his temper. How it had flared up and he had struck me on the cheek on two occasions, the second only a few days before she had arrived here.

She peered at me with tears in her eyes. 'You know, I thought I saw a mark on your face. That's why you've been wearing so much makeup, isn't it?'

I nodded and let my tears fall. She put her arms around me and we cried together. 'You must come and live with me. Come back with me tomorrow,' she said finally, releasing me and straightening up.

I shook my head. 'I can't do that. I've got to stay here. I've got to try and make it work, Rose.'

'But don't you see, Juliet? It's never going to work. And you could be in danger here. Who knows what he might do to you.'

'But what about you and Rob? You need to be alone together. I couldn't possibly intrude. And I couldn't go back to Auntie in Penang either. Imagine how triumphant she would be that everything she had said about Gavin actually turned out to be true.'

'Look, if you won't come back with me now, just promise me one thing. I want your word that if it happens again, if he hits you again, you'll come. You'll get on the very next train and come to us. Please promise me that, Juliet.'

I promised, but I wasn't at all sure that I would keep it. Then Rose told me something about her own life that surprised me. 'I have to tell you this. It has been weighing on my mind. Rob and I have been trying to have a baby. Nothing has happened all these months. In the end I went to the doctor. After lots of horrific tests and examinations he said I had some internal problem that would make it difficult to conceive. But that I was to keep trying and mustn't give up.'

'I'm so sorry, Rose. What a worry for you and Rob. Why didn't you tell me before?

'I didn't want to alarm you, and I kept thinking I might soon have some good news.'

'But surely, if you keep on trying it will happen one day?'

'That's what I'm hoping. And I'm sure that's right. I tell you, if I do conceive, Juliet, that baby will be so wanted, so precious.'

I bit my lip, fighting back tears again. I knew Rose had always wanted babies, and how much her problems must be hurting her. I was sure though that one day it would happen for her.

That evening at supper, Rose was noticeably frosty with Gavin. She did not smile at him or respond to his anecdotes as she had before. When he spoke to her directly, she answered curtly. I stared at my plate, dreading that she would challenge him about what I had told her. I could not bear to think about how he might react if she did do that. I knew Rose had an impulsive side, and that she might not be beyond blurting something out. But I need not have worried: Gavin soon tired of being rebuffed and left to go down to the estate.

After he had gone, Rose turned to me. 'How can you just let him go like that without saying a word? You know where he's going. You could stop him, tell him that you know and that you're not putting up with it.'

'Hush, Rose. Please don't. It would only make things worse. Let me handle it my way, please.'

'You are too good and gentle, Juliet. I can't bear to see it happening to you.'

'Please leave it to me. I will challenge him one day. I just need to find the right time and way to do it.'

Rose tutted impatiently. 'I don't like seeing you like this.'

'I will do something about it, don't worry. I promise. It won't be long.'

Rose went home the next morning. She kissed me on the station and said, 'Just remember what I said. You can always come to us. Anytime. All you have to do is to just jump on the train and leave. And please write to me often. Let me know how you are feeling.'

I promised that I would, but as the train pulled out of the station, and drew her away from me again, I felt lonelier than ever. I walked slowly back to the car where Abdul stood waiting for me, holding the back door open. I realised that confiding in Rose had not made me feel better. Instead it had put renewed pressure on me to do something about my situation. And the thought of that terrified me more than just living with it, accepting my unhappiness and surviving from day to day as I had been until then.

15

B y now the little ferry had entered the mouth of the great Musri River and was heading upstream towards Palembang. The river was so wide at this point that the far bank to the south was just a smudgy line on the horizon.

'It won't be long now,' said Mary. 'A few hours at the most. Then we can find a guesthouse and get some rest.'

Juliet stared out at the river bank, where rice-fields stretched as far as the eye could see, interspersed with tiny villages of wooden houses on stilts. It was very hot on the deck in the full glare of the sun. The wooden bench, where they were squeezed in between an old woman clutching an enormous bundle and a man holding a plastic bin full of lobsters between his knees, was hard and unyielding. Juliet, sweating and aching with exhaustion, longed for the journey to be over.

After a while the banks of the river became more densely populated, with houses crowded together over the water. From the ferry it was possible to see right into these houses, where washing was hung out on poles, naked children dived from steps into the muddy water, and women sat on platforms over the river preparing food.

As they drew closer to the centre of the city, the landscape changed continually. They passed huge modern warehouses and towering factories built right on the banks of the river, then chugged past dockyards where cargo ships were being unloaded by labourers bent double under the weight of the sacks they carried. To Juliet this felt like a huge, alien place. She glanced at Mary, who sat with her eyes half closed, a gentle smile on her face, basking in the sun. Juliet realised that to Mary it would be a different experience, that it probably felt like a homecoming.

The ferry docked at a rickety wooden jetty and as they scrambled ashore hauling their bags behind them, they were instantly surrounded by touts, clamouring for their trade. Mary took charge straight away and singled out a reasonably priced rickshaw-wallah. He pedalled them through the potholed streets that fanned out behind the little port, past ramshackle houses and rows of street stalls, until they came to a stop in front of a modest little hotel, nestled in a terrace of houses opposite a bazaar.

'This place will do,' said Mary. 'I've been past it a few times. It looks cheap so it should be good.'

'Mary,' began Juliet, 'I don't mind paying if you'd like to stay somewhere a bit more ... '

'Don't worry,' cut in Mary proudly, lifting her chin. 'I don't want you to pay for me. I have my own money, thank you.'

'Oh, Mary, I didn't mean it like that. Please don't be offended.' But she had already turned away to pay the rickshaw-wallah. Then she hoisted her bag on her shoulder, turned and marched into the hotel reception without looking back. Juliet was forced to follow, feeling rebuffed and rather foolish.

It was a very basic hotel but the rooms were clean and well kept. They both had little shower rooms and windows that looked out over the road. Juliet suddenly felt homesick as she sat down on the saggy bed after taking a shower. The water had been a cold trickle and the creaky fan in the ceiling turned too slowly to cool the air. She sighed. She wished Mary had not taken offence at her offer of paying for somewhere a little better. She could hear Mary's shower running in the next door room through the thin wall. She felt exhausted. The early start and the sea air on the journey had left her sluggish. She lay down on top of the bed in her towel and closed her eyes, letting the voices of passers-by and the sounds of hawkers in the street below lull her to sleep.

Singapore 1942

I felt awkward having realised that the soldier who stood before me was the officer I had met all those years before in Kuala Lumpur. I felt self-conscious that he was here with me now in such different circumstances. Nazira offered the men the soup I had prepared.

'That is very kind of you,' said Patrick, an Irish lilt in his voice. 'But first we need to find a doctor. Adam was shot when we escaped this morning and he is losing a lot of blood. We've been hiding in a storeroom at the canteen all day, and there was no chance to get any medical help. We've just walked about five miles to get here and he's in a lot of pain. Do you know a doctor we can trust?'

'Let me look,' said Nazira. 'I am a nurse. Come, please lie down on the bed.' Adam manoeuvred himself onto my little bed, and Nazira rolled his sarong back to reveal a huge wound on his thigh, oozing blood and pus. His leg was caked in dried blood.

'I don't know any doctors near here,' she said, shaking her head. 'The Chinese doctor in the next street was taken away by the Japanese in the *Sook Ching* and has not come back. Let me see what I can do ...'

'Are you sure? Perhaps it could wait until we can find some-one,' said Adam.

'The wound is already swollen, and an infection is setting in.

If we don't remove the bullet quickly you could get septicaemia. You might lose your leg.'

The three men exchanged glances. 'I guess there's no choice then,' said Adam.

Nazira went to the wall cupboard and after some rummaging produced a pair of tweezers and an old cotton sheet. 'Juliet, could you bring some boiled water please?' she asked, beginning to rip the sheet into strips.

I boiled some water over the little stove and brought a bowl of it to the bedside. Nazira soaked some pieces of cloth in it. Then she took the tweezers and passed them through the flickering flame of the stove. She turned back to Adam, handing him a twisted rag. 'Put this between your teeth and bite down on it. I don't have any anaesthetic, I'm afraid. Are you ready?'

Adam nodded, a grim look on his face, and lay back on the bed, the cloth between his teeth as instructed. I held the candle above Adam as Nazira got to work with the tweezers, digging away at the wound, removing the infected tissue and easing out the bullet. I held my breath and could hardly bear to watch, as the tweezers dug deeper and deeper into the flesh. Adam began to writhe around in pain.

'Keep still please,' said Nazira. 'If you move it will slow things down.' Sweat was standing out on Adam's brow. I mopped it with a damp cloth.

A few tense minutes later there was a squelching sound: Nazira drew out the blood soaked bullet and held it up. 'It's a big one,' she said, laying it down on a cloth. 'Now I need to sew up the wound. I only have sewing cotton, I'm afraid, but it should hold it together while it heals.' As she stuck the needle into his flesh and pulled the cotton through, Adam twisted and turned in pain again. He screwed up his face, but he didn't cry out. At last it was over. Nazira quickly cleaned and bandaged the wound then stood up and went to wash her hands.

I looked down at Adam, but his eyes were shut and his face completely grey. He had passed out. Nazira shook her head. 'I will try and get some painkillers in the morning. He will just have to get through the night without them.'

They left him there on my bed that night. Richard and Patrick climbed the ladder into the loft, and I followed Nazira down the staircase to the space behind the shop. We spread out sheets on some wooden pallets amongst the shelves of pots and pans and tried to sleep. I lay awake listening to Adam turning restlessly on the bed and uttering the odd moan of pain in his sleep. I thought back to that day when we had met in Kuala Lumpur in 1939. It felt so long ago, almost like a different lifetime. I remembered his kindness towards me and the way he had distanced himself from the boorish behaviour of his fellow officer in the hotel. I remembered, too, the way he had watched my taxi as it drew away. As I lay awake watching the moon out of the high window at the back of the shop, I found myself hoping that he got better quickly, that he did not succumb to infection and die.

The next morning, after her morning prayers, Nazira went out early and came back with a bottle of pills. 'I got them from the Chinese medicine shop round the corner,' she said. 'He needs to take ten of these three times a day. And could you dress his wound when he wakes up? You'll need to boil a cloth and clean the wound, then bandage it up with some new strips of that sheet.'

'Of course. But where are you going?'

'They still need my help with the food parcels. I'll be back early evening as usual. I'll bring back some food. There's still some soup and some *chapatis* left for today.' She peered into my eyes and put her hands on my arms. 'You're feeling anxious again, aren't you? Please, please don't worry, Juliet. Nothing has changed. Things will be fine here. Things will go on just as before.'

'Do you think he will live?'

'Our soldier? Yes I think so. He will be in a lot of pain for a few days, but we got the bullet just in time. I'm sure he will live.'

16

A fter Nazira had left for her day's work, I went upstairs to the flat. Adam was just beginning to stir, but I could hear the other two already moving about in the roof-space above. An unfamiliar sound of some sort of electronic tapping and bleeping came from the loft and I stood still listening, wondering what it was. Then I heard Richard's voice saying over and over, 'Hello? Do you read me?'

The hairs stood up on my neck. They had a radio transmitter. I had heard stories of people being bayoneted to death, or beheaded and their heads displayed about the city for simply listening in to the BBC World Service. But a radio transmitter ... I could hardly bear to think of the consequences of it being discovered.

Adam was awake now. 'Good morning,' he said, lifting his head and smiling at me.

'How are you feeling? Did you manage to get some sleep?'

'Yes, thank you, I'm fine.' But I could see from the pallor on his face and the strain in his eyes that he was not telling the truth. 'I'm very sorry to have driven you from your bed,' he said. 'Most un-gentlemanly of me.' He sat up and I noticed him wince with pain. He tried to hide it with a smile.

'Here are some painkillers,' I said, handing him the bottle of pills. 'You need to take ten of these. I'll get you some jasmine tea. And Nazira asked me to dress your wound. I'll just boil some water.' I topped up the paraffin in the stove, noticing that the supplies were alarmingly low, lit the wick and put a pot of water on above the burner. When the water boiled I made a pot of tea, and with the rest of the water, I soaked a rag. I brought a cup of tea to Adam, and he swallowed the pills with a gulp of it.

'Do you mind?' I asked. 'I'll need to dress your wound.'

'Of course not.' He sat up in bed and pulled his sarong up above his knees. I was relieved to see that he was wearing a pair of tattered shorts underneath it. Even so I felt a little awkward at the intimacy that dressing his wound would involve. I removed the bandage, knowing that this meant leaning over him and winding it under his leg several times. I was so close I could smell the heat and sweat of his body. When the bandage was finally off I drew back and looked at the wound. It was oozing pus and swollen and was an angry red around the stitches. I stared at it, horrified, but remained silent. I had no real idea what it should look like and didn't want to alarm him.

I began to dab at it with the damp rag, and felt him tense at my touch. 'I'm sorry,' I said, drawing back.

'Don't worry, you go ahead. It's nothing really.'

I tried to be gentle as I wiped away the worst of the pus, but each time I touched him he tensed up in pain. It made me nervous and cack-handed, and when it came to bandaging the leg up again, my hands felt clumsy and slow. Again I had to lean right over him and pass the bandage under his bent leg. I felt the colour rise in my cheeks. I couldn't look at his face.

I had finished and was just washing my hands when a face appeared through the trap door above. 'Good morning, Mrs.

Crosby,' said Patrick. 'We're in a bit of a fix, I'm afraid. They gave us a radio at the canteen yesterday. We need to get in touch with our contacts in the resistance, but the batteries have drained down. I don't suppose there any batteries here are there? We might be able to use portable ones if they're the right voltage.'

'I don't think so, I'm afraid,' I said, 'I've never seen any here, but I can look.' I opened Nazira's wall cupboard and looked on the shelves, then I went into the kitchenette and searched the cupboards there.

'Nothing here, I'm afraid. I could check down in the shop if you like.'

'Could you, please? It is important.'

I went downstairs. The boy who ran the shop had arrived and was just opening up, setting out the remaining stock of pots and pans. He stopped and stared when he saw me. I knew that Nazira had spoken to him about me in case he ever happened to come up to the flat, but we had never met face to face before. He looked straight at me with unblinking eyes.

'Good morning,' I greeted him in an unsteady voice. He carried on staring. 'Do you have any batteries down here?' He didn't answer. I tried again, this time in Malay. He shook his head and turned his back on me, returning to his task of setting out the wares. My palms were sweating as I scanned the shelves behind the shop for batteries. What if the boy were to inform on me? He seemed unfriendly, hostile even. There were rewards for informers, I knew that much.

There was nothing there that even resembled a battery so I went back upstairs. 'I'm really sorry, but I can't find any downstairs,' I called up to the loft.

Patrick came down the ladder. 'I'm sorry to have to ask this, Mrs. Crosby, but do you think you could possibly go out and buy some for us? We came past a line of hardware stores yesterday. They're only a couple of streets away.'

I swallowed. My heart began to beat faster. 'Don't be stupid, she can't go, Paddy,' said Adam. 'She's a white woman. Someone would spot her and tell the Japs.'

'She could wear a headscarf and darken her skin. It's less likely that she would be spotted than we would. We need to contact Special Opps. Headquarters today. There's a chance they might want to do the pick-up tonight. If we don't get in touch they'll think we didn't make it through and they'll leave us here. It could be weeks before there's another chance.'

'Let's wait until Miss Syed comes back,' said Adam. 'It's not worth the risk.'

'I'll go,' I said in a firm voice, standing up and turning to face Patrick. 'I can wear a *niqab*. There is one hanging up on the back of the door. I've never seen Nazira wearing it, but it is more of a disguise than a headscarf. I'll wear a long tunic too.'

'You don't have to, Mrs. Crosby,' said Adam. 'You'd be risking your life.'

'Didn't you all risk yours yesterday?' I asked vehemently. 'Aren't you going to be risking them daily when you're in the jungle fighting against the Japanese Occupation? Doesn't Nazira risk hers for other people every day? I've done nothing so far to help anyone. All I've done is hidden in this flat and let other people take risks for me. I'd be more than happy to go.'

Adam began to protest, but Patrick said quickly, 'Thank you. Here, take some money. The batteries need to be 1.5 volts. Go to the end of this road, turn right then second left. That street is full of shops selling tools and hardware, but whether they'll have any stock left now is another matter. It is worth a try though.'

With shaking hands, I took the *niqab* and a long black tunic from the back of the door, and as I slipped on the tunic over my clothes and pulled the *niqab* over my head, I wondered if they had belonged to Nazira's mother. Nazira had told me her mother had been very strict in her religious observances and used to cover her face. The *niqab* and tunic were very old and traditional, and had a musty, unused smell. It was the best chance of a disguise there was. My eyes were blue, and there was no way of disguising that. I realised I would have to walk with my eyes cast down towards the ground, and avoid looking directly at anyone.

I left the flat carrying a shopping basket. It felt strange stepping out on to the street for the first time in weeks. It was sweltering being swathed in dark cotton like this, but I was glad of the disguise. The atmosphere on the street was very different from when I had last walked along it on that first day. Now, the stalls were virtually bare, save for a few meagre offerings of shrivelled vegetables and some washed out second-hand clothes. There were few people about.

I walked quickly along the road, following Patrick's directions, keeping my head down. It seemed a long way to the street of shops, but as I turned into it, sure enough I saw there was a row of hardware stores on my left. Some were shuttered up but a few were still open. I went into the first one, ducking under the forest of tools hanging from the ceiling. It was unlit, but dusty shafts of sunlight penetrated from the street, and the place smelled strongly of creosote. The old Chinese proprietor came stooping forward to greet me. He wore a dirty white vest and a pair of shorts.

'Do you have any batteries?' I asked in Malay, keeping my voice low.

'What you want?' he snapped in English, peering at me.

I repeated the request in English. He gave me a puzzled look and turned to the shelves behind him. 'What voltage you want?' he shouted and I told him, wishing he would keep his voice down, hoping that no-one was listening on the pavement. I kept nervously checking the doorway, willing no-one else to come into the shop, but as far as I could see there was no-one outside.

After what seemed an age, the old man turned back and thumped two huge dusty batteries on the counter. I hurriedly paid and put them in my basket. Retracing my steps was even more nerve-racking than going to the shop. I could now feel the dead weight of the batteries in the basket over my shoulder. I felt as if every eye in the street was scrutinising me, and I could not control the pounding of my heart. If I were stopped and searched, I knew that would be the end of everything.

I had almost reached the end of Nazira's road when what I saw ahead made me freeze on the spot: A Japanese army jeep was parked there, and two soldiers were standing on the road, stopping people as they passed. On their uniforms I recognised the white arm bands of the *kempeitai*, the secret police. I stood there aghast, and in my panic, everything in my vision turned into a blur. I took some deep breaths and tried to get a grip on my nerves, then turned quickly about, prepared to make a run for it. I rushed away, but it was difficult to do so in the long robe, and in the intense heat. I came to a quiet turning that seemed to be a parallel street to Nazira's and quickly walked the length of it, continually checking over my shoulder. When I had reached the end, I took a right turn and entered Nazira's street from the other side. But glancing down the road, my heart did a somersault: two more officers stood at this end, too, and were stopping people and questioning them. I thought about retreating and waiting until they had gone, but one of them had already spotted me, and was beckoning me forward.

My heart was hammering as I walked slowly towards the roadblock. I could feel the eyes of the officers on me, but I kept my own eyes lowered to the ground. Sweat was pouring from my brow. I could feel it trickling down my cheeks beneath the *niqab*. I moved through and took a couple of steps towards Nazira's shop-house. My heart began to slow, but then I heard a shout behind me, 'Hey you! Stop!'

My heart lurched again, my stomach tightened, and I turned: it was not me they were shouting at, but a young Chinese man who had slipped through the checkpoint behind me. I quickly turned away, and heart still thumping, moved towards the shop-house steps. I darted up the stairs and hammered on the door.

Patrick opened it straight away. 'Are you alright?'

I sank down on the stool and, pulling off the *niqab*, burst into tears of relief.

'What happened?' asked Adam from the bed, his face full of concern.

'*Kempeitai*,' I managed to say, 'At both ends of the road. They're stopping everyone. They let me through though, thank God.' I fumbled in the basket and handed Patrick the batteries. He thanked me and dashed back up the ladder.

'Mrs. Crosby, you're a very brave woman,' said Adam, reaching out and putting his hand on mine. 'We won't forget this.'

'It was nothing,' I said, 'and please, please, call me Juliet.' His hand lingered on mine for a few seconds. It felt warm, reassuring, and when he took it away, I wished he had left it there for a little longer. His eyes, filled with admiration, were appraising my face. His gaze was so intense it made me look away, embarrassed, but despite that a calm feeling spread through my whole body, dispelling all the fear and tension of the past half hour.

'We'll need to check that the *kempeitai* aren't coming to check the houses,' said Adam. 'Could you do that?'

I pulled the *niqab* back over my head and opened the balcony door then looked up and down the street. I noticed that it was unusually empty and quiet. People must have gone inside, fearing the *kempeitai* and what they might do. I could just about see the checkpoint at the far end of the road; the one at this end was too close for me to see properly. Were the police here because someone had told them about Adam and his friends? Did they have a tip-off that there were three escaped prisoners sheltering in this street? Despite the heat a chill ran through me at the thought that they might search the building. I thought about the Chinese boy in the shop downstairs and the way he had looked at me. Would he keep quiet if the Japanese came to the shop asking questions? My heart began pounding with fear once again.

'What's the scene out there?' Adam's voice broke into my thoughts.

I turned back into the room. 'They're still at the end of the road, but they haven't moved.'

'Probably just a routine check,' he said. I knew that they had never searched people coming into this street before, but I didn't mention that.

'We've managed to make contact with Headquarters, Adam,' Richard said, appearing on the ladder from the loft. 'The pickup is going to be this evening. A good job you got the batteries Mrs. Crosby. Ten o'clock rendezvous in the next street. We're sailing at high tide. Paddy and I can go. We'll leave you the radio, Adam, so you can keep in touch. When your leg's better they'll try to get you across too.'

So that evening, after the *kempeitai* had finally disappeared, Patrick and Richard prepared to leave. When Nazira returned with food supplies and fuel for the stove, she and I cooked a vegetable stew with rice, and we all ate it by the flickering candle-light. Then Nazira gave the two men some fruit for their journey, which they stowed in their packs. They were dressed once again in the sarongs they had arrived in the day before.

When they said goodbye to Adam, I noticed the emotion in his eyes and how he swallowed hard as he shook their hands. And then they were gone. Adam hauled himself out of bed and stood beside the window as Richard and Patrick left the flat, their footsteps barely audible on the stone steps. I went and stood next to Adam. We watched the still dark street but even though I was straining my eyes to see them, I could not make them out or see any movement down in the street.

'Where are they?' I asked Adam.

'They've been trained to be invisible when they move in the dark,' he said, smiling. 'They will have darted from doorway to doorway and then disappeared down a side alley. If you didn't see them, it must mean that the training worked.'

Despite his upbeat tone, I noticed the sadness in his eyes. 'They mean a lot to you, don't they?'

He nodded. 'We've been through a hell of a time together these past few months.'

17

That night Nazira and I moved to sleep up in the roof-space, and a new routine established itself. Nazira would leave in the mornings as before, but I was no longer lonely and terrified during the daytime.

Adam and I would eat a breakfast of bananas washed down with green tea, and then I would dress Adam's wound and prepare vegetables for our lunch. There was no awkwardness between us after that first morning. We sometimes played cards and sometimes just talked. He wanted to improve his Malay, so I taught him some basic conversation. Sometimes I read him passages from the Koran. We exchanged stories about our lives, although I was very careful about what I told him. There were some things I simply could not talk about, through shame that he might judge me, and through fear that he might not understand. I sometimes wondered if he too had secrets he did not want to tell me.

'I thought you were in the Indian Army, not Special Operations,' I said one day.

'They asked for volunteers from amongst the officers last year to train in jungle warfare. We all went into the jungle to get special training in survival and guerrilla tactics. Some units were "left behind" enemy lines as the Japs advanced down the Malay Peninsula.'

'Really? I didn't know that.'

'It was all very hush, hush, but they are still there, as far as we know, trying to sabotage the Japanese Occupation. Our unit was about to set off to join them, but we were thwarted by the invasion. We were all rounded up with the rest of the army and marched into Changi. But as soon as we were captured, we began to plan our escape.'

'That must have been difficult. How did you manage it?'

'Through the brave people who deliver food and medicines to Changi, we managed to make contact with the resistance movement. Every day we were taken out into the city on work parties. Our job was to clear and rebuild the bomb sites, or bury the Chinese people who had been murdered by the Japanese. That was a truly dreadful job ...' He stopped himself, and the shadow of the memory crossed his face.

'There was not much security for some of those work parties, and one day the three of us simply left. The Japs in charge noticed when we were at the end of the road, and started to fire at us. We then ran, of course. The other two were quicker than me, and I got hit in the thigh. We realise now that we should have been more careful, more covert in our escape,' he said.

I knew that my stories were no match for his. As I listened to him, it struck me what a sheltered life I had led thus far. I told him about my life in London, about my beloved father and about Rose. How Father had died and we had come to Penang. I told him about Auntie Maude and Uncle Arthur and the ex-pat community in Penang. I told him how Rose had met Robert and about their wedding, so full of pomp and splendour. He listened attentively, smiling and nodding, asking questions as if my story was as interesting and remarkable as his own. I avoided speaking about Gavin, or about the estate and what had happened there. I deflected every question he asked about it, and always steered the conversation carefully in the other direction. Being naturally polite and sensitive, after a while Adam must have realised my discomfort with the subject and stopped asking about it.

One day I asked him about how he had come to be in the Indian Army.

'I left school when I was seventeen, in 1932. I lived in London with my parents, like you. Father was a school-teacher. There was no money for me to go to university. The Great Depression was hitting home and there was no work at all. I tramped the streets of London looking for work, any work, but there was nothing. In the end I saw an advertisement for young men to go to India and join the Indian Army. I'd never been abroad and it all sounded very exotic and exciting. Without saying a word to my parents, I went to one of the recruitment centres in Paddington, took a medical, swore an oath of allegiance and signed up. Within a few months I was in Quetta, on the North-west frontier, the wildest, most breath-taking landscape you could ever imagine.'

'Tell me what it was like there.' It seemed a world far, far away from the steamy heat of this tiny apartment, from life in this beaten, oppressed city, spent cowering in fear of the brutal Japanese.

'It was truly astonishing. The cantonment, where the officers and their families lived, was like an English garden city. It was built in a flat valley surrounded by huge mountains. Row upon row of neat bungalows and barracks set amongst trees and gardens. The fort, where we soldiers were stationed, was on a hill just outside the city. That was pretty bleak and formidable and often very cold. In the winter the peaks would be dusted with snow. We used to go on patrol up the mountain passes. It was the most inhospitable but somehow the most majestic place on earth. The barren beauty of that landscape on the North-west frontier is like nowhere else: mountains of black rock reaching into the clouds, wastes of tundra where only the hardiest yaks can survive, land that is barren and too steep to walk on.'

As the days passed, he told me of skirmishes in the hills with fearless Pathan and Pushtan tribesmen, of living in the mountains where he and his fellow soldiers had to sleep with their rifles tied to them in case they were stolen in the night, of being ambushed by hostile tribesmen and having to take shelter in ditches for several days. I found myself transported by his stories and the vivid memories of his past. The days flew by now, and I realised that I had begun to live for those tales, which spirited me away from this time and place. But gradually Adam's leg healed and he was able to walk around the flat. He took to going up and down the steps to the backyard for exercise. I realised with a sinking feeling that his leg would soon be better and he would have to leave.

He had never spoken about any women in his life, and I had been wondering about it since he arrived. He didn't wear a ring, but I knew that many men in Changi had pawned jewellery for food. Finally, one afternoon, as we sat side by side chopping vegetables for the evening stew, I plucked up enough courage to ask him: 'Have you never married, Adam?'

Suddenly his dark eyes filled up with pain, and I instantly regretted having asked the question. He put down his knife and shook his head. 'I nearly did once,' he said quietly, 'but it wasn't to be.'

I assumed that he would change the subject, and that he would find it too painful to keep talking, but he carried on, his eyes fixed on the table in front of us. 'There was someone special in Quetta,' he said. 'It was several years ago, when I first arrived from England. I wanted to marry her but the army stopped us.'

'Whatever for?'

'Soldiers had to get permission if they wanted to marry. My fiancé was half-Indian. It was not allowed, getting married to her. I was at rock-bottom for months. In the end I transferred away from Quetta to Peshawar. I couldn't bear to stay there. Later on the chance to come out to Malaya came up, and with that I would be made up to be a non-commissioned officer, so I volunteered. I just had to get away.'

'What was she like?'

'She was beautiful and clever and spirited. She was the governess of the children of one of the officers in my regiment. We were all invited to a reception on the cantonment soon after I arrived, and I met her there. We hit it off right from the start. I walked her home that first evening and managed to find the courage to tell her I liked her. We used to ride out together on her days off to discover the local countryside. She showed me some wonderful things. A crumbling palace buried in undergrowth and inhabited only by monkeys; bazaars deep in the Indian quarter of the city where normally no Europeans ventured; lakes high in the mountains that formed perfect reflections of the surrounding peaks.' His eyes took on a faraway look now, as he remembered.

'It sounds very romantic.'

'It was. We fell in love and after a few months I asked her to marry me. I was over the moon when she accepted, but when I asked my commanding officer for permission, he refused point-blank.'

'Because she was not British?'

'Precisely. There are undercurrents of racism running through every facet of life in British India. She was devastated, of course. She took a lot of time off work, and eventually she was asked to leave. She went back to Delhi to live with her family.'

'What a very sad story,' I said, looking into his eyes. 'I'm so sorry for you.'

He smiled, picked up the knife again and began attacking a potato with gusto. 'As I said, it's a long time ago. And the old saying is true – time can be a great healer. But what about you?

You haven't told me anything about your husband. Where is he now, for instance?'

'He's still on the rubber estate near Kuala Lipis,' I said, avoiding Adam's eyes, looking down at the potato I was peeling.

'Did he not sign up?' I shook my head, still looking away. I could sense his eyes on my face. 'He wanted to make sure the estate kept going. Lots of people's lives depend on it, you see. I came down to Singapore to stay with my sister when it looked as though the Japanese might invade. People thought it would be safer here,' I said, trying to keep my voice steady.

I realised that he was staring at my hands, which were clenched around the knife, the skin stretched tight over my knuckles. I quickly let go of the knife, and it clattered to the floor.

'I'm sorry,' he said, with a look of concern. 'It must be very difficult to be separated like that.'

I swallowed hard and bent down to pick up the knife. I began chopping again, very fast, still looking down. Nothing would induce me to tell him the truth about why I had packed my bags and fled to Singapore, about the torment I had suffered during those months at Windy Ridge, about the hideous memory of my last day there.

'You must miss him dreadfully,' Adam was saying. He looked at me in silence for a while, awaiting a response, then cleared his throat and changed the subject. I sensed he knew I was holding something back.

After a few more days, Adam's leg was strong enough to climb the ladder up to the loft. I sat on the bed down in the flat and listened, holding my breath as the radio crackled and buzzed into life above me. I could hear Adam speaking into the microphone, and then the sound of a fuzzy distorted voice from the other end, but I could not make out any of the words. When Adam came back down, he said, 'They can collect me in three days' time. They need to bring the boat to Kranji Point to pick me up. They need to be sure the tides are right and it's as safe as it can be.' He was not smiling, however.

'Oh,' I managed to say, my voice choked with sadness. I suddenly realised how much his being there had meant to me, how much comfort I had drawn from his presence. I felt a wave of panic at the thought of him leaving, at the thought that I might never see him again.

He came and sat down beside me. 'I shall miss you, Juliet,' he said.

I looked into his eyes, and I was aware of how close we were sitting, how our arms were touching, how I could feel his breath on my face, could smell the sweat on his skin. 'Perhaps, when this is all over ...' he began, but there was a sudden rumpus in the street, raised voices, shouting in Japanese. We rushed to the window.

Down in the street a group of Japanese soldiers had surrounded two young Chinese men, they were hardly more than boys. An officer was leaning forward and speaking angrily to one of them, jabbing him in the chest with his finger. The boys looked bewildered, shaking their heads, trying to back away. Then the officer began slapping one boy's face over and over, and the other soldiers started punching the other boy. Soon all the soldiers had joined in. The boys both collapsed to the ground, and were being kicked and pummelled by the whole group.

A sick feeling was spreading in the pit of my stomach. 'How can they do that? It's dreadful.'

'They're a brutal bunch. My few weeks in Changi taught me to never underestimate their capacity for cruelty.'

'I wish we could do something,' I said, feeling my fists clench.

'There's nothing we can do.'

The boys were being dragged away now, their broken bodies floppy and bloody. We stood for a long time at the window, staring at the blood stains on the pavement, paralysed by the horror of what we had witnessed. Then I noticed something that sent a fresh chill of fear through me: *kempeitai* officers were going from house to house, knocking on doors, questioning occupants.

'We'd better get upstairs, quick,' Adam said in a strained voice. We scrambled up the ladder. I was shaking so much that I thought my legs would give way. When we got into the loft, Adam pulled the ladder up behind us, and stowed it along the wall. Then he pushed the trap door into the hole.

'Sit very still and be as quiet as you can,' he whispered, crouching beside me. Through the open skylight we heard snatches of conversation from the street, and soon we could hear Japanese voices in the shop-house directly beneath us. The *kempeitai* must be questioning the boy who looked after the shop. I felt all my muscles tense up, remembering the boy's hostile stare the day I had gone down for batteries. I felt as though my heart would burst, it was hammering away so fast.

The conversation went on. Voices were raised but I could not make out the words. It sounded like a mixture of Chinese and Japanese. Perhaps the Japs had interpreters with them. I looked nervously at Adam, and he gave me a reassuring smile. He slipped his arm around my shoulders and held me close. I could hear his breathing and it was far steadier than my own. 'Try to stay calm,' he said. I could not respond. All the saliva had disappeared from my mouth and a painful lump had formed in my throat. We stayed there like that for what felt like an age. It reminded me of crouching in the cupboard in the hospital with Nazira.

But then the street grew quiet again, and Adam got up and looked through the tiny skylight. 'They've gone, thank God.' He leaned forward and peered down the road. 'They've moved on. They're probably doing a spot check on Chinese residents for papers.'

I felt weak with relief; all my muscles relaxed, and my eyes suddenly filled with tears. Adam knelt down in front of me. 'Don't cry, Juliet. It's over.'

I couldn't stop the tears welling up and running down my cheeks, the silent sobs shaking my body. Then I felt his arms around me, and his lips kissing my eyelids, my cheeks and finally my mouth. He was drawing me close to him, pressing his firm body against mine. I opened my mouth and kissed him back, put my arms around him, drawing him closer. But after a few minutes he drew back.

'I'm sorry, Juliet. Forgive me. I couldn't help myself. You're married, I know that. That shouldn't have happened.' I looked into his eyes, and saw the depth of his feeling in them.

'Please don't be sorry, Adam. I wanted it to happen. I've been wanting it to happen ever since you arrived.'

'But what about ...'

'My husband?' I asked bitterly. 'You must have guessed there was something wrong. When I came to Singapore, it wasn't just because of the Japanese. I came because I was running away from him and from ... from my life with him. I'll never go back.'

Adam sat back on his heels and stared at me. 'Do you want to tell me about it?'

'Not now. One day, perhaps. I feel too ... too ashamed. It's hard to explain.'

'Then there's no need to.' He kissed me again, tenderly and slowly this time, and I kissed him back, and slipped my arms around his shoulders, but the kiss was interrupted by the sound of someone moving about downstairs in the flat. We sprang apart. Had the *kempeitai* come back and managed to get inside? We sat frozen to the spot for a few minutes and then came the sound of Nazira's voice, gently calling our names. We breathed again.

Adam opened the trap door and called down to Nazira, 'We're up here. We had a bit of a scare.'

'Yes, I know,' she called back. 'Ah-Cheng down in the shop told me. He said the *kempeitai* were going to every house, checking papers. It's very lucky they didn't search the place.'

That evening, as we prepared the evening meal with Nazira

and listened to her stories about her day, I found it difficult to concentrate. I kept thinking about Adam's lips on mine, the feel of his body against my own. My eyes kept wandering to his face, lingering on his strong features, his square jawline, those soft brown eyes, the dark stubble on his chin, and the way his dark hair curled in the nape of his neck. But I didn't want Nazira to suspect that anything was different. That would be very awkward for all of us, so I was very careful only to gaze at Adam when Nazira's back was turned. I noticed that he was making an effort to behave normally too. He told Nazira about his radio conversation with Headquarters and the plans for him to leave.

'We will be very sorry to see you go,' she said, looking up from stirring the pot. 'It has been so good to have some extra company here, hasn't it, Juliet?'

'Oh, yes,' I said, unable to peel my eyes away from his face. 'Very nice.'

Occasionally, as that long evening drew on, I caught Adam's eyes lingering on me and it made ripples of pleasure run through my body. Once, as he handed me a plate of sweet potatoes, our hands touched for a second longer than necessary, and it felt as if an electric current had passed between us. That night I lay awake on the thin mattress on the attic floor, watching the stars through the skylight and thinking about him, remembering the way his warm lips had felt against mine.

In the morning I felt oddly nervous as Nazira dressed and prepared for her day at the canteen. After she had gone I climbed down the ladder. Adam was already up and making tea for breakfast. He turned and smiled at me, and I could tell from the way he lowered his eyes that he too was apprehensive about what the day might bring.

We ate our breakfast in silence. Every attempt either of us made at conversation trailed off awkwardly. When we had finished, I took the cups to the sink, wondering how I could break through this uneasiness, but as I washed the cups, I heard his step behind me and felt his arms encircling my waist, his lips on my neck. My whole body tingled to his touch. I turned around to face him and we kissed for a long time. Then, he half carried me to the little bed and lay me down. He knelt down beside the bed and unbuttoned my blouse, caressing my skin and covering my body with kisses. They he was lying next to me on the bed, and I slipped my hands inside his clothes, exploring his firm body, drawing him closer. Soon our limbs were entwined, and he was moving on top of me, and my hands were around his back, willing him on, feeling the heat of his skin and the strength of his muscles as we melted into each other, becoming one.

Afterwards we lay together on the bed, silently contemplating the momentous thing that had happened between us. We listened to the familiar sound of the voices in the street, the cries of vendors, the chattering of cicadas. Nothing outside had changed, but for us everything had.

'*Saya cintakan awak*,' he whispered into my ear, breaking the silence. 'I love you.' I had taught him the words. He kissed me again, pulling me closer.

'I can't believe you're leaving in a couple of days,' I whispered.

'I know. I can't either. I'm sorry, but I have to go. I'll come back for you though, Juliet. If you'll wait for me, I'll come back.'

'But when will that be?' I propped myself up on one elbow and looking into his eyes, panic setting in again at the thought of losing him.

'The war can't last forever,' he said. 'A few months, maybe a year'?

'Do you promise you'll come back?'

'Of course. I promise,'

'But what if you ...' I couldn't bring myself to finish the sentence, to speak this horrifying possibility aloud.

'I'll be careful. I've been well-trained you know. You're not to worry,' he said, smiling and stroking my hair.

But I did worry. How could I stop worrying? Now that I had at last found happiness it felt so unjust that it was about to be snatched away as suddenly as it had arrived.

The next two days were charged with emotion. We made love urgently when we were alone in the flat. We knew we had so little time together, and that it was important to cement what we had, to make the most of those short few hours. But our passion was tinged with sadness, with the knowledge that we had to part. For me, these encounters were completely different from the muted, almost clinical acts I had experienced with Gavin at the beginning of my marriage, and from the other time ... The time I had blotted from my mind completely. Adam was loving and tender, always putting my pleasure before his own. I had not realised before what it was to really love, to be loved, to be at one with another human being, to give in to passion. As we made love he would look deep into my eyes and say, 'I love you, Juliet.'

He said it over and over again on that last afternoon as we lay together. 'Don't forget me, Juliet. *Saya cintakan awak.*'

'Forget you? How could I ever do that?' I murmured. 'You're the only man I've ever loved.' The thought that we might not be together again for months, maybe years, was almost impossible to bear. I clung to him, knowing I would not be able to say goodbye properly when the time came for him to leave.

'Can't you take me with you?' I asked desperately, looking up into his eyes. I thought he would laugh at me, but he looked at me sadly, shaking his head.

'I'm sorry, Juliet. I would love to, but it would be too much of a risk. You need to be trained for jungle survival and warfare where I'm going. You would never make it.'

When Nazira returned, we ate our meagre meal in tense and gloomy silence. I could hardly bear to look at Adam. I did not trust myself to be able to hold back the tears.

All too quickly it was ten o'clock, time for him to leave. He had stowed the radio parts and some food in a backpack Nazira had given him. He swung it onto his back. He said goodbye to

Nazira and kissed her hand. 'Thank you, Nazira. Thank you so much for all your bravery and your tremendous kindness in letting me stay in your home these past weeks. I cannot thank you enough.'

She shook her head, smiling, tears in her eyes. 'Please, don't speak of it. Good luck, and please, be careful in the mountains. We will meet again when this dreadful war is over. May God go with you.'

He then turned to me, and kissed me on each cheek, as if we were old friends, nothing more. 'You will come back, won't you?' I asked, my voice shaking.

'Of course. As I said. I promise.'

And he turned and went out through the door. I rushed to the window. This time the moon was bright and I managed to catch a glimpse of him moving along the walls of the buildings opposite. This worried me: who else might have seen him go?

I sat down on the bed and hid my face in my hands. I did not want to cry in front of Nazira, but my chest and throat were constricted with the effort of holding back the tears. Nazira sat down beside me and slipped an arm around my waist. 'You are in love with our soldier, aren't you?'

I turned to her, shocked. 'How did you know?'

'It would have been hard to miss. I've seen it happening over these past weeks. I don't mind if you cry, you know.'

So I let the tears fall, and I sobbed and sobbed until I felt I had no more tears left. But still they came.

18

The following days were an ordeal. I didn't have enough energy to get out of bed. I could hardly eat even though my stomach gnawed with hunger. I tried to put on a brave face and appear to Nazira as if I was coping, but she knew as well as I did that it was all an act.

Once Nazira had left for the day, I lay there staring at the cracked, grubby ceiling, trying to imagine where Adam might be and what he would be doing. The first day, I pictured him making his way through the streets of the bombed-out city to Kranji Point on the north of the island. He had been vague about how he would get there, but I guessed that his comrades in the resistance would provide some sort of transport. Would he be hidden in a delivery van, or crouched in a rickshaw, hoping to slip through the dark streets unnoticed? I tried to imagine what sort of boat would be waiting for him at Kranji to take him up the Malay coast. Would it be a fishing vessel, or a rowing boat? I guessed it would have to be fairly large to make that journey. Would he be hiding in the bottom of the boat under cover, or would he be able to look out, breathe the salty air and watch the moonlight dancing on the water as the boat slipped along the causeway and made its way north up the coast?

As the hours crawled past, I wondered whether he had made it to the jungle on the mainland and what he would be doing. He had not spoken much about what his duties would be, but I knew that whatever he would be doing would be dangerous, camping out in villages or in the jungle with the guerrillas, blowing bridges, sabotaging checkpoints, railway lines, and all the time trying to remain hidden, to avoid discovery and capture. I found myself shivering when I thought about him being caught by the Japanese. I tried to put those disturbing thoughts out of my mind, to replace them with memories of our days together. When I thought about lying in his arms, feeling his flesh on mine, listening to the soothing rhythm of his breathing, or to his spirited voice as he told his stories of India, a warm feeling crept over me, dispelling my fear if only for a few moments. '*Saya cintakan awak,*' I breathed to myself over and over again.

Nazira carried on leaving early in the morning. She rarely spoke about how she spent her days, and I often wondered what sort of risks she was taking to get food and medicines into Changi. I knew that sometimes Nazira went to the docks where prisoners were forced to work unloading ships, and sometimes to parts of town damaged by the bombing raids, where prisoners were made to clear rubble from damaged buildings. She never took a day off, even through the long hot month of Ramadan when she had to fast from sunrise to sunset. I tried to support her as best I could. It was the one thing that kept me going after Adam had gone.

I tried my best to keep the flat clean and tidy, prepare any food there might be for the evening meal. But as the Occupation wore on, Nazira brought home less and less food. One day, Nazira set off as normal, with her anxious smile and brief wave. But that evening, she did not return home. The sun went down and it grew completely dark outside, but there was no sign of Nazira.

I began to worry. Had something happened to her? By eight o'clock I had grown very anxious. My stomach began to churn with nerves and I could not sit still. I kept going to the window to check the street, then sat by the bed and stuffed down a couple of cooked potatoes and an overripe banana. It was the only food left in the house, and I forced myself to eat it. But instead of satisfying my hunger, it just made me feel nauseous.

I spent the rest of the long evening with my forehead pressed against the window, staring at the street below, looking out for any sign of movement that might signal Nazira's return. But the hours passed and still she did not come.

After midnight I went and lay on the bed, exhausted with worry. I drifted off into a fitful sleep, waking up with a start many times, instantly remembering. Eventually it was daybreak, and I heard the sounds of the stalls being set up in the street and of Ah-Cheng opening the shop below. My body ached with fatigue, and I felt weak with hunger and lack of sleep. I would have to find some food from somewhere. I also noticed that the water in the enamel container Nazira filled each day from the standpipe was getting worryingly low.

I emptied the remaining water into a jug, took the container and slipped out of the door and went down the stone steps to the shop. The boy was there setting out the pots. There were hardly any left now. I wondered why he still bothered to come. When he saw me, he stiffened visibly.

'Good morning, Ah-Cheng,' I said in Malay, 'I have some really bad news, I'm afraid. Nazira did not come home yesterday. I don't know where she is. Do you have any idea where she might be?'

His mouth turned down at the corners, and he looked away, avoiding my eyes.

'I not know,' he said.

'I'm sorry to ask you this, but do you think you could fetch me some water? And if you have any money, might you be able to get me some food? I wouldn't ask, but I have no money and no food left, you see. I will repay you as soon as I can.'

He scowled at me. 'I not want trouble,' he said. 'You bad trouble.'

'I'm sorry. I know it's difficult for you.'

'Why you no go? You go before.' He was referring to the time I had gone to get the batteries. I had not trusted him then, so had not suggested asking him. But I had felt reassured by the way he had dealt with the Japanese patrol when Adam and I had crouched in the attic.

He held out his hand for the container grudgingly. 'I go now,' he said without smiling. 'Will get food this one time, but today my last day. Tomorrow I no come. Nothing to sell here now. Nobody buying.'

A wave of panic went through me at his words. If he didn't come and if for some reason Nazira did not return, how would I survive here alone? Without a further word, he rushed off into the street in the direction of the standpipe, and I went into the back of the shop and hid myself behind the empty shelves while I waited, in case the *kempeitai* chose this moment to return to the street.

It seemed an age had passed by the time he returned. 'I have water. Here,' he said putting the container down on the floor. 'And some rice and onion.' He handed me a paper bag. 'That all there is.' He did not meet my eye.

'Thank you,' I said taking the bag and picking up the water container. 'Thank you so much. I will pay you back one day.'

'No need. I not come back here.'

Still he would not look at me. I returned upstairs and set to work chopping the onions and cooking the rice. I decided to save a portion for the next day, although there wasn't really even enough for one meal. All the time I thought about Nazira. Where could she have gone? Had she fallen ill? Had she been captured by the Japanese? If so, was she in Changi herself now? Had she been questioned? I shuddered and tried to put that thought out of my mind. I was desperate to find her, but didn't even know where the canteen was that she worked from. And even if I had known where it was, how could I possibly get through the city without being apprehended myself?

I lay on the bed and waited restlessly. The hours passed and still there was no sign of my friend. When it grew dark, I forced myself up and ate a little more rice and made some tea. I was conscious that I had to conserve the paraffin, though, so decided to limit myself to two cups. I heard Ah-Cheng putting the stalls away and the rattle of the metal shutter as he pulled it down over the front of the shop. Shortly after that I heard footsteps on the stairs. My scalp tingled. Could that be Nazira? But there was a knock on the door. Nazira never knocked. My mind raced with possibilities. Could it be the *kempeitai*? They had not come upstairs last time, and I hadn't seen them in the street today. I even wondered fleetingly if it could be Adam, but quickly put that from my mind.

The knock came again. With my heart in my mouth I opened the door a fraction. It was Ah-Cheng. I pulled it open further and smiled at him. He handed me a cloth bag.

'This money from shop for this week,' he said, his face still stern. 'I take my wages. I no come back.'

'Thank you. Thank you very much,' I said, wanting to ask him if he would go for food and water again, but from the way he avoided my gaze and shifted about on his feet, I could tell that he was desperate to leave. He turned and ran back down the steps.

I shut the door behind him, then went to the table and poured the money out. It was only a few coins. I counted them out. At least they were Singapore dollars rather than the virtually worthless banana money the Japanese had tried to introduce since the Occupation. There were about ten dollars there. It was probably enough to buy food for a week or so.

Early the next morning my hunger forced me out of my bed.

My head pounded from sleeping fitfully and from the extreme heat in the flat. I knew I had not been drinking enough water. I caught sight of myself in Nazira's cracked little mirror on a shelf above the sink. I hadn't looked in the mirror for weeks, and noticed now how thin and sallow my face had become, how it was marked with dark smudges under my eyes. I took a few sips of water and ate the remainder of the rice that Ah-Cheng had given me. Then with a feeling of dread in my heart, I pulled on the dark robe and the *niqab* that still hung on the back of the door.

The street was almost deserted. Piles of rubbish had built up on the pavements. Most of the stalls were unmanned and held no stock. The empty frames and tables had a forlorn look, like skeletons picked clean by vultures. I felt nervous about walking to the end of the road where the impromptu checkpoint had been the last time I had gone out. So I turned and went in the other direction, remembering that Nazira had spoken about a kindly old woman who sold vegetables a couple of streets away on the way to Chinatown. Before I had gone many steps, my body was running with sweat under the dark veil and robe, and I felt weak and breathless. It felt strange to be outside again, to not be enclosed by walls, to be so visible to any eyes that might be watching me. I edged along close to the buildings, every so often putting my arm out to steady myself, taking deep breaths to calm my nerves.

I soon found myself in a street where several houses had been destroyed by bombs. The front walls had collapsed, piles of masonry and rubble blocking the road. I picked my way past that towards a shabby little market at the other end of the road. I was not sure if this was the place Nazira had mentioned, but I noticed an old woman behind one of the trestle tables. She had a kindly face furrowed with age, and smiling eyes. I spoke to her in Malay and she answered cheerfully. I tried to keep my eyes cast down, but could not help giving the old lady a grateful look as she handed me a bag containing five potatoes and some stringy kale, all for one dollar. Before I left, I asked where I might find paraffin.

The old lady gave me a strange look. 'You not go already?' she asked.

'Oh, my sister usually goes, but she's … She's ill with fever, so I didn't want to wake her to ask for directions.'

The old woman gave me directions to a shop that sold paraffin a few streets away. It was a long walk and the shop was hidden in a side alley. The transaction went smoothly, but there were several people queuing in the shop. I was glad that I had spent so much time perfecting my Malay on the rubber estate, for I was fairly sure my accent sounded like a native's and didn't give me away. I returned to the flat congratulating myself on a successful shopping trip, and making sure not to deliberate on what would happen when my money ran out. I had already spent three out of my ten dollars. Perhaps Nazira would come back before that? Remembering my friend brought back all my anxieties, and my eyes filled with tears at the thought of what might have happened to her.

I had just one more trip to perform that day. I took the water container and went down the road to the standpipe. There was a queue of women carrying jars and bottles, gossiping as they waited to use the pipe. They stopped and stared at me as I approached. One of them turned and said, 'You're new here, aren't you? I haven't seen you before.'

My heart began to pound again. I kept my eyes on the ground. 'Yes. I was living in another part of town, but my mother died so I came here to live with my sister,' I spoke again in fluent Malay. Yet the woman eyed me suspiciously.

'And your sister? Where is she?'

I nodded in the vague direction of the end of the road. 'Up there. But she isn't well today. She has fever. So I came for water.'

The woman continued to stare at me, but moved aside to let me fill my container from the pump. I felt all their eyes on my hands as I turned the screw on the pipe. Mine were obviously a white woman's hands; they were not even suntanned any more. I filled the container and left quickly, my face burning with anxiety under my veil, sensing the women's eyes on me as I walked back up the street.

Back in the flat I threw off the robes and *niqab*, and lay on the bed to cool off, to let my racing heart settle. My mind kept returning to the way the women at the pump had stared at me. How could I go back there day after day and face them with my lies?

I did my best to make the food last and eat as little as possible at each meal so that I would not have to go out. It was easier to conserve the food than it was water though. Two days after my trip to the stand-pipe, the container was almost empty again, even though I had tried to limit the amount of water I used. It was so hot in the flat, it was difficult to get through the day without drinking much. I decided to go to the standpipe after dark so that fewer people would be there.

When the sun went down that evening, and the street was empty, I ventured out again, wearing the robe and *niqab*. This time I brought a large jug as well as the usual container. As I approached the standpipe and saw that there was nobody there, my nerves eased a little. I put the container and jug down and fumbled with the nozzle. It was stiff, but soon the water was gushing forth. Gratefully I filled up the container and jug and switched the tap off, but as I turned to leave, I realised with a shock that the woman who had questioned me the day before was standing in front of me, hand on hip, an accusing look on her face.

'What do you think you're doing coming here at this hour?' she said. 'I saw you from my window.'

'I'm sorry,' I muttered, barely able to form the words.

'Don't you know there's a curfew?' You'll get the whole street into trouble. You're not meant to be out after dark.'

I stood there quietly, not knowing what to say.

'Well don't do it again. You should come and get water in daylight, like everyone else.'

'Of course. I'll do that.'

The woman tutted to herself and vanished into the darkness, and I hurried home on shaking legs. I had known about the curfew, of course. Nazira had mentioned it, but my friend had frequently broken it herself, coming home at all hours of the evening. It hadn't seemed that serious.

I went to bed that night racked with worry about Nazira, and when I eventually fell into a fitful sleep, I dreamed about her. Nazira was running through the streets, her breath coming in gasps. At first I didn't know what she was running from. I ran beside her, and when I looked behind us, I saw a group of Japanese soldiers chasing us, bayonets drawn. I tried to warn her, to shake her and tell her about the danger, but she couldn't hear me. No words would come from my mouth. I was shouting frantically, but the shouting had no sound.

A loud hammering on the door woke me just after dawn. I scrambled out of bed, my heart thumping, but had the presence of mind to pull the *niqab* over my face. I hesitated before pulling back the bolts. Should I open the door? From the urgency of the knocking, it sounded as though whoever was outside would break the door down if I did not. Was it Nazira? The nightmare was still vivid in my mind. Was my friend in trouble? I drew back the bolts and turned the handle, but before I could pull it open, the door was shoved back towards me violently, almost knocking me off my feet. Three Japanese soldiers burst into the flat.

'Remove your veil,' barked one in English. I was paralysed with shock and did not respond immediately. He reached out and pulled it roughly off my head.

'English woman!' he yelled, leaning towards me, flecks of spit hitting my face. 'You defy word of Emperor. European civilians report to Padang day of surrender. Why you here?' I stared at him, open mouthed, quaking from head to toe. I could not speak. I flinched as he slapped my cheek, making my skin smart and sting.

'Pack bag now. You go Changi.'

I had no bag but I bundled a couple of blouses and spare sarongs into a pillow case from the bed.

'You come now!' The soldiers pushed me through the door of the flat, down the stairs and out onto the street. I almost stumbled and fell as one of them shoved his rifle butt between my shoulder blades. A small crowd had gathered outside to watch. I saw the fear in their faces, noticed that none of them wanted to look me in the eye.

A truck was parked a few doors down the street. The soldiers pushed me towards it, then bundled me up the ladder at the back of the truck and over the tailgate. They got in and surrounded me. 'We go Changi prison now. You like it there,' said the officer who had slapped me, and laughed heartily. The others joined in. He leaned over and banged the side of the truck with his hand. The engine roared into life.

As the lorry drew out of the street, I caught sight of the woman from the pump. She stood apart from the crowd, hands on hips as before, a malicious smile on her lips.

The lorry drove erratically and dangerously through the streets of the beaten city. People stopped and stared as we passed, no doubt wondering who was being taken away, secretly relieved that it wasn't them. Many buildings had been reduced to rubble, and the streets that had once been thronging with markets and activity were now unnaturally empty and quiet. Eventually the buildings began to thin out as the lorry headed east towards Changi. Would they question me when I arrived about why I hadn't given myself up with the rest of the Europeans? Would they torture me? I gripped the bench as the motion of the truck threw me from side to side, my mind and body frozen with terror.

We were soon roaring through the outskirts of the town,

through the European quarter where mock Tudor mansions stood shaded by trees. The houses that had once been elegant and cared for with well-kept gardens were now reduced to bomb-damaged rubble with great holes blown in their roofs, their walls collapsed. Vegetation had been allowed to grow unchecked, creepers covered paths, and bushes and thickets of bamboo threatened to engulf the buildings. Soon we were passing crowded ramshackle neighbourhoods of the Indian and Chinese workers, and then on were soon clear of the town and passed through native villages built of wood and bamboo.

As the lorry was nearing the very edge of the city, the guard who was sitting next to me on the bench nudged me and looked at me with an evil smile on his face. Then he pointed upwards to the telegraph wires suspended high between the poles along the street. There, hanging from the wire on lengths of rope were five human heads, the necks grotesque black stumps of congealed blood. I stared up at them mutely, my brain unable to process what I was seeing. Despite my revulsion I was transfixed, unable to look away. The features on the faces were swollen and discoloured, and dried blood had oozed from mouths and ears. Their mouths hung open bizarrely, making the heads look like ventriloquist's dummies. Two of the heads belonged to women, judging by the length of the hair that hung down in matted clumps. The guards stopped the lorry for a moment right under-neath the heads so I could see them more clearly. They continued to nudge and laugh at me mockingly, but I ignored them. I could not take my eyes off one of the heads with long hair.

Distorted and swollen as it was I could still recognise who it had once belonged to. It was the face of my dear friend, the woman who had saved my life, the kind and generous Nazira who had cared for me and sheltered me from harm, had risked her own life to help countless others.

'Nazira!' I finally snapped out of my daze, and let out a piercing shriek that seemed to rip straight from my soul and take on a life of its own. To my stunned and confused mind it sounded as though the scream was coming from a long way away, and not from my own mouth. Everything around me was suddenly swimming out of focus, black spots were then obscuring my vision and I was falling forwards, plunging down into a void of darkness.

JULIET WAS SITTING up in the bed, sweating. She looked around her at the bare little room and remembered where she was, in the worn out guest-house in the back streets of Palembang. She glanced at her watch. She had been dozing for over an hour.

She dressed quickly and went to Mary's room next door. She knocked on the door tentatively. The girl emerged after a few moments, wearing a clean but crumpled dress, her face looking fresh and her hair damp. She looked younger without makeup.

'I'm sorry, Mary, I must have dropped off to sleep. I had no idea of the time.'

'No problem. There's still bags of time. I came and knocked on the door a while back, but there was no reply. I guessed you needed to relax.'

'Yes, I had no idea you had knocked.'

'Look, I'm really sorry about being moody earlier on,' Mary said, putting her hand on Juliet's arm and looking into her eyes. 'It was kind of you to offer to pay for a better hotel. There was no need for me to be so rude. Forgive me?'

'Of course,' said Juliet. 'Please forget about it. Perhaps it was tactless of me.'

They began to walk down the concrete staircase. 'It's just that, when I first came to your place, I had the impression that you thought I was some kind of gold digger. I don't want to give you any reason to think that.'

'Oh Mary, I was so confused when you first came, I didn't

know what to think. But we know each other a little better now, don't we? I trust you now.'

'I know,' said Mary, tucking her arm into Juliet's. 'We'll ask reception to call us a taxi. The orphanage is miles away. I don't think a rickshaw would make it there before dark.'

They crossed town in a battered blue Toyota taxi. The roads were choked with traffic and they crawled along the shabby thoroughfares, past markets and bazaars, mosques and shopping malls. It was a busy city, heaving with people and pulsating with energy. Juliet thought back to how amazed she had been at the atmosphere of a large Asian city when she had first experienced Kuala Lumpur all those years ago. Now she just felt exhausted by the pace, wishing they were out of the traffic and away from the crowds. Being here made her long for the peace and order of her life on the plantation.

At last they were through the centre of the city and out on the other side, heading west through a suburban district where the houses were neater and set further apart, surrounded by gardens and shaded by trees. The car turned into a drive off a main road and drew up in front of a long two-storey concrete building with a flat roof. There was a painted sign above the main entrance: 'Convent and Orphanage of Our Lady.'

Juliet had not expected a modern building like this. The word 'orphanage' had conjured in her mind visions of Victorian institutions built of red-brick with towers, gothic windows and arches. She couldn't have been more wrong. As they paid the taxi driver, a couple of nuns dressed in long black robes and head-dresses emerged from the door and smiled at them. Then one of them stepped forward and walked towards Mary holding out her arms. 'Mary Batari! I can't believe it's you. You look so modern now. How is life in Singapore?'

'Sister Theresa!' said Mary, and the two embraced.

'What brings you back here, Mary? We haven't seen you for a long time.'

'This is Juliet Crosby,' Mary said, turning to Juliet and putting her arm around her. 'I think she is my aunt. We're trying to do some research into my early life. I was wondering if there was someone in the office we could talk to about the orphanage records?'

'Well actually, there is someone archiving our material at the moment.'

'Really?'

'Yes. A new Mother Superior arrived last month, and she thought the records should be more organised. So she hired an intern, a university student, to look through the files and catalogue what is in there. She might well be able to help you. But I'm afraid she has left for the day now. Why don't you both come and look around the orphanage and have some tea with us. Then you can come back tomorrow and speak to our student. Kezia is her name.'

'But weren't you about to go out?' asked Mary.

'Yes, but we do not have visitors every day. We would like to welcome you, wouldn't we, Sister Saviour?' The other nun nodded and smiled, and beckoned them inside the orphanage.

As they walked through the front entrance, Juliet caught a whiff of that old institutional smell of stale cooking, disinfectant and polished floors that took her back to her own school days.

'Come, come this way,' beckoned the nuns. 'The children are just having tea. You can join them if you like.'

They followed the nuns down a bare echoing corridor and into a huge double-storey dining hall. There, dozens of children of all ages were seated at low tables, shovelling noodles into their mouths. The sound of their chatter, bouncing off the concrete walls, was deafening. Juliet looked up. There were walkways lining the walls above, with rooms opening off them, and above their heads, a net was suspended, presumably to catch any children who might decide to climb over the balconies. A shiver went through Juliet. It reminded her of another place, where similar nets had been placed to stop people from falling. But she put that out of her mind immediately and smiled at the sister who was asking her to sit down at a low table amongst a group of children. They were already smiling excitedly at the sight of the visitors, and they laughed merrily when Juliet sat down on one of the tiny chairs and joined them for tea.

Juliet guessed that the children at the table were all around four or five years old. She was unused to children and found it overwhelming that their little faces were all turned towards her, wide-eyed, expecting her to say something funny or interesting. She smiled, feeling awkward, wondering what to do. Finally she asked, 'Do you speak English,' and they all chorused. 'Yes, madam. Very pleased to meet you, madam. How do you do?'

'Oh, very good!' she said, clapping. 'Now you must all tell me your names. Let's go round the table, one by one.'

As the children took turns to shout out their names, Juliet glanced at Mary, who was sitting at the next table. The girl was relaxed, smiling and laughing with the children, her cheeks slightly flushed. Again Juliet reminded herself that this environment was completely normal to Mary, that she had grown up like these children. Her heart contracted with pity at the thought that these children didn't have any family and that Mary had spent her childhood here just like them, believing that she too had no family to love her or care for her. The image of that baby in Rose's arms surfaced again.

'Madam, you're not listening. What is your name please? Tell us your name,' the children were calling her back to the moment, and she smiled and joined in with their conversation.

Later, Juliet and Mary said their goodbyes to the children and the nuns, promising that they would be back the next day, and hailed a taxi to take them back to the hotel. Mary asked for them to be dropped at a covered market a few streets away from the hotel.

'Look at these fantastic clothes, Juliet,' said Mary, ducking into the sweltering darkness of the bazaar, darting towards a stall in the centre that sold tie-dyed kaftans. As Juliet arrived she was already holding one out. It was bright orange with swirling white patterns.

'How groovy is this? I've just got to have it!' said Mary. 'Do you think it would suit me?'

Juliet smiled weakly. 'Hold it up to your face.' Mary did, and Juliet saw that the orange of the garment emphasised the dusting of freckles across the girl's nose and cheeks. Mary was smiling widely, and for a split second, Juliet caught a fleeting glimpse of someone else in that smile. Someone long gone. She clutched the stall to steady herself.

'The colour suits you,' she said, recovering herself. 'But is it your style, Mary? I thought you liked more tailored clothes.'

'Well, I do, but this is the future. I'm sure things like this will come into fashion very soon.'

'Do you think so?' asked Juliet uncertainly.

'Of course. Hey how about this for you?' Mary said suddenly, and pulled out a white cheesecloth shirt with an embroidered yoked neckline.

'I'm not sure it's my style.'

'Of course it is,' said Mary holding the shirt against Juliet. 'It would look great on you. Why don't you try it on?'

Reluctantly Juliet went behind the curtain the stallholder was holding aside for her and, in the tiny cubicle, changed out of her plain blue blouse into the white one. It was a difficult manoeuvre; she was sweating in the heat and her clothes stuck to her, but with some wriggling she managed it. There was no mirror in the cubicle so she stepped outside, feeling self-conscious.

'That looks beautiful, Juliet, really!' said Mary, clasping her hands together in genuine pleasure. The woman who owned the stall was smiling and nodding in agreement. She gestured to a mirror behind the stall. 'Come and look, stand here please,' she said.

Juliet stood in front of the mirror and was amazed at what she saw. The bright white of the blouse contrasted with her tanned skin, and made her look healthy and glowing. It brought out the blue of her eyes. It gave her a relaxed look, a contrast to her safe, inconspicuous, old-fashioned clothes in greys and blues.

'You look lovely,' said Mary standing behind her. 'See, I knew it would suit you.'

Juliet smiled at her. 'You were right. How did you know?'

'I have a gift for these things,' said Mary.

'You certainly do! I'll buy it.'

As the stallholder wrapped their purchases, Juliet remembered shopping with Rose, all the trips to Oxford Street they had made together, the visits to Rose's tailor in Singapore. Juliet had never really cared about clothes, and since Rose died she had cared even less. Rose always knew what would suit her, far better than she knew herself. She would pick out swatches of cloth or dresses and hold them up to her face and say, 'This would suit you, Jules. Why don't you try it?'

For dinner, they went to one the stalls in a food-hall in the middle of the market.

'So now you've seen the orphanage, what did you think?' asked Mary as she attacked a huge plate of beef *rendang*.

'I was surprised at how modern it was. But all the children seemed very happy, and so loving,' said Juliet, remembering how they had clung to her as she had tried to leave.

'Mealtimes weren't fun at all when I was there. Things are much more relaxed now,' said Mary, her eyes suddenly serious. 'We used to have to eat in silence, and boys and girls had to sit at separate tables. You had to eat every scrap of food on your plate or you'd be punished.'

'Those children looked as though they would eat it all anyway,' said Juliet.

'The food wasn't so good then either. It was often just rice and vegetables when I was a child. It was just after the war, and I think food must have been scarce. I remember hating the taste of boiled cabbage. It was revolting, and they served it every day. I used to squash it in the pocket of my uniform so I wouldn't have to eat it. Once, a nun caught me doing that, and I had to sit in Mother Superior's office and write five hundred lines as punishment,' Mary said, her face slipping into a frown.

'Was it all bad though? You seemed very happy to see Sister Theresa,' Juliet put her hand on Mary's to comfort her.

'There were lots of happy times, of course,' Mary said, brightening again. 'And Sister Theresa was great. Wonderful and caring. Unlike some of the others. Some of them were cold and hard.' Juliet saw a shudder go through Mary. For a moment her eyes clouded over as if she were re-living some dreadful memories, but she quickly recovered herself and returned to her food.

19

I came to on the floor of the lorry. I was lying directly on the metal, and the heat of it was burning my bare arms and legs. I felt something prodding my back. I rolled over and I saw that I was being kicked awake by one of the guards. Their boots looked odd, like the hooves of strange beasts, with a single compartment for the big toe. With difficulty, I sat up.

'Wake up,' said a guard gruffly.

I looked around and realised with a fresh chill of fear that the journey was almost over. There, up ahead, loomed the forbidding grey walls of Changi Prison.

Within moments the lorry was lumbering through the stone gates and into a courtyard enclosed on all four sides by prison blocks. The guards on the back of the lorry sprang into life. 'Get up, get up, speedo,' the leader barked at me. I struggled to my feet, my mouth dry and rough as sandpaper, my body covered in sweat and dirt from the floor of the lorry.

'You come now.'

They shoved me off the back of the truck, and half carried me across the courtyard and into a room on the ground floor. My body went weak with dread. This was it: an interrogation room. A stony faced Japanese officer stared at me from behind a desk in the centre of the room. I noticed the white band of the *kempeitai* on his arm.

'What you name?' he asked.

I could not focus properly on what he was saying. The image of Nazira's severed head was still swimming in my head. The man was waiting for my answer, tapping a pen on the table.

'Juliet Crosby,' I muttered, shaking my head, trying to clear it. The officer wrote it down painstakingly then looked back up at me.

'Why you not go Padang with other Europeans on February 15, day of great Japanese victory?'

'I was very ill. Unconscious. I knew nothing about ... about the victory.'

'Everyone know,' he snapped. 'Whole city of Singapore know. It was broadcast on radio by Governor. When you get better why you not give yourself up? Why you hide?'

I shook my head. 'I did not know what to do,' I whispered, looking at the bare brick floor.

'You stay in house of enemy of Japanese Emperor,' the officer said. 'This woman.' He slid a photograph across the desk towards me. It was of Nazira. It must have been taken when she had been captured. Her face was a mass of cuts and bruises and she was looking down, defeated.

'You know her? Miss Syed.'

I remained silent. Should I deny knowing Nazira and betray the memory of my friend? No, I could not do that. In any case, what use would there be in denying it? They must know where Nazira lived, and they had found me asleep in her flat.

Suddenly at a nod from the officer, one of the guards standing next to me slapped my cheek hard. I flinched. 'You do know this woman.'

I nodded, my cheek stinging from the slap.

'And you know three British prisoners escape from Changi POW camp?'

My scalp tingled at the thought that Adam and his friends might still be in danger. Did the Japanese know that they had stayed in the flat? Had Nazira broken down and talked under torture? I shook my head vehemently and said, 'No, I don't know any prisoners.'

'You know men. They escape Changi. They stay with you. In Kampong Glam. Tell where they go.'

I looked him straight in the eye. He was glaring at me, his jaw set grimly, his eyes narrowed with contempt. 'I do not know anything about any British men,' I said. 'I stayed with Miss Syed, yes. She was a nurse. She cared for me, helped me to get better. But I know nothing about any prisoners.'

The officer nodded at his guards, and they pushed me backwards onto a hard metal chair and bound my arms and legs quickly. They pulled the rope so tight that it cut into my flesh. Then one of the guards began to slap me, again and again, first one cheek then the other. Soon my face was burning with pain and I felt dizzy with the force of the blows.

The officer came out from behind the desk, strode over and leaned towards me. 'You do know those men and you will talk.' Flecks of spit landed on my face as he spoke, but I could hardly pay attention to what he was saying. I was swooning from the slapping and thought I was about to pass out.

'I know ... I know nothing,' I mumbled and then closed my eyes. Adam's face swam before me, his gentle brown eyes searching my own. He was smiling at me now, the skin at the corners of his eyes crinkling. I felt his arms wrapping around me, enveloping me until the heat of his body was all I could feel. It was getting hotter and hotter, and once again I was falling into a dark void, down and down into nothingness.

I had no idea for how long I was unconscious. When I came round I was still in the chair, my head flopping forward onto my chest, dribble from the corner of my mouth caking on my chin. My face was throbbing with pain and my eyes swollen so I could not open them fully. With an effort I lifted my head and looked around. I was alone in the room. A square of bright sunlight coming in from a window high up in one wall made me blink, and close my eyes again. My tongue was dry and swollen and I realised that I had not had anything to drink since the previous evening. Not even a sip of water. I sat there like that for a long time, exhausted, unable to move.

Then the door opened and one of the guards came in and untied the ropes from my wrists and ankles. The guard did not speak to me or even look at me. He took hold of one arm and forced me to my feet. Then he half dragged me out of the room and into the courtyard for a few paces, then back into a concrete passage lined with metal doors. He stopped at one, opened the door and shoved me inside. He slammed the door shut and bolted it before striding away.

The cell was narrow and bare, with a hessian sleeping mat in one corner and a metal pail in another, which was the first thing I smelled as I entered. As in the interrogation room there was a tiny square window on the far wall with bars and no glass. It was too high to see out of properly, but I was grateful for any glimpse of the cloudless blue sky. I sank down on the mat and put my head in my hands. I was beyond tears. After a while a metal hatch in the door was pulled across.

'Food. Take it!' a guard said and shoved a metal plate through the hatch.

I got up unsteadily and took the plate. On it was a small portion of grey-looking glutinous rice swimming in grease with a few lumps of fatty meat nestling in it. A tin cup of water was also pushed through. After the last few days of near starvation in the flat, I was glad of the meal, however revolting it looked and smelled. I sat down on the mat and ate it as slowly as I could bear to, chewing every mouthful several times. The meat was so fatty it couldn't be broken down by chewing so I had to force it down in one lump, but this only made me gag. I sipped half the cup of water and saved the rest. I had no way of knowing when there might be more.

When I was finished, I slept for a long time, but the sleep did not refresh me, it was a sleep interrupted by terrible haunting dreams.

It lasted for several days, perhaps a week. I was questioned every day, was taken to the interrogation room early in the morning, and kept there for hours, was asked exactly the same questions and beaten up in various different ways. The days and the sessions all merged into one, each one indistinguishable from the next, forming one dreadful memory that I would never forget.

I distinctly remembered the last time I was interrogated, though. It had started with the usual questions about Adam and his friends. I denied any knowledge of the men, and was rewarded with slaps and threats from the guards. This went on for well over an hour. Then, suddenly, on that last morning, the officer came out from behind his desk. He came up close to me and took hold of my filthy blood-stained blouse and pulled me towards him. He stared at me, eyeball to eyeball, and I stared back, determined to show him that despite all those days of beatings he had not dampened my spirit.

He stared for a long time with narrowed eyes. Finally he said quietly, in a voice that was more sinister than when he shouted, 'We know you know those men. We not forget you, Mrs. Crosby. One day you talk to us.' His mouth was so close to my face that I could smell his last meal on his breath. Nausea rose in my throat but I carried on staring back. He then let go of my shirt and hit me once with the back of his hand, across my mouth. I felt the sharp pain of my lip splitting and tasted the sickly sweet blood trickling into my mouth. After that the two guards took me by the arms again and dragged me out of the room. This time I was not taken along the passage to my cell. Instead they dragged me outside and across the great courtyard and along another line of cells inside the block on the other side. I felt the presence of other people as we passed, could smell and hear them, crowds of them, their voices filling the air. The guards opened one of the doors and shoved me into a cell, slamming the heavy metal door behind me.

The first thing that hit me was the smell of the latrine bucket. It filled the cell and made me gag. Although I was expecting it, I was shocked to see other occupants. There must have been fifteen women and children in there, but only two metal bunk-beds. The women were all sitting silently along the lower bunks and on the floor. They were all staring at me. Even in my confused and nervous state I could tell from their eyes that they were all thinking the same thing, that there was no room for anyone else in here. One woman got up from one of the beds and moved slowly towards me, peering at my swollen face. Instinctively, I drew back.

'You alright, love? You look as though you've been in the wars. Here, come and sit down on the bed. I'll get some water and bathe those cuts.' The woman looked a rough type, with lined, raddled skin and dyed red hair greying at the roots. She had tired, cynical eyes. Anywhere else, I would have found her appearance intimidating, but at this moment I was grateful for her concern. As I moved towards the bed, the others moved aside grudgingly for me to sit down.

'I'm Elsie,' said the woman, coming back with a bowl of water and a torn rag. 'Used to run a bar down in Geylang. You lot here wouldn't have been seen dead anywhere near it a few months ago, but we're all in it together now, my love.'

I remembered overhearing a whispered conversation between two scandalised women at the swimming club when I had first come to Singapore. They had been talking in hushed tones about the goings-on in Geylang, a red-light district on the edge of Chinatown, frequented by visiting soldiers and sailors. I wondered how this ordinary-looking woman, clearly a Londoner like myself, had ended up in such an unlikely place, thousands of miles from home.

Pursing her lips and shaking her head in disbelief, Elsie dabbed at my swollen cuts and bruises with the damp cloth. 'Those guards are bastards. Fancy doing this to a woman,' she kept repeating under her breath. When she had finished, she emptied the bowl in the latrine bucket in the corner of the cell and returned to sit on the bed. The other women automatically shifted up for me and I sensed that they were a little in awe of Elsie, perhaps viewing her as a sort of leader.

As Elsie squeezed in between myself and another woman, I sensed that not so long ago she would have been a large woman. Her shabby floral dress hung off her shoulders and she still moved carefully and deliberately as if she had a bulky frame to manoeuvre around. 'What's your name, love?' she asked.

I told her, and Elsie then introduced me to everyone else in the cell. There was Janet and Pat, two middle-aged women who looked me in the eye and nodded to me as they shook my hand. All the others were interchangeable in my memory: they all looked unhealthy, pale and defeated. They each simply nodded to me listlessly as they were introduced, avoiding my gaze. Again I had the sense that they resented my presence. All I meant to them was further overcrowding of their cell and discomfort. The last one to be introduced was Doris Jones. A younger woman who held a grubby, whining baby to her chest. She smiled as I was introduced, and I instantly realised that out of all the women, only Doris, Elsie, Pat and Janet were still fighting for survival.

The others seemed to have given up. They were the wives of officers, civil servants or businessmen. Most were older than me. They seemed to have already crumbled, frequently dissolving into tears, had given up on caring about their health or appearance, stumbling through the days in a trance, isolated in their own private hell.

On that first evening the guards threw an extra sleeping mat into the cell, and I took it and stretched it out in a corner, under the window. There were only a few inches of floor-space for me to lie in. It was sweltering inside the cell and no air circulated. The smell of sweating and unwashed bodies and of the filthy latrine bucket made me feel nauseous. Throughout the night, women would pick their way past the others to use it. Some had diarrhoea, but were still forced to use the bucket several times a night in full view of all the others.

I lay there on the mat, worrying that I might suffocate, concentrating on trying to get enough air to my lungs. The stinking air was heavy and clammy. I wondered how enough of it could filter through that tiny window to sustain all of us. I was unable to sleep in such close proximity to so many other sweating people, all coughing and snoring, sobbing and whimpering, tossing and turning on their mats. I stared up into the darkness and could not stop myself from thinking about Nazira. I could not rid my mind of the dreadful image of her bloodied face dangling from the telegraph wire. I was plagued by imaginings of what might have happened to my friend in those few days before her death. How had she been discovered and captured? Had she been tortured and beaten? I thought of Adam too. Had he escaped to the mainland as he had planned? The Japanese were clearly still looking for him. I prayed fervently that he was safe somewhere, hidden in a camp in the jungle or deep in the hills in Central Malaya. But I knew instinctively that wherever he was, what he was planning to do would surely put him in danger.

I was awoken from a fitful doze by the sound of a siren wailing. The other women had already informed me that in Changi everything was done to Tokyo time, which was two hours ahead of Singapore. It was still dark outside. Yawning and rubbing our eyes, we all hauled ourselves up and out of the cell, prodded on by guards holding batons and bayonets. We joined a crowd of other women and children shuffling down the corridor. The press of bodies moved slowly forward and eventually emerged into a huge open area several floors high with metal walkways lining each floor. Looking up, I noticed great nets stretched across between each walkway.

'That's to stop people throwing themselves off,' said Elsie, following my gaze. 'A couple of women couldn't take it during the first few weeks and jumped off the top floor balconies. Dreadful it was. But now people just use those nets to sleep on when there's no room on the floor or in the corridor.'

Breakfast consisted of a sticky concoction made of rice and water, supposed to be porridge. An attempt had been made to sweeten it, but I still found it hard to force down my throat despite the hunger that gnawed away at my stomach. It was followed by a slice of stale bread, with a slick of greasy margarine smeared on it, and a tin mug of plain black tea.

'You'll get used to it, my love,' said Elsie, spooning her own porridge down with gusto.

'You stop noticing it after a couple of days,' Doris offered, forcing a spoonful of the goo into her baby's mouth. 'But if you don't eat, you'll get sick. Simple as that.'

In the months that followed, I got to know Doris well. She was a planter's wife of about my own age. Doris's baby was a boy, only a few months old. She told me that her husband was in the male wing of the prison, in another block, and that she had only seen him a few times for an hour each time since they were first incarcerated in February. They had been able to pass notes to each other from time to time though, by bribing one of the guards. Doris kept those letters in the top pocket of her dress, pressed to her chest day and night. Sometimes, when the baby slept, she would take them out and read them, mouthing the words silently with a dreamy look in her eyes.

I noticed the way Doris's whole existence was focused on ensuring the comfort and survival of that tiny scrap of humanity. How she would go without food to make sure the baby ate, sleep on the very edge of the bed to ensure the baby could stretch out and sleep peacefully, how she would never let him out of her sight, not even for a moment. I realised that for Doris the baby was the only reason to carry on the struggle for survival day after day. Despite the hardships, unlike many of the others, Doris bore it with optimism.

But every time I looked at the baby, I could not stop myself from thinking about Baby Claire. It seemed an age since I had last held her in my arms. I couldn't help wondering how Rose was coping, wherever she was with the baby. Was she having to make sacrifices like Doris was? Was she hungry and dirty, lacking in creature comforts? I hoped with all my heart that Rose had made it to Australia, and that she and the baby were now safe and well, away from the Japanese and the war.

There were two children in the cell too. A boy of about eight and a girl of eleven, brother and sister. They were both pitifully thin and listless, their skin sallow and covered in insect bites. They seemed to have lost their zest for life, not wanting to play or even to talk. In the mornings they would go to a 'school' in another cell run by a prisoner who had been a schoolmistress.

Some of the women had jobs in the prison too: cleaning or cooking, sweeping the corridors and the courtyard, clearing the drains, tending the vegetable patch. They went off each morning, and those who remained would clean the cell as best they could and empty the latrine bucket in the overflowing communal latrines across the courtyard.

The days wore on in the same fashion. Three meals a day were taken in that great hall beneath the wire mesh. After meals we were allowed out into the courtyard to walk about in the shadow of the prison walls. I was glad of the fresh air after the foetid stench of the cells. I would stare up at the cloudless blue sky. It gave me some comfort to think that somewhere out there, the same blue sky sheltered Adam, and Rose, and Baby Claire.

20

After a few days, when the swelling on my face had started to subside and my bruises were a little less painful, I volunteered to join one of the work parties, working outside on garden duties. After breakfast, I went with a group of women to a large patch of ground outside the prison walls that had been cleared and planted out with vegetables. Someone handed me a hoe and told me to clear the weeds from an area that had been planted with potatoes.

I began to dig the heavy clay soil, realising that it was years since I had done any physical work. From the time I had stepped off the boat in Penang and had been chauffeured to Auntie Maude's house, there had been servants to do everything for me. On the plantation, the most I'd ever done was some light cooking and that was through my own choice. If I had wanted to go riding, the horse had been saddled for me by the groom. The car had been brought to the front door if I wanted to go out. My clothes had been washed and ironed by Surya and the house cleaned and tidied by the houseboys. At Rose's home on the airbase, it had been the same. Despite the bungalow being small, Rose and Robert had a houseboy, a cook and a gardener. I had been careful not to take advantage of them, but I had noticed how Rose had become very untidy and had got into the careless habit of dropping her clothes onto the floor of her bedroom in the knowledge that someone would always clear up after her.

After only a few minutes of activity, I was sweating profusely and all my aches and pains from the beatings were beginning to resurface. I straightened up and wiped a grubby hand across my forehead. I scanned my surroundings. The vegetable garden consisted of a square field bordered with a high barbed wire fence, with a sentry hut on stilts at one corner. There were guards standing inside the fence holding bayonets watching us women as we worked. There were guards inside the sentry hut too.

I noticed that beyond the perimeter fence on the southern side was another similar stretch of land, in the process of being cleared and planted, except, instead of women, men were working there under the supervision of more guards. I resumed my hoeing and as I did so, I watched the men out of the corner of my eye. They wore ragged khaki shorts or loin cloths. Many of them had no shirts and their bodies were burnt brown by the sun. They were all very thin, as thin as the women, but they were labouring with vigour and discipline. Whereas the women worked randomly and fitfully, either alone or in little groups, some barely making an impression on the soil, the men worked their vegetable strips in regimented lines, spaced evenly apart, moving up the field in parallel, slowly and methodically.

'Who are those men?' I asked Janet as we made our way back to the dining hall at lunchtime.

'They're soldiers. They're being kept in the Selarang Barracks next door to the prison. Sometimes work parties of them come into the prison to make deliveries, or sometimes they come to do repairs or building work in the prison. We're not allowed to talk to them, though.'

'I think my brother-in-law might be there. He was in the air-force,' I said, suddenly hopeful. 'Do you think I'd be able to make contact with him?'

Janet laughed bitterly. 'I can tell you're new here,' she said. 'Firstly, there are thousands of them in there. And secondly it's impossible to even speak to them, let alone make contact with a particular person.'

'Maybe I could try working near to the fence. I might be able to speak to them then.'

'You could try, but people have been caught at that game before and have been punished.' A chill went through me. I did not need to hear details of the punishments. I could imagine them well enough, but Janet went on, 'Some of them severely, too. Beatings, solitary confinement, starvation rations.'

I did not want to risk another beating. I did not know if I could withstand that either mentally or physically, but the knowledge that Robert could be close by was tantalising. It gave me renewed hope. If I could only make contact with him he might be able to give me some news about Rose and Baby Claire. I wondered how he was faring in captivity. He was tough and strong and well-trained, but judging by the state of the prisoners I had seen toiling on the vegetable patch, he could well be stick-thin and possibly sick by now. I began to worry about him, on top of all the other painful thoughts and memories that already plagued me. The thought that he could be so close by and that I might be able to make contact with him if I tried began to eat away at my mind.

The next morning as we started out in the direction of the vegetable garden, I asked Pat, who seemed to be in charge of the allocation of work, if I could work on the far side near the fence. Pat was tall and gaunt with straggly grey hair. She stared at me with sceptical eyes.

'I don't need to ask why,' she said raising her eyebrows. 'I'm sure you've got your reasons. Other girls have got into trouble with the Japs for talking to the prisoners, so be careful. If you're going to try to speak to them, make sure you aren't spotted, for God's sake.'

'Of course,' I said. 'Thank you.'

When we reached the field, I headed quickly towards the area near the far fence and began to hoe the weeds away just as I had done the day before, but as I worked I watched the soldiers through the lines of barbed wire. They were working further away this time, too far away for me to even contemplate trying to attract their attention. It would mean shouting, and that would be far too risky. Feeling thwarted, I bent back to my task, but each time I stood up and leaned on the hoe to catch my breath, I looked in the direction of the prisoners, straining my eyes to see if I could pick Robert out in the lines of men working away on the soil in the far corner. I went through them by a process of elimination, checking their hair colour, height and build. It took me all day, because there were dozens of them. By the end of the day, I knew that he was not there.

I repeated the process almost every day for a fortnight. Occasionally Pat would say to me, 'You've got to work somewhere different today. The Japs will get suspicious,' and I would dutifully trudge to an area under the sentry hut or near the prison walls. One morning after more than two weeks had passed, my heart began to beat faster when I entered the field and saw that the men were working close to the fence again. Pat shot me a warning glance, but then nodded for me to go and work in that area.

I watched the men discreetly as usual. They were moving closer to the fence, and after a time, one of the men was only a couple of yards away from me. He was so close that I could hear his breathing, steady and deep as he worked. I stopped working and glanced back at the guards. They were chatting to each other, not watching us women at all, but I could not see inside the sentry box. I decided to take a risk.

'Hello,' I hissed in a stage whisper. 'I'm Juliet Crosby. What's your name?' The man did not look up, nor did he stop digging.

'I can't talk to you,' he muttered. 'It's too dangerous. Don't draw attention to yourself.' He moved on, and I carried on working, disappointed. I tried the same thing with the next man who moved near to the fence, and the next, all with the same reaction. It was nearing lunchtime, and I was beginning to despair of talking to any of the men. I decided to give it one more try and hissed to the next man who came near to the fence: 'What's your name?'

The man did not stop working. He carried on digging vigorously, his eyes on his task. 'I'm Harry. Harry Baines. Northumberland Fusiliers.' He was small and wiry, burnt brown by the sun. He worked neatly and efficiently. Next to him worked a taller man, much younger. 'That's my mate, Ian.' I said hello, and Ian just nodded.

'Do you think you could help me?' I asked Harry. 'I'd like to try and find someone.'

'I could try. It wouldn't be easy.' Still he didn't look up.

'It's my brother-in-law. Robert Thompson. He's a captain in the RAF. I'm sure he is here somewhere.'

'There are some RAF men in the barracks, I'll ask around later. Not sure when I'll be back here, though. Try tomorrow, same time.'

'If you find him, could you please tell him that Juliet sends her love?'

'Will do. If I find him, that is. I have to move down the line now, lady.'

He moved on without even having glanced in my direction.

The next day Pat let me work next to the fence again, but there was no sign of either Harry or his friend. For three days it was the same, but on the fourth day he was back. I spotted him working in the middle of the field. I tried not to stare at him, but with every breath I took and every movement of the hoe I willed him to come closer. Eventually, towards lunchtime, the men began to pick up their tools and walk back toward their barracks. My heart sank, but then I felt hopeful again when I saw that Harry had detached himself from the group and was coming towards me. I glanced round at the guards, my heart thumping. How could he be so brazen?

Harry made a show of picking something up near the fence. 'I've asked around,' he said, speaking quickly. 'Someone did know an RAF captain of that name, but he's not here anymore. He's gone up north with a work party. Bound for Thailand they are, building some sort of railway for the Japs.'

Disappointment and fear flooded through me. What did that mean for Rob? Was it good news that he was out of here? I knew Harry was waiting for me to say something, but for a few seconds I had no words. Eventually, I whispered, 'Thank you for your trouble. You're very brave.'

'Don't mention it. Now I'd better go before the Japs are on to us. You'd better carry on with your work.'

With a heavy heart, I went back to my task, but I could barely find the energy to push the hoe through the soil, and a film of tears blurred my vision. Soon the other women were gathering by the gate to walk back to the prison for lunch, and I joined them, dragging my feet, my heart heavy.

Some of the women tried to entertain themselves by organising a choir accompanied by a small orchestra. A few had smuggled instruments in their luggage when they first came to the camp. I was not very musical, but Elsie persuaded me to join in, and I accepted, as an attempt to overcome my grief for Nazira, my longing for Adam and my disappointment about Rob. Under the supervision of one of the older women who had been a music teacher, we put together a medley of recent popular songs, and practised three times a week. Elsie was the soloist. The first time I heard her sing, goosebumps covered my arms. Her voice was strong and gravelly, like a jazz singer's. It reminded me of the bands I had watched playing at the Majestic in Harrow or at the Penang Club.

We put on a few concerts in the courtyard, with the permission of the guards. The rest of the internees were invited, including the men from the other wing. The occasions were a great success, greeted by clapping and cheering from the audience. Even the guards, standing at the back, dropped their usual stern expressions and applauded enthusiastically.

For the most part though, the days were bleak and tedious. I got so used to life at Changi that I even stopped longing for a decent meal or a comfortable bed after a while. Many of the women and children around me got sick with malaria, dengue fever or dysentery. They were taken off to the hospital wing where doctors, themselves prisoners, did their best to care for them with virtually no medicine or equipment. Many of those women died, and everyone who was well enough would troop to the cemetery on the edge of the camp where the padre would say a few words before the body was lowered into a grave. The loss of each of them further undermined my already fragile emotional state. I was not very close to any of the women there apart from Elsie, Pat and Doris, but I still felt a bond with all of them, which I knew came from sharing this dreadful experience. Because of that their deaths hit me harder than I thought possible.

After a few months, I, too, succumbed to a bout of malaria. I was carried by Elsie and some other women to the hospital wing and have a vague memory of living through those days in a state of delirium, of the doctors and nurses moving around me like ghosts. When I began to recover, it was as if I was waking from the most bizarre and longest dream I had ever had. I awoke to the realisation that I was still in prison, away from the people I loved, and that nothing would change that, even if I did manage to survive the illness.

As the months wore on I began to think that despite their warnings, the Japanese had forgotten about me, especially when rumours began to circulate in the camp that the tide of the war was turning. Some people had home-made radios carefully concealed in hiding places, and were able to listen to the BBC World Service. With that news the mood in the prison began to lift. Women would go about smiling, talking about what they would do when they were released.

'Not long now,' they would say to each other, out of earshot of the guards.

But one day, just when I had finally started to hope again, I was seized by two of the guards as I was walking out to work on the field. I noticed the terrified faces of the other women as the guards took me roughly by the arms and dragged me away.

'Chin up, girl!' shouted Pat as I was hauled off. 'Don't let 'em get to you.'

The two guards dragged me back to that bleak little room where I had been interrogated and beaten all those months ago. Nothing had changed. The officer sat there behind the desk as if he had never left, as stony-faced as before. 'Sit down, Mrs. Crosby,' he said, gesturing towards the chair as if I were an honoured guest. 'You look afraid.' The two guards pushed me down into the hard chair. I waited for them to bind my arms and legs, but they did not. The officer contemplated me, leaning back in his chair and putting his fingertips together as if in deep thought.

'No need to be afraid, Mrs. Crosby,' he said, leaning forward. 'I have news for you. News that interest you, from mainland Malaya. About men you know. The escape prisoners.' My heart lurched and missed a beat, but I stared straight back at him trying to keep my eyes from betraying any emotion.

'You look interested, Mrs. Crosby. You *did* know those men?' I frowned and shook my head vehemently.

'No, I did not. I've told you that.' What was this? Were they trying to trick me?

'You lie. I know. But no matter. No matter now. We find the men. We capture them.' He hesitated, and looked straight at me, waiting for a response. 'You know they went into jungle, don't you?' I did not respond. He came out from behind the desk and leaned over me, thrusting his face close to mine. 'They go to jungle, no? To camp in jungle.'

He carried on like that for half an hour or so, trying every subtle trick to get me to betray anything I might know about where the men had gone. 'I don't know. I don't know those men, and I don't know anything about them,' I kept repeating, doing my best to keep my voice steady.

His eyes never left my face; he was watching for any slip I might make. In the end, he went back behind the desk and sat down. Then he said, 'Mrs. Crosby, I have something else to tell you about those men.' He sat perfectly still, watching me, making sure he had my full attention. Then, with a malicious smile he said, 'We execute them. We kill those men.'

The words echoed around the bare walls of the tall room. I stared back at him. I could feel my body start to shiver, and an icy feeling starting in the pit of my stomach, moving upwards towards my heart. I swallowed hard and did my best to quell the feeling. I knew I must not faint now. 'I thought you should know. I know you interested,' he said smoothly, still watching me. 'You can go now.' The guards lifted me out of the chair and pushed me out of the room.

I could not believe what was happening. I didn't resist as they dragged me down the corridor and pushed me back into the cell. I stumbled across the floor and collapsed on to the bed.

I lay there and stared blankly at the concrete ceiling. For the first time I understood why those nets were suspended between the walkways, why some women had felt driven to put an end to their suffering, to climb over those railings, teeter on the edge, stare down at the dizzying view of the concrete floor below, and finally to let go.

21

'Juliet, my love, whatever's the matter?'

I heard the older woman's soothing voice, but it sounded a long way away. I opened my mouth but could not speak. I could do nothing except clench my fists and take a deep breath, then let that great roar that had been building up inside my lungs escape through my mouth. I turned over and lay there, sobbing into the dirty mattress. Elsie sat beside me, stroking my hair, trying to calm me.

'Tell me what's happened,' she asked, but I shook my head, unable to speak, unwilling to say the words. If I didn't say them perhaps it wouldn't be true. 'It might help to talk about it,' said Elsie.

Eventually I drew a deep breath and muttered, 'They've killed Adam.'

'Adam? Your friend? The one you met when you were in hiding?'

I nodded. Over the months, I had told Elsie snippets about the past, about how I had escaped with Nazira from the hospital, about the flat in Kampong Glam where I had hidden, and about Adam. 'It's not true,' said Elsie immediately.

'It must be. Why would they say so otherwise?'

'Two reasons. Either they were testing you. Thought you might crack and give something away, or maybe it was just out of spite. They know they're losing the war, and they'll have to let us all go one day. They probably want to inflict as much damage on us as they can while we're still here.'

The news about Adam affected me deeply. My hair, which had grown very long over the months in the camp, now began to fall out in great clumps. Even though I knew I should eat, I no longer had any appetite and at mealtimes passed most of my food to others. I grew thinner than ever. It hurt to sit down because my hips were just skin and bone now. I stopped going out to work on the vegetable patch; I had no energy for that any more. I just lay listlessly on one of the bunks all day staring up at the bare brick ceiling, thinking about Adam, about the precious moments we had shared and about what might have been.

A month or so later, we civilians were told to pack our belongings and to assemble in the courtyard. Rumours had been circulating in the prison that if the Japanese lost the war they would kill all their prisoners. Perhaps this was it? We were made to wait a long time, standing there in the stifling heat of the courtyard, shuffling nervously in the shadow of the great walls. Eventually the Japanese commandant climbed onto a box, stood in front of the crowd and addressed us: 'You all going to new quarters. Prison camp on Sime Road. Better place. Good conditions. Good food. You march there now.' With that the guards prodded us forward, and we moved slowly in straggly columns out though the towering gates of Changi Prison. Most of the others were retracing their steps back along the same road they had walked when they had first entered Changi, more than three years before. We were to walk to the city in the full heat of the noonday sun. I shuffled forward with everyone else. I was astonished that the villages and plantations dotted along beside the road were still there. They appeared just the same as before the war when

Rose and I had driven along this road on a leisurely day trip around the island. It was odd to see that normal life had continued outside the prison.

The months at the Sime Road camp passed in a kind of daze. The camp consisted of dozens of long wooden huts built on a hillside. The huts were dilapidated. They had tin roofs, most of which leaked. There were far too many prisoners for the available space and conditions were very cramped. We had to endure the extreme heat, the discomfort of sleeping on a wooden platform without bedding, and being bitten from head to toe by mosquitoes. The thing that struck me most about the camp was its colours; the endless, enervating greens and browns all around, the trees, vegetation and mud. Even my fellow inhabitants, listless and ragged after years of internment, seemed to take on a sepia tone.

Soon after we arrived, the monsoon broke. It rained constantly for days on end and the camp became a quagmire. Food was even less plentiful here than in Changi. The rice was full of maggots and weevils, and we had to resort to catching snails, mice and even snakes to supplement our diet. That mattered little to me though, for I still could not summon any appetite.

During the first month in the new camp, Elsie contracted malaria and was taken, delirious with fever, to the hospital hut. I spent my days nursing her, sitting beside her night and day, sponging her brow, feeding her food and water. I was suddenly terrified of losing this strong, caring woman who had helped me through my darkest days at Changi. But ironically it was Elsie's illness that gave me back the feeling that there might be some sort of purpose in my own life. I started to force myself to eat the unappetising rations, so I could stay alive to help my friend.

After several days Elsie did begin to recover, and the two of us started to spend time outside, between downpours, walking slowly around the camp, arm in arm, so that Elsie could regain her strength. During those walks Elsie became nostalgic for what she termed 'the old days', and began to reminisce about her life in Geylang before the war. She told me her story, of how she had come to Singapore in 1925 with a small jazz orchestra from the East End in London, touring the Far East.

'We'd been all over the place – Aidan, Delhi, Calcutta, Bombay, Colombo, Rangoon, before we got to Singapore. I wasn't too bad a singer in them days, didn't look too bad neither in me time. That was before I started to put on weight, of course, and before me heart was broken and my skin started to sag. We'd only done a couple of nights in Singapore when the band leader got knocked down by a bullock cart and had to go to hospital. Can you believe it! The band couldn't keep it together without him. They were always arguing and fighting. Heavy boozers most of 'em. Most of 'em disappeared off back to Blighty, but I didn't have enough money for the passage. I had to stay. Got myself a job in a bar, hostessing as they say.' She gave me a sideways look. 'Earned a good wage I did, what with tips and extras. In a couple of years I'd earned enough to rent me own place. It did well and after a while I bought it outright. I'm proud of that bar, means everything to me.'

'Who's looking after it while you're here?'

'I've got a little Chinese man, my manager. Good business head he's got on him. Practical type. He'll keep the place running as best he can. Lives behind the bar he does, so he can keep an eye on the place. I've got a little flat upstairs. Can't wait to get back there. It's what keeps me going in this god-forsaken place. That, and friends like you of course.'

There was another camp adjoining the women's camp. The two areas were separated by a high-barbed wire fence. Each day as we walked along the boundary, we noticed new occupants arriving in the other camp. They were all men, soldiers, but they were like no soldiers I had ever seen before. These men were like walking skeletons. Virtually none of them had any clothes, and wore only loin cloths, and most of them went about barefoot. They were all burnt dark brown from the sun. None of them ever ventured near the fence. They seemed to be fully occupied repairing their huts or digging a new vegetable patch. I was intrigued by these newcomers, wondered where they had come from and why they were so emaciated.

Gradually rumours began to trickle around that these were the remnants of the British Army who had been working in Thailand and Burma, building a railway through the jungle to supply the Japanese army. I overheard some women talking about them in hushed tones in the queue for food. 'Why are they so thin?' one of them asked.

'They've been treated like slaves according to the one we spoke to,' answered another. 'Beaten and starved, forced to do hard labour. Thousands of them died. Of starvation, cholera, malaria.'

Would Robert have survived such an ordeal? Perhaps he was right here in the next door camp.

The next day after breakfast, I went to the camp perimeter and looked through the fence. Two men were repairing the roof of the hut nearest the end. There did not seem to be the same rules against speaking to the prisoners in this camp as there had been in Changi, so I called out to them, 'Excuse me. Please could I ask you something?'

One of the men stopped working and approached the fence. His arms and legs were stick thin, the bend of his bones visible through his leathery skin. His eyes stood out from hollow cheeks and I could have counted his ribs. My instinct was to look away in embarrassment, but I resisted that urge and kept my eyes on his face as if nothing was wrong. 'I'm just wondering if you men are British?'

He smiled, revealing gaps in his blackened teeth. 'Of course. We're from the Royal Norfolks.'

'Someone said you've been building a railway in Thailand. Is that right?'

He nodded, and his smile faded. 'I'm afraid that's right, lady.'

'I think my brother-in-law was there. Might you have news of him?'

The man laughed, but not unkindly. 'I doubt it. There was a hell of a lot of us there. The camps were all spread out up the line for miles. If he was in our camp I might have known him, though. What was his name?'

'Captain Robert Thompson. He was in the RAF.'

The man shook his head. 'Sorry, there were no RAF men in our camp. Not sure where they ended up. I'll ask me mates. Come back here tomorrow evening. If I've found anything out I'll let you know then.'

I waited nervously by the fence after the evening meal the following day. My heart lifted when the man approached. I had spent all day worrying that he wouldn't come, but he had kept his word. 'There aren't no RAF here,' he said. 'Most of them were taken to River Valley Road camp and they're being shipped out from there.'

'Shipped out?'

'Yes. Taken to other parts of the Jap Empire. Japan, Formosa. Not sure why. Probably to be used as slave labour again most likely.'

My heart sank again, but by now I had become used to not knowing. And at least this knowledge gave me a flicker of hope that Robert could still be alive somewhere.

The final months in the camp were harder than ever. Food supplies dwindled further, and the Japanese guards became nervy and unpredictable. If any of the prisoners stepped out of line they were slapped or beaten. The guards would often spend hours drinking cheap whisky in the guardhouse, becoming noisier and more belligerent as the day wore on. Then they would stagger down the steps of the guardhouse and rampage through the camp, pushing prisoners, slapping them and shouting at them, 'You all die. We kill you all'.

Then, for several days, air raids rocked the city. I stood and watched with the other internees in stunned amazement, as planes bearing the stars and stripes screamed low over the city. We listened to the crash and boom of explosions, some so close that the ground in the camp shuddered with the force. We knew the end had finally come when one morning we awoke to the sight of a group of strange soldiers at the camp gate. These men walked through the camp with the Japanese commandant. Their uniforms looked clean and new, their faces so pink and clean and fleshy-looking. It was as if I had never seen anyone look as healthy as these men before. But the soldiers did not stop to talk to any of us. They visited the camp hospital, had a cursory look around the camp and then left.

The next morning we awoke again to the sound of aircraft flying over the city. We ran out of our huts just as a group of planes flew right over the camp. As the planes flew over they released dark objects that rained down on the camp and landed in the spaces between the huts. We ran for cover at first, thinking that these were bombs, that the Japanese were carrying out their threat to eliminate all the prisoners. But when we eventually examined the objects, we realised that they were enormous food parcels. Eagerly we tore them open, marvelling at the contents.

Elsie and I shared a small tin of peaches. We had to bash the tin on a stone to break it open and then we sat there, enjoying the succulent texture and sweet taste of the fruits bursting on our tongues. But afterwards our stomachs rebelled against the unfamiliar richness, and like many others we had to lie down until the pains and nausea eventually passed.

The parcels had been dropped along with thousands of pieces of paper that fluttered around the camp, lodging in the trees and bushes, sticking to the roofs of the huts. I read one out loud to Elsie: 'Although peace was declared on August 15, the

British Army advises all internees to remain in the camp until the administration is fully re-established in Singapore. The situation in Singapore is not stable at present, and the streets are not safe, particularly at night. A curfew is in place from sundown to sunrise. Japanese Soldiers will parade the perimeter of the camp for your protection.'

'Well, I'm not staying,' said Elsie, her old spark returning. 'I need to get back home, see whether me bar's still standing. What about you?'

'I haven't really got anywhere to go. There's only the flat in Kampong Glam, and that's not my home.' I thought about the plantation, and realised that staying here in the prison camp was preferable to going back. I could not bear the thought of seeing either Gavin or Scott. Even after all these years and everything that had happened to me here.

'Why don't you come along with me then?' Elsie was saying. 'You're welcome to stay at my place until you get yourself sorted out.'

'But if the streets aren't safe ...'

'Nonsense girl,' chided Elsie. 'Where's your spirit? I'm not going to stay in this filthy place a moment longer than I've got to. They only say we're *advised* to stay in the camp. That doesn't mean we have to stay.'

'You're quite right,' I said, smiling warmly at her. I was glad that the old feisty Elsie had emerged again. For months after her bout of malaria she had been a fragile shell, shaken and wasted by the illness.

'Let's get our stuff then.'

I bundled my few ragged belongings back into the threadbare pillowcase that I had brought from Nazira's flat. Elsie packed herself a battered leather suitcase. We said our farewells to the other women in our hut and set off towards the gate.

'You no go!' said the Japanese sentry on duty, and stood in

front of us trying to bar our way. But now he had no weapons to threaten us with.

'We're free to go wherever we like,' Elsie said to him, looking him in the eye defiantly. 'You've got no right to stop us.'

He stepped back. 'It not safe,' he said. 'Lot of fighting.'

'We'll manage. No need to worry about us,' said Elsie pushing past him, and I followed her.

We were soon out through the gate and stood staring down the length of Sime Road, that steamy morning in August 1945, free for the first time in over three years. I had no wish to look back at the camp, but the sight of that straight tree-lined road stretching out in front of us filled me with a different type of uneasiness, with the fear of the unknown.

22

In the morning, Juliet and Mary took breakfast together in the small café on the ground floor of the little guest house. The other guests were all backpackers, barefoot and unwashed, poring over tourist maps and guidebooks as they trowelled their breakfast. Mary appeared subdued. She ate her food slowly, staring down at her plate.

'Are you alright, Mary? You look pale,' said Juliet at last.

Mary looked up. 'I was going to say the same about you. You look washed out, too. To tell you the truth, I didn't sleep very well.'

'Me neither,' said Juliet. 'The road was quite noisy, wasn't it? It didn't seem to quieten down all night.'

She wasn't going to reveal that she had spent a turbulent night, reliving the horrors and hardships of her wartime internment. Mary stared down at her porridge. 'It wasn't the noise,' she sighed at last. 'I was thinking about today. Wondering whether we will find anything at the orphanage. I've waited so long for this.'

Juliet felt a twinge of guilt that she herself had not felt able to be so honest. She reached over the table and squeezed Mary's hand. 'Don't worry about it, Mary. Let's go there straightaway. Get it over and done with, shall we?'

Mary nodded, brightening a little. When they had finished their food, they went out onto the busy street and hailed a taxi.

Sister Theresa greeted them warmly on the steps of the orphanage. 'Good morning! Let me take you to meet Kezia, the intern I mentioned yesterday. She is working in the office.' They entered the cool of the building. The place was quiet this morning.

'The children are all in lessons or in nursery at the moment,' Sister Theresa explained, leading them down the long corridor again. At the end she opened the door to an office filled with filing cabinets and shelves of box-files. Behind a desk covered in folders and papers sat a serious-looking young woman in a white veil and heavy glasses. She rose to greet them.

'Sister Theresa told me you were coming. She asked me to look for your records,' she said to Mary. 'It has been an incredible task to archive the old records here. And it's not over yet. In the past, to save space, only the most basic information on the children was kept up here in the main office. The rest was stored in the basement. It had all been locked away for years when I arrived. Some of it had been eaten by mice or mildewed beyond repair. Your file has just about survived though. I dug it out this morning, but it is a bit moth eaten at the corners, and some of the pages are mouldy.'

She selected a buff-coloured folder from the top of the pile and handed it to Mary. Juliet watched Mary's face, as she took the file and stared down at it intently, holding it at arms' length as if it were an unexploded bomb.

'Would you like some time alone?' Kezia asked getting up from the desk. 'I've got some work to do down in the basement. I'll give you half an hour or so.'

Mary sat down at the desk and put the file down in front of her. She stared at it for a while, then she reached out a trembling hand and opened the front cover. She sat there, head bowed over the desk, turning the pages, peering at each one and reading carefully. Juliet came round and stood behind Mary, reading over her shoulder. There were the girl's early school reports, her medical records, records of dental appointments. At the very end, tucked behind the rest, was a single sheet marked 'Admissions Record'.

Similar information was written along the top of the page as was recorded on the certificate that Mary had shown Juliet that first time she had come to Windy Ridge: 'September 1942. Admission of baby girl of approximately ten months old.' But underneath that was a note, written in flowing handwriting, signed 'Sister Xavier, September 10, 1942.' The ink was now faded and pale.

'This baby girl was brought here today from Bamboo Island by an Indonesian man named Darma Tan, a missionary based on the Island who had made the journey to Palembang to buy supplies for his Christian mission. She is believed to be a European child, probably British. She was taken to the mission by some villagers from Desa Kelapa on the north coast of the island. They had tried to care for her, but food was scarce because of the Occupation. According to the villagers she had survived the sinking of the *Rajah of Sarawak*, but they seemed afraid to give details or even to speak about it. The baby was found wearing a small amulet that appears to be of little value and which was brought with her. Mr. Tan had given her the name "Mary" and an Indonesian name "Batari". Her real name is not known.'

Mary looked up at Juliet, smiling, tears in her eyes. 'So it's true then. Proof of who I am and where I came from.'

Juliet could not answer. She stared at the paper, unable to take in what was written there. She read the words again and again, until they danced before her eyes, merged together in a blur. 'But it doesn't tell us much more than we already knew, Mary,' she began gently. 'It isn't really solid proof, is it? The amulet could have come from someone else. You could be someone else's baby altogether.'

Mary stared at her, and her smile faded. Juliet could see that she was getting angry.

'Are you serious?' Mary said, raising her voice. 'This is as much as we're ever going to get. Why won't you see the truth? Why don't you want to believe it?'

Juliet was silent, trying to understand her own feelings. Ever since Mary had appeared on her front drive, Juliet had been avoiding confronting the truth behind what the certificate from the orphanage had said. At first she had not wanted to believe it, afraid of Mary's motives. But once she had got to know Mary and even to become fond of her, she had not wanted to think about those words for another reason, for fear that her hopes would be dashed. That there had been some mistake and that this young woman whom she had begun to think of as her only family in the world was no more than a stranger. That the baby she had last seen in Rose's arms in the hospital that morning in February 1942 had perished with Rose on that remote beach after all.

'I'm afraid, I suppose, Mary,' she confessed.

'Afraid of what, for goodness' sake?' Mary's voice was loud, impatient.

'Oh, Mary,' she began, 'I want to believe it so much that I'm terrified of finding out that it might not be true. Don't you see? I want to be sure that there's no room for doubt. To eliminate any possibility of that.'

'But there isn't any room for doubt anymore,' said Mary, her voice pleading. 'It's written here,' her finger stabbed at the page on the file. 'I just don't understand you.'

'Look, why don't we just go there? To Bamboo island? We were planning to go anyway. We know the name of the village now. We could go there and see if anyone remembers.'

'No-one will remember. Why would they? It's twenty years ago,' said Mary. She looked disconsolate now, her anger dissipated. 'Look, let's not bother. Let's just forget it. You're never going to believe it's true whatever proof we find. You've set your mind against it. I don't even think you want it to be true.'

Juliet bit her lip. 'Of course I want it to be true. I just need to be sure that's all. I need to be absolutely sure.'

'But why? It's enough for me. Why can't it be enough for you?'

'Because ... Because there can't be any room for doubt. I can't explain why exactly.' Juliet saw the anguish on Mary's face and her heart turned over with sympathy for the girl. They stared at each other for a long time, then Juliet became aware of someone standing in the doorway.

'Are you finished?' asked Kezia. She looked flustered. Juliet wondered how much of the conversation she had overheard.

'Of course, of course,' said Juliet quickly. 'We mustn't take up any more of your time. Thank you very much for all your help.'

'Did you find what you were looking for?'

'Yes,' said Mary, firmly, standing up. 'We did. Thank you very much. Can we take the file with us?'

'I hope you don't mind, but Mother Superior wants us to keep all the originals at the orphanage. I've made copies for you to take.' She rummaged in a drawer and handed Mary another cleaner folder.

Juliet and Mary retraced their steps to the front entrance, said their goodbyes to Sister Theresa and Kezia and went out onto the road to hail a taxi.

All the way back to the hotel, Mary stared out of the taxi window, her face turned obstinately away from Juliet. The girl's silence unnerved Juliet, increased the guilt she felt at not being able to accept the words in the file at face value.

Back at the hotel, Mary rushed straight in and up to her room, slamming the door behind her, without looking at Juliet and without saying a word. Juliet followed her up the stairs, but remained standing on the landing, staring at Mary's door. It tore her heart to see Mary unhappy. She bitterly regretted the fact that she had not been able to tell Mary everything about the past. Should she try to explain to Mary the real reasons why she needed to have absolute proof?

She stepped forward and knocked on Mary's door. There was no answer so she tried again.

'What do you want?' Mary's voice sounded sulky.

'Can we talk? There's something I need to explain.'

'Not now. I'm going to have a shower.'

'Please, Mary. It might help you to understand.'

'Look, I'm going out soon. We can talk later.'

'Out? Where are you going?'

'I'm going to see Zaq, as a matter of fact. I promised that I'd look him up if I came back to Palembang.'

'What time will you be back?'

'I'm not sure. Evening sometime.'

'Shall I go down to the boat quay and book the tickets while you're out?'

'Tickets?'

'To Bamboo Island. We might as well go now we're here.'

There was a long pause and then came a grudging reply, 'I'm not really that bothered. You can book them if you like.'

'Alright. I'll do that then. Shall we go there tomorrow?'

'Fine. Whatever you want.'

'I'll see you later then. Have a nice time.'

Juliet went into her room, feeling helpless, and sat on the bed. She listened to the shower running in Mary's bathroom, and after a few minutes she heard the sound of her door slamming and her footsteps running down the concrete steps. A feeling of loneliness swept over her, something she had not experienced in years.

Later she took a rickshaw down to the boat quay, queued up at a kiosk and bought tickets for the ferry to Bamboo Island. She decided to walk back to the guesthouse to kill time. She enjoyed the noise and distractions of the streets, the throng of rickshaws and mopeds, the ever-moving crowds of people, the street markets overflowing with fresh produce, and the delicious smells of spicy cooking. It made her forget, for a moment, Mary's mood and her own dilemma. She stopped at a street stall for some fried rice, enjoying eating on the street at a plastic table, watching the people go about their business. Then slowly she made her way back to the hotel, sweating from the heat, her senses overloaded with the sights and sounds of the city. Lying down on the bed under the fluttering ceiling fan, she closed her eyes and allowed herself to slip gradually out of consciousness.

WE SET OFF SLOWLY, unused to walking long distances, both weakened by years of hunger and ill- health. At the end of Sime Road, we turned into Adam Road and as we walked through the streets, we saw that the devastation of the bombing raids of 1942 had been left unchanged. If anything the streets looked even more rundown now, after three-and-a-half years of oppressive rule. Little had been repaired, bombed out buildings still crumbled into the streets, vegetation had sprung up on the heaps of rubble, gardens were overgrown and unkempt. But people seemed to be going about more freely now, not cowed and afraid as they had done before. I even noticed a few Union Jacks flying from roofs and telegraph poles.

It was several miles from Sime Road to Geylang. There were few rickshaw pullers about, but those we tried to flag down ran past us after a quick glance at our dishevelled appearance. Eventually one stopped, but on finding out we had no money, he set off shaking his head.

We walked on, trying to flag down passing taxis and even private vehicles, but no-one would stop. We had to make frequent stops to rest and catch our breath and gather strength. The sun beat down mercilessly and the air was steamy and unbearably hot. At last an army truck rounded a bend in Thompson Road and ground to a halt beside us. An officer jumped down from the cab. 'Are you two ladies alright? Can we take you anywhere? We're taking some supplies to POWs in Changi.'

'We've just come out of Sime Road camp. We need to go to Geylang.'

'We could make a bit of a diversion for you. You look all in. Come on, jump up on the back.'

We clambered onto the back of the lorry and sat on the bench next to a couple of soldiers. Like the soldiers who had come into the camp a few days before we had left, these men seemed to exude health and vitality. I felt self-conscious being in such close proximity to these men and kept my eyes on the floor of the lorry as it bumped and rattled along. I tried not to think about the last time I had ridden on the back of an army truck, making that dreadful journey from Kampong Glam to Changi.

The truck dropped us at the end of Elsie's road. The captain jumped down from the cab again to help us down. 'If you two ladies should find yourselves stuck for somewhere to stay, Raffles is the place. They've set up a dormitory there for people in transit from the camps or whose homes have been bombed.'

'I can't afford that place,' said Elsie, laughing.

'I think you'll find it's a bit changed from the old days. And I don't think it would cost you much, if anything. It's become a reception centre. It's just a thought.'

We stood on the pavement holding our meagre little bundles and watching the truck disappear down the road. 'Here goes then,' said Elsie, sighing apprehensively. We made our way slowly along the street, past former bars and shop-houses, many of which were shuttered or derelict. From one or two came the sound of hammering and sawing, and glancing inside we caught sight of coolies at work, rebuilding or restoring the buildings.

Halfway along Elsie stopped outside a shuttered building. 'This is my place,' she said, going up a couple of marble steps and pushing open an unlocked saloon-style door.

23

The shutters were down, and when we first stepped inside we could not see much. But as our eyes adjusted to the gloom, it became clear that the place had been ransacked. The floor was a mass of smashed glass. Broken chairs and upturned tables were strewn about, and the bar itself had been smashed and splintered. Elsie let out a cry and dropped her suitcase.

The front door opened slowly and a Chinese woman appeared in the doorway. She was petite and exquisitely beautiful. Her hair was done up in an old-fashioned bun and secured with knitting needles. Her face was white with powder and her lips painted bright red. She wore a tight-fitting red silk dress embroidered with silver butterflies.

'Tina!' cried Elsie going to her and throwing her arms around her.

'I'm so sorry, Elsie. Japanese soldiers did this.'

'Where's Chun Lao?'

The woman's smile vanished and she looked down at the floor. 'They took him away in a lorry during the *Sook Ching*. No-one has seen him since. We think he might be in prison some-where, or maybe worse.'

'But why? He wasn't political. He was just a barman.'

'I'm not sure. They made lots of mistakes. No-one knows ... I'm so sorry.'

Elsie sat down heavily on a low coffee table, the only upright thing in the room. She put her face in her hands and began to cry quietly, sobs shaking her body. I looked at the Chinese woman, who held out her hand. 'I'm Tina. I run the massage parlour next door. Elsie and I were friends before the war.'

'I'm Juliet. Elsie and I were in the camp together. She helped me so much.'

'She's a wonderful person, I'm so sorry this has happened to her.'

My heart went out to my friend. I went over and put my arms around her. 'We could clear this up,' I said. 'I could help you.'

'Why don't you both come into my place for something to eat?' asked Tina. 'Then we can decide what to do. I'll go and ask the boy to prepare something now. Come on in when you're ready.'

'Poor, poor Chun Lao,' said Elsie shaking her head. 'I just can't believe it. He never did any harm to anyone.'

'It's dreadful Elsie,' I said, feeling helpless.

'This was my life, this place,' she said, giving a great sniff, trying to control herself. 'You should 'ave seen it on a Saturday nights. Buzzing it was. Full of soldiers, sailors, businessmen. I used to hire a little jazz band and they would play in that corner.'

'I'm so sorry,' I repeated.

'You know this was what kept me going in there. The thought of coming back here and getting this place up-together again. It's just so cruel.' She cried for a few minutes more. Eventually she dried her eyes and heaved herself up. 'I suppose tears ain't going to solve anything. Let's go and have that meal.'

We left the shattered room and went next door. Tina showed us through some red velvet curtains on the ground floor into a lounge, with a red deep-pile carpet, button-back velvet chairs, and elaborate lace curtains festooning the windows. As we entered I caught sight of a young girl in black underwear and stockings dash up the stairs. The place reeked of heady perfume. I could sense immediately that it functioned as a brothel.

'Come through, come through,' motioned Tina, smiling, ushering us into a back kitchen where a young boy was frying chicken on a wok over a gas stove. 'I bet you two ladies are hungry,' said Tina. 'Here, sit down. Drink some tea, please.'

I shall always remember that meal we had at the bamboo table in that tiny kitchen behind that Chinese brothel, which smelled of sandalwood smoke and exotic spices. The meal was served on simple blue and white china. It was fried rice with chicken, and we ate with chopsticks from china bowls. Green tea was served in tiny cups.

'I'm so sorry,' said Tina, looking at us anxiously, 'We have rationing. Not much food.'

'It's absolutely delicious,' I said, and I meant it. I ate as slowly as I could, trying to prevent myself from bolting my portion down in seconds. It was as if I had never tasted such powerful flavours in my life before. The tangy taste of fresh garlic and onion burst onto my tongue, and the chicken was succulent and flavoursome. There were no weevils or maggots or little stones in our rice to contend with.

Tina did not ask us about the camp, and we were only too pleased not to have to speak about it. Over the meal Tina told us about how there had been rioting on the streets since the Japanese surrender, how the Chinese population of Singapore had rebelled against the Indians for siding with the Japanese.

'They are very angry because many Indians went over to the Japanese army. They helped them punish and kill many Chinese people during the *Sook Ching*. You know thousands of our people were massacred. We cannot forgive the Indians for helping with that. But we are angry with the British, too. The British just let them walk free.'

'What a dreadful situation,' I said, trying to find some words of comfort for Tina.

'We didn't see any trouble when we were coming here,' said Elsie.

'It is usually alright during the daytime. It starts up in the evening after dark. There has been a curfew these past few days. Very bad for business.' Tina shook her head gravely.

At the end of the meal Tina put down her chopsticks. She opened her mouth to say something, then hesitated. Finally she looked down at the table, avoiding our eyes and said, 'I would like to invite you both to stay here, but I'm afraid there is only one free bed. I can only ask one of you to be my guest.'

'Well, Elsie must stay of course,' I said immediately.

'But what would you do?' asked Elsie. 'I'm sure we could manage if you stayed. I could sleep on the floor,'

'No. I could go down to Raffles. You know, the soldier mentioned it. I don't mind in the slightest.'

'If you're sure. But you mustn't walk there,' said Tina, looking anxious. 'As I said before, it is not safe on the streets. It is a long way, and it will start to get dark before you can get there. I will ask my boy to take you.'

I accepted Tina's offer with gratitude. 'I will come back tomorrow. I can help you clear the bar up,' I said.

'There will be no need for that,' said Tina firmly. 'My girls can sweep the place, and my boy can mend the broken furniture. We would have done it before, but the Japanese often patrolled this street and we were afraid to go there in case they punished us or took us away. But they have no power to hurt us now, thank goodness.'

'Of course I will come back tomorrow. And if you do need help, I'm willing to lend a hand.'

Tina looked at me, smiling. 'You look as though you need to build yourself up a little before you start working.'

An hour or so later I found myself perching precariously behind a Chinese boy on the pillion seat of an old motorbike, clutching his wiry body with both hands. We wound our way through the streets towards Beach Road, past bomb sites, around piles of rubble, darting through traffic jams of cars, rickshaws and carts. The streets were busy; everyone was trying to get to where they were heading before the curfew at nightfall. The boy rode quickly, and rather dangerously, but I couldn't help feeling exhilarated at the unaccustomed feeling of speed and at the sensation of the wind rushing through my hair.

When we finally stopped on the circular drive of Raffles Hotel, I got off the back of the bike carefully, my face flushed and my hair a frizzy tangle. I was amazed that we had actually arrived without having had an accident, but I thanked the boy and made my way towards the hotel entrance. I felt apprehensive walking past the uniformed doorman, acutely aware of my untidy hair and ragged cotton dress, which Doris had donated to me when I had arrived in the camp. I thought about the last time I had been to Raffles hotel in 1941, to attend a ball, when I had been staying with Rose and Rob. The whole place had looked magnificent that evening, floodlit and shimmering with fairy lights. I remembered a procession of cars drawing up on the circular drive, disgorging passengers in evening dress and being driven away by uniformed staff. But those days were gone, for now at least.

As I walked up the front steps, I saw that the chandeliers had been taken down, the floor tiles were scuffed and the paint faded and chipped. There were no glamorous people at the hotel today, just others who were poorly dressed, and wandering about looking pale, thin and a little lost. I asked the man at reception about the dormitory accommodation.

'You are welcome to stay, madam. British Government is paying the bill. Meals are provided in old ballroom. No need for cash unless you eat in veranda or restaurant.' He pushed a form and a pencil across the desk to me and asked that I complete it.

'Resettlement form,' he explained. The form asked a lot of details about dates of internment and close family. I completed it all. I hesitated over the question about my 'next of kin' before putting down Gavin's name. I assumed that his life had not changed since I had left, that he was still on the plantation, working long hours and amusing himself with the woman in the village just as before. I also wrote down all the details I could about Rose and Robert and Baby Claire. I found my stomach knotting up and my hand shaking as I did so. Would filling out this form mean that we would soon be reunited? I stifled the thought, not even daring to hope.

The man at the desk took the form back and explained that officials would try to match my details with details on all the other completed forms. He then directed me to the stairs. 'Dormitory on third floor, madam. Only camp beds there, I'm afraid.'

'A camp bed sounds just perfect, thank you,' I said with a smile, thinking of the countless nights I had spent on a hard concrete floor or wooden platform in the camps. As I turned towards the stairs, a familiar voice called out from across the lobby.

'Juliet! How wonderful to see you. I have been wondering where you were for years.' I turned to see Beatrice bearing down upon me.

I was shocked by the change in my old friend. No longer stout, she was now skin and bone, her face deeply lined. She, too, looked pale. We embraced and held each other for a long time. Then Beatrice held me at arms' length and peered at my face. 'So what happened to you? I got your letter saying that you had gone to stay with your sister. Why did you run off like that and not come back?'

'It's such a long story, Beatrice. I'll tell you later, of course, but I need to get my bearings first. I've only just come out of Sime Road prison camp. What about you? Where have you been?'

'I've been interned in a jungle camp somewhere in the hills up-country. I arrived here a few days ago. My poor Henry didn't make it.'

'Oh Beatrice, I'm so sorry.'

Tears glistened in Beatrice's eyes then one rolled down each cheek. 'I know. It's rotten luck,' she said, wiping the tears away with her hand. 'He'd been ill for a long time. He couldn't take the conditions, you see, and the dreadfully poor diet. It was diphtheria that took him in the end. I'm quite lost without him,' she said, trying to force a smile. 'Come – let's go to the veranda and get a cup of tea. We can have a long chat and catch up.'

'I don't have any money, Beatrice, I'm afraid.'

'Don't worry. Most of us here are in the same position. They don't tell you on the desk, but the management are quite happy to run tabs until people have sorted themselves out.' I felt Beatrice's firm hand on my elbow, propelling me forward.

'I was very sorry to hear about Gavin, by the way,' Beatrice was saying. 'Never saw eye to eye with the man, but no-one could wish that fate on anybody.'

I felt the colour drain from my cheeks and my knees go weak. 'Gavin? Why, what has happened to him?'

'Oh my dear, didn't you know? I assumed that ... How silly of me. How could you have known? I'm so sorry. How insensitive of me. Come on, let's get you to a chair.' I walked in a daze through to the veranda. Once we were seated at a table, Beatrice said, 'He was shot, I'm afraid. Shot dead by the Japs. I'm so sorry, Juliet.'

I stared at the table, nausea rising in my throat, and clutched at the edge of the table to keep myself steady. The room began to revolve around me. I focused on the table top, willing myself not to faint.

'Deep breaths, dear,' said Beatrice. 'Waiter? Could we have some water here please?'

'Why? Why did they shoot him?'

'Well, you know he had that bee in his bonnet about staying on the estate? Nothing could shake him from that.'

I nodded, remembering his insistence on staying back. 'It was why he wouldn't join the Volunteers.'

'Well, the Japs decided that they wanted the place for themselves. It was the house they wanted most of all, to have their officers stay in and use as a sort of regional headquarters. When they turned up and told him to pack ready to go to an internment camp, he refused. Things got nasty. Rumour has it that he threatened them with his shotgun. They shot him on the front drive. I'm so sorry, Juliet.'

On the long walk from Sime Road, before I had been picked up by the army truck, I had started to mull over what to do with my freedom. I had decided then that I could never go back to Gavin. I had also decided that I would try to find out if it was true that Adam had been killed, and if it was, I would go back to England. But this shocking news threw me into a fresh turmoil. 'I can't believe it. How did you find out?'

'Bush telegraph, my dear. News travels fast in the East, especially at times like these. The servants and the rubber tappers all around the district knew what had happened. It filtered through to us before the Japs came to get us. We were ready for them, and we didn't even try to resist. They took our house, too, you know. Bundled me and poor old Henry into a lorry and off to that beastly camp.'

The waiter brought a pot of English Breakfast tea. I watched Beatrice pour it into the porcelain cups and for the second time that day I was stunned by the delicious flavour of a drink I used to find commonplace. I sipped in silence for a while. I was glad that it was Beatrice who had broken the news to me of Gavin's death. With Beatrice I knew that I could be absolutely honest, and I did not have to act, or pretend to have feelings I did not possess.

'And what about Scott?' I asked Beatrice. I could hardly bear to say his name.

'Nobody knows. The last anyone heard of him, he was sent to build that railway in Thailand. Many men died there.'

For a fleeting moment I found myself hoping that Scott would not come back. Was it wrong to hope that he didn't?

I looked around at the other people sitting at the tables in the veranda. British families mainly, still looking shell-shocked. They all looked as though they had suffered some sort of hardship or heartbreak. Some looked as though they were anxiously waiting for news. This dreadful war had changed the lives of everyone in the colony, not just my own. No-one had escaped unscathed.

'What are you going to do now it's all over, Beatrice?' I said, turning to my friend.

'I'm planning on going back to England. That's why I'm here in Singapore, waiting for a passage. I never thought I would leave this country, but everything's changed for me now. Without Henry, there doesn't seem any point in staying ...'

'But what about your house? Your dogs and horses?'

'The house belongs to the mining company, Juliet. They will waste no time installing a new manager now the war is over. There won't be anywhere for me to live. We had the dogs destroyed when we were sure the Japs were coming to take us away, and the horses died during the war. So, you see, there really is nothing for me here anymore. My sister lives in Brighton. She's a widow, too, so we'll be good company for each other.'

'I thought I might head back to England, too,' I said after a pause.

Beatrice squeezed my arm. 'You don't need to think about it now, my dear. You've just had a dreadful shock. You must give it time to sink in before you make any decisions.'

I stared out over the tops of the palm trees lining Beach Road, many of them with their tops dangling down, damaged in the bombing raids. Even they had not escaped the effects of the war. My mind felt empty. I had no idea where I was going or what I was doing next. Beatrice was right. I needed time to think.

24

———

Juliet showered and dressed quickly, then went out onto the hallway to knock on Mary's door. There was no response. She put her ear to the door, but all was quiet inside. She tried to turn the handle but the door was firmly locked. As she went downstairs she began to worry. What had happened to the girl? Where had she gone last night anyway? Juliet berated herself for not having insisted on having Mary leave an address, but things had been so awkward and strained between them that the girl probably would have refused to tell her anyway.

She went down to breakfast in the little café overlooking the busy street. She sat down at a simple plastic table. The waiter shuffled over with porridge and coffee. He looked as tired as she felt, moving about slowly with bags under his eyes. Juliet tried to force down some porridge but found she had no appetite. It had become unfamiliar to her to feel anxiety for another human being. The person she was closest to now was Abdul, she supposed. She was fond of him and felt protective towards him, worrying about his occasional illnesses and about the way his face sometimes tensed up with pain from his rheumatic joints.

She often told him to leave the physical tasks to her or to others, knowing that he could no longer do the things he had done as a young man. But she knew that however close they were, their relationship was ultimately one of servant and employer, rooted deep in the past, in the customs and hierarchies of a long-gone empire.

Her concern for Mary was different; it was troubling and immediate. She found it hard to concentrate on her food or even to sit still. She kept looking up and craning her neck to see if she could glimpse Mary on the pavement, making her way towards the hotel. Perhaps she had gone over to the bazaar again to search for outlandish clothes? But there was no sign of her amongst the people coming and going between the stalls. Juliet glanced at her watch. It was only a couple of hours until the boat was due to depart and they would need to leave in enough time to get down to the quay. Perhaps Mary had decided that she didn't want to go to Bamboo Island after all.

Juliet wondered what to do. Should she tell the police? She felt vulnerable and unsure of herself in this huge, alien city. But she had to do something. She could not bear this feeling of not knowing. She thought about it for a long time, and had more or less decided to go to the desk and ask the receptionist to telephone the local police when she glanced outside and caught sight of Mary dismounting from a rickshaw.

Leaving her half-eaten breakfast, Juliet jumped up from the table and rushed through to the lobby. Mary was just coming in through the glass front door. She looked tired. She wore the orange kaftan she'd bought in the bazaar and blue jeans, but they looked dishevelled.

'Mary! Where have you been?' Juliet could not keep the scolding tone out of her voice. 'I was worried sick about you.'

Mary stopped and stared at her. 'Hey, cool it. Please don't make a scene, Juliet. I've been at my friend's house. Zaq. You remember? I told you where I was going last night.'

'But you said you were coming back *last night*.'

'Did I? Well I'm not a child, you know. I can do as I please.'

'I know that, of course. Come on, let's not stand here in the lobby. Come and have some breakfast.' They walked through to the café and sat down back at Juliet's table.

'You're not answerable to me, Mary. It's just that we're here together in a foreign city, and I just think we should look out for each other. Let each other know where we are, that's all.'

'I'm not though, am I?'

'You're not what?'

'I'm not in a foreign city. This is my home. My city. You seem to be forgetting that.' Bitterness surfaced in Mary's voice again. The waiter appeared, and Mary ordered herself eggs and bacon.

'Look,' began Juliet when the waiter had gone. 'Can't we just forget the difference of opinion we had yesterday? Let's hope the trip to the island will tell us more. It might even resolve matters once and for all. Can't we just agree to get along with each other until the end of the trip?'

'Of course, we can,' said Mary. 'Look I've done some thinking. I talked it all through with Zaq, too. His parents and family are all dead, and there's never been any hope for him of finding them. I told him about my research and how I had tracked you down. I told him how angry I was with you for not believing that I'm Rose's baby.'

'It's just that I need to be sure, that's all. I explained that to you ... Well, what did he say?'

'Oh, he's very wise. He is training to be a doctor, you know. He has a lot of insight into human nature. He helped me to think a bit about how you must feel.'

'And?'

The bacon and eggs arrived and Mary tucked in hungrily. Juliet smiled in admiration. Mary's unbridled appetite had surprised and impressed her from the start. For someone so slim, she could certainly eat.

'Well,' Mary said, looking up, her mouth full. 'He explained it like this. You buried yourself on that remote rubber estate all those years, didn't you? You shut yourself off from the world, thinking everyone was dead, and in a way you got used to that. You were even quite happy with it in your way. But when I came along, I was dangling some sort of hope in front of you, wasn't I? Some hope that someone, something, had survived from all that death and devastation. But on the other hand, there's a chance that I might not be that baby after all. And you're afraid of that. You don't want to have your hopes dashed, so you're reserving your position, keeping a bit of yourself back. Is that right?'

Juliet was surprised that Zaq had so much insight about the way she felt. 'I suppose your friend might have a point,' she admitted. 'And you're right. He's got great wisdom.'

'So I'm not angry with you anymore. I understand how you feel. Let's just see what happens on the island, shall we?'

'Yes. Let's do that ... And did you make any decisions about him?'

'About Zaq? Yes. I've been thinking a lot about what you said the other day. I've realised that Li was just a passing fancy. I was just attracted to him, that's all. I know now that Zaq's the one I truly care about. He's the one who can make me happy.'

'That's marvellous.'

'When he's finished his course, he's going to get a job in Singapore so we can be together.'

Juliet took her hand across the table and squeezed it. 'I'm very happy for you, Mary. I'm sure you've made the right decision.'

The little passenger ferry moored up on the jetty was already crowded; dozens of locals swarmed up the gang-plank carrying children and babies and luggage of all shapes and sizes. Juliet watched as chickens in cages, fish in plastic dustbins and huge baskets of fruit and vegetables were brought on board. She and Mary squeezed onto a bench on the deck, and after the usual unexplained delays that seemed inevitable on all these journeys, the boat cast off onto the river, and started back towards the sea. It chugged past the factories and warehouses that they had seen on the way up to the city, past whole neighbourhoods of houses on stilts built out over the river, where small children played, diving into the murky water with yelps of delight.

They chatted about the scenery for a while. Juliet sensed that Mary felt a certain pride for this great dirty city that had become her home. Her face shone with pleasure as she pointed out local landmarks she remembered from her childhood, mosques, villages, distant hills.

Juliet stared out at the far bank. The river was already widening out as they chugged on towards the sea. The land on either side was flat and green for miles, stretching towards distant hills. The little boat made its way steadily down river towards the Bangka Straits and towards the island that held so many secrets.

Malaya 1941

AFTER ROSE HAD GONE HOME I tried my best to avoid Gavin. By this time he spent the nights in a different room. I would sleep on after I had heard him leave in the mornings, have a late breakfast and usually be out riding when he came back from lunch. In the evenings we might sit down together for supper, but he would be off out again as soon as he had finished. When I was with him I was usually careful to avoid mentioning anything that might trigger his anger. But sometimes, the humiliation was too much to bear and I could not resist asking him where he was going in the evenings. He would inevitably say, 'What the hell's it got to do with you?' and his temper would flare up in an instant. Sometimes, if I dared to remind him that he was my husband and I had a right to know where he was spending his evenings, he would reward me with a back-handed slap around the face. I think he knew that I had found out about his lover in the village, and that in itself enflamed his temper.

Life went on like that for a long time. I carried on pretending to everyone else that things were fine. Although I had confided in Rose when she had visited, I found it easier to go back to pretending in my letters to her that everything was alright. And eventually in her letters back to me, Rose stopped asking. Perhaps I had finally convinced her that things had changed for the better. I saw Beatrice from time to time. She always wore that concerned expression on her face when she was with me, and asked me how things were at home, but I never managed to tell her the truth.

Scott made an appearance every few months. He would arrive to stay at the bungalow, sometimes with a couple of fellow officers in tow. I gathered from overhearing the houseboys' gossip that they would spend their time drinking and playing cards. If he was on his own he would amble up to the house on the pretext of visiting. If I spotted him coming up the drive I would retreat to my room and I made sure that I was never alone when he was around. Fortunately his visits were infrequent and short. Any exchange he had with Gavin was usually tense and filled with animosity.

War was coming, that much was obvious from the news reports, the rumours running rampant in the colony and the build-up of troops on the Malay Peninsula. Everyone at the club was talking about it. The general feeling was that the Japanese would be no match for the British troops.

One evening, Gavin had insisted on me accompanying him to the club. I knew he was doing it for the sake of appearances, but I went along, hoping that Beatrice would be there. The Federated Malay States Volunteer Force was recruiting in the area and the other men asked Gavin if he was going to join up. It was late in the evening by this time and he had been drinking steadily since we had arrived.

'Not bloody likely,' he said, in a loud voice, his words slurred. 'I'm not about to risk life and limb. There are plenty of other chaps eager to do that. My place is here. I've got over a hundred tappers on my payroll. Can't let the estate go to rack and ruin. I've only just got it up to scratch again after the last fiasco.'

His words were greeted with silence from some and muttered incredulity from others. I noticed people shaking their heads and looking away. 'You bloody coward, Crosby,' said Ron, another planter. 'Stand up and defend your country, man. It's your duty. Even your own brother's had the decency to join up. Why don't you follow his example?'

'You calling me a coward, Bailey?' The room fell silent. 'Come here and say that.'

'Alright, I will,' said Ron, slamming his drink down on the bar. Everyone was watching now, holding their breath. Ron walked over to where Gavin stood beside the bar. I was sitting with Beatrice at one of the tables nearby. She reached out and put a comforting hand on my arm.

Ron stood right in front of Gavin and leaned towards him, looking straight into his eyes. 'You're a bloody coward, Crosby,' he repeated. 'We've all joined the Volunteers. We're ready to defend our country and take what happens. You damned well should, too.' Gavin stared at him for a second, lurched backwards, then lunged at Ron and punched him full in the face with his fist. We could hear the crack as Ron's nose broke. Blood spurted everywhere. Ron staggered backwards, but Gavin lunged towards him, about to punch him again. A couple of the other men grabbed Gavin and pulled him away, but he soon struggled free, and started kicking Ron who had collapsed on the floor. A couple more men came up and managed to pull him away. They had to hold him back. It took three of them. Gavin was very strong and the drink had fuelled his aggression.

'Get him into his car. Can you drive him home, Mrs. C?'

'Of course,' I said getting up quickly. My face was aflame with embarrassment. I kept my eyes on the floor as I went out, I was so ashamed. Beatrice came out to the car and stood beside me as they bundled Gavin into the back seat.

'Are you going to be alright, my dear?' she asked.

'Of course. Don't worry. He'll probably go to sleep on the way home.'

'Do you want me and Henry to come back with you, just in case ... ?'

'It's very kind of you, but things will be fine, Beatrice, thank you,' I said.

Despite my brave words, my hands were shaking on the steering wheel as I drove off out of town and onto the jungle road that led to the plantation. My nerves were in such a state that I ground the gears and nearly stalled several times as I drove through town. I was right though; although he was shouting and swearing as we pulled out of the club car park, Gavin soon slumped forward and fell asleep, snoring loudly, occasionally waking with a start and muttering angrily to himself. As I drove through the jungle in the dark, I wondered what I would do when we got back to the house. I hoped that Mohammed would still be up. I decided that I would run in and get him and Abdul to help me. They were used to Gavin's ways and to his occasional drunken behaviour, and they were fiercely loyal to him.

But as I drove through the gates at around midnight I saw that the living room lights were on. Normally the servants would have turned them off, especially as we had been out for the evening. I parked the car beside the front steps and went inside. As I entered I stopped with a start. Scott was there again, lolling in his favourite armchair in the corner, whisky glass in his hand.

'Well, well, if it isn't my adorable sister-in-law. Long time, no see. I see you are looking as lovely as ever. Where's my big brother?'

I didn't want to tell him the truth, anticipating another ugly scene, but there was no choice. He would find out anyway. 'He's in the car. He's a bit the worse for wear, I'm afraid. I was going to ask the houseboys to help me bring him inside.'

'There's no need to bother them. I'll help you,' he said, getting up unsteadily.

'Are you sure you're alright?'

'Of course. I might have had a couple of stiff ones, but I'm not incapable you know.' He pushed past me, through the front door and to the car. He opened the back door, and I saw him shake Gavin roughly. I heard raised voices, but after a few minutes, he hauled Gavin out of the back seat and helped him up the steps.

'I won't be able to get him upstairs. I'll take him through to the dining room sofa. Can you bring a blanket? He can sleep there.'

I dashed upstairs to get a pillow and blankets, and as I did so, I noticed that the door to my room was open. Scott must have been poking around while we were out. I hoped he had not read the letters Rose had written me.

Scott heaved Gavin onto the sofa, and I tucked the blanket around him. Although he had been swearing and grumbling at Scott on the way in from the car, Gavin fell asleep straight away. 'Come and join me for a night-cap. You look as white as a sheet,' said Scott, 'I saw blood on his knuckles and on his shirt. He's been fighting, hasn't he?'

'I'll go to bed, Scott, if it's all the same to you.'

'In a moment. But I insist you have a brandy first. It will help you sleep. You look as though you've had a nasty shock.'

I sank down in one of the living room chairs and Scott poured me a generous glass. I took a sip and was grateful for the comforting warmth that spread through my limbs. Scott sat in the opposite chair, and I was aware that he was watching me and scrutinising my face while he toyed with his glass.

'You're not happy,' he began. 'I can tell that. Each time I've been back here I've seen it getting worse. I knew this would happen.'

'Scott, things are fine.'

'Is that the little lie you tell yourself to get through each day? Believe me, I can tell the signs. My father was just the same. I saw it happen to my mother, and it's like history repeating itself. How often does he hit you, Juliet? Don't bother to deny it. I know what he's like.'

'Scott, I don't know why you're saying these things. It's really no concern of yours.'

'You even sleep in separate bedrooms, don't you?'

'I see that you've been nosing around,' I said, getting angry now, 'You've absolutely no right going into my room you know.'

'I just wanted to check on you, make sure you were doing alright.'

I got up from the chair and put the glass down. 'I'm going up to bed now, Scott.'

'You don't deserve to be treated this way, you know.' He stood up, too, and came towards me. 'You deserve to be loved, Juliet.' He was close now, and I could smell the sweat on his skin. I moved aside to go upstairs but he grabbed me by both arms and kissed my hard full on the lips. He tasted of sour whisky and bad breath. I struggled free.

'Leave me alone.' I ran towards the stairs.

'Why don't you let me love you? A woman like you needs to be loved, Juliet. Loved properly.'

I ran upstairs and into my bedroom, slamming the door shut behind me and locking it. I sat on the bed shaking. Soon, though, I heard his footsteps on the stairs. He knocked on the door. 'I'm sorry Juliet. I'm so sorry. I didn't mean to alarm you. Let me in. I want to explain myself.'

'No. Just go away. Go to bed, Scott. You're drunk and you have no idea what you're getting into.'

He laughed at me. 'I think it's you, Juliet, who doesn't know what you've got into. I always knew that Gavin's little plan would end in disaster.'

'Little plan?'

'Oh, you still don't know? Hasn't he told you? Well let me enlighten you then. You know why he married you don't you?'

I was silent.

'Don't you?'

'Of course,' I replied weakly. 'He loved me. We were in love.'

Scott laughed. 'He's never loved you. He's in love with that little tart down in the village. Wife of one of the tappers. But the poor fellow upped and left years ago. Couldn't stand the humiliation. You know all about her, don't you? Obsessed with her, he is.' By now, the tears were streaming down my cheeks. 'He's been under her spell since he was a teenager. She's a bit older than him, quite a looker in her own way. Bold as brass. Gavin used to go down there when Father was in one of his rages. It was his refuge, I suppose. Father knew and was furious about it. Did everything in his power to stop it, but it still carried on. Father was determined they wouldn't marry though. So do you know what he did?'

He waited for an answer, but I had no words. I tried to picture Gavin's Malay lover. I had never seen her face but in my head she looked like an exotic goddess, flawless, with a perfect figure, beautiful brown eyes and long glossy black hair.

'He changed his will. Gavin was left the estate, but Father left the rest of the money on trust for him, stipulating that no funds would be released until he married an Englishwoman. The estate was going to rack and ruin after Father died. Gavin had run out of funds. He had no money to replant, couldn't pay the workers. When he came down to Penang to visit Cousin Johnny, he was looking for a wife. And he found you. That's why he married you Juliet. I just thought you should know.'

I was stunned. I knew Scott wasn't lying. It all made perfect sense to me now. All the concerns I had before I married Gavin were completely justified. Gavin hadn't told me he loved me because he didn't. He just needed me to think that he was genuine, and a few words of flattery had been more than enough. Even his lovemaking had been clinical and passionless. I now understood why he had cut our honeymoon short to go to Kuala Lumpur and see his lawyers. He would have taken the marriage certificate to them as evidence, ensuring they drew up the papers so that his father's money would come to him without delay. He had even alluded to it himself at the time, but I had been too blind to see the truth.

25

The next morning I packed my bags and asked Abdul to take me to catch the early train to Singapore. I didn't have time to send a telegram, to let Rose know I was coming, but when the train finally rattled into Keppel Road Station in Singapore that evening, I saw to my astonishment that Rose was there waiting on the platform. Gavin had telephoned during the afternoon to ask if she had heard from me. He'd said he couldn't understand why I had left, but that Abdul had taken me to the station. Rose had guessed that something dreadful had happened and that I would be coming to Singapore on the next train.

When I saw her on the platform I just dropped my bags, rushed over and threw my arms around her. We both stood there clinging onto each other, tears streaming down our faces, unable to speak for a while.

Gavin wrote to me during the first week, asking why I had left, and telling me to come back to the estate. I wrote back explaining that I had found out all about his father's will, and had known for a while about his mistress. He wrote again straight away, trying to get me to return, promising that he would change, that he would leave his lover. When I didn't reply, he wrote again, begging me not to seek a divorce. I finally wrote back to him, assuring him that I had no desire to get divorced for the time being. After that he stopped writing, and I realised that what he was really worried about was getting divorced, since that would mean that the trust fund would stop paying out.

It was April when I arrived in Singapore, and within a few months the Japanese had invaded Malaya. I stayed with Robert and Rose on their bungalow on Tengah Air Base. I was an emotional wreck when I arrived, reeling from the events of the past few months. I was full of self-loathing and misery. I hadn't been eating properly, so I was thin and unhealthy, and my skin was sallow.

Rose prepared the guest room for me, and we spent hours together, walking in the garden, or sitting on her veranda sipping tea as I unburdened myself. Robert made himself scarce, dining at the officers' mess and keeping out of our way. Rose was very patient for the first couple of days, but on the third day at breakfast she said brightly, 'I think we should go out today, Jules. Let's get the syce to take us into town. We can do some shopping and have a spot of tiffin in Raffles. I'm going to take you to my Indian tailor and get you fitted up with some nice outfits.' My sister was determined that I should not stay in the bungalow and mope, that I should go out and about. She was desperate for me to be part of her social set.

'I don't have the money for that, Rose,' I said, alarmed. The thought of leaving the airbase, or even going very far from the house filled me with dread.

'Don't worry about that. You know Rob's parents aren't short of money. We don't have to rely on his RAF salary alone. If you're coming out and about with me, you'll need a few pretty dresses.'

I gave her a pleading look. 'I'm not sure I want to be out and about, as you put it. I'd much prefer to stay here in the house. If you want to go out that's fine, but can't you just let me be? I really don't mind staying here on my own.'

I could see a stubborn expression forming on her face. She pursed her lips and raised her eyebrows. It had always been the same, ever since she was a child. She always wanted to have things her own way. 'Look, I know you've had a dreadful time, Juliet, but the best cure for unhappiness is to distract yourself from it. You need to put it all behind you, and the best way to do that is to start enjoying yourself.'

'But I'm not sure that I could enjoy myself, not the way I feel at the moment.'

She stared at me, looking puzzled. 'Well, why don't you at least give it a try? For my sake, Jules? Now, come on. Let's get ready. I'll ask for the car to be brought to the door in half an hour.'

It was the last thing I wanted to do, but I went into the bedroom and selected the most presentable cotton print dress I had. It was several years old. I had bought it in Selfridges in London in 1937. I knew that the cut and the shape were out of fashion and that Rose would not approve but it was the best I could do. I hastily made my face up and put on a summer hat. Rose smiled as I emerged from the bedroom, but she didn't say anything. She must have been biting her tongue, staying silent because of my fragile state. But in the car on the way into town she clearly couldn't hold back any longer. She looked at me and said briskly, 'I was quite right, we really ought to get you down to the tailor as soon as we can.'

The Tengah Air Base was on the north-west side of the island, and a fairly long drive into town. I stared out of the open window, glad of the breeze in my hair, staring out at the plantations and villages of *atap* and bamboo as they rolled past. As we neared the city, they gave way to leafy suburbs where huge colonial houses stood shaded by trees, some of them with mock Tudor beams on the eaves, others with white stuccoed pillars and porticoes. Rose instructed the syce to drive us around the town, and as we entered the centre, I was astonished by the symmetry of the place, the beauty and grandeur of the colonial buildings. We passed the palatial municipal building, the Victoria Memorial Hall, the ultra-modern Fullerton building. We drove along Connaught Road, a tree lined boulevard bordered by beautifully manicured municipal gardens and running along the seafront. I stared out at the great ships moored in the busy harbour, where lighters were being rowed or poled to and from them carrying cargo.

'You see, it is beautiful isn't it? I knew you'd like it,' said Rose, watching my face.

I followed my sister into the great lobby of Raffles Hotel and through to the veranda, where the hubbub of conversation from fifty tables seemed to pause and hover in the air as we entered. People turned to wave at Rose, women came up to kiss her on both cheeks and exclaim at how well she looked. I realised she was in her element, and that she was determined to try to get me involved, to love this life as much as she did.

Rose and her friends seemed to lead lives of endless trivia, of lunch parties, swimming parties, tea dances, evening dances. The social round went on and on, even though everyone knew that war was imminent. It was as if they didn't want to face up to it. For me, the endless socialising was a huge effort and even more painful than the lonely days I had spent on the plantation. Except that here, in Singapore, I felt safe.

The talk was all of war. At dinner parties and dances, people speculated about when the invasion would happen and how long it would take to defeat the Japanese. But no-one seemed to take it very seriously. They all seemed confident that if the Japanese did invade, they would very soon be overwhelmed by the might of the British. 'Singapore is a fortress, everyone knows that': this was repeated in bars and clubs throughout the colony. It was like a mantra, a palliative for everyone's fears.

On the airbase, Robert and his fellow officers were busy practising for an invasion. Extra pilots were being drafted in and hastily trained, the barracks on the airbase was full of young men who looked to be barely out of their teens. Despite that, Robert was worried that there weren't enough aircraft.

'The ones we do have are old and slow,' he confided in me and Rose one rare evening when we dined together in the bungalow. 'The Japs have new Zeros. Fantastically manoeuvrable and quick. Our lumbering old Brewster Buffalos would be no match for them in a dogfight.'

'Don't talk like that Rob. It will be alright, won't it? Everyone says so,' said Rose in alarm.

'I'm sorry, my darling. I didn't mean to frighten you.' He spoke indulgently, slipping his hand on top of hers on the table, but I could see the anxiety still lurking behind his smile.

When the first air raid finally came in December it was a massive shock. It was in the middle of the night. We were woken by aircraft screaming overhead and the crash and boom of multiple explosions. Japanese planes were bombing and strafing the airfield. We expected the bungalow to be hit any second, but although it shook and trembled, it was not hit directly. In the morning we went outside and surveyed the devastation. The airfield was full of bomb craters. Buildings had been blown apart and fires were still burning. What everyone had said would never happen was actually happening. We were terrified.

Once they had started, the bombing raids continued night after night. It went on for weeks like that. There were reports from the centre of the city that many people had been killed. Bodies were lying in the streets, buildings devastated. Rose and I were desperate to get away. We had received a telegram from Auntie Maude to say that she and Uncle Arthur were sailing to Ceylon on the next boat, hoping that from there they could get back to England. Everyone who could do so was leaving.

Eventually Robert drove down into town. He did the rounds

of offices of various shipping lines. Everyone else was doing the same thing, and the queues were phenomenal. He had to wait for hours, but he finally managed to reserve and pay for a passage for Rose and me to sail to Australia.

THE LITTLE BOAT was making its way along the coast of a jungle-covered island. Juliet looked at the tangled creepers and palms that covered the hills. This must be it. This was Bamboo Island. They passed strips of white sand fringed with palm trees, and forests of bamboo, interspersed with rocky outcrops, where huge grey boulders lay scattered on the sand.

The little ferry port on the western tip of the island was no more than a village, and when the boat moored up at the end of a ramshackle wooden pier, a crowd of locals wearing sarongs and sandals waited impatiently with their boxes and bundles to board for the return journey. There were no touts here. Tourism had barely touched this place. Confusion reigned, with much shouting and gesticulating, as the passengers clambered off the boat and waited for the crew to pass their luggage from the hold.

Mary quickly found an open-backed truck, which she told Juliet was called a *bemo*, to take them to the only town on the island. The driver told them that he knew about a guesthouse that catered to local businessmen and that it would probably have a room for them. Mary negotiated a price for the driver to take them there and wait while they checked in, then take them on to the beach, Pantai Kelapa. He seemed pleased with the bargain they had struck and shook hands with Mary, a beaming smile spreading across his face.

'My name Basir,' he told them, inclining his head in a bow. 'Pleased to be of service.' They climbed on board and settled themselves on the wooden benches on the back of the truck. It bounced through the dusty little ferry port and out into the countryside.

They passed through long stretches of untamed jungle where bushes and creepers encroached onto the narrow road. It reminded Juliet of the old familiar road between Kuala Lipis and the plantation. After a few miles the jungle gave way to rubber plantations on either side. In some places the land was scarred with great swathes of barren earth, where the vegetation had been ripped away and where no trees grew. Disused mining equipment lay rusting in the sun.

'Tin,' shouted Basir, noticing in the mirror that they were staring. 'Big industry here.' After a few more miles they arrived in a small town, of mainly single-storey buildings. A few shops and cafes lined the main street.

'This our capital,' said Basir proudly, swerving between bicycles and rickshaws. 'Kota Timah.' They drew up outside a modern guesthouse that looked even more down at heel than the one they had stayed at in Palembang. A crowd of curious locals gathered to watch them get down from the truck and go into the hotel with their luggage.

'Don't worry about it, Juliet,' said Mary, seeing her expression. 'We're only sleeping here. We don't need luxury.'

They checked in and left their bags in a gloomy twin room overlooking the street. The beds were narrow and there was little else in the room besides a faded photograph of an elaborate mosque. 'You go Pantai Kelapa now?' Basir asked as they emerged from the lobby.

Juliet nodded and smiled nervously. The prospect of seeing the place where Rose had died made her feel apprehensive. She could hardly speak, her heart was beating so fast. She clambered back on the truck and it set off smartly, belting black smoke from the exhaust and raising a cloud of dust in its wake.

Once out of town, the driver turned off the main road, drove over a rickety wooden bridge and onto a narrow dirt track that ran along the coast beside mangrove swamps, stretching for miles, where the shallow sea washed under the exposed roots of the trees. When they rounded a headland, they passed through a small village of stilted wooden houses, where people stopped and stared as they passed, and naked children ran out onto the road to wave. Just beyond the village a wooden pier was built out to sea, and a fleet of brightly painted wooden fishing boats were moored up alongside it. Beyond that was a beach, the most beautiful one she had ever seen. A perfect curve of white sand, bordered by low scrubland, and fringed with a single row of graceful coconut palms that leant over graciously as if bowing to the sea. Beyond that was another headland. They were on the very tip of the island.

Basir pulled the truck off the road and parked up on the scrubland beside the beach. 'This called Pantai Kelapa,' he said. 'It mean coconut palm beach.'

Juliet nodded and found her eyes were moist with tears. It was just as she had imagined it. This place had lay buried in her head for almost twenty years. She had thought for a long time that she would never come here, but now it was right before her eyes, the place where her beloved sister had died.

26

Juliet clambered down from the back of the *bemo* in a daze. The sun was high in the sky now, and her body was bathed in sweat, her clothes sticking to her. She kicked off her shoes and left them beside the vehicle. Then, she moved forward onto the hot sand without any conscious thought. She could feel Mary by her side but all her senses were focused on this place, on the smooth white sand, on the tiny waves lapping and sucking at the shore, on the gentle breeze rattling the leaves of the coconut palms. She stared in front of her, at the sun shimmering on the constantly moving sea that stretched as far as the eye could see.

She was aware that Mary was saying something to her, but she didn't catch the words. She closed her eyes and visualised the events of that dreadful day in 1942 as she believed they had happened. Japanese planes swooped overhead and there was the stricken ship on the horizon, slipping beneath the waves. There were people out there in the water, swimming frantically or floundering about in life jackets. A lifeboat was rowing for the shore. It moved quickly, the oars beating in rhythm. And then it was here on the beach, and the people were climbing out. They were making their way up the sand towards the shade of the coconut palms. Juliet opened her eyes and then, shading them, peered towards the far headland. That was where they would have come from, the Japanese soldiers. They would have come carrying weapons of war, advancing on the little party of survivors, moving closer and closer.

Her eyes suddenly filled with tears, and she sunk down to her knees on the sand, her face in her hands, sobbing. Juliet felt Mary slip a comforting arm around her shoulder. She tried to control the tears, but found that she could not stop them.

'I think you need to be alone here for a while,' Mary said. 'I'm going to wait by the *bemo*.'

Juliet tried to collect herself, but the tears kept coming. She had suppressed them for a long time, for all those years when she had hidden herself away on the plantation, shutting her mind to the past. The tears had been building up inside her all that time, and now her chest was so full of them that it ached.

She remembered when she had first heard the news. She had been staying in the dormitory at Raffles at the time, and she had asked around for news of Rose's ship, but no-one seemed to know anything. So she had decided to find out for herself. She had gone to the offices of the shipping line on Orchard Road. It was above a pharmacy, up a narrow staircase. The place had been in a state of chaos, papers everywhere, people moving boxes and furniture about. They were just opening up again after the Occupation had closed them down for three and a half years.

When she had enquired about the *Rajah of Sarawak*, the man behind the desk had given her a sympathetic look and had gone to fetch a more senior colleague.

'Step this way please, Mrs. Crosby,' said a man in shirtsleeves and a tie. He spoke with an Australian drawl. He had greying hair and wore glasses. From his fleshy face and ample midriff Juliet instantly knew that he must have arrived in Singapore very recently, that he hadn't been anywhere near an internment camp.

He sat her down in a tiny office. The window was open and a fan stirred the humid air. 'I'm afraid I have some very bad news for you,' he began. She had felt a wave of shock pulse through her body. 'The ship was attacked by Japanese aircraft. It went down, I'm afraid, and there were only a handful of survivors. Your sister and her baby are on the list of people who were witnessed getting onto a lifeboat that landed on a beach on Bamboo Island, near the village of Desa Kelapa.'

She had stared at him, open mouthed, trying to digest the news, but her brain was working very slowly, as if stunned by a physical blow. 'Well that's good, isn't it?' she had said at last, swallowing.

'I'm sorry, Mrs. Crosby, but it isn't good news at all. This is going to be very painful for you, but I have a duty to tell you what we know. It seems that all the survivors were marched into the sea and shot by a group of Japanese soldiers.'

She had not been able to process this information. She was dimly aware of life happening outside on Orchard Road, of people chatting on the pavement below the window, of hawkers touting their wares, of traffic crawling past, of engines and horns.

'People in one of the other lifeboats saw what happened. They turned round and rowed back out to sea. They were finally picked up by another vessel bound for Australia. A few others made it to another beach and were captured and put into a prison camp. I'm very, very sorry. If there is anything we can do...'

'No. There's nothing. I need to go now.' She had rushed out through the office, blinded by tears, down the narrow staircase and out onto Orchard Road, where she walked a few yards then stopped and leaned against a glass shop-front, weeping. Crowds of strangers had jostled past, jabbering away in different languages, and she had felt so alone in the midst of the teeming crowd. So utterly alone.

And now, here on the beach she cried again. It came back to her, the memory of Rose's terrified face as she emerged from the fortune teller's tent at the temple in Ceylon back in 1938. The ominous words of the strange old woman had finally come true, just as Rose had feared, and Juliet had been helpless in the face of the prophesy, had been unable to protect her sister. Juliet closed her eyes and tried to blot it all out of her mind. At last the tears stopped coming. She sat still, breathing deeply for a few minutes more, then hauled herself to her feet and walked slowly back up the beach, her limbs aching and her head thumping in the relentless heat from the sun.

Back in the *bemo*, Juliet splashed her face with water from a drinking bottle. Basir turned the truck around and drove them back the hundred yards or so into the village. He parked up under the shade of a spreading banyan tree, alongside a couple of battered vans and mopeds on what must have been the village square. There was a crowd of villagers on the little jetty, clustering around something lying on the boards. Basir nodded, gesturing for Juliet and Mary to go ahead and look. As they drew closer, Juliet could see that the excitement was caused by a leopard shark, which lay in bloody chunks on the jetty, its beautiful black-and-tan patterned skin already dull, tarnished by death. Its head had been severed and it lay there, its eyes blank, its mouth gaping open, exposing needle-like teeth. Blood was splattered everywhere, all over the boards of the jetty, dripping into the water beneath. A wave of nausea rose in Juliet's throat. She wanted to walk away, but the people had already turned and noticed them. They were beckoning them forward, with broad white smiles of welcome.

Juliet and Mary stood there with the villagers, pretending to admire the catch for a few minutes, then Mary took one of the younger men aside to ask him questions. Juliet could not make out what they were saying, but the man was nodding and smiling. He turned to Juliet, 'You come with me,' he said in English, 'I show you lady who might remember. She very old now. I show you lady's house.'

They followed him along the village street to the very end, where the houses petered out and the road became a mud path, running between clumps of bamboo on one side and mangrove swamps on the other. He turned to them, smiling, as he walked. 'Lady very old. She is our village wise woman. If anyone remember, it is her.'

The house was built on stilts over the mangrove swamp. It stood alone, apart from the village, and was approached along a long, raised walkway made of duck boards. As they walked along the boards towards the house, there was a shout from within, and an old woman appeared on the porch. The young man looked at them, smiling. 'This is Mawar,' he said. 'She pleased to see you. She love visitors.'

The old woman waited for them as they climbed the wooden steps to the porch. She was very thin and walked with a stoop. She held out her hand to her visitors; her leathery skin was turned almost black from the sun. She wore wooden bangles that rattled together as she moved, and a bright orange sarong in a traditional Indonesian print, patterned with songbirds and dragons. She took Juliet's hand and smiled broadly, displaying a row of broken and blackened teeth.

'Selamat datang,' she said, welcoming them, speaking in a high, cracked voice.

'These ladies would like to know about the day the ship went down in 1942,' said the young man. 'If you know anything about it, they would like you to tell them what happened.'

'Please tell her that my sister was on the ship with a baby,' said Juliet. She could understand the words that they spoke. It was very close to Malay, but she did not have enough confidence to try to speak the language. The young man translated Juliet's words and the old woman's smile vanished and was replaced by a troubled, anxious look. She motioned them to come inside.

'I will tell you what I remember,' she said, 'but first I will make you some *teh manis*.' They sat down on cushions around a low table while the old lady busied herself on a small stove in the corner, boiling water and setting out cups.

'None for us, thank you, *Ibu*,' said the young man. 'Basir and I will wait back by the pier. We will leave you ladies to speak alone.'

Juliet looked around at the hut. It was tiny, with just one room for living and sleeping, but it was clean and well-kept, with possessions stacked neatly on shelves, and clothes hung on a wooden rail in one corner. The wooden walls were decorated with brightly coloured batiks. At one end, shutters were thrown back and there was a view of the sea. In another corner was Mawar's bed, covered in colourful throws.

She brought them the drinks, and Juliet took a sip. It was strong and sweet, and had an immediate calming effect on her nerves. She felt ready now, to hear the old lady's story.

Mawar settled herself on a cushion opposite Mary and Juliet. She looked them straight in the eye and began her tale. Juliet leaned forward to concentrate, to understand the words in the unfamiliar tongue.

'We heard the planes attacking the ship. It was mid-morning, I suppose. Some of our menfolk were out fishing, so we were afraid for them. But it wasn't unusual. Over the past few days there had been many, many air raids on ships passing through the straits beyond the island. But most of them were further out to sea. Some of us women went down to the beach to watch. There was no pier in the village then. We watched the planes dropping bombs onto the ship. The sounds of the explosions and of the ship breaking apart were terrifying. We were horrified to see the ship going down, quite soon after the air raid. There were people in the water. There were some people in lifeboats too, and one of them was heading towards our beach.

When we saw it coming, we were afraid. Japanese soldiers were occupying the island, and we had heard stories of how they had dealt with people who opposed them. Torture, beatings, beheadings. They had already built a camp near the main town and taken all the Europeans there, people who managed the mines or the plantations. They had even taken the man of God there, the missionary, Mr. Owen. So when we saw these white people coming ashore, we were afraid. We ran and hid amongst the bamboo thickets behind the beach and we watched from there. We decided to see what they did and offer to help them once they had moved off the beach. We watched them come up the beach and sit in a little group on the edge. They were mostly women and children. A couple of old men. They looked exhausted and afraid.'

The old lady's rheumy eyes kept filling up with tears, and she wiped them away with the back of her hand. Juliet had no tears now, she had cried herself out. She just wanted to hear the story as the old woman told it. She wanted to fix it in her mind, to remember it.

'Go on,' Mary urged. She was listening intently, too.

'One of the women in our group stepped forward to help them, but I gripped her arm to stop her,' the old woman went on. 'I knew it wasn't safe for us. I had seen them coming, you see. The soldiers. They were coming around the headland to the west. They were carrying weapons. We froze and stayed where we were. There was no time to run back to our houses.

It was a few seconds before the survivors saw the soldiers, but when they did it threw them into a panic. They started to argue. Some of them burst into tears. They didn't know what to do. Two or three of them broke from the group and started to run for the village, but the soldiers were on them within seconds. They fired shots into the air and then rounded the people up. They split them into two groups. The men and the older women into one group, the others into the second group. The soldiers were shouting at them, yelling and screaming, pushing them with their rifle butts and bayonets. Then they told the first group to spread out in a line and to walk into the sea. We were dreadfully afraid by this time, clinging together.

The group walked into the sea and kept on walking. None of them looked back. When they were up to their thighs in the water, the soldiers started to fire on them. They all fell instantly, splashing under the waves, silently. None of them screamed or shouted. The rest of the group were clinging together crying and shaking. One of them was holding a baby. She had long blond hair and a bright blue dress with white flowers on it.'

Juliet's hand flew to her mouth. 'I remember that dress,' she murmured. She thought of Rose picking out the swatch of luxurious material at the Indian tailor's on Serangoon Road and holding it up to her face. 'It matches my eyes, doesn't it, Jules?' And Rose had worn that dress when she had brought the baby to Alexandra Hospital to say goodbye. How lovely she had looked then, the colour of the dress emphasising the blue of her eyes and the healthy tan in her cheeks. She had smiled and turned as she had prepared to leave, clutching the baby to her breast: 'Don't fret, Juliet, it won't be long. We'll all be together again in no time, you'll see.' Those were the last words she had spoken to Juliet.

'I will always remember her,' Mawar continued. 'She must have known what was going to happen, and when the soldiers were coming back up to the beach for the second group, she slipped behind a tree and quick as a flash popped the baby on the ground, hid it under a bush. We watched her take a locket from around her neck and put it round the baby's. Then she turned and stepped back onto the beach. She didn't look back. The guards made the rest of them, the young women and children, stand next to each other in a line and told them to walk into the sea just like the others.

As they moved forwards, the baby began to cry. We looked at each other. Then one of the women in our group darted toward the bush and grabbed the baby. She brought it back to where we were crouching, and rocked it and soothed it until it stopped crying. The guards were too busy to notice. The women were in the sea by this time, and the soldiers opened fire again, just like on the first group. Round after round. When the women and children had all fallen, the soldiers turned round. They were laughing and joking. They hoisted their weapons onto their shoulders and marched back the way they had come. It had all taken less than ten minutes.

We crouched where we were, amidst the bamboo, terrified and shocked by what we had seen. We stayed there for a long time, until we were sure that they weren't going to come back. Then we went down to the edge of the water. We were planning to bury the bodies, but they had already been washed out on the riptide. We could see some of them bobbing on the waves. There was still blood in the foam that was washing up on the sand. Apart from that there was nothing to show that anything had happened here. Except, of course, the baby.'

'That baby was me,' Mary burst in tearfully. She took the amulet from around her neck and showed it to Mawar. The old lady gasped and clasped the amulet. She looked at it in wonder for a few minutes.

'I always wondered what had happened to that little girl,' she said. 'Thank God you have survived, my dear.'

'What happened to me that day?' asked Mary.

'We went back to the village. We were all stunned by what had happened. The woman who had carried you from under the tree took you home. She already had four children of her own, but she did her best to feed you and care for you. The family looked after you for a few weeks, but one day some Japanese soldiers came to the village. They searched all the houses, ransacking some of them. They were looking for survivors. They questioned us to see if we knew anything about what had happened, but we all denied having seen anything. The family were able to hide the baby ... You, I mean, my dear, in the cot with their other ones. Luckily you had thick black hair so they believed you were Indonesian. But the incident terrified them. It terrified us all.

The family kept you for as long as they could. It must have been for a few months, then they took you to the mission in Kota Timah. They made sure you went with the amulet you had been found with. The missionary was in the prison camp, as I said, but he had left the mission in charge of a young man, an islander who had converted to Christianity. His name was Darma ... Darma Tan. He could not take you in himself, but he said he would take you to the nuns in Palembang when he next went to the city. That was the last we heard of you. But we prayed for you, and we often spoke of you.'

'Can I go and see the family? The woman who saved me?' asked Mary.

'The father died about ten years ago,' said Mawar, 'and the mother and children went to live in Jakarta. She had a sister there. She was hoping to get work in a clothing factory. We haven't heard from them for a long time.'

'Perhaps I could go there and look them up one day. You must tell me their name.'

'Batari,' said the old lady. 'That was the father's name. Yes, Batari.'

'But I thought ...' Mary trailed off. 'Never mind. At the orphanage, I was told that the missionary had given me the name. But they must have got that wrong.'

'Thank you. Thank you for telling us,' said Juliet. The old woman's story had filled her with pain, almost physical at times. She could not get over the fact that this woman sitting here in front of her had seen Rose, and had witnessed her death all those years ago.

'We have waited so long to know the truth. We owe you a great debt. How can we repay you?'

'Please don't think about that. It is nothing my child. I am only sorry that the story is such a sad one.'

When they had finished their tea, they stood up to leave. Mawar embraced them warmly and stood on the porch waving as they retraced their steps over the walkway.

They walked back towards the village in silence for a few minutes, then Mary turned to Juliet. 'So we've heard the truth now. Do you believe it now? You must believe that I'm Baby Claire surely?'

Juliet nodded. 'Yes, Mary. Yes, I believe it. Of course I do. The old lady's story confirms everything.'

'Well, aren't you pleased?'

'Of course I'm pleased. I feel stunned. I'm in shock, that's all.'

'So that's it then. You're my aunt. I'm Rose's baby. It's what I've been saying all along.'

Juliet stopped walking and turned to look at Mary, at the girl's honest open face with its sprinkling of freckles, her blue eyes, which had turned serious now. They were in sight of the village. She knew the time had come. She couldn't hide the truth anymore.

'Let's go down to the beach again, Mary. I want to see it again. I want to be there again before we leave. Will you come down with me? There's something I need to tell you.'

27

Juliet and Mary walked in silence towards the little bay, over the coarse grass and between the thickets of bamboo. They sat down under the leaning coconut palms on the edge of the sand. Juliet looked out to sea. She felt a strange calm descend on her, now that she had finally heard the truth and knew what had happened to Rose. She felt as though the tears she had wept earlier had somehow purged her of her anguish, and she was now ready to grieve properly.

But now that she had finally decided to tell Mary what she had been holding back from revealing, she could not find the right words. In fact she couldn't find any words at all. Her mind was suddenly empty. She couldn't even look at Mary, who was sitting beside her, watching her, waiting for her to speak. Juliet's calm soon deserted her, and she could feel her heart thumping against her ribs, her palms sweating. Her eyes followed a flock of white-tailed birds as they flew across the little bay together, fluttering and flapping in the breeze like a flag. Juliet watched them as they swooped over the village and headed east.

'What did you want to say?' asked Mary at last. She sounded

distracted though, as if she was musing over Mawar's story and as if nothing Juliet had to say could possibly interest her.

'I ... I haven't been completely straight with you, Mary,' Juliet began, looking down at her hands. 'I haven't told you everything yet. I was waiting until we knew the truth. And when I do tell you, I hope you'll understand why I couldn't before.'

'Why? What else could there possibly be to say?' asked Mary, turning to her with a smile and a dreamy look in her eyes.

Juliet took a deep breath. 'This is going to come as a shock to you, I'm afraid, but the fact is, you're not Rose's daughter, Mary.'

Mary's smile disappeared. Irritation clouded her eyes. 'Oh, for goodness' sake, don't start that again!' she burst out. 'Didn't you hear the old lady? I was there on that beach. I was that baby. Rose gave me that amulet, and it came with me to the orphanage. What more proof do you need?'

Mary was glaring at her, waiting for her response. 'Well?'

'Mary,' Juliet went on gently, 'you *were* the baby on the beach but you're not Rose's daughter. Rose couldn't have children. She mentioned having difficulty when she visited me on the estate. She had it confirmed shortly before I arrived in Singapore.'

'But that's crazy! All this time, you've led me to believe ...'

'I haven't really led you to believe anything,' Juliet said quietly. 'I suppose I could have told you before. But all along you've believed what you wanted to believe, and I don't blame you in the slightest for assuming this.'

Mary's eyes filled with tears. 'Fine. Then whose daughter am I?'

'Mine. You are my daughter, Mary,' Juliet said, mustering up some courage. 'I didn't want to tell you this until I was absolutely sure, until there was no doubt at all that you were the baby that Rose had taken on board that ship.'

The colour drained from Mary's face. 'It's not true,' she muttered. 'It can't be true. You're just making it up because you're lonely. You're sad and lonely, and you're jealous of Rose, so you're lying.'

The words stung Juliet. 'I don't blame you for being angry,' she said. 'You've every right to be. But you are my daughter, Mary. I am not lying or saying this out of spite. I was pregnant when I arrived in Singapore although I didn't realise for months.'

'But ... But in your journal ... I thought that you and Gavin ...'

'It was very hard for me to write down everything about the end of my time at Windy Ridge. There are things about that time I just couldn't describe.' She clenched her fists. She wanted to tell Mary everything now, but she was afraid to burden her with the full truth. She couldn't do that. Not now. Not yet. Mary needed to get used to this news first.

'You must understand, Mary, that at first I was very shocked at finding out I was pregnant. I was in no position to bring a baby into the world. I had no home, I had left my husband. But as the months went by, and you grew inside me, I gradually forgot my unhappiness and all the trauma I'd been through. I found I was looking forward to being a mother, to having something to live for. It would be a new start for me.

Rose was delighted, of course. She wanted me to carry on living with her so that she could help me look after the baby. It was like a dream come true for her. The next best thing to having her own child.

You were born in Rose and Rob's bungalow during an air raid. You were about a month early, and it was a long and difficult birth. I remember holding you in my arms for the very first time and looking down at your perfect, innocent little face and loving you instantly. But within a few hours of delivering you, I became very ill. There were some complications during the birth. There was no midwife or doctor on hand, only Rose to help me. I contracted septicaemia. I was delirious with fever for days, and it just got worse. Eventually Robert carried me to his car and drove me down through the bombed out city to the military hospital.

After I had been there a couple of days, two places came up on a ship sailing for Australia. The *Rajah of Sarawak*. Rose was desperate to go. Her house had been bombed, and she was sleeping on the floor in the officers' mess, trying to look after you as best she could. I was far too ill to travel, so Rose and I agreed that she would go, and take you with her. It seemed the only solution. We agreed that she would say you were her baby in case anyone tried to stop her, but in the end I don't think she ever gave your surname. We hadn't even had time, and it was too chaotic, to register your birth.

Robert said he would look after me and make sure I found a place on another ship. I remember saying goodbye to you on the ward. I held you close for as long as I could, just so I would remember the smell of your hair, the warmth of your little body close to mine. You looked so sweet and so beautiful, it tore my heart to see you go, but I knew it was for the best. I cried and cried after you had left. I missed you so much and I was so worried about you, but I knew you were with Rose and that she would care for you whatever happened.

Over the days I started to get a little better. I waited for Robert to come to take me back to the airbase. But by that time the Japanese had crossed the causeway and were on Singapore Island. Robert must have had to stay with his unit and fight. He never did come for me.'

Mary was leaning forward, drawing circles in the sand with her finger, her eyes following a group of delicate white hermit crabs scuttling across in front of them. They both sat in silence for a while.

'You know, Mary, I let you think you could be Rose's child because I thought it would make things easier for both of us if it all turned out not to be true. I'm so sorry. Perhaps it was unfair on you. Perhaps I shouldn't have done that. But it was self-preservation in a way.'

Juliet put her arm around Mary's shoulders and hugged her

close. It was hard to believe that this strong-willed young woman was that tiny vulnerable baby she had loved so fiercely, and for whose loss she had mourned all her life. How could she ever breach the gulf that twenty years of separation and the devastation of war had wrought between them? Could she ever make up for all those lost, empty years? It seemed like a huge mountain to climb, an almost impossible journey, like setting off to cross a continent without a map or a compass.

As they sat there, each absorbed in her own thoughts, the sun began to go down on the far horizon, streaking the sky and sea red, orange and purple. 'Come on, Mary,' Juliet said, getting to her feet. 'It's getting dark. It's been an exhausting day. Basir is waiting in the *bemo*. Let's get back to town. We can find somewhere to eat and try to get some rest.' Mary said nothing, but stood up slowly. They started to walk back through the long grass towards the *bemo*. And as they walked, Juliet slipped her arm through the crook of Mary's elbow. She felt Mary stiffen for a second, but in the end she didn't resist.

Basir drove them back along the narrow rutted road to Kota Timah. They remained silent for the whole journey. As they entered the stretch through the jungle, the squawks and whoops of night creatures could be heard loud and clear above the hum of the engine. Again, Juliet thought of home, of the road near the estate. She watched Mary anxiously. A new worry now entered her mind, making her stomach tighten with anxiety. What if Mary rejected her? What if her daughter went back to Singapore and severed all contact with her? How would she possibly bear that? Mary sat opposite Juliet with her eyes closed, but Juliet could tell she was not asleep. She wondered what Mary was thinking. She longed for some words from her, some indication that she would forgive Juliet for not having told her the truth earlier. But there was no sign of that. Juliet knew she would have to wait; Mary's anger and frustration were inevitable, understandable, and she would have to give her time.

On the edge of town, Juliet knocked on the window of Basir's cab. He slid back the glass and she asked him whether there were any cafes nearby.

'I take you,' he shouted, smiling over his shoulder. 'Very nice seafood stalls by port-side.' He dropped them at the end of a busy little street, beside a concrete pier where fishing boats were moored up, bobbing and jostling each other on the high tide. The street ran alongside the seafront. It was lit up brightly and thronging with locals. One side was lined with market stalls, piled high with all kinds of wet fish and shell fish, and the other side was filled with cafés and food stalls.

Juliet approached one of the fish stalls manned by a smiling young woman. Mary lagged behind. Juliet managed to bargain for half a kilogram of prawns and two slabs of monkfish. They took them to a restaurant across the street, where the owner whisked the fish away to be barbecued. For a few extra rupiah he told them that he would also provide beer, rice, and stir-fried vegetables.

They sat down at one of the little tables overlooking the street. Juliet watched the busy scene: children playing, families out for an evening stroll, or bargaining for fish at the stalls.

Still Mary had not spoken. The owner brought them bottles of beer, and Juliet took a sip gratefully. 'Are you alright, Mary?' she asked at last, looking at her face, searching for a response.

'Of course,' said Mary, looking back at her with a rueful smile. 'I'm just trying to get used to things, that's all. It's all been quite a shock to me. You know that.'

'I know. I'm so sorry. I understand, of course I do, and I feel dreadful that I couldn't tell you before. I hope you can try to understand why.'

Mary shrugged, and then looked away. 'Look, let's not talk about it now. I feel wrung out.'

The owner brought plate after plate of barbecued seafood, smothered in butter and garlic, perfectly charred.

'Look, I know this has been hard for you, too,' Mary suddenly said. 'But I just need some time to process all this. To get used to all this new information I've come to know about myself.'

Later, as they walked back through the streets of the little town towards the guesthouse, Mary slid her arm through Juliet's. The air was hot and steamy. Shops and stalls were packing up for the night, with much shouting and clattering.

'You know you should try to find out what happened to him,' said Mary. 'Adam, I mean. I read what you wrote about him in your journal.'

Juliet stopped walking. 'I believe that poor Adam is dead. I did everything I could to confirm this for myself. He might not have been executed by the Japanese, but I'm sure he must be dead. Otherwise he would have been in touch.'

'But you don't know for sure.'

'If he did survive, if he'd wanted to see me again, he'd have been in touch. If he didn't die, then perhaps he met someone else. Who knows?'

'You'll never know until you know,' Mary said, smiling. 'Look at me. I didn't give up, did I? I persisted, and look what I managed to dig up.'

Juliet smiled. Was this a signal that Mary had accepted the situation? She quickly decided it would be too risky to pursue the point. The girl had asked her for time, and Juliet would respect her request. Instead she shrugged. 'I'll think about it tomorrow, Mary. So much has happened today. I'm so tired.'

ADAM DIDN'T COME BACK for me. I never saw him again. I never really believed that he had been executed by the Japanese. I thought the officer at camp were just fishing for information, trying to shock me into giving something away. But then, when I didn't hear from Adam again, I had no choice but to believe that

he died fighting with the guerrillas in the hills in central
Malaya.

After the war had ended, while I was staying in the dormitory
in Raffles, I went back to Kampong Glam. It was a few days after
Elsie and I had walked out of the camp at Sime Road. It was
really difficult for me to go back there, but I knew I had to. I had
to try to find out if Adam had been back to look for me. It was
strange returning to that part of town, bumping along in the rickshaw down that familiar street full of shop-houses where so
much had happened to me, both good and bad. By then the street
was already getting back to normal. Stalls were set up on the
pavement and the place was full of people browsing for goods
and bargaining with the stallholders. The atmosphere was so
different that day from how I remembered it. It felt happy and
boisterous, carefree almost.

I stopped outside Nazira's shop-house and looked up at it. It
looked exactly as it had when my friend and I had arrived there
on the very first day of the Occupation. I was surprised to see that
the shutters were rolled back and the stalls were set up in front of
the shop. A few pots and pans were displayed on tables just like
the old days. An old Malay man sat behind the stall. I approached
him and told him that I was a friend of Nazira's, that she had
helped me during the Occupation.

He was very friendly. He got up and shook my hand warmly,
and asked me to come and sit down on the stool beside him. He
even called upstairs to his wife to bring me tea. He told me that
he had arrived a few days before from Johor Bahru. He had
worked on a rubber plantation that had been taken over by the
Japanese and run down badly during the Occupation. All the
workers had been laid off when the owners returned from internment. He and his wife had come to Singapore to find his brother
as they had nowhere to go, no-one else to turn to. He had found
the place shut up. The neighbours had told him that Nazira and
her family had not survived. He had decided to stay and open up

the shop again. There was still a bit of old stock stored in the back.

His wife came downstairs. She was dressed in a traditional tunic and headscarf. She was full of smiles and very welcoming. She carried a pot of tea and two china cups on a metal tray. She sat down beside us at the front of the stall. I recognised those old chipped cups from all those weeks I had spent in that flat. The sight of them sent a chill through me. I remembered drinking from them countless times, and the terror I had sometimes felt during that time. I remembered watching Adam take his last drink from one of those cups.

'The neighbours told me that a British woman was hiding in the flat,' said Nazira's uncle, 'and that she was taken away by the soldiers.'

'That was me,' I said. 'Your niece was a wonderful woman. Kind and good and very brave. I was ill, and she nursed me back to health after the invasion. She sheltered me here for months. She helped countless others too, soldiers and other prisoners in Changi. But she paid a heavy price for her bravery and kindness.'

There were tears in his eyes. 'They told me she was executed,' he said, shaking his head in disbelief. 'War is a truly terrible thing.'

We sat there in silence for a while, sipping our tea, reflecting on the dreadful changes that the last few years had wrought. 'Has a man been here asking for Nazira?' I eventually asked, breaking the silence. 'A tall Englishman, a soldier?'

He shook his head. 'No. No-one has come. Not while we have been here. I'm sorry.'

I wasn't surprised. It was not long since liberation, and Adam might not have had a chance to get to Singapore from wherever he was in the jungle on the mainland.

'If he does come, please could you give him this letter?' I had scribbled a note to Adam on Raffles notepaper before I had left that morning.

'Of course, I will. You can rely on me.'

I went back to see them a couple of weeks later before I went back to Kuala Lipis. The old couple were pleased to see me again, but Adam had not been there and they still had the letter. 'If he comes, we will make sure he gets it,' Nazira's uncle assured me.

Later that day I went to the headquarters of the armed forces. It was housed in the Municipal Building, an imposing place on Connaught Road where the records were being compiled for those who had served in RAF, the army and the navy. I needed to find out what had happened to Rob. I had already taken a taxi out to the Tengah Air Base and seen the devastation there. Robert and Rose's bungalow had been completely destroyed in an air raid and was now just a pile of rubble. No-one there had any news of the servicemen. 'There's an office in town with all the records as details come in,' an officer had told me, handing me a piece of paper with the address on Connaught Road.

When I got there the man at the desk scanned his records. His finger stopped dead as it ran down a column. He looked up, and I knew what he was about to say from the expression of apology on his face. 'I'm very sorry to have to tell you this, but Captain Robert Thompson died in June this year, in a shipwreck. He was being transported to a POW camp in Formosa. The ship was sunk by US forces off the island of Luzon in Philippines. There was only a handful of survivors.'

'Formosa?' I asked weakly. And then I remembered what the prisoner-of-war in Sime Road had told me over the wire fence, about how thousands of POWs were being shipped to Japan and to their colonies. 'They were being shipped to work in the mines there. I'm very sorry, lady.'

Without a word, I left. The fierce sun made my head throb. I walked for a while along the pavement then when I could walk no further I sat down on the wall. I could not cry. I kept thinking how strange it was that both Robert and Rose had both been in ships that had gone down. I felt oddly detached from the news. It was as if I had no capacity to feel anything anymore. I thought about Adam. Perhaps they had news of him here, too? I suddenly needed to know if he was alive. I needed to find out the full extent of my loss.

I went back inside the office. The man behind the desk looked up in surprise. 'Mrs. Crosby? Is there something else?'

'I need to know about someone else. He was in the Indian Army, India III Corps. Then he was moved to special operations.'

The man looked flustered. 'We can't give out any information about special operations, I'm afraid. Officially it doesn't exist.'

I leaned forward and looked him straight in the eye. 'Please. It's important to me. I really need to know. I've lost so many people.' My voice broke, and I stifled a sob.

'What's his name? I'll go and see what I can find out, off the record. But this must go no further. I won't tell anyone you asked, and you must not say how you came by anything I can tell you.'

'Of course. I understand. His name is Adam Foster.' He disappeared into an office. I paced about on the tiled floor in an agony of anticipation. When the man came back to the desk I was clenching my fists hard.

'I'm afraid it's not good news, Mrs. Crosby. Captain Foster has not reported back to his regiment. We've got him down as missing. Presumed dead. That's all I can say. I'm very sorry.'

28

I gave up any thoughts of going back to England. I had to stay in Malaya, for a while, at least, until I knew for sure about Adam. Now that Gavin was no longer there, I could go back to the estate. I needed to have somewhere to put down roots again, and I wanted to be somewhere I could wait for Adam. Also, in the letter that I left with Nazira's uncle, I had asked Adam to contact me at the estate.

I went to Geylang for the last time and said goodbye to Elsie. It was the day after the re-opening of her bar. She had an opening celebration and invited as many of her old customers as she could track down. Tina and the girls from the massage parlour came. Elsie had hired a small jazz band who played long into the night. The bar was thronging with partygoers all night and the evening was a great success. But it felt all wrong to me somehow, to be celebrating when so many had suffered and died. I wasn't ready for that, but I was happy to see Elsie behind the bar in a red sequinned dress, serving drinks and laughing and joking with customers.

That night I took the train from Keppel Road Station and left the city that had been my home throughout those turbulent years. I vowed to myself to never return.

It was raining hard when I got off the train. I took a taxi from the station in Kuala Lipis. When Abdul saw it draw up on the drive in front of the house, he came out to the car with an umbrella to help me inside. He was overwhelmed that I had come back. We both cried once we were inside the house.

'You look very thin, madam. A lot happened here. Dreadful things,' he said, shaking his head sadly. 'Japanese soldiers were living in house. They not good men.'

We walked around the house. It was shabby now, and showed the wear and tear of having been lived in by many people who had been careless of the paintwork and of the furniture. Most of the antiques and ornaments had disappeared. There were faded patches on the walls where the paintings had been taken down.

Abdul followed me, wringing his hands as I walked around examining the damage. 'Japanese soldiers live here,' he said again. 'They not treat the house well. Or the servants. Surya ran away. So did gardener, and cook. Only me and Mohammed stay. We take care of place for when you return, madam.'

'What about Mohammed? Where is he?'

'He very tired and very old now. He go back to his village when Japanese leave. I all alone here. Only one visitor. Mr. Scott came back last month. He stay two days.'

My heart stood still, and I felt the blood drain from my face. I had not expected this news. I had been assuming that Scott was dead, that like so many others, he had not survived the harsh conditions on the death railway. If I had stopped to consider that he might come back here, I might not have returned at all.

'Mr. Scott very, very thin now. And he very angry at the way Japanese damage house. He drink very much for two days, then leave again.'

Early the next morning Abdul showed me Gavin's grave under the *angsana* trees in the corner of the garden. It was marked by a simple wooden cross, tied together with twine. I stood there in the morning sunlight, with steam rising all around from the wet garden. I stared at it for a long time but I felt nothing. As I turned away, I saw Abdul wipe away a tear.

He showed me around the estate, too. It was neglected and forlorn, no longer working. Clumps of weeds and thickets of bamboo grew in the avenues between the trees. In some places the jungle had completely reclaimed the land. The rubber trees had grown beyond control. They had not been pruned for years. Many trees had died, their lifeless shells still standing without leaves, others had blown over in high winds. The office and latex sheds were deserted, thick with dust, windows broken. Machines sat rusting under leaky roofs, papers and files covered the floor, filing cabinets stood open, drawers ripped out and thrown aside.

'Japanese soldiers come here to search,' Abdul explained, seeing my dismay.

We walked down the hill to the tappers' village together. Many of the workers had fled and some of the houses stood empty, some of them derelict, bamboo and creepers growing up through the *atap* roofs. I stood outside the house where I had seen Gavin kiss his lover, that fateful night in 1939. It seemed a lifetime ago. The doors were padlocked now and the windows boarded up.

'That woman leave,' said Abdul with a frown of disapproval when he saw me looking. 'When Mr. Gavin die, she run away. Nobody knows where. She not liked in village.'

Some of the tappers came out of their houses to talk to me. They looked listless and malnourished. 'They have no food. Only what they grow here,' said Abdul, pointing around him. I saw that every available patch of land between the houses had been turned into vegetable gardens.

Gavin's old foreman, Jalak, shouldered his way to the front and emerged from the little crowd to speak to me. 'Mrs. Crosby. You must get this estate working again like in the old days,' he said, looking me straight in the eye, his face stern. He was a proud man. He was not begging, he was telling me facts. 'Many people depend upon this estate for their lives. We need to eat. Our children need a future.'

My heart went out to this little crowd of destitute people who had worked so hard to build up the estate, and upon whose goodwill and hard labour my own life had once depended. That evening I sat down at the bureau, found some old writing paper that had been shoved to the back of a drawer, and wrote to Gavin's lawyers in Kuala Lumpur. I had no idea if they were still in business. I informed them of Gavin's death and asked them about his will. I knew that if the estate now belonged to Scott, I would have no choice but to leave, but I needed to find out my position. Abdul drove into town to post the letter for me.

I heard back from them within a few days. Gavin had left the entire estate and all his money to me. He had made the will just after our marriage, in accordance with his father's wishes. They asked me to visit their offices 'at my earliest convenience', to sign some papers. The estate would then be transferred into my name. It seemed that the estate needed me, and it suited me to stay. There was nothing for me back in London. Here I could bury myself away from the world and nurse my sorrow. And I could be useful at last. I could rebuild the estate and give all those people some hope for the future.

So that's what I did. It took months, no years, to bring the estate round. I re-hired all the workers and recruited still more. Soon all the houses in the tappers' village were repaired and fully occupied again. I set the people to work clearing and weeding the land, resurrecting the trees that were still viable, replanting where necessary. I learnt so much about the industry in the space of a few months. I plumbed strengths and resources in myself that I didn't know existed. I threw myself into it body and soul. It became my whole life.

And I found that I began to heal, in a way. I began to think less about the past and of what I had lost, and more about the present, about the work I had to do, and about the future. If troubling thoughts or memories did enter my mind I blocked them off, forced myself to think of other things. I became quite adept at that. But there was always a tiny corner of my heart that didn't give up on Adam. I never stopped hoping against hope that he would return. Whenever I sat down for tiffin on my veranda and watched the sun go down over the hills, I was watching those gates at the end of the drive, watching and waiting.

THAT NIGHT after Mary had gone to sleep, Juliet lay awake on her bed in the guesthouse, watching the patterns of lights from passing cars dance on the ceiling of the tiny room. Old memories troubled her, the darkest memories, the ones that she thought she had buried years ago. She hadn't written about these memories in the journal she had used to record her past, the book she had given Mary. She had been too ashamed, too horrified, to put it down on paper, to let anyone else know about it. For the first time in years she went back to that night, that dreadful night in April 1941, the last night she had spent at Windy Ridge before she had left for Singapore.

After Scott had gone back downstairs, she had fallen into a troubled sleep, tormented by images of Gavin and his lover. She had been sleeping fitfully for a couple of hours but had then woken up with a jolt. She had found herself sitting bolt upright, bathed in sweat, breathing quickly.

She heard a squeak from the direction of the door and realised that someone was turning the handle, trying to enter her room. She froze, terrified. Too terrified to move. Before she could gather her thoughts, there came the sound of a key turning in the lock, and the door burst open. Scott appeared in the doorway. He held a key up on a string, he swung it from side to side. She could see that he was smiling, taunting her.

'Careless of you, Juliet, my love. You forgot the spares in the kitchen cupboard,' he said with a cold smile.

Juliet scrambled out of bed and made a dash for the bathroom. She had the wild thought that she could lock herself in there. But he was across the room and upon her in seconds. He grabbed her by both arms. He was strong. His fingers were tight around her arms, hurting her flesh, bruising the skin.

'Not so fast, Juliet. I know you want it, and I'm here to give you what you want.' Then he was pulling her towards the bed, and she was resisting with all her strength, struggling, trying to break free. 'I've always wanted you, Juliet. But you know that, don't you? That I've always admired your perfect poise, your ice-cool beauty.'

He shoved her onto the bed. 'Please!' she gasped. 'Please don't do this.'

He held her down. 'Get off me,' she screamed, writhing about, trying to break free from his grip.

'There's no-one to hear you. Gavin's unconscious, and the servants are safe in their quarters. You can scream all you like. But you and I both know what's going to happen. And I know you're going to like it.' He was still holding her down with one hand. He was fumbling with his trousers with the other. She felt his rough hands rip her nightdress, then push it upwards around her hips. He forced her legs apart and stood between them, while she thrashed around, screaming and sobbing, crying for him to let her go. She was horrified by what was happening, what was about to happen.

He leaned forward, pressing himself onto her, and she could feel the weight of his body on top of her, his hard lips on hers. She turned her face aside and spat into the pillow. He covered her face in clumsy kisses; she could smell the alcohol on his breath, the reek of sweat on his body. He moved even closer, and she could feel him now, hard between her legs, and even though she twisted and turned and tried to break free, he was forcing himself inside her and then, grunting with the effort, he was moving on top of her. She was gasping and yelling, unable to bear the pain and the humiliation.

It was over in a matter of seconds, and he collapsed on top of her. She instantly wriggled free and slid out from underneath him. She scrambled for the bathroom, sobbing and gasping and shivering with shock. She slammed the bolt back and dashed for the lavatory, retching repeatedly, but she could not rid herself of that sick feeling deep inside her stomach. Then she sat down on the lavatory, and stayed there for a long time, trying to calm down. Then, quivering and weak, she got up and turned on the shower. It was freezing cold but she forced herself to stand under it. She stood there, rubbing herself all over with soap, trying desperately to get clean, examining the fresh bruises on her arms and thighs.

When she had dried herself, she crept back into the bedroom and, her heart hammering, dressed as quickly and as quietly as she could. She could see the shape of Scott still lying on the bed face down. She thought he was asleep, but when she glanced over at him to make sure, she realised with a start that he was watching her, and that his face was wet with tears.

'Forgive me, Juliet,' he murmured. 'Please forgive me. I love you. I was drunk. I didn't know what I was doing.'

She did not reply, but quickly pulled her suitcase from the wardrobe, and flung in a few random clothes.

'Don't hate me, Juliet. Please. Don't hate me for this.'

Without looking at him, she dashed out of the room and downstairs and into the back kitchen. She left her suitcase there and let herself out of the back door and into the yard. She had hardly ever ventured into the servants quarters before, but now she ran across the yard and knocked frantically on Abdul's door.

There was a light on inside, and he was already up and

dressed. He opened the door quickly, but she saw the look of affront on his face. He was shocked that she had come to his room.

'Madam?' he said stiffly. And then he peered at her face, and his expression changed.

'Could you take me to the station please, Abdul?' she asked breathlessly. 'Straight away. I need to get away from here as quickly as I can.'

Two months after the momentous trip to Bamboo Island, Juliet's days were virtually back to normal, had resumed their old rhythms, except that there was a new joy in her life. She would remember each morning, as soon as she woke up, that she had a daughter, and the knowledge would fill her with fresh pleasure and fuel her with energy for the day ahead. She and Mary spoke every day on the telephone. She had even had a line run up to the house from the office so that she could speak to Mary from the living room.

Mary had been back to the estate once since their return, to spend her days off. Those days had been bliss for Juliet. They had spent them in easy companionship, strolling around the estate arm in arm, chatting on the veranda over cups of tea, shopping in the bazaar in Kuala Lipis. On her other weekend off, Mary had been back to Palembang again to see Zaq.

During her stay at the house, one evening, Mary had said, 'Next time I come I'll give you your journal back.'

Juliet hesitated, 'There's no need to do that. You can keep it if you like.'

'But it's yours. It's where you wrote down all your memories. Are you sure you don't want it back?'

'Quite sure, thank you. I wrote it down to try to make sense of it all. I don't need to do that anymore. Not now that I've got you. You keep it, Mary. As a reminder of everything, as a gift from a mother to a daughter.'

Mary had persuaded Juliet to think about starting to ride again. Juliet asked around at the club, and had managed to buy a horse from one of the neighbouring estates. It was a bay Arab called Monty. She had taken to riding again as if she had never stopped, and as she rode around the estate, the two dogs trotting behind her, she would think about Mary, and about speaking to her in the evening. She would sit beside the telephone at six o'clock, waiting for Mary's call. Usually they would just exchange news about their days, how they were feeling, what they had eaten, who they had spoken to. It was mundane conversation, but to Juliet it became her new life-blood, as essential to her well-being as food and drink and fresh air. She began to wonder how she had existed alone through all those empty years.

One day Mary's voice sounded different on the phone, breathless and excited. 'There's something I need to tell you. Are you sitting down?'

Juliet laughed. 'Of course. In the armchair by the window.'

'I've been to Indian Army Headquarters. I managed to find out some information about Adam Foster.' Shock waves coursed through Juliet. She could not reply. In her confusion, the phone slipped from her grasp.

'Juliet? Are you there?'

Juliet picked up the receiver again, her hands trembling. 'Yes,' she whispered. 'I'm here.'

'He's alive. Isn't that fantastic? I managed to persuade them to give me an address. He keeps in touch with the regiment from time to time. He's still in Malaya. They said he was discharged a few months after the war ended. On grounds of incapacity. He'd been injured apparently and could no longer serve. Shall I read out the address? We could go and see him.'

'No. No,' said Juliet thinking fast. 'It would be better if I wrote to him. If he doesn't want to see me, it would give him a chance to explain. We can't just turn up at his doorstep out of the blue.'

'Okay,' Mary said, sounding a bit disappointed. 'Here's the address ...' She read out the address of a post office in a village deep in the Bukit Sembilan hills.

Later that evening, with a lot of trepidation, Juliet sat down at her old bureau and wrote Adam a letter. She made several false starts and tore up many drafts, but she finally settled on something very short.

My Dearest Adam,

I have recently discovered that you survived the war and that you are alive and still living in Malaya. I went to Kampong Glam after liberation and left a letter for you there. I have been waiting to hear from you ever since. The Japanese soldiers at Changi told me that you had been executed, but I did not believe them at the time. But because I did not hear from you, I thought that you must have died. I assumed you were killed in action.

I fully understand if you have no wish to have any contact with me. After all, it is twenty years since we said goodbye. If that is the case, please write soon and let me know, and I will try my best to forget.

With love as ever,

Juliet.

She waited breathlessly for a response for over a fortnight, and finally, one morning, the postman from Kuala Lipis dropped a letter in the box at the end of the drive. Her heart was pounding as she opened it.

My Dearest Juliet,

You can't imagine how surprised and overjoyed I was to receive your letter. I have been thinking you were dead for so many years ...

Towards the end of the war I was badly injured in a bridge-

blowing exercise. The device went off early and blew the bridge before I could get away. The bridge collapsed on top of me and my leg was crushed, the leg that had already been injured in Singapore. This happened in Pahang, not too far from Kuala Lipis. I was laid up in the jungle for a few days, and by the time I could walk, the people in the villages were telling me that the war was over, that the Japanese were withdrawing from the region. On the off-chance that you might be nearby, I decided to see if you had gone back to the estate before I went back to Singapore to report to the regiment. I asked around for the Crosby estate, and the villagers directed me to Windy Ridge. I took a taxi from Kuala Lipis, and as I drew up at the house, someone came out onto the drive to speak to me. At first I thought it was Gavin, but when I asked him, he said he was Gavin's younger brother. He was really hostile and obviously drunk. I asked after you, said I had met you in Singapore during the Occupation. He leaned right into the car window and said, 'She's dead. Died in Changi. Dreadful business. Malaria or cholera or something like that. She always was a weak one.' There was something malicious about the way he spoke, as if he was pleased to be delivering such dreadful news.

I left as quickly as I could. I couldn't think straight. I was devastated. I went back to the village where I had camped with the guerrillas for most of the Occupation. It was a long way from Kuala Lipis, up in the Bukit Sembilang hills. I managed to hitch rides with lorries and vans going that way. It suited me to be a long way away from your estate. I wanted to try to forget all about you.

The villagers were pleased to see me again. They helped me recover. I wrote to the regiment in the end, telling them about my injury. I had to go down to Kuala Lumpur for a medical and then they discharged me from the army. I never went back to Singapore. I couldn't face it. It would have brought back too many memories.

I went back to the village, and I've lived there like a native ever since. The villagers built me a simple wooden house, and then together we built a school for the children. I became their teacher. I must have *taught generations of village children the basics of maths, science and English. That's how I've spent the years since the war.*

But try as I might, I never could forget you, Juliet, and the love we shared. You are in my thoughts each day. I need to see you now. As soon as I can get to you.

Unless you send a telegram to say it is not convenient, I will arrive on the 17:45 train in Kuala Lipis on Friday. We have to make up for all the lost time.

With all my love,
Adam

JULIET PUT the letter down with trembling hands. Her heart was thumping even harder now. She looked again at the date. The letter must have been held up in the post; the very next day was Friday. She thought about dashing to the post office in Kuala Lipis to send a telegram, asking him to wait. But there was no real reason to do that, not after all these years, but the fact that she would be seeing Adam within twenty-four hours threw her into turmoil.

She went upstairs and stared at her face in the bedroom mirror, tracing the lines with her fingers anxiously, examining the grey streaks in her hair. Would he recognise her now? Would he still find her attractive now that she was no longer young?

She thought about the evil, vengeful deed that Scott had done when he had told Adam that she was dead. She felt bitter that he had tried to ruin her life, again, that he had chased away the only man she had ever loved. How could he have done such a cruel thing? But she knew the answer. It was because he loved her himself, he'd always loved her in his own covetous, envious way. It was a twisted type of love, the only type of love that he could experience, but it was love all the same. She remembered his eyes appraising her, his words of flattery, the way he had looked at her when they had gone riding on the plantation together. With a shudder she thought of him watching her as she had dressed quickly, shivering and sick with loathing, on that last dreadful night before she had left. 'Forgive me, Juliet,' he'd said. 'Please forgive me. I love you.' He must have realised, in those few seconds that he had spoken to Adam, perhaps it was something in Adam's eyes that told him, that Adam loved Juliet too. Scott would have sensed the threat, that Adam's love was real and that she loved him in return. It must have been that fear that drove Scott to say what he did. He couldn't bear for her to belong to another man. Juliet clenched her fists in anger. She understood why he had said what he did, but she could never forgive him for that.

She recalled the day that he had come back to the estate on leave, a few months after her own return. She had seen him walking up the drive. He had grown thinner, but still walked with his unmistakable military swagger, and she had rushed to the front door and bolted it, had stood with her back to it, breathing hard. He had stood on the porch and banged on it, shouting to be let in. Abdul had come through from the kitchen but she had put her finger to her lips and shaken her head at him.

Eventually, when Scott had refused to leave her alone, she had gone and shouted through the letter box, 'Go away. You're not welcome here.'

'You can't stop me from coming in there. This is my home.'

'Not any more. The estate is mine. Gavin left it to me.'

'Well, the bungalow is mine, you bitch. You can't stop me going there. I'll be staying there whenever I like. I'll be keeping an eye on you.'

She had forgotten about the bungalow. The father's will had originally left the old bungalow and surrounding land to Scott, and it still belonged to him. She went to the window and watched him stride off defiantly in the direction of the bungalow. She felt anxious. She knew there would be more trouble from him. That this was just the start.

He came over to stay in the bungalow for a few days every couple of months. He would always come up to the house and bang on the door first, pleading with Juliet to let him in. He would even apologise for the way he had treated her the night she had left for Singapore, would profess his love for her. Juliet never responded to him, never spoke to him. Sometimes she would go upstairs and lie on her bed, her head buried under the pillow, to block out the sound of his whining, cajoling voice. He was nearly always drunk, sometimes he could barely stand up. Sometimes he was tearful, sometimes angry. He would call through the letter box, 'Juliet, forgive me for what happened back then. I did it because I love you. I didn't want to hurt you.'

Eventually he was discharged from the army and moved to live in the bungalow full time. He hired a woman from the village, the wife of one of the tappers, to look after him. Juliet would overhear scandalised conversations between the servants and the tappers about Scott's drinking and his brutish slovenly ways. She learned to ignore his presence, but the fact that he was just over the hill and might appear near the house at any time forced her to live constantly on edge.

Things went on like that for a few years until the Malayan Emergency reached a critical phase. There was fighting between the British forces and the guerrillas, who wanted independence. It had reached the Kuala Lipis area, and several local plantations had been attacked by guerrillas. A British estate manager on the other side of the town had even been killed. Consequently, the chief of police in Kuala Lipis had sent armed guards to the Windy Ridge estate to protect the plantation. They would patrol the perimeter day and night, so the tapping and production could carry on as before. At night an armed policeman would be stationed on Juliet's veranda. If she awoke during the night, she would hear his reassuring footsteps pacing the boards below.

One day she was down in the latex sheds, supervising the presses, when she heard a shot from the bottom of the hill. She glanced out of the window to see a group of armed guerrillas spread out in a line, swarming through the undergrowth towards the sheds. She turned to the women working the presses and said to them calmly, 'I need to get out of here. They won't harm you. It's me they want.'

She rushed out of the sheds and up the hill towards the house. Her breath was coming in pants and her heart was leaping through the effort of running in the heat. She was at the junction of the track where it forked to go down to the bungalow. Glancing behind her, she could see the guerrillas emerging from the trees, only a hundred yards or so behind. There was no time to get up to the house. She took a decision to run down to the bungalow. She ran down the hill, up onto the porch and hammered with her fists on the front door.

'Let me in, Scott, please! The guerrillas are on the estate! They must have broken through the police lines.' He opened the door. He was wearing a dressing gown and looked unshaven. He already smelled of whisky. He looked at her squiffy-eyed.

'What the hell?'

Juliet pushed past him and ran to find somewhere to hide. 'Scott, come inside. It's not safe out there. They want to kill us,' she panted. 'Where's best to hide?'

'Sod that,' he said, swaying on his feet. 'I'm damn well not hiding.' He went to a cupboard and pulled out a shot gun. He clumsily loaded it with bullets from a drawer then stumbled out onto the veranda.

'Come on, you little yellow bastards,' he yelled. 'I'm not afraid of you. Come out and show your faces.' He fired a shot into the air. Juliet crouched behind his settee, quivering with fear. She could see one of the guerrillas through the open door, advancing stealthily through the undergrowth, his weapon poised.

Suddenly there was a volley of shots. Juliet covered her ears and crouched motionless behind the sofa, dreading what might happen next. More shots were fired, and she heard the ping of bullets against the wall of the bungalow and the smash of glass as a pane in the door broke. Then silence, followed by the sound of footsteps in the grass, running away from the bungalow. She stayed where she was, not daring to show herself, fearing a trap. Was Scott hurt? Was he lying on the boards of the porch? Then she heard his footsteps on the boards and he came inside.

'They've gone now, the little bastards. They didn't bargain on me being tooled up. I got one of them. He's gone down in the grass out there. That sent the others scampering for cover.' He came behind the settee and peered down at her. 'It's safe now, you can come on out.'

Juliet got to her feet slowly and dusted herself down. Her mouth was dry. She felt Scott's hand on her arm. 'Come on,' he said, 'you don't need to be afraid. They've gone.'

'I'll go back up to the house then,' she said, not looking at him.

'I wouldn't do that just yet,' he said. 'They might be waiting over the hill. I would wait here for a bit. Come on. Sit down here, won't you? I'll pour you a drink. You've had a hell of a shock.'

He put his gun down on the table beside the settee, and moved the jumble of newspapers and dirty clothes onto a chair to make room for her. Reluctantly she sat down and watched him pour brandy from a bottle on the cluttered chest.

'Here,' he said, handing the glass to her, 'drink it down in one. It'll do you good.'

Silently, she took the glass from him and took a gulp. She felt the burning sensation on her tongue and the fire in her throat as the brandy slid down, and within seconds she felt its warmth stealing over her, dulling her shock, calming her nerves. A numbness took over her senses and she closed her eyes for a moment. Then she felt Scott sit down on the settee beside her. She snapped her eyes open, immediately tense.

'Juliet, please. There's nothing to worry about. Please, relax.'

'I need to leave,' she said, moving to get up.

'Don't be silly. You can't leave yet. They might take a pot-shot at you.'

She sat back, but as soon as she had done so, she felt Scott's arm slip around her shoulder. Then his other hand was on her thigh and he was leaning in to kiss her.

'Just relax. Please,' he said, and she felt his breath on her face.

'No! Scott, stop it,' she said, trying to push him away. 'Leave me alone. Don't do this!'

But he carried on, pawing her, pulling at her blouse, kissing her face. She turned her face away from him, struggling to get away, but he strengthened his grip on her, pushing her down, tearing at her clothes, pulling at the buttons of her trousers. She tried to squirm sideways to get away, and it was then that she noticed the gun on the table. With an effort, she managed to pull her right hand out from Scott's grasp, and felt for the handle of the gun. Her heart was thundering against her ribs as she closed her fist around it and lifted it up.

'Leave me alone,' she said, her voice trembling. 'I've got the gun.'

He stopped and stared at her. For a second he looked astonished, then he started laughing.

'Don't be silly,' he said.

He lunged sideways, leaning across her, for the gun, and as he did so, she brought it towards him. She felt the weight of him top of her.

'Get off me, I'm warning you,'

His hand was on the barrel of the gun now and he was pulling it towards him. 'Let go of it, Juliet. You know you're not going to fire it. Be sensible now. I'm not going to hurt you. Please, let me show you how much you mean to me.'

He gave the gun another tug, and she pulled it backwards, away from him. There was an ear shattering bang as the gun went off. Scott leapt backwards with a grunt. He stood up, staggered back a few paces, clutching a wound on his stomach, blood spreading over his dressing gown. He stumbled towards the door, his eyes locked on hers. In them she saw a mixture of shock and hurt. Then he crashed onto his back on the floor, through the door of the bungalow, and lay there, half in half out of the door, still clutching his stomach.

'Scott!' She ran towards him, but before she could get to him, there was another round of shots from the direction of the trees. Another pane in the front door shattered, showering glass over Scott.

Juliet dropped to the floor trembling. She could see Scott twitching, hear his moans. She was paralysed with shock. But within a few seconds the noises had stopped, and he lay there motionless.

There were footsteps on the path, 'Stay there Mrs. Crosby. We'll be right with you,' It was the voice of the police officer. 'We've got them all now. You're safe.'

She dashed across the floor to Scott, and knelt down beside him. She felt his brow and listened to his chest, trying not to look at the glutinous entrails spilling from his stomach onto the boards. He was completely still and lifeless. She collapsed beside him, weeping.

Within seconds the two policemen were with her, lifting her gently by her arms.

'Come on, come on up to the house, Mrs. Crosby. We can look after things here. You've been very brave.'

DAYLIGHT WAS JUST STARTING to fade, and the jungle creatures were gathering momentum for the night. The rattle of cicadas and the whoops of jungle birds rang loud and clear from the undergrowth.

Juliet drove along the old jungle road she knew so well. She drove slowly. She had left plenty of time for the short journey.

Abdul had offered to drive her to the station to meet her visitor, but she had insisted on going by herself. She needed to be alone.

She recalled the short but fervent time that she and Adam had spent together. In reality it had only been a few days but it had been a time of such intensity, it felt as though they had lived a lifetime together in that tiny flat in Kampong Glam. She could remember everything about it: his touch, his smile, the way he had looked at her that had made everything around her fade into nothingness. She remembered how his stories had transported her to magical places, and how being with him had given her an overwhelming sense of well-being. Her whole body tingled with anticipation, but her excitement was also tinged with nerves. Would he still feel the same way about her after all this time? Would the years have changed him, put some distance and barriers between them?

She was out of the forest soon and driving through the outskirts of Kuala Lipis. She drove over the bridge and along beside the Jelai River and into the little town. As she drew closer to the station, her nervousness increased. Perhaps she should have sent a telegram to stop him after all? It would have given her more time to adjust. She pulled into the station yard, parked the car and checked her face in the driver's mirror. She had put on her makeup carefully, and twisted her long hair into a French pleat secured with a silver comb. But the lines on her face were still there, the grey streaks in her hair. Perhaps she should have taken Mary's advice and had her hair done at a salon. Too late to worry about that now, though.

She got out of the car, her body taut with anticipation, and walked through the station hall and onto the platform. The station master recognised her and gave her a cheery wave. She waved back but was glad that he was busy and didn't come over to speak to her.

She was a good ten minutes early, so she paced up and down the deserted platform, watching the light fade over the distant hills. It felt as though she was waiting there an age. She kept checking her watch. The seconds crawled by. At last she heard the shrill sound of the train's whistle and turned to see it puffing in alongside the platform. It ground to a halt, squeaking and rattling, with a hiss of steam and another sudden blast of the whistle.

She watched, holding her breath as the passengers got down, local families returning from shopping trips with packages and parcels, a few local businessmen in suits and carrying briefcases. Adam was the last to get down. He stepped off the end carriage and emerged from a cloud of steam from the engine. She knew instantly that it was him, the shape of his tall frame, the way he walked with a slight limp. He carried a small suitcase and walked slowly towards her, shading his eyes against the setting sun with one hand.

Juliet began to walk towards him from the other end of the platform. Hesitantly at first, then more quickly. Finally she was running. Then she had reached him. He caught her by the arms and held her to him. She looked up into his face. It was tanned from all his years in the East, and now bore the lines of age. His dark hair was streaked with grey like her own. He smiled, and she noticed again the little crinkles at the corners of his eyes that she loved.

'Juliet,' he said gently. '*Saya cintakan awak.*'

She looked up at him and smiled. Her nerves evaporated. Everything around her melted away, and for a split second, it felt as though she and Adam were the only two people on earth.

I hope you enjoyed reading *Bamboo Island: The Planter's Wife* as much as I loved writing it.

Would you like to read *The Tea Planter's Club*? (a heart-breaking novel of love and survival set in Burma during the second world war).

Please sign up to my website (annbennettauthor.com) for news, updates, giveaways and freebies. You can also follow me on Facebook, for information and previews of future books.

Please turn over to read the first chapter of *The Tea Planter's Club*.

THE TEA PLANTER'S CLUB
CHAPTER 1

Edith Mayhew stood on the hotel terrace amongst the potted geraniums, waving goodbye to the last guests as their rickshaw wobbled out through the wrought-iron gates and turned left onto Bunder Street, disappearing instantly into the crowds. With a deep sigh, she turned back into the empty lobby. Anesh, the receptionist, was behind the counter making his final entries in the ledgers.

'All finish, Madam?' he asked, opening the till and starting to cash up.

'All finished, Anesh,' Edith said, forcing a smile, while a great feeling of emptiness washed over her. She looked around the deserted lobby; the cushions on the basket chairs still bore the indents from the last occupants; two half-finished cups on the coffee table, one with a lipstick stain, the only evidence of the recently departed guests. How many people had passed through here down the years since Edith had arrived on that fateful day back in 1938? For a moment, it was as if she could see faint shadows of them all converging on the lobby at once; arriving with their luggage, sipping welcome drinks on the basket chairs, leaning on the reception desk, returning hot and flustered from sight-seeing, rushing for a taxi. But now there was only silence. The old place was finally empty.

Edith wandered absently through the lobby, plumping cushions, straightening magazines, automatically running her fingers along sideboards and the backs of chairs on the lookout for dust, forgetting that today it didn't matter. She went into the dining room, with its linen tablecloths, potted aspidistras and framed prints of hunting scenes, where the two elderly "boys" dressed in starched aprons were clearing up from breakfast for the very last time. She watched their slow, stooping progress, as they loaded dirty dishes onto trays and removed the hotplates, as she had every day for the past forty years, only today she had tears in her eyes. She knew that neither of these faithful old gentlemen would ever find another job; that they'd given their lives to this place, asking for so little in return, and that tomorrow they would travel back to their villages in the hills for the very last time.

One of them, old Roshan, looked up, put his hands together.

'Namaste, Madam,' he said, inclining his head, and she returned the greeting.

It all felt so final now, but it was what she'd been planning for some time. Trade had been dropping off for years and, a few months ago, she'd finally had to admit that the business could no longer make ends meet. There was so much competition now from the guesthouses and hostels along Bunder Street, attracting backpackers with their rock bottom prices, pool tables and cheap beers. No backpackers ever came to stay at the Tea Planter's Club, nor would Edith have welcomed them, with their bare feet and filthy T shirts. There was a dress code in all public parts of the hotel which had been rigidly maintained since the glory days of the Raj. But even the better-heeled travellers now tended to head for the big chain hotels on Chowringhee Road with their swimming pools and happy hours. No, no one seemed to want to partake of "gracious colonial living" anymore. The world had changed so much since

Edith had come here as a young woman and she knew she hadn't moved with the times.

What would Gregory say if he was here, not lying six foot under in that war cemetery in Singapore? He would never have sanctioned her selling the place, but Edith normally got her way in the end.

She closed the doors to the dining room, leaving the boys to their final clear-up, wandered through the hallway and started climbing the wide, sweeping staircase. This was where Edith had hung framed portraits of interesting or famous guests; the faces of several tea planters stared down at her, from the days when the building really had been their club. They stood stiffly with their rifles next to their elephants or dead tigers. There were members of the British Raj peering solemnly from under their solar topees, a few lesser-known actors, a couple of Indian film stars.

The man from Clover Hotels, the multinational chain that was buying the place, had asked Edith to leave the pictures; 'So redolent of a past era, Mrs Mayhew. They add a certain olde-worlde charm,' he'd said. 'We're going to try to keep that if we can, whilst tastefully upgrading, of course.'

'Of course,' she'd echoed in a whisper, pleased that not everything she held dear would be ripped down or painted over.

But there was one photograph that she wouldn't be leaving behind. She peered at it now; it was of Edith and her sister, Betty, taken the week they had arrived at the hotel. Aged 26 and 24; fresh-faced, straight off the ship from England and bursting with enthusiasm for their Indian adventure. She could still see it shining in their eyes all these years later. The raw energy and sheer exuberance of youth.

She took the framed photograph off the wall and traced the line of her sister's jaw with her finger.

'How beautiful you were... you *are*, Betty,' she said, speaking directly to those dark, liquid eyes, the perfectly formed mouth she'd always envied.

'Why didn't you come back?'

Saying those words out loud now, made Edith experience another rush of nerves at the thought of leaving the place behind; the place where Betty knew to find her and where they'd last been together. It was 38 years since she'd received her last letter from Betty, telling Edith that Rangoon was falling to the Japanese and she was setting off for Calcutta, travelling on foot if needs be, that she would be with her as soon as she could. But the weeks had passed and Betty had never arrived. Weeks turned into months and months into years without any word.

During those first few terrible, empty years, Edith had often sat on the edge of the terrace, her eyes glued the gates. She expected Betty to stroll through them demanding a chota peg as cool as cucumber, but as the years had slipped by, she'd stopped watching quite so much. But she'd never quite given up hope. In fact, if she'd heard Betty's strident tones in the lobby now, she wouldn't have been at all surprised.

She knew that selling up and leaving the hotel would be severing that final link with her sister. It would amount to admitting that Betty was never going to stride across the terrace issuing orders. Butterflies besieged Edith at the thought of leaving all this behind. It was so much a part of her. How would she ever survive without it?

She looked again at Betty's smile, at her dancing eyes, and felt that familiar pang of guilt she always got when looking at that picture.

'I'm so sorry, Betty. I let you down. I know that and I regret it deeply,' she whispered, but no amount of apology could wipe away the guilt of decades, or the nagging feeling that perhaps the true reason Betty hadn't returned was because she'd known all along about Edith's betrayal.

Suppressing those thoughts, Edith put the picture down on the step beside her and let her mind wander back to the day the two of them had first arrived at the hotel. It was pure chance that they had stumbled upon this particular establishment. She'd often wondered how their lives would have panned out if they'd chanced upon somewhere different.

They'd come out to India after both their parents had died within a few months of each other. That might have been a blow to many people, but to Edith and Betty it had been a blessed release. Both parents were incurable alcoholics who'd drunk their way through the family money and incurred substantial debts on top. Edith and Betty had left home long before the final descent, to find jobs and to live together in a flat in Clapham. She remembers the squalid apartment in Kensington where her parents had ended up, having sold successively smaller houses along the way. It was dark and smelly and crammed with heavy furniture. Every surface was covered in empty bottles, over-flowing ashtrays and dirty glasses. She shudders, even now, remembering the horror of it.

Edith and Betty had to sell the flat to pay off the debts. An uncle had taken pity on them and had paid for tickets to India so they could both have a new start. Having spent his own youth in India in the army, his house in Hampshire was filled with memo-rabilia; animal skins, a tiger's head, a hollowed-out elephant's foot and a lot of heavy, teak furniture.

'Endless opportunities on the sub-continent for bright young women like you,' he'd told them. 'Head for Calcutta. Streets paved with gold. You can't go wrong there.'

He hadn't expanded on what those opportunities might be, but neither of them had bothered too much about that; they were just glad to get away and to leave London and its ugly memories far behind.

They'd boarded the British Indian Navigation Company's *SS Nevasa* full of hope for the future, and the voyage had shown them that their hopes were not misplaced. The generosity of their uncle meant that they travelled First Class. On board were many young men returning from home leave, or travelling out to take up jobs in the Indian Civil Service; planters, officers, merchants, engineers, box-wallahs (as businessmen were known). There were a few other young women like themselves, but the women were far outnumbered by the men. They were never at a loss for a dancing partner, or someone to walk out onto the moonlit deck with to look at the stars. During the voyage, Betty received no fewer than four proposals of marriage, but although she flirted mercilessly with all her suitors, to Edith's mind giving them false hope, she turned them all down.

'I'm not going to give up this adventure for life in some bungalow on some stuffy British station, playing cards in the club and complaining about the servants,' she'd said, as they lay awake side by side in their cabin one night, talking over the evening's events. Edith hadn't received any offers of marriage, but she took that in her stride. She was used to standing aside for her more attractive younger sister. It was just how life was back then.

When the ship docked at Kiddapore Docks in Calcutta, they took a rickshaw to Bunder Street where their uncle had told them they would be able to find a reasonably priced hotel. The rickshaw brought them all the way from the docks and the two of them had been entranced by the sights and sounds of the city; they passed exotic temples, where discordant bells chimed and incense and smoke wafted from archways, vibrant markets where exotic fruits were piled high on stalls and women in brightly coloured sarees squatted on the pavement gossiping, where the air was filled with the smell of cooking and spices mixed with open drains, and where whole families camped out under tarpaulins on the pavements. They passed Fort William, a massive, fortified structure on the banks of the river, then they crossed the maiden, a huge expanse of open grassland, where sprinklers pumped out precious water and lawnmowers pulled by bullocks made perfect stripes in the lawn. In contrast to this show of colonial elegance, at every crossroads, ubiquitous beggars who lived in makeshift shelters beside the road, would emerge with hands held out and pleading eyes, desperate for a coin or two.

Bunder Street was a busy, crowded road off Chowringhee, the main thoroughfare that ran all down one side of the maiden. The rickshaw moved slowly along it. They passed a couple of hotels that looked promising; Queen's Lodge and Park Hotel, but had already agreed to go the length of the road before making any decisions.

They were just passing the gates of the Tea Planter's Club when there was a disturbance on the pavement beside them. A fight had broken out between two men, and others were joining in, punches were being thrown in every direction, hate-filled faces loomed, shouts of anger filled the air. Suddenly the mob spilled off the pavement and onto the road in front of their rickshaw, forcing their rickshaw-wallah to stop dead. At that moment, to her horror, Edith saw the flash of a blade, a knife raised then plunged into soft flesh. One man fell to the ground yelling, clutching his stomach, and the mob surrounded him, but not before Edith had seen the blood gushing from his wound, spreading quickly over his white tunic.

She turned to Betty, but Betty's face had completely drained of colour and her eyes were flickering. Edith leaned forward to the rickshaw-wallah.

'She's going to faint. Can we go into this building?'

He turned into the gates of the Tea Planter's Club and drew up beside the entrance just as Betty collapsed into Edith's arms. Within seconds they were surrounded by uniformed staff. They quickly lifted Betty from the rickshaw, carried her gently under the covered portico and laid her out on one of the sofas in the reception area. A blanket was brought to cover her. Edith followed gratefully and when she looked back at the rickshaw, saw that their luggage had been unloaded and had been brought into the lobby.

A tall white man dressed casually in linens strolled towards her.

'I'm sorry,' began Edith. 'There must be some mistake. We're not guests here. It's just that there was a stabbing outside and my sister fainted.'

'I'm so sorry to hear that,' said the man mildly. 'The police will be along shortly to break up the mob. Things like that aren't uncommon around these parts, I'm afraid. There's quite a lot of feuding between factions. I hope my staff are looking after your sister.'

Edith glanced over at Betty. One of the uniformed bearers was kneeling beside her, fanning her face furiously, another was bringing a glass of water.

'They've been wonderful. So kind. It's just that... we can't stay here.'

'Of course you can. We have spare rooms.'

'But it's a club, isn't it? We're not members. Nor are we tea planters, I'm afraid.'

'Oh, that doesn't matter anymore. I've just kept the name. It started out as a club for tea planters and everyone knows it by that name. We've been letting rooms out to other people for quite a few years now. You have to pay a nominal fee to be a temporary member, that's all. It's just a formality.'

Edith heaved a sigh of relief. 'Well then, if you don't mind, we'll take a twin room if you have one.'

'Of course. We have a lovely suite upstairs. How long will you be staying?' he asked.

'I'm not sure. We've come to live in the city and we need to have a base until we've found somewhere permanent to stay.'

'That sounds perfect,' said the owner, smiling at her. She noticed the wrinkles around his eyes as he smiled and the fact that his skin was deeply tanned. 'Stay as long as you like,' he added.

And she had stayed. She'd stayed for forty-two years to be precise, and that first impression of Gregory had stayed with her down the years. It had told her everything she needed to know about him; that he was an open, kind, generous-hearted and gentle man with no side to him.

Thinking back now, it struck her that the end of her extended stay was fast approaching. And that fact filled her with mixed emotions.

She took the photograph, brought it down the stairs and laid it on one of the coffee tables in the lobby.

Taking a deep breath, she walked through the hotel to the back of the building, past the kitchen where the chefs were clearing up for the very last time, and into the back yard where the servants rooms opened off a concrete courtyard. Tentatively, she approached the one at the far end. It was the best room; the biggest one, given to the most senior member of staff.

Outside, on the step, lay the stray dog whom Subash, the chief bearer, had loved and fed with scraps from the kitchen. The other servants still fed him, but he refused to leave Subash's doorway. As she approached, he looked up at Edith with soulful eyes. She patted the dog, then felt a little nervous as she turned the handle and pushed the door. She'd rarely ventured into the servants' quarters, and never into this particular room. Now she stepped inside and closed the door behind her.

'Oh, Subash,' she breathed, sitting down on the bed, her eyes filling with tears again. She pictured the old man coming in here to rest, to pray and to perform his puja, to wash and to change, every day of his working life, which had started well before Edith had moved here. This was his private, inner sanctum and even though he was dead, she felt as though she was stepping over some invisible boundary to be in here. He'd served her faithfully for decades, he knew everything about her, her likes and dislikes, her habits and foibles, and yet she knew so little about him. But looking around her, she realised that there was nothing to see anymore.

He'd died two months ago and it was partly his death that had prompted Edith to think seriously about selling up. It was the end of an era, the passing of such a stalwart figure. She hadn't been able to bear to come in here. Not until today. She'd felt his loss so keenly. The other servants had cleared his room, packing up his meagre belongings into a trunk and shipping them off to his home in the village near Darjeeling. He'd always intended to retire there one day, but now he never would. Professional to the end, he'd served Edith her breakfast on the very last day and returned to his room to lie down for the last time.

Absently, she opened a drawer, partly checking to see if the boys had been thorough. There was only one thing inside and she stopped and stared at it. It was an envelope, addressed to *her* in spidery writing. Her heart beating fast, she snatched it up and stared at it. The postmark was Assam, and judging by the smudgy date, it was at least two years old. But why ever had Subash not given it to her when it arrived? It had already been opened by the receptionist, as all hotel post was. That wasn't a surprise. She fished inside and pulled out a single sheet. The address was at the top; *Dapha River Tea Plantation, Ledo, Assam*

My Dear Mrs Mayhew,

I hope you don't mind me writing to you out of the blue. I was recently installed as manager at the Dapha River tea plantation in Assam after the death of the previous owner, Mrs Olive Percival. My company, the Assam Tea Corp, bought the plantation from her estate. Whilst renovating the house, we found some documents including a diary that I believe may have belonged to your relative, Betty Furnivall. They date back to 1942. I have not looked at them in detail. If you would like me to send them to you, please let me know. I wanted to check I had the right address etc before putting them in the post.

Yours sincerely,

Richard Edwards.

Edith sank down on the bed, her heart thumping fit to burst.

'Why ever did you hide it from me, Subash,' she said into the emptiness.

ABOUT THE AUTHOR

Ann Bennett was born in Pury End, a small village in Northamptonshire, UK. She read Law at Cambridge and qualified as a solicitor. She started to write in earnest during a career break to have children. Her first book, *Bamboo Heart: A Daughter's Quest* was inspired by her father's experience as a prisoner of war on the Thai-Burma Railway.

Bamboo Island: The Planter's Wife has previously been published both as *Bamboo Island* and *The Planter's Wife*. It is the second book in a Southeast Asian WW2 collection which includes *Bamboo Heart: A Daughter's Quest, Bamboo Road: The Homecoming, A Daughter's Promise, The Tea Planter's Club* and *The Amulet*. All books are standalone stories, and they may be read in any order.

Ann has also written *The Lake Pavilion,* set in British India in the 1930s, *The Lake Palace,* set in India during the Burma Campaign of WW2, *The Lake Pagoda,* and *The Lake Villa,* both set in Indochina during WW2. Ann's other books, *The Runaway Sisters*, bestselling *The Orphan House, The Child Without a Home,* and *The Forgotten Children* are published by Bookouture.

ACKNOWLEDGMENTS

I'd like to thank my writing buddy, Siobhan Daiko, who's been a constant source of help and support for many years now. Helen Judd, and all my sisters, in particular Mary and Dot for reading and commenting on early drafts. I'd especially like to thank Sujatha Sevellimedu, who edited this book, for her inspiration and dedication.

Bamboo Island: The Planter's Wife was inspired by research into my father's experience as a prisoner of war on the Thai-Burma railway during WWII. I'd like to thank the Thai Burma Railway Centre at Kanchanaburi, the Taiwan POW Camps Memorial Society and the Far East Prisoner of War Community. That research led me to write *Bamboo Heart: A Daughter's Quest* but it also inspired me to find out more, especially about how the Japanese invasion and Occupation of Malaya and Singapore affected the lives of civilians, which is the focus of *Bamboo Island: The Planter's Wife*.

The following books have been sources of inspiration and information:

Sheila Allan, *Diary of a Girl in Changi*
Charles Mc Cormac, *You'll Die in Singapore*

Peter Thompson, *The Battle for Singapore*
Colin Smith, *Singapore Burning*
J.G. Farrell, *The Singapore Grip*
W. Somerset Maugham, *Collected Short Stories*
Michael Barthorp, *The North West Frontier: British India and Afghanistan – A Pictorial Record, 1839–1947*
Brian Moynahan, *Jungle Soldier*

OTHER BOOKS BY ANN BENNETT